Cristal's Revenge

Ian M. Ferguson

Paperback ISBN: 978-0-9917589-5-1

1St paperback version published June, 2014

e-book ISBN 978-0-9917589-4-4

Other works by Ian M. Ferguson

Books

Unintended

Elephant Theory

Operation Counterpunch

Short stories

Culpeper

Dedication

To Colton, Kylie and Cooper. You make my life so much richer.

Acknowledgements

I would like to thank Cristal and Tiffany Huyghe for lending me their names, and all the others I stole names from (Norm Lulham, Chip Atwood, Jim McGuire, and Walt Gargaro).

Thanks to Humphrey Pickering in the UK for his exceptional and tireless editing, proof reading and information on MI6 and Germany.

Thanks to Ruediger Steffen in Cologne for all the help on German scenes.

Thanks to my other editors and reviewers Stephanie Ferguson, Natalie Lelievre, and especially Bob Glass and Zul Abbany.

And finally, thanks to Dan Ferguson for assistance in plot development and the cover art.

Disclaimer

This book is a complete work of fiction based solely on a 'what if' premise.

None of the events are real and nothing relating to people, places, entities or events is based on anything but my imagination.

In some places I've used real names simply as a geographical or corporate reference and no inference should or can be drawn beyond that.

Contents

Kidnapped

The damned rain had started again. Looking out the small barred window at the back of the Cincinnati police station, he could see puddles forming in the parking lot.

It was a cold damp Tuesday morning, Thanksgiving week as senior Detective Bert Wilson turned back to the witness. The witness who was starting to give him heartburn.

He had just about had it with this guy and his frustration was uncharacteristically starting to show. The rain and the stale coffee had put him in a foul mood. His wife had risen too late and he had missed her great coffee. What a way to start a morning he thought to himself.

They had been at it for almost an hour now and it wasn't only what this guy said, it was more his style, his look, attitude, and posture. Something made his cop's nose twitch.

The guy was arrogant too. Looked like a body builder, dressed like a gigolo with tight pants and a flowery shirt open too much at the neck, especially for this time of year. Wore lots of gold and probably had one of those insincere but dazzling smiles. But he was not smiling today. Sizing him up once more, 'Vegas Baby!' came to mind.

Bert stretched his aching back and faced him straight on, "You'd better start making some sense right about now, mister!

"Your wife disappeared and you claim she has been kidnapped. You say you had no warning that she might be leaving on her own. No note from her. No ransom demand and you've no idea where she might be.

"And then you go and pull this Amber Alert stunt. Now start from the top again and leave nothing out this time. I want to try just once to get the whole story without all your detours and commentary. Let's start with last night. You came home yesterday and what?"

Greg Wiggins exasperated, squirmed in his seat. Whatever it was he was doing, he was not getting through to these numb skulls. The older one, Bert something, almost spitting in his face, was an ogre. The other younger one sitting by the door hadn't said much.

"OK", he said speaking slowly and deliberately, "I'm trying to do as you say and be very specific.

"As I told you, I'm a trucker. I've been working in town for the last week doing short hauls and I came home about 5:30 yesterday and the phone was ringing and no one was home.

"The woman on the line from the daycare said that Cristal hadn't arrived to pick up the baby and I needed to get over there pronto, 'cause she was lockin' up'.

"I called Cristal's number at the TV station on the way over and it went to voicemail. I tried her cell too and the same thing.

"I picked up Tiffany at the daycare, came home, fed her, had dinner, put her down and started calling Cristal's girlfriends, her sister and her parents to try to find her but no one had seen her. Her cell just kept going directly to voicemail.

"So, as the hours went by I started to panic. Around ten, I called the police and got the runaround from your desk guy. He took some details but said no one would do anything until 48 hours had passed for a missing adult.

His hands were shaking as he continued, "Obviously I couldn't sleep so about 2 am I tried to phone in an Amber Alert figuring you might at least start looking for her car and that might get your asses moving but they told me they already had a missing person's call at my address, not a missing child and if I was making it up I was committing a felony. So I just hung up.

"Then this morning I called her office and they said she was not at work all day yesterday and had not called in which really made me panic.

"I dropped Tiffany off at Cristal's parents' home and I was back and just calling work to tell them I would not be in when you guys showed up because of the Amber Alert."

He was starting to show signs of getting impatient and agitated, "And here we are, wasting time while my wife is God knows where. Why are you guys giving me the gears? Why aren't you trying to find her?" his voice rising.

Bert's younger partner Colt Baker could see the exasperation on his partner's face and quickly stepped in, "Calm down. You see Mr. Wiggins, we're trying to help you here but your story changes a little each time. Each time you add a little or leave something out or change something slightly and that's not a good sign. Details are important. This time you added a call to her office number last night and calls to her girlfriends. If you really want to help us find your wife then you need to give us ALL the information."

The younger Baker pushed a notepad and pen forward, "Now start writing and list everyone that may have seen her, where they live or work and their numbers if you have them.

"We're not accusing you of anything but frankly, you're a very inconsistent witness to this disappearance so far.

"So please," he pleaded, "be very careful that you give us EVERYONE she might have seen whether you've already checked with them or not. We're the pros at this and we ask different questions than you would. Understand?

"Now, I'll get you another coffee while you're writing that down. We'll be back in a few minutes."

As they stepped out of the interrogation room, they could see that Greg Wiggins was pissed and maybe a little scared but that was to be expected if he feared for his wife.

Colt was first to speak, "What do you think?"

Bert sneered, "I think he's lying, about what I don't know, but there's something about his evasive attitude and changing story that raises the hair on the back of my neck. He's had lots of practice at making up stories would be my guess. He keeps hopping all over the place and did you notice the lack of eye contact? This guy is afraid of the cops for some reason.

"He hasn't done or said anything yet to make me think he off'd his wife but still there's something he's holding back. Given that most of these cases have something to do with the husband, he's either really smart calling it in early and trying that Amber Alert stunt, or he's truly shook up about her disappearance and due to that, he's totally panicked and therefore a lousy witness. I mean we must have gone over his story four times and I'm still not sure we're getting the whole picture.

"He doesn't even know if he left before or after his wife yesterday morning or what she was wearing. How does that work?"

Colt who had been preparing a coffee for the witness nodded, "Yeah, I know exactly what you mean.

"You know we can dump this one for another day. The forty-eight hours are not up yet and if it wasn't the need to check out the Amber Alert thing we would still not be on it.

"Still I'm with you, this disappearance seems fishy somehow. My first thought was whether she had a reason to leave on her own, like another guy.

"I know nothing about her but I could see where a woman might grow tired of that piece of work in there. But she left the baby. From his description of her, I don't see her leaving the baby behind. We'll know more when we speak to some of her friends and neighbors."

The older Bert reluctantly poured himself another stale coffee. "I'm not going back in there. I'll just blow my cool.

"I don't think we're going to get any more out of him anyways.

"Get the list from him and we'll make a few calls. Ask him to get us a current picture of her too. Send him home but fingerprint him first. Tell him it's for exclusionary purposes if we find her car and we'll take it from there."

***

Detective Bert Wilson was just wrapping up some paperwork when Jr. Detective Colt Baker came back to his adjoining desk, "He gave me about 10 names to check including the parents and he said we can get a picture off the TV station's web site but get this, no fingerprints. Says it's his right to refuse, which of course it is but man that doesn't feel right."

Bert looked up from the paperwork he had seemed engrossed in, "I told you there was something off about this guy so I'm not surprised he ducked the fingerprinting. No way we're waiting for the 48 hours. This guy just pushed this to the top of the heap. I want the neighbors first. Let's hit a couple of them right after lunch. I took the credit card numbers off that stuff he gave the desk last night as well as her SUV info and I've set tracers on them."

***

Lunch was a hurried affair as usual. Today was Colt's turn to pick and they ended up at one of the Penn Station East Coast sub shops for Philly Cheese Steaks which they both loved.

The 30-year old Jr. Detective Colt Baker was in great physical shape spending at least an hour a day at the gym so he figured he could eat whatever he wanted and he loved the way 'The Penn' made them.

Philly Cheese Steaks on the other hand were bound to go straight to the 50-year old Detective Bert Wilson's mid section but he loved them too.

They made it over to the neighborhood where the Wiggins lived by about one thirty.

Mrs. Roberts was in her sixties and the next door neighbor of the Wiggins. As it turned out Mr. Roberts had taken early retirement and was home too.

After being invited in and offered a coffee, which they both declined, they were seated in the small cozy living room when Bert opened the questioning.

"As I mentioned, Mrs. Wiggins next door has not been seen since yesterday and Mr. Wiggins has asked us to look into it. We'd like to ask you a few questions in total confidentiality. If we need anything on the record, we'll do a formal questioning later but today we're just looking for some cursory information.

"Hopefully Mrs. Wiggins will return soon and solve our little mystery. Can I ask you when you last saw her?"

After glancing at his wife, Mr. Roberts took the lead, "Well, I'm home most of the time and we would normally see her coming and going, but now that I think of it we didn't see her yesterday," again glancing at his wife, "or even over the weekend. We saw her return from the daycare with little Tiffany on Friday and waved hi but I don't think we saw her after that."

Mrs. Roberts nodded agreement.

Colt was scribbling notes as Bert continued, "Would you normally see them on the weekend or daily going to work?"

"Well Greg is a long-haul trucker so there are times we don't see him for a week or so. We usually see Cristal frequently but not seeing her for a day or two is not entirely unheard of."

"I see. Can you tell me anything about their relationship? How do they seem when they are together."

This time it was Mrs. Roberts who responded, "I'd say they are like any other young couple. They seem friendly enough and seem to have a decent marriage but I've heard the odd raised voice from over there recently but nothing to get alarmed about."

"So you have a good relationship with them too?"

It was apparent Mr. Roberts had something on his mind, "I would say yes, but we have a better relationship with Cristal than Greg. We occasionally babysit that tiny angel Tiffany and Cristal is a devoted mother and just a darling herself, but Greg has always given us pause. Nothing you can really put your finger on, but just something a little deceitful if you know what I mean. Someone once described it to me as being 'economical with the truth'."

Colt smiled at that, stopped writing and jumped in, "Can you be a little more specific?"

Mr. Roberts hesitated, looked at his wife and then continued, "Well I don't see how this will help find Cristal and it's really nothing serious, but Greg told me one time that he had done two years at Stanford University before he dropped out and got a real man's job, as he called it, driving long-haul transports. But during a cookout over at their place, I asked him how he liked Palo Alto and he said he had never been there. It was clear to me that the Stanford story was made up.

"So as you see, nothing important, but just enough to give you pause about any story he tells you. I mean it could simply be that he's embarrassed about his level of education."

A big red flag for the two detectives. Pathological liars were common in police work and lying in casual conversations was a prime indicator. Greg Wiggins was starting to look a lot like the picture Bert Wilson had in his head.

It was still early in their investigation and Cristal could show up at any moment so after finding out the Roberts had nothing more to add they made their way to the door thanking them.

As they walked down the steps, Colt said to Bert in a hushed voice, "Did you notice the car in front of the

Wiggins' house? There's been someone sitting in it since we arrived."

Bert held Colt back for a moment and turned away from the suspect car, "Good catch. I noticed that too. Let's go find out who it is but have your service weapon ready and keep your eyes open for any movement up or down the street and pick some fast cover in case we need it."

As they approached the rather old Ford on both sides, the occupant who had his hands on the steering wheel made no attempt to escape their attention.

"Good afternoon sir. My name is Detective Bert Wilson with the Cincinnati Police." Bert said flipping open his badge, "Could I ask to see some Identification please?"

Looking distraught, the man in his sixties asked, "Have I done anything wrong officer", reaching for his wallet under the careful eye of the two Cincinnati cops.

"Not yet, Mr. … Serpe. Can I ask you what you're doing here?"

With a voice almost cracking he said, "My daughter lives in this house and her husband told us she's missing. I've called the cops but you guys just brushed me off, so I'm sitting here to see if she returns or if that jackass of a son-in-law is up to something."

"Mr. Serpe, we are the ones investigating your daughter's absence. We were just talking to their neighbors.

"I don't see a car in Mr. Wiggins' driveway so assuming he's not here, could I ask you to join us in our car to answer a few questions?"

"Thank God someone is on the job. I'd be happy to help. I'm seriously concerned over Cristal's disappearance and I'll do absolutely anything to help," he said as he started to get out of the car.

They put him in the back of their car and started right in on the questioning with Bert taking the lead again, "Sir, when was the last time you heard from your daughter?"

"Last Thursday after dinner. We usually speak more often but there was no reason to call this past weekend. It was cool and rainy so we didn't drop by either, which we often do."

"I see. Can you think of any reason she may have had not to return home yesterday?"

"No. No way. And leave Tiffany all alone? Couldn't happen. She's devoted to that child. There's no way she would take off and leave Tiffany. Not in a million years."

"Does your daughter have any medical issues?"

He looked surprised and maybe hurt at the question, "None. She's as healthy and strong as a bull. She's an expert in several martial arts disciplines and spends lots of time at the Health Club. Last time we saw her she seemed happy enough."

"OK. We just have some standard questions we have to get through. Understand?"

Serpe simply nodded as Bert continued, "How's your relationship with her husband, Mr. Wiggins?"

He swallowed hard, "I'm sorry. This is really hard for me. I've never had to deal with the police before and I'm terrified something has happened to Cristal.

"As to Greg, we get along OK I guess, but I can't say we were thrilled when Cristal married him about a year ago. The baby is not his. She used to work overseas and married a US Marine over there. He was killed in Afghanistan shortly after they were married. We actually never had the chance to meet him. It all happened so fast. So she came home to have the baby. They must have gotten pregnant on their honeymoon. His death was a terrible shock to her having been married a little over a month at the time.

"About a year later, after she had the baby she met Greg who had a part-time job as an instructor at that health club where she goes. She was trying to work off the baby fat and get back into shape.

"Six months later, they were married. Of course, we thought she rushed into it a little too fast and in fact her first marriage was a really hurried up affair as well, which I've always thought is out of character for her, but what does a father know?

"I'm really concerned. What do you think has happened to her?"

Colt sympathized, "Sir we're just starting to look into this now. In many of these cases the person shows up with a rational explanation, so it's a little early to get too excited about an unannounced absence."

He continued, "What was your daughter doing overseas in terms of a job?"

"She started out as an intern at CNN and because she speaks Arabic she was quickly assigned to the Middle East and Africa and soon became a full producer for most of the news coming out of that area. She was one of their youngest and brightest producers ever. Had quite a career going. She flew around a lot. Did some really big international stories. She met her first husband at an embassy event where he was stationed at the time. I don't remember what country it was."

"Her Arabic was strong enough to deal with the locals?"

"Yeah, she had done a year as an exchange student in Jordan living with a family there and was fluent. She seemed to love that part of the world. God knows why. All we see on TV makes it look so completely backward."

"I see. Back to Greg. You don't sound too thrilled about their relationship. "

"Well she seems to like him or love him. Who knows. Maybe it's just a parent thing but we thought she could have done a lot better than a truck driver who gives body building classes on the side. We've always thought it might be a beefcake fetish or a rebound thing after losing her first husband.

"I hope you won't repeat that to Greg."

Bert shrugged it off.

"Anyways, she didn't want to go back to her job in Africa with a young baby to look after and CNN doesn't have much of a presence in Cincinnati so now she produces the news for the local TV station, WKRC-12.

"She wanted to be close to us as the baby grew up. We love getting the odd opportunity to babysit little Tiffany. She's a gem.

"Greg brought her over this morning when he told us Cristal was still missing and we're looking after Tiffany right now. But I'm really afraid that something has happened to Cristal. You men have got to find her for us!"

"Mr. Serpe, we've no reason to believe that Cristal won't walk back in the door at any moment but just to be thorough, can you think of anyone who would want to do harm to either Cristal or Greg."

The sixty-something father clearly paled at the thought, "No. There's the odd tough story on the news that would clearly upset some of the characters in her reports but I don't even think her name as the producer is easily available and there's been nothing of any significance in the news lately that I'm aware of.

"Everybody loves Cristal. She's a really sweet girl but no push over if you know what I mean. Because of her martial arts expertise, if anyone did tangle with her she could probably handle them. She won several state and national championships in college."

He thought for a second looking for something to add and then replied, "As to Greg. Who knows? We know very little about him. Apparently, he was orphaned a few years ago when his mother died. He never knew his father. He has no siblings or even relatives that he keeps in touch with. But I've never seen any evidence that he might have enemies or people who would want to hurt him or his family. No, I can't say there is anything there but gentlemen I'm really scared for my daughter. This is totally unlike her to disappear with the love of her life, Tiffany left behind. Please take this very seriously and do everything you can to find her. I fear something really terrible has happened to her."

"Thank you very much for your assistance Mr. Serpe. You can be assured that we'll do our best. No promises but many of these situations turn out to be some sort of domestic turmoil and the parties get back together within a day or two. We spoke to Greg earlier and he gave us your number so we'll call you if we need anything more."

Frank Serpe shook their hands and went to open the car door in the rear of the detectives' vehicle, "Oh, someone broke your handle?" he suspected something different before the words were out of his mouth.

"It's made that way", Colt said as he stepped out and opened the door for the gentleman who was now red in the face.

They watched as he returned to his vehicle and set up his own surveillance in front of the Wiggins' home.

"So what did you think?", Colt asked.

Bert put the car in drive and drove off, "Nice guy, not much to offer except they didn't see or hear from her all weekend either and the number of people who don't like Greg Wiggins just got bigger. He has no family and no history too. That's always a red flag for me. Maybe that has something to do with not allowing us to collect his fingerprints. I really don't like this guy."

The Investigation

Bert continued, "Let's swing by the daycare, it's not far from here. I want to find out if they saw or heard anything when she dropped off the toddler. At least they'll have seen her, what she was driving, how she was dressed, her mood, and if there was anyone with her."

Five minutes later they pulled into the parking in front of the 'Tiny Tots Daycare' on the main drag in this middle class suburb.

It looked like an old Pizza Hut renovated for the purpose with a manicured lawn and gardens in front and four-foot fences surrounding a play area toward the back of the property. They had to show their badges to be buzzed in and were met by an attractive, classy looking woman who had just walked out of an office strategically positioned to see all comings and goings.

"Hi, I'm Detective Bert Wilson and this is Detective Colt Baker of the Cincinnati PD. I'm not sure if you know this but Mrs. Wiggins, mother of Tiffany Wiggins has been reported missing and we're looking for some information on her. Can I get your name and your position here please?"

The smartly dressed forty-something woman smiled as she spoke, "Of course Detective. My name is Martha Cox and I am the manager of this facility and yes, we're aware and concerned about Cristal's disappearance. Mr. Wiggins informed us and told us this morning that he was leaving Tiffany with her maternal grandmother for a few days. How can we help you?"

"Well, first off, did you see Mrs. Wiggins drop Tiffany off yesterday morning?"

"I'm afraid I did not. I was not at this post yesterday. For the morning for drop-offs, we always have someone assigned here at the desk and yesterday it was Nancy's turn. She's in one of the classes right now. I can replace her for a few minutes if you wish to speak with her."

"That would be excellent."

The pretty director disappeared down the hall soon to be replaced by an even prettier girl who could not have been much more than eighteen. She introduced herself as Nancy Trudel.

Colt found her embarrassment of speaking to the cops charming and jumped in before Bert could get a word out, "Nancy. Can I call you Nancy?" as she nodded.

"Nancy did you see Mrs. Wiggins drop Tiffany off yesterday morning?"

"No."

The two men seemed puzzled. Colt continued, "Can you say more. Why didn't you see her?"

"I'm sorry, I'm new here and I don't know all the parents. I just focus on making sure we have the children in our custody and they get headed off to the right playroom. I really couldn't tell you who dropped off any child yesterday or any other day. I've only worked here since last week and yesterday was only my second day doing incoming. I do know Tiffany by now. Cute little two-year old but I paid no attention to who dropped her off."

"Well can you at least tell us if it was a man or a woman?"

After a moment of reflection she said, "Sorry, I have no memory of who dropped her off at all. It's just something I don't pay attention to. Often there are several arriving at the same time and my only concern is not to lose track of one of the kids. Sorry".

"Thank you Nancy. If you think of anything else please call me at my personal number." Colt said as he handed her his card. "Could you ask the director to come back now?"

"Sure", she said blushing even more as she turned and walked quickly down the hall, Colt's eyes following her little wiggle.

"Nice move", Bert said, "You're a young single guy, go for it".

As Martha Cox returned Bert took over the questioning, "Well I'm afraid Nancy was not much help. She saw Tiffany but has no idea who dropped her off."

"I'm sorry about that. She's new and sometimes the job here can overwhelm the newcomers for a few weeks. Is there anything else I can do for you?"

"Do you know either Mr. or Mrs. Wiggins at all? Do you know anything about them, their family, their relationship, their normal routine?"

"I've spoken to Cristal on occasion and she seems very sweet. I think she's involved in TV or something. She normally drops Tiffany off in a white SUV and picks her up. I think I saw Mr. Wiggins only once before last night when I had to call him after Cristal didn't show up. I'm afraid I have nothing else to offer in that vein."

"Thank you Ms. Cox. We'll be in touch if there's anything else. Have a nice day."

***

They were quickly back at the office and just about to check up on some other files they were working when Colt Baker's phone rang and the caller ID said it was Greg Wiggins.

Wiggins snapped at him, "So what have you found out?"

"I'm sorry Mr. Wiggins we have nothing to report yet."

"Well one of the kids on the block told me you were interviewing neighbors today and I just want to let you know that the Robert's don't like me.

"And while I'm at it, that old buzzard Serpe is sitting in front of my house and he won't even talk to me like I've got something to do with his daughter's disappearance."

His voice was rising, "I want some action here! Get that old buzzard off my property and find my damned wife", he yelled as he slammed the phone down.

***

Greg Wiggins spent the rest of his day driving around places they had been together to see if he could find Cristal's car. He even checked out the shopping centers and headed over the bridge to the airport but no luck.

He was wondering if there was anything her friends at WKRC could think of. He didn't know a lot of people over at the TV station but he had met her boss at the Christmas party. Harry something was his name.

When Greg got home after dinner time, he found that Harry had left two voicemails simply saying he wanted Greg to call.

Initially Greg was reluctant to speak with him but finally gave in and called him at the number he had left, "Harry, good of you to call, I guess you're going to want an update on Cristal."

"Well of course Greg. Have you heard from her yet? We're all worried sick about her at the station."

"No, not a word and I'm going out of my mind. The cops are on it but I'm not impressed with the way they're going at this. Do you guys over at the TV station have any ideas on what could have happened?"

"No, but it's the only thing we're talking about around here. We're just as perplexed as you.

"Listen Greg, we're in the TV business and we want to help. This is going to go public at some point and likely sooner than later when some media outlet picks up the fact that a TV producer has gone missing. You just said the cops aren't doing much. Let us help you. Let's go on air with her disappearance. At a minimum you'll have about a million more people looking for her and more when other stations pick it up. Seriously we can more than double the efforts of the cops if you're ready to do this."

"I'm in. Anything to help get a message to her or whomever has taken her. What do you want me to do?"

"We have head shots of her for publicity and any time we have to show her face on TV but we need something more natural and personal to get the viewer's attention so we need a recent photo of her. A good one that captures her entire face if possible. Then we need a satellite truck out at your house to film the home and you making an appeal out front."

"I'll get the picture off her computer and mail it to you and the filming of the house is fine but there's no way I'm going on camera. That's just me. You guys do it as her employer."

"It really needs to be you Greg. We won't ask any questions or anything and you can say as little or as much as you want. We want you to be comfortable so we'll play it any way you want within reason."

"No deal. No camera on me. You do it."

There was a long pause and then Harry reluctantly agreed.

"I'll have a team over there within the hour," he said as the call ended.

Greg knew just which picture he wanted to send. It was a great shot of her on vacation last summer in a terrific bikini. She looked really sexy in it.

He barely knew how to send an e-mail. That was more Cristal's domain. He didn't know how to trim the picture so he wrote a cover note to ensure they would crop the photo to just her head for TV and sent it off to the station's main mail address, attention Harry in the Newsroom.

The TV crew came and got their shots of the home with a reporter standing in front of the house. By the eleven o'clock news, it was near the top of the broadcast and to his horror, they had not cropped the photo. The good news was that they had treated the whole thing with some dignity; 'beloved producer of the news for Channel 12 had gone missing ... foul play suspected ... leaving behind a two-year old baby and a distraught husband ... anyone seeing her or knowing anything about her whereabouts to call the Cincinnati Police'.

***

Detective Bert Wilson was in the office early and woke Greg Wiggins at 7:30, "So you've had a ransom note." he said rather than asked.

Greg struggled to clear his throat, "No, not yet. What would make you think that?"

"Well, I caught the news last night and apparently foul play is suspected. That usually means the police are investigating a crime. Do you want us to get a subpoena, kick you out of your house and send in a forensics team?"

"Hey those were not my words. They made that stuff up over at the TV station. They want to help to get her back too you know. You guys have nothing to show yet."

"Well maybe you should talk to us before you go off half cocked. If there are kidnappers involved then you may have just eliminated a few of our options. What are you going to do if they had planned to tell you not to involve the media or the police and all you've done is really pissed them off?

"You need to leave this investigation to us. This thing will be all over the Cincinnati media outlets by lunch. Call us if you get a ransom demand," he said as he slammed the phone down.

Bert was just fixing his coffee near his cubical when Colt rushed up, "Ran into the chief on the elevator. Wants to know why he didn't know about the Wiggins case until he saw it on TV. He wants a briefing for the press calls he's expecting."

"What did you tell him?"

"Just what we know. It's not even forty-eight hours yet since he phoned it in. A woman doesn't come home and husband says she has been kidnapped but we have no evidence of that. Could be a domestic dispute. He still wants the briefing though."

Colt continued, "Hey, by the way did you notice Wiggins was not videotaped? They had a local reporter do the piece in front of his house. I'm guessing he's the one that didn't want to be on camera. He doesn't seem shy to me. Could be that he doesn't want to be identified by someone who may have seen him up to something over the weekend."

Bert nodded, "You could be on to something. Anyways, I'll handle the briefing with the chief. In the meantime get that jackass Wiggins back in here. I want to know why he was not on TV and also who might have seen her over the weekend. We could be dealing with him not reporting her disappearance for three days which really changes things.

"Also, now that it has gone public and the boss is asking, we'd better open an official file. You handle that part but remember those files are shared with the FBI through the Homeland Security linkup so be careful what you put in there, just the minimum. There is no reason to think the FBI might get involved unless we declare it as an interstate kidnapping or her car is found on the other side of the bridge and that brings them in."

***

Bert spent the next 15 minutes in the chief's office bringing him up to date on what they knew about Cristal Wiggins' disappearance.

The fact that it was very little was only offset by the fact that the 48 hours since the call came in had not yet elapsed so they could call it an alleged disappearance for now if the press were pushy.

Still they knew she had been missing for at least 48 hours, given she never showed up at her office on

Monday, and maybe much longer if Greg Wiggins had delayed reporting it.

One of our own

Greg Wiggins was more than aggravated at being summoned again to Police HQ by these two clowns of cops. As a long-haul trucker, he had lots of experience with cops and no real love for them but these two were incompetent in addition to being a pain in the ass.

Given the previous day's testiness between Greg and Detective Bert Wilson, and after all three were seated with a coffee, Colt took the lead, "Mr. Wiggins we found it curious that you didn't choose to be on TV last night, making an appeal for your wife's return. Why did you leave it up to a reporter? They were right there at your house after all. Usually a family member carries more weight and I'm sure the station wanted you to make a personal appeal?"

It was obvious to the two cops that Wiggins was instantly uncomfortable, "Look I want my wife back NOW! I'm just a little shy with the TV thing if you really want to know. And what the hell does that have to do with anything? I'm a private person and I've never been the center of attention so I didn't want to be videotaped. I don't want guys coming up to me and saying 'I saw you on TV last night and you looked stupid dude', that's all there is to it."

The two detectives glanced at each other and it was clear to everyone in the room that they were not buying this lame excuse. Greg Wiggin's didn't come off as the shy, retiring type or even easily embarrassed by other truckers.

Colt continued, "OK, most people would be more concern about the missing loved one than any embarrassment caused by a TV appearance but let's leave that for now.

"You said that your wife dropped your daughter off at the daycare around eight am on Monday, right?"

"Yeah, so what?"

"Well no one there saw her do that. No one there saw her Monday morning."

"Hey, I told you I didn't see Cristal leave with Tiffany. I must have been in the shower or something. She always leaves just before eight. Hell, Tiffany got there right, because I'm pretty sure it was her I picked up at five thirty and she's now with Cristal's mom! What's your point? It's my wife that's missing, not my step daughter."

Bert stepped in, "OK let's move on. What did you and your wife do on the weekend?"

"Where is this going? She disappeared on Monday. Not on the weekend."

"Just answer the question if you will."

"Listen, I don't know what she did on Saturday because I had to drop off a load in Dayton, so I took it up there, dumped it in the holding yard and came back home around three or four in the afternoon. I usually park my tractor at a local body shop. I know the guy. So I left it there, got in my car and drove home. She was watching some sappy movie on the Hallmark channel as I remember."

"And Sunday?"

He looked at them like this was never going to end, "Let's see, we got up late, and just vegged out all day between munching on snacks and watching more of that sappy Hallmark crap that she loves. I did a bit of paperwork in the afternoon but she was watching the movies. It must have been some sort of marathon movie thing or something. Anyways, she monopolized the TV all day. Where is this going?"

"Did she phone anyone or receive any calls on Saturday or Sunday?"

"Not that I saw. It was a quiet weekend. Why are you asking all of these questions?"

"We are just closing some open ends and frankly no one we've interviewed so far, other than yourself, saw your wife after 5 pm on Friday. No one saw her on Monday. So between Friday evening and now, you're the only one who saw her."

Wiggins had been getting a little redder each minute he had been in the hot seat, "OK, I can see where this is going. You think I did something to her over the weekend, right? I want a lawyer?" he said turning even redder in the face.

"You guys are clearly focused on me having done something to my wife and you couldn't be further from the truth and now I'm starting to believe you've done nothing to find her.

"I spent most of yesterday afternoon and evening driving around looking for her car. What the hell did you guys do. I think it's time for me to have another discussion with my friends in the press. Maybe they can get the ball rolling on finding her.

"Have you even put out her car description or traced her credit cards? Have you done anything to try to find her?"

Bert was thinking this guy was either being honest, unlikely, or he was putting on a great act, "Mr. Wiggins, we've done everything we normally do in a case like this and yes we've flagged her car and her cards.

"That will be all for now so you can leave but remember, the more you get the media involved, the more you potentially complicate getting your wife back if she's in the hands of kidnappers."

Just as they led him huffing and puffing out into the main office the TV tuned to CNN at the end of the room had a full body picture of Cristal Wiggins in a sexy bikini.

"Turn that up", Colt yelled to an officer standing by the TV.

The screen quickly shifted to a reporter standing in front of the Wiggins' home, "So that's it Candy. A wonderful young mother of a two-year old daughter, Cristal Wiggins, a former CNN producer and more recently news producer for our affiliate in Cincinnati, has apparently been abducted and the police have no idea where she is or who has her. As far as we know there has been no ransom demand yet."

The officer turned the volume down as the channel went on with other news.

Colt turned to Greg Wiggins, "Wow, now the whole nation knows and we just invited in the FBI because they will be under pressure to find a way to take over this investigation now that it has gotten national attention and CNN has declared it an 'abduction'. Your wife is in the TV business and you didn't realize that a local story would get picked up nationally, especially with a picture like that?"

"They were supposed to crop that picture. Who cares anyway. I'd rather have the FBI in on this. You guys are doing no good", he turned and stomped out of the room.

The two cops stared at each other and then turned back to the coffee cup on the table in the interrogation room.

Colt smiled, "At least we now have his fingerprints."

***

An hour earlier, just three minutes after Colt Baker had hit the submit button on the Wiggins file, an automated alarm went off on a CIA analyst's screen in Langley.

At first, he was not concerned. They had triggers set for all kinds of entries into the Common Intelligence Database.

The code on this one was one that he didn't recognize. He looked up the general code which was listed on the reference web page as an alleged 'Kidnapping of a Watched Person'. His first thought was that it might be someone in a witness protection program who had been discovered and nabbed.

He did a search with the full alarm identifier on the National Security Database Warning codes. There it was, 'Kidnapping associated with an undercover law-enforcement officer.'

Still pretty cryptic so he went back to the alarm and clicked on the source report. Someone named Cristal Wiggins in Cincinnati was the subject of a missing persons police report.

He did a secure search on the name and was shocked to find out that a Cristal Wiggins aka Cristal Serpe had once worked for the CIA in covert operations and not that long ago.

He double checked his work just to be sure. It was all there, a former CIA undercover operative had been listed as missing and possibly kidnapped in Cincinnati. That was big and had to go up to his controller right away.

Five minutes later, the young CIA analyst sat in a small conference room in Langley waiting for what he was not sure. His boss had simply told him to get a conference room quick, be prepared to brief, and wait for him.

Two section heads that he barely recognized filed in with his boss and took seats facing him. By the name tags he identified them as Philip Harris and Chip Atwood. He had brought five hardcopies of the file as he had not known what to expect and now slid three of them across the desk to each of the new arrivals as they took their seats.

He cleared his throat and sat up straight as he spoke, "My name is Jim McGuire and I work in internal intercepts and this alarm came over my system about ten minutes ago. The file I just gave you is a brief with our most recent photos of a Cristal Wiggins aka Cristal Serpe.

"According to our records this Cristal Wiggins was a deep undercover agent working for us until about three years ago. She was assigned to various Ops in Africa and the Middle East and was responsible for the capture of at least one major Al Qaeda operative in Africa, one Daniel Boone."

No one in the room even smiled, "According to the local police in Cincinnati, it's starting to look like someone nabbed her two days ago. All we have is what they entered into the National Crime Database because no one from Langley has yet contacted them to get any additional info. There is a possibility it's a domestic violence affair but our protocol requires I escalate this as she was apparently one of ours."

36

Chip Atwood nodded slowly as he reviewed the file, "Jim, you've done a great job here. Unless you have anything else to add I think we can let you get back to your post. Please let us know immediately if anything additional comes in on this file but this is 'eyes only' for now and no one should contact Cincinnati PD. We'll take it from here. Thank you."

Jim McGuire indicated by a nod and quickly gathered his papers and left the room.

Once the door was closed, Chip turned to the two remaining, "I've never heard of her, is that her real name or was that a cover?"

Philip Harris responded, "I knew her briefly and yes Cristal Serpe was her real name, Looks like she married.

"She was recruited right out of college. Her cover was as a CNN producer all over Africa and the Middle East and she did bring in a big fish about three years ago. We called him Daniel Boone internally, don't ask me why. He had another Arab war name but it escapes me for the moment. I'll bet you he's still in Guantanamo.

"I seem to remember she was a real tiger and actually did some serious wet work for the agency. It's a long shot but maybe someone figured she set this Daniel Boone character up, tracked her down and is looking for some pay back. It says here the husband has been interviewed and has not been eliminated as a potential perpetrator so far. But that may not be our first concern.

"Believe it or not, she was a personal recruit of the Deputy Director. They were pretty close throughout her career. By close I mean father daughter style or coach protégé, nothing more. It says she has a two-year old child and it must be about that time that she left the agency so there may be a connection on why and when she left. I was never read into the whole story. I only met her once or twice because she was always overseas. Real looker too as I remember.

"I know she was being fast tracked and there was some jealousy in the ranks with what seemed like favoritism from the DD but you didn't hear that from me. She had moved up the ranks pretty fast and was still in her late twenties, which is young for someone running full undercover solo Ops in-country. One way or another this is going to heat up fast given her connection to the DD unless she shows up home with some sob story."

Just then, there was a knock at the door. It opened and it was Jim McGuire again. "I thought I should inform you that CNN has picked up the story and is running it hourly I would imagine. They have a really sexy picture of her and you know how that goes, so they're making a big thing of it."

Chip spoke first, "Great, just what we needed. Nancy Grace will be on 24/7 with 'Missing Tot Mom' before this is over. I had better get on the Deputy Director's calendar right away."

The Deputy Director was the real muscle and ran all operations in the CIA. The Current CIA Director was more of a figure head and he left all operations to the DD. A political appointee with no CIA background, he kept his nose for the most part out of the daily business of the organization. He did have to be briefed though, every morning before the National Security meeting known internally as NATSEC, which he attended in the Whitehouse with the President.

It was nearly two hours later when Chip Atwood caught Deputy Director William Carter, known internally as the DD, hustling out of one apparently urgent meeting and into another, "Sir I thought you should hear about this right away. We have reason to believe that someone you know named Cristal may have been kidnapped."

The DD stopped dead in his tracks, "Our Cristal? Cristal Serpe?"

"Yes. Well actually her name is Cristal Wiggins now sir but it's her and the local cops have no leads. CNN picked it up because she's very photogenic and they have her in a bikini so it's a national story already and they can be expected to milk it for ratings. There is a chance that it's a domestic violence case but given her history of special Ops I think we need to be cautious on this one."

"I would have to agree. She was into some heavy stuff back then and there could be some hurt feelings out there.

"Damn it, I begged her to change her name and go underground. If you're right and someone from her past has snatched her, I have a feeling who it might be. Watch for a strange ransom demand, probably out of Spain and it will be directed at us not the locals or her husband.

"I'll bet I can guess what they want too … Shit … I have no time for this. Get Phil Harris on this NOW! He knows some of the history. I'm up to my eyeballs in a potential bigger problem so I can't deal with this at the moment. I'll be in these meetings most of the day."

"Harris was in on the briefing so I'll hand this off to him and of course we'll keep you updated."

"I don't know if you know it but I recruited Cristal right out of college and she is very special to me. All I can think is that those morons may not know much about her and how much trouble they may be in themselves. She did some real wet work for us. If they turn their back on her for a second, it'll be a bloody mess. They'll be dead and she'll be the one calling us. Don't let this one get loose."

He turned to leave and then stopped abruptly thinking for a second and then turning back to Chip said, "Shit, we may have a much bigger problem here.

"If my guess is right about who has gone after her, and we'll confirm that if we get something out of Spain, then we may have at least one foreign Jihadi on our soil out of central Africa and there's no way he's going to leave the US without racking up some points.

"This is Thanksgiving week and I'll bet he'll launch an attack around Thanksgiving before he leaves but not before the Cristal affair is resolved.

"I want a meeting in an hour and I want us to go to internal YELLOW on this. We have no actionable Intel on this to share with anyone so doing a full Homeland Security YELLOW is not possible.

"You raise the alarm internally. See Phil Harris if you need help. Mention we've reason to believe that we have an imminent threat from a foreign Jihadi who has already entered the US. He may be here from Burundi. Get a scan going on all fronts for any suspicious entry activity in the last two weeks. And find out if the African desk has anything on movement of principals over there."

At that, he turned and hurried into his next meeting.

Chip's first thought was "Wow, am I going to be popular. A Yellow Alert will cancel everyone's Thanksgiving plans for this weekend. Why me?"

Loose Nuke

As DD Bill Carter entered the room, he was surprised to see about fifteen people already seated and ready for the briefing. He turned to his Ops manager Carole Glass and whispered, "Too many".

She nodded and turned to the room, "Sorry ladies and gentlemen, this is a new situation yet to be given a classification and therefore it is eyes only at the moment. I want major section heads and the two people from the Pakistani desk to remain. The rest of you are dismissed at least for the moment. We'll call you if and when we need you."

This was taken as normal modus operandi for high level Top Secret meetings and the room was quickly weaned down to only the eight of them.

Carole kicked it off, "Samir, as head of the Pakistani desk maybe you can brief us."

"Yes Ma'am." He passed out packages marked 'EYES ONLY.'

"Two days ago we picked up information that there was a young man in a hospital in the Waziristan region with what could have been radiation burns. We dispatched one of our agents up there and he reported back this morning that the young man died yesterday with all the signs of acute radiation poisoning.

"He was interrogated by the local police before succumbing to his injuries but they were unable to get anything out of him and they have yet to identify him but we think from the pictures that he is Mohammed Sadoum, a known bomb maker in Pakistan whom we've been looking for for some time. Our guy is still in Waziristan trying to collect any additional evidence."

He paused and then continued, "As you know we've had increase chatter that the head of Al Qaeda, Khalil al-Adel is determined to get his hands on a nuke or at least a dirty bomb. So our best guess is that he's the one behind this.

"We've been watching the Afghanistan routes out of Turkmenistan and Uzbekistan in case they are able to smuggle something out of Kazakhstan or beyond, cross country to Pakistan and this is the first indication that there may be a device that has made it that far."

On the screen at the end of the room a grisly picture appeared of a corpse covered in ugly lesions.

Samir continued, "Our medical staff says these pictures and the radiation reading our agent took of the remains would indicate that this person was in the presence of an exposed core for thirty minutes or more within the last 5 days. Alternatively, it could have been longer exposure to a lower grade nuclear source, up to a month ago.

"If it was a nuclear core we're not sure why he would have been exposed to it. Could have been lack of knowledge of handling or working on a damaged package or transferring the core from one package to another.

"Either way we're pretty certain this was a weapons grade device due to the level of contamination and it was in or near Waziristan recently. As you know, Khalil al-Adel has many agents in the area so another reason he's our prime candidate for the lead on this even though he's about twenty five hundred miles away in Somali. Or so we think.

"One other thing, our orbiting radiation monitoring systems have picked up nothing in the area recently so the package has been shielded most of the time."

Assistant Deputy Director Glass pointed to the file, "Do we have anything on this Sadoum's affiliations. Is he in Khalil's operation and how high up would he be?"

The second briefer spoke up, "The latest Intel we have on Sadoum, which is about six months old, is that he's a top level mercenary. A bomb maker for hire. Clearly he is sympathetic to Jihad but our best information is that he will work with whatever radical group can pay. But if you wanted a bomb constructed or modified there's a short list and he's likely top three on that list. Of course, none of the top bomb makers has ever dealt with nuclear material to our knowledge. Until now.

"He has stayed on the loose because he never anchors himself to one place or one group for long, like many of these mercenary types."

It was the Deputy Director's turn, "So we may have a bomb in play and it may have been in Waziristan in the last five to thirty days. Well this is an easy one. Get ALL of our assets who are not anchored on something important, and even a few of them, onto this immediately. Use every means possible to find, track and neutralize this threat.

"Tell them only we're tracking a suspected nuclear device. Nothing about how we got the info. You have carte blanche on contractors in the region. Security at airports is too tight in general so they are likely shipping this overland and out by sea. Get all of our assets looking in those directions. Carole, you are the lead on this."

He stood, "I'll speak with the Air Force to get a drone with radiation detectors focused on the area. If you get any better focus on the locale let me know. Let's hope they are dumb enough to leave it unshielded at some point.

"Carole, get a watered down version of us chasing down a lead on some loose nuclear material, potential active threat, into the Director's briefing book for tomorrow and make sure we have the latest before he heads over to NATSEC. Let's get going."

At that the meeting ended.

Immediately the DD called a meeting of his top team. All ten of them were assembled around the large conference table in his office. All surveillance countermeasures were activated, as they were in all of the building now which was constantly going through upgrades to block any kind of snooping on the CIA.

"Ladies and gentlemen, we may have some major action with Khalil al-Adel. Bob, bring us up to date on Mr. Adel."

Bob Boutet had been point man on Al Qaeda's leader for the last three years. "Well, just to remind us, he's number one on our most wanted list. Just like all former Al Qaeda leaders, he's a radical Islamist who thinks he's doing Allah's bidding through Jihad but he has more of a political agenda than religious. He hates the US and wants our influence driven out of all Islamic countries. He's used our actions, especially drone attacks, as fodder for recruiting and he has maintained a wide network of loosely connected cells worldwide.

"Our last known ... let me take that back ... our last suspected location for him is Mogadishu, Somalia but it's hard to confirm any sighting of him as unlike his former Al Qaeda leaders we have no idea what he looks like now.

"From about the age of 4 to 20 he lived in the US, so his English is excellent and we have pictures from that era that are likely useless. He is thought to be a master of disguise and we're pretty sure he has excellent forgery support.

"Our Intel says he uses no electronics, no laptops or internet or cell phones. He never sleeps in the same house more than one night at a time. He is a master at organization and is hands-on for the planning of many of their ops.

"Pretty much no one knows anyone else in the organization by name. They all use war names that sometimes change for a specific operation. All communication seems simplex or one-way in the sense that you can never backtrack anything. It's highly likely that they don't use permanent or even repeating couriers after the Osama thing.

"For all we know they use carrier pigeons or smoke signals to communicate but whatever they do they must be doing lots of it in a fashion that we have not yet uncovered.

"The few people we've interrogated have different and puzzling stories to tell of communications. They don't understand it themselves. They might randomly get a phone call from someone they don't know who is likely using a disposable phone, probably with a spoofed sim card telling them to go down a certain street and turn when they see a chalk mark on a sidewalk. Then pick up a package somewhere there and take it to another street and put it in a trash can with another chalk mark on it. Presumably someone else has been given instructions to watch these transactions to pick up any tails. Their communications strategy keeps changing and remains a mystery but our best estimate is that it's working for them.

"Some of his far flung affiliates seem to be able to run their own Ops without his direct involvement. Often he simply provides the financing and moral support and possibly defines targets or strategies from afar.

"However he has been known at least in the past to do some of the hands on dirty work himself and he can be brutal. Over the years he has been personally tied to some pretty gruesome and videotaped assassinations. A few years ago in the Sudan, in front of some of his followers and a group of hostages, he buried a western journalist up to her neck and stoned her to death himself as her fellow hostages were forced to stand and watch with AK-47's in their faces."

The DD stifled a shiver when he remembered that episode. Cristal had been one of the journalist onlookers. The group had apparently been lured into a well laid trap. She had barely escaped with her life. The victim was a very close friend and it had really affected her but that was not widely known. He saw a big change in her after that.

Boutet continued, "We believe the leader and executioner in that attack was Khalil himself but as usual he was in a very comprehensive disguise and witnesses we interviewed later could not even agree on his height except that he was a little taller than most Arab men.

"You've seen the stats. We think he's behind over 60% of the attacks around the world including a couple of the foiled ones on our own soil.

"He has operatives in Pakistan, Afghanistan, Kazakhstan, Kurdistan, Yemen, Oman, Somalia and several small African nations. We think he may have a sleeper cell or two in Europe and the US but we've never been able to verify that. They also have sympathizers and fund raising operations pretty much everywhere you can find a couple of radical Muslims.

"We now know he was behind the failed bombings of the Amtrak trains in Philadelphia last year."

A few in the room chuckled at the CIA's most recent win in the war on terror. They had panicked for a short time when they had lost track of a box of doctored detonators in their attempted sting but celebrated when the detonators turned up in lethal bombs that refused to detonate on three trains in Philly.

The Deputy Director smiled himself, "OK Bob, I'll take over.

"The reason Khalil has popped back up to the top on this particular day is that we just came out of a meeting with our Pakistani group where they've turned up a corpse in the Waziristan region who looks like he has recently been messing with an open core of a nuclear weapon. We think Khalil is behind it."

Those in the room who had not been in the previous meeting looked startled and sat up straight.

"Are you saying Khalil has a bomb?" asked one of his direct reports.

"That's our fear. At this point, it could be anything nuclear and it could be someone other than Khalil but I think at the end of the day this will lead to him at the head of whatever operation they are planning.

"Whatever it is, active weapon, dirty bomb, loose radioactive material we need to find it and neutralize it. We are putting all free resources we have on this, so I need each of your departments to have an action plan to Carole for review by the close of business today. This thing is live and our Intel says that probably within the last five days or so, this thing whatever it is, was in Waziristan. We have to assume that the US mainland is the target with such a prime weapon as this and it has, or will be weaponized and is or will be on its way here.

"We will go to Red Alert nationally if we get specific Intel that it's really on its way here. Until we have some actionable Intel we won't raise a Homeland Security alarm but that could be imminent. Before that I need something Homeland can act on so get me something. A name, a ship, a target, a timetable anything.

"I want particular focus on entry points. How could he get it in here? We know the scenarios. It's time to pick up the pace of detection and interception. Hell it could be here already. So get on this immediately.

"Just before we break up, I've just ordered an internal Yellow Alert on an unrelated matter which you will be briefed on later today. We may have a foreign Jihadi who has recently penetrated the US with intentions of a major attack. Let's not get the two situations mixed up."

***

Greg had just returned from the police station steamed at the way he was being treated and targeted by the two cops assigned to Cristal's disappearance.

As he opened the door his home phone was ringing. He ran to the closest phone just before he thought it was going to voicemail.

It was a muffled woman's voice, "Is this Mr. Greg Wiggins?"

"Yes it is".

"Mr. Wiggins, you don't know me but I knew Cristal Serpe a few years ago."

"Yes?" He was starting to think this was a sympathy call.

"Well …", there was a long hesitation, "I worked with Cristal. I was actually a secretary in our group and while she has changed her name after marrying you, I was sure that was her when I saw her on TV this morning.

"Mr. Wiggins, I'm breaking the law with this call so I'm afraid I can't give you my name or contact information. I don't know if she told you but Cristal used to work with us at the CIA."

Now he thought this was turning into a prank call although the woman sounded elderly and sincere, "I don't think we're talking about the same person. Cristal has always been in the TV business."

"That was her cover. She worked at CNN. Even they didn't know she worked for us. She was stationed in Africa and something went wrong over there. All I know is that she came back very upset and I think she was pregnant but I can't be sure, woman's intuition and lots of rushed trips to the bathroom in the mornings.

"Now I read she has a two-year old which ties out with the date of her pregnancy. Anyways she left not long after returning from Africa without a cover story or new identity and I left not long after that for unrelated reasons."

There was just enough truth in this that he let her go on.

"Anyways the reason I called is that I suspect she didn't tell you about the CIA and if in fact she has been kidnapped then I'm sure it has something to do with her

African assignments. If I'm right, these are not people who want money and I don't want to scare you anymore than you already are but if you want to see her back home your only chance is to get the CIA involved.

"They owe it to her.

"They may deny her service in Africa but you need to push on them to get involved and save her. It's your only chance.

"I'm sorry but that's all I can do for you. I've already broken my non-disclosure agreement so good luck Mr. Wiggins."

At that the line went dead and Greg was left standing there wondering what had just happened. He pressed some keys on the phone and saw that there was no caller ID available on the last call.

After thinking about it for another ten minutes he jumped in his car and head for the police station.

Bert Wilson and Colt Baker could see he was animated about something and ushered him into an interrogation room.

"OK you guys, maybe now you'll believe me. I just got off the phone with a lady who told me that she used to work with Cristal at the CIA and she is sure that her kidnapping has something to do with Africa."

Colt was listening intently and Bert started to smile, "Let me guess. She didn't leave a name or number and she offered no proof that Cristal was in the CIA."

"That's true. She said she would get into trouble by telling me but she knew everything. She knew Cristal's maiden name. She knew Cristal worked for CNN in Africa before we met. She knew she was pregnant when she left the CIA. I'm sure this woman was telling the truth."

"Listen Mr. Wiggins," Bert started, "We warned you about the press. Now that this is on CNN we're going to get prank calls. Most if not all of what she told you is probably available with a Google search. Your wife used to be a CNN producer and now produces the news for WKRC so there's likely all kinds of info available on her on the web. And besides that, CNN already announced that she worked for them and your baby is two years old."

"You're just going to let this slide? You're not even going to try to check it out?"

Colt chimed in, "We are duty bound to chase down every lead and yes we'll make inquiries with the CIA but I would not hold out too much hope that we find anything."

"She said they would deny it but you're going to have to push them."

He could see he was not making an impact, "You know what, you guys are a total waste of time," He said as he rose quickly and stormed out of the room.

The two cops were left looking at each other.

Bert was the first to speak, "If he had something to do with his wife's disappearance, this is a pretty lame way to throw us off the trail. I'll get the boss to call our contact at the CIA and get them to check it out just in case."

Within an hour they had their answer. The CIA didn't know anything about someone named Cristal Serpe or Cristal Wiggins.

Over lunch the two cops mused about Greg Wiggins' antics of the morning. Colt finished with, "I suspect we might find that his fingerprints are in our database. This guy just does not feel right. I really fear for the wife."

Bert simply nodded as he finished his second Philly sub in the last couple of days. He liked it with lots of hot peppers, especially on these cool autumn days.

The only thing he liked better than Philly Cheese steaks was a full turkey dinner with all the trimmings and he knew his wife would not let him down with Thanksgiving upon them.

Cristal

She felt like she was working off a tremendous hangover as her eyes started to open in what seemed to be the dimly lit basement of some industrial building. She recognized the taste of some anesthetic gas and tried to piece together where she was and what had happened but nothing was coming to her.

There was a window on the far wall and it was nighttime. Her legs were cramping and the smell of the dank basement mixed with the anesthetic and the smell of her own urine was sickening.

As her head began to clear she remembered something about her SUV. She had just dropped off Tiffany at the daycare, jumped back into the driver's seat without checking the back as she used to do and was putting her seat belt on when a hand with a sponge clamped over her face from somewhere behind her.

Normally her training would have kicked in. Maybe she was out of practice but the person behind her was a pro too and the first deep breath told her she had made a big mistake. Before she could reach her face her arms felt like lead and it was all over.

She could feel that her hands were well tied behind her and then to her feet in a hog-tied fashion and she was lying on her side in a dirty, wet bed in some basement. The fact that she was not gagged told her they were in a remote location and calling out would do no good.

Her first thoughts went to Tiffany. Surely the daycare would have called Greg and he had her. She missed her precious little girl but knew instinctively that she had to focus first on getting free before she could get back to her.

Tiffany would be OK for a few days. Between Greg and her parents, she would be in good hands.

Instinct told her this kidnapping was all about her and her past and had nothing to do with Greg or Tiffany although there was always the chance that whoever had grabbed her would use threats against one or both of them to pressure her into whatever they wanted.

She was pretty sure Greg would not think to take precautions like disappearing with the baby until this kidnapping was resolved. He had no reason to think he needed to. He knew nothing of her past and how it could put them all in jeopardy.

Her mind went to Bill Carter's warnings that she should have taken defensive steps and changed her identity to make it a lot harder to find her. All of her work had been in the Middle East and Africa so she mistakenly figured she was essentially safe at home in the US.

Her mind then went immediately to who she could be dealing with. There was nothing in her current life that would point to a professional abduction and these guys were pros because they had kept her drugged from around 8 am until at least nightfall and they sure knew how to tie up a hostage.

She could think of no reason Greg could have gotten into trouble to the level that would cause such an action and there was no reason for him to have turned on her and planned this, so it had to be her past career overseas.

Someone had pieced together her CIA connection and she had made it easy for them to track her down. She had been determined to return to Cincinnati to where her parents lived when she had the baby. She wanted Tiffany to grow up in the best of environments with her grandparents close by.

Back to the present, she thought. What in her past could account for this? Most of her operations especially the nasty ones had been done in a way that she could not be tracked. She had used false identities that were likely unbreakable coming out of Langley.

She had usually used disguises. In the few cases where she had to use ultimate force there was no one left alive to track her down.

A mole in the CIA was a possibility but who would want her years after active service. No, this definitely had to do with something from her past and she was starting to see that there was really only one op where there were survivors that might hold a grudge. Her last one.

After what she reasoned was two hours of lying there with nothing else to do but reason her way through her circumstances her fears were verified when the door opened and a familiar face entered the room.

"Well I see you have awoken Miss Cristal. I suspect your Arabic is a little rusty by now so I'll speak English because I think your French is not so good, n'est-ce pas?

"I don't think you knew that I spoke English, did you? It might surprise you to know that I was educated for a few years here in the US."

She had only met him once in Burundi. She remembered him as Samir something or other but she had later found out from a CIA file that he was actually Jabir Habib, a Somali pirate turned jihadist and linked to some real nasty people back in Somalia.

US educated was a surprise. She had not known that he spoke English and suspected the CIA had never tied him to whatever name he had used when he lived in the US. From memory his file had always had him as Africa based.

"We'll have lots of time to talk but for now you must be very hungry. You've been here a long time so let me get you some water and humus. I seem to remember you like it with a little lemon."

She suddenly realized she was famished and dehydrated as he turned and left the room. So it was true. Her last operation in Burundi was behind all of this.

This was not good. Either they planned to kill her in retaliation, or more likely they might want to try to trade her for their leader Daniel Boone who was probably still in Guantanamo. If they planned to negotiate, they had zero chance of success. Whether it was assassination or negotiation neither was a good scenario.

Habib was back shortly with the promised humus, a bottle of water and a guard with an AK-47.

"Now here is how this is going to work my little whore. I'll untie you and bind one hand to the bed. Your feet will remain tied – you may feed yourself and I've brought some clothes for you, as I'm afraid we were unable to wake you while we were traveling to use the facilities.

"There is a toilet and a shower in the next room but again your feet will remain tied so you'll have to figure out how to dress and undress. Sadly there are no windows in that room and my friend here will be a short distance from the door with his weapon. You will be allowed only 15 minutes. If you behave yourself we won't shoot you … yet. As I see you've already figured out, calling out won't help as we are far away from any other people."

Snarling she said, "I would prefer to use the facilities before eating if that is allowed."

Habib smiled and said, "Of course. We are quite civilized here even for bitches like you." He mumbled something to the guard in French who took up a strategic position so he could shoot her at the simplest infraction.

"You must untie my feet if I am to clean myself. Please. I promise I'll behave myself."

Habib thought for a second and removed a revolver from his waist band. "I think this is a reasonable request but I assure you, we will kill you at the slightest sign of any funny business. You are still valuable to us dead."

Within 15 minutes she was back at the bed, showered and wearing oversized men's working clothes. She flipped the mattress over and sat while she was expertly tied up once more by Habib. Her feet were bound to the bed but her hands were tied in front of her so she could eat.

So far these guys knew what they were doing. The guard was always well positioned and always out of reach. Any kind of lunge on her part would be fatal.

The food and water were welcomed as the guard sat in the corner 15 feet away hardly blinking with his AK-47 leveled at her mid section.

Habib returned and re-tied her hands behind her before he started to talk.

"My first question is why did you not try to hide? It was not so difficult to find out your new name."

"I didn't think anyone would be looking for me or trying to kidnap me."

"Well surprise!" he said spreading his arms like a stage performer. "Here I am. There is no point in denying it. I know you are CIA and you were responsible for the CIA capturing Daniel."

He turned to motion to the guard seated in the corner, "Oh, by the way, my friend here does not know a single word of English or Arabic for that matter. He, unlike you and I is a native of Burundi and is fluent in French and some of the local dialects so we can speak freely. We must be careful however. I would not make any sudden moves. I've told him you are a demon witch and that he should shoot you at the slightest sign of trouble. He's very superstitious, you see and he fervently believes in demons and witches," he smiled.

He continued, "Once we knew where to look we just had to come and say howdy, as some of you yankees say. Getting my team into the US across your southern border was a little tricky but I have enough of a team here to take care of you for a few days. They are all aware of your treachery and would love the opportunity to end your miserable life."

He got up and paced back and forth, "You know what really puzzles me is how your government and your CIA always gets it wrong. They are always on the wrong side of the fight. You knew the government of Burundi was one of the most corrupt in Africa. You knew they were guilty of untold war crimes, massacres, and atrocities and yet you support them and target freedom fighters like us?

"Daniel, or Abu Nistal as he was known to us, had only been in our organization a few months but he had galvanized us into a focused force and even some of the other factions of the FLN were joining our cell in our fight to liberate that beautiful country. Why did you have to go and mess it up? Why does the CIA always pick the wrong side?"

Cristal just stared at him.

He could see he wasn't going to get any kind of a response from her.

"Now I know in your culture men and women are sometimes treated as equals but the Holy Koran warns of whores like you and your tricks. Your deceit and manipulation of Daniel and the damage it caused to our organization will not go unpunished.

"How could you throw yourself at him and trick such a man into caring for you, and then set up a trap, betray him and bring him to your US torture site in Guantanamo? How could you do this? How could any human being do such a thing? What kind of a demon are you?"

She had heard enough. He was working himself up into a murderous tantrum and she had to get him off this ramp.

As part of her advanced psychological training she had attended a Transactional Analysis class which taught her to snap someone out of a childish tantrum mode by asking a direct question requiring a rational answer forcing them into adult and rational mode. With a straight face, confident voice and calm demeanor she said, "What are your plans for me?"

He finally hesitated and seemed to calm down just a bit. He reasoned he was not going to get any answers at all from her which in the big picture didn't really matter. He knew who he was dealing with and he had all the information on her he needed. What he really wanted was a chance for Daniel to get a crack at her while she was still breathing.

"OK. Tomorrow, friends of ours in Europe will try to make direct contact with your CIA. We will offer to release you to them in return for Daniel."

Cristal smiled nervously, "I was afraid of that. Do you know anything about the US government or the CIA? They would never negotiate with terrorists especially if it was to release another terrorist. They would not even do it for a really important person like a General. Please tell me this is not your only plan. Please tell me you have something better than that. Otherwise this is a total waste of time and you've put yourselves in grave danger by coming here."

Habib smiled, "Then for you and me, let's hope you're wrong.

"I think they will negotiate as long as we don't make everything public. But, now that you mention it, yes we do have another plan but I don't think you are going to like it," he smiled.

"If we get any resistance from your CIA we'll carve off little parts of your body and ship them to your former employer, CNN. If CNN refuses to report it or tries to hide or downplay the fact then we'll send pictures of the body parts and your bleeding body to your FOX News and Al Jazeera and tell them your former employers the CIA and CNN have abandoned you.

"One of them will gladly report the story to the world. I think then the CIA will have to negotiate.

"We'll plan it so that the pictures make the evening news and they will present it side by side with a picture of you and your delightful child in stark contrast. I think the pressure from the American public to rescue you will be quite overwhelming, especially when they find out through Al Jazeera why Daniel is in

Guantanamo; for fighting a US government propping up a despot in Burundi guilty of raping and murdering his own people.

"What do you think of my plan B?" he smiled.

She just stared at him in rage. She kicked herself for not being able to hide her fury any better. She felt like spitting in his face but figured that would not get her anywhere. What she really wanted was two minutes alone and untied with this jerk.

Jabir was enjoying himself, "But I would not worry about threats for now. I think the CIA will see the wisdom in negotiating in private over the public display of your body parts.

"Your biggest worry should be if they find us here and we're forced to kill you if they storm the building. We are all ready to die a martyr's death. But don't worry, we're quite certain they have no idea where you are.

"So I would suggest you pray to your god that they don't want to make a public spectacle out of this. We will see if they really do not negotiate with terrorists.

"I love a good plan, don't you?" he smiled.

She was still convinced the US could never negotiate with terrorists, especially Al Qaeda, even if they did promise secrecy. It was bound to get out at some point and they would not want to be caught breaking their own rule of no negotiations. Washington was still smarting from the 'Arms for Hostages' fiasco with Iran of decades earlier. That had not stayed quiet for very long.

As he left he said, "Enjoy your short stay with us."

Cristal just sat there silently. She needed a plan. She needed to find a way to take control of this situation herself. The only good scenario was for her to find a way to escape.

There was no telling how long she had. Apparently they were going to get a message somehow to the CIA tomorrow through Europe but that told her nothing. It could take hours to days for any kind of back and forth communications given that it would not be direct.

That communication would drive her timeline to deal with these kidnappers because as soon as contact was made, the CIA was bound to tell them to take a hike.

From watching carefully and listening to voices from the other room she knew that there were at least four of them. They might have some other kind of local support in this area but they didn't seem to be at this location.

So all she had to do was figure out a plan to get the jump four heavily armed terrorists, while she was tied hand and foot.

A Message

It was late afternoon on the day before Thanksgiving before the Deputy Director, Bill Carter could get back to his office and the kidnapping of Cristal Wiggins.

At the short meeting earlier in the day that the DD had asked Chip Atwood to set up, the domestic group had been briefed on the theory that a Jihadi or Jihadis from Africa had likely penetrated the homeland and all was being done to track them down before they did any damage.

The FBI and Homeland Security had been given the theory as well but there was very little information to go on. They were only told about an anonymous tip but were not told about the related kidnapping as the CIA were worried about leaks and jeopardizing any negotiations for Cristal further as well as other National Security issues such as the CIA's past connection to CNN being leaked.

Phil Harris was back on the case and reported they had had a call from the Cincinnati police asking if they knew anything about Cristal.

"We gave them the standard answer that we had no knowledge of her but clearly someone pointed them to us. Possibly Cristal had told her husband that she used to work for us."

Carter thought for a second, "I don't think so. Has the FBI been in on the kidnapping side of this yet?"

"No sir. I think we should expect they will be though. Kidnappings often end up in their bailiwick and it's already a national news story. It won't be long before they connect the dots."

"Yeah, but there are national security issues here so we need to deflect attention from her background. No good would come of it being leaked and broadcast that we use CNN producers and other press people as spies. Everyone assumes that happens from time to time but we cannot allow the verification of that particular scenario. Besides that, public knowledge of her being CIA might kill any negotiating room we might be able to create.

"For now I don't want the local cops or the FBI for that matter finding out she was one of ours or had operations overseas that may have put her in jeopardy. We may need a complete cloak of secrecy over this.

"This has to be made to look like something of a domestic dispute for the moment, until we can get some control over it. See what you can come up with."

Just then the phone rang and he could see it was Walt Gargaro from his European HQ. A shiver went down his spine.

He looked at Phil and said, "This could be the corroboration I feared."

"Bill it's Walt in London. We just received a cryptic communiqué from a confidential source in our Spanish office."

"Yeah, I was half expecting that."

"It's addressed to you and it simply says 'We have you know who and we want you know who in return.' Does that mean anything to you?"

"Sadly, yes it does."

"They say they want an answer in 48 hours to a temporary e-mail address and as to deadlines, there's no telling when they sent this message as it probably came through several relays."

The DD thought for a moment, "Give them the standard answer, something like 'We don't need 48 hours, we do not negotiate with terrorists.'"

It was late in London and Walt Gargaro was not sure what to say next. Apparently the DD was not going to clue him in on what the message meant. "I'll send that back right away and let you know if we get any response." At that he signed off.

Bill Carter turned to Phil Harris. "Well we're in it now. I hate it when I'm right sometimes. It is in fact the gang from Burundi and they want the infamous Daniel Boone out of Guantanamo in return for Cristal."

Phil Harris laughed out loud, "Daniel Boone? Is that really his name. I thought that was an inside joke."

"Yeah, that's the only name we have on him. His nom du guerre in Burundi was Abu Nistal but he's an American going by the name of Daniel Boone. He burned off his fingerprints so we've never been able to really get to the bottom of who he is and what he was doing there aside from the fact that he was helping Al Qaeda. If I remember correctly they water boarded him down there and got nothing useful out of him."

He leaned back in his chair, "So this makes the internal threat level go to Red. It looks like we really do have Jihadis on our soil. I guess I'll have to read you into the whole mess.

"I think you knew that I recruited Cristal Serpe right out of college; Northwestern's Medill School of Journalism. She was a perfect candidate; fluent in Arabic, intelligent, attractive brunet, looks meek, mild and fragile except for the subtle signs of an athletic build and calluses on her knuckles because she held championships and top belts in just about every martial arts discipline there is.

"She was at Northwestern on a full athletic scholarship and won lots of awards. The amazing thing is that she looked a lot more like a cheerleader than a Chuck Norris or Steven Seagal type.

"We helped her get the job at CNN and with some creative work got her assigned to the mid-east. For almost 8 years she moved up the ladder here and at CNN and started running major Ops for us all over the Middle East and Africa. She excelled at combat training and did some real solo wet work too without complaint. She's one focused agent and a walking killing machine when she needs to be. What I would call an extreme patriot and you would not want her on your tail. She could kill you in many different ways and has done so on several of her assignments. Cristal was a real gem while she worked for us. She looks vulnerable but man that's a mistake you only make once.

"She seemed to lose the edge a month or so before she quit when a bunch of media types including Cristal were tricked into an ambush by some Jihadis. To this day, we think it was Khalil himself who buried Cristal's best friend up to her neck in the sand and stoned her in front of the other reporters as an object lesson.

"As I remember it, he pulled the girl's crucifix off of her dead neck, covered in blood and stuffed it into Cristal's hand telling her she was next if she didn't get out of Muslim lands. The other journalists were left alive to spread the fear. They all headed home but not our girl although she was never the same after that. If I remember correctly, the dead journalist was named Tiffany something and worked for the BBC. Apparently Cristal had been a lot closer to her than we knew, so we dialed back some of her assignments for a couple of weeks.

"Then there was this one report that an American had infiltrated one of the rebel groups in Burundi and was causing a big stink. Somehow, he had taken over one of the cells of the FLN in Burundi and was making life really difficult for the local government, who by the way are a bunch of thugs themselves.

"But it looked like this branch of the FLN was financed by and had deep connections to Al Qaeda and the last thing we wanted was another Jihadi with American roots like Khalil.

"Anyway we sent Cristal in to see what she could find out. Don't ask me why she was assigned. She didn't speak the local language but then again they were looking for an American who spoke English.

"Anyway, one of her first contacts was an American businessman she met in the restaurant in the hotel. One thing led to another, he claimed to know all the westerners in the country, so she pursued him.

"Frankly I'm shocked the crazy name, Daniel Boone did not tip her or the rest of the CIA off to a cover. I think he must have had some explanation that made sense at the time.

"Anyways, I think they fell for each other and then lo and behold a couple of weeks later, we get reliable Intel that he's actually the one we're looking for. He's been hiding in plain sight.

"For some unknown reason he's spending two or three days a week in a suit rubbing elbows with businessmen and government types in the biggest hotel in the country, and the rest of the time he's leading an Al Qaeda cell, crawling through the jungle and creating mayhem for the government."

Phil was taking this all in as Carter continued, "About this time, just after she finds out that he's the guy, she overhears a plot that he wants to hit a government train on a bridge over a ravine in a neighboring country that is bringing cash into the corrupt government of Burundi. Hundreds of innocents could be killed so we had to move fast.

"There was no way to get her out of there fast enough and the operation was time critical so she stayed and set up the trap. We got him out of there clean and whisked him off to Guantanamo and the train was never hit. We just missed picking up some of his lieutenants at the time but we got the big prize. I'm guessing his prime lieutenant, Jabir Habib, is either the guy now making the threats on Cristal or at least he's behind it.

"Anyways, all of this had just gotten to be too much for her. She was near a full collapse so we authorized an early retirement for her with the hope that she might come back some day when her life had stabilized a bit.

"I see by the reports she has a two-year old baby named guess what, 'Tiffany', so I'm thinking the thing with Daniel Boone might have been more than we thought at the time. I suspect now that she was pregnant when she left us.

"In retrospect, that really adds to the breakdown she was having. Imagine, within a month or so she sees her best friend Tiffany stoned to death right in front of her, falls for this guy, finds out he's a terrorist and about to kill hundreds, has to set him up, loses him, and finds out she is pregnant by him I'm guessing. She's lucky she did not have a complete breakdown. I can see now why she was so determined to get out of the CIA, she most likely had a baby on the way.

"I tried to get her to accept a new identity but she insisted on being close to her parents in Cincinnati. Now we know why. Looks like that was a bad call and some of his old gang have found her. I told her she would be the obvious snitch if she disappeared at the same time as him.

"It wasn't long before someone leaked to the media the fact that we had 'Daniel Boone' in custody in Guantanamo. I guess the name was all they needed for the media to jump on that one. Until then his cell may have thought he had just run off with her but after they found out he was in Guantanamo and she had disappeared, well it wouldn't take a brain surgeon to put that scenario together.

"If you've looked into this today like I expect you have, then you know she was like a daughter to me. I want to be involved in every step of this.

"That message I just sent back will be returned by some outrageous threat but it will set the stage and buy me a few hours to get something going on this.

"First thing I want to do is have a face-to-face with Daniel Boone. If they had a kid together, he likely does not know about it and he may have had some legitimate feelings for her at the time. So call transport and I'll fly down there first thing in the morning.

"Mr. Daniel Boone may be in for a big surprise and there is an outside chance I can use that somehow to find out something that might lead us to Cristal."

A Suspect

Bert Wilson was in early as usual at his desk in the Cincinnati Police headquarters. He was catching up on some paperwork as Detective Colt Baker arrived looking excited with a bunch of papers in his hand, "You're not going to believe this. We've got him."

"We've got whom?"

"Wiggins, who else. The fingerprints paid off. Greg Wiggins is not Greg Wiggins after all. He is really Bobby Watson of Wichita, Kansas who incidentally died almost four years ago."

"What?"

"Yup. After I saw the name on the finger prints, I checked for any national watches and warrants. Wichita has a cold case on his disappearance. He was reported missing about 4 years ago. Looked like an accident. They found his pickup in the Arkansas River but never recovered a body. Left a wife and two little girls.

"I downloaded the synopsis of the cold file. Their theory was that he ran up some big gambling debts using someone else's money and decided to take a walk but they had no real evidence to support it.

"His wife collected the insurance money. Looks like the local cops think most of the money went back to the mob. I knew it, the guy is a pathological liar!"

Bert leaned back in his chair, "Wow! I wasn't expecting that. So is he legally still married to the first wife too?"

"I guess so. Usually in the case of a death they don't go to the trouble of dissolving a marriage. Best guess is she knows nothing about this. He's a self-employed long-haul trucker so I don't know how he got a driver's license and he must file taxes under a Social Security number for Greg Wiggins that is probably fraudulent. This guy has built a whole new life for himself. My guess is Cristal Wiggins knows nothing of this either. And while this says zip about her disappearance specifically, I just got a lot more suspicious of Bobby Watson."

"Yeah right. Let's keep this under our hat for the moment but looks like we've got him on at least bigamy, insurance fraud, fraudulent acquisition of a Social Security number and driver's license and probably more. It's also grounds for some warrants. I want to see his current bank accounts and maybe even a sweep of the house.

"But before you go getting all excited, this is not good news for Cristal Wiggins. Looks like he pulled an insurance fraud to fix a gambling problem once before so maybe he has done it again but this time it's the wife who disappears and she may really be dead so he can collect the insurance."

"Shit, I never thought of that," said Colt wondering if they could now be searching for a body and a crime scene.

***

It was very early in the morning when Phil Harris knocked on the DD's door and entered without waiting for an invitation, "Sorry to barge in sir but I wanted to get this to you before your trip to Guantanamo. I thought you would want to see this.

"On the Cristal matter, the locals did a fingerprint check on the husband and amazingly he is in the system as dead. Apparently he faked his own death, probably to avoid large gambling debts. He's now living under an assumed identity. His real name is Robert 'Bobby' Watson of Wichita, Kansas.

"Clearly after the ransom demand last night out of Spain there's no reason to think he has anything to do with the kidnapping but you were looking for a way to deflect attention from a CIA connection and I think I have it."

Harris sat down in front of the DD's desk and continued. "Given that Greg Wiggins is a heavy gambler and he's often hauling loads to or through Vegas where he may be assumed to take breaks in the Casinos, I suggest we make a rather large deposit in his bank, back-dated to when he was last there and then an immediate withdrawal. It will look like he borrowed a large sum of money and lost it and now is in some trouble with the mob. We have access to the Vegas hotel records so it shouldn't be too hard to find a time when he was there. We will have to act quickly before the locals get a warrant to check his bank records.

"I also checked the insurance database and he has a substantial insurance policy on Cristal so that could be the basis of a deflection for the local cops and the FBI if they get involved.

"He'll deny the whole thing but if I read between the lines the local cops seem to think he's involved already. Given that there's no evidence that he actually did anything to his wife he won't be charged but this would definitely serve to distract the local cops and the FBI for a while and keep Cristal's predicament secret as you requested. Our safety valve is of course to fill in local law-enforcement or the FBI of some subset of the real situation, should the need arise."

The Deputy Director hesitated, "I don't like getting civilians tied up in a mess like this but in this case he's already a bad guy and I think it's best to keep everyone away from Cristal's kidnapping. God knows what we may have to do to spring her. We may be forced to keep it really quiet so go ahead with your plan."

Carter spent the next twenty minutes on the phone with the Director who was walking into the daily NATSEC meeting. He took him through the latest on the loose nuke situation then he took a quick chopper flight over to the airfield for the flight to Guantanamo.

***

The search for a loose nuke was getting nowhere. It was now Carter's top priority but he had to do something about this Cristal affair before it got out of control.

There was a slight chance that if Cristal and Daniel Boone had really been an item at one time, he might be able to get the prisoner to tell him something that could be used to rescue her, assuming there was still some residual love there.

If he couldn't get Boone to talk and give him something he could use to save Cristal, she was doomed because there was no way they would release one of Al Qaeda's men especially when they were so focused on trying to track some of them down and the bomb that he was certain they possessed.

If Boone didn't talk that spelled a very tragic and probably painful and soon to be public death for Cristal. He would be powerless to help her. The terrorists would be sure to make it very public and there would be enormous public outrage on an ex-CIA agent being tortured and beheaded inside the US, especially given she was a very photogenic mother of a two year old. His career would be over once the Senate and House had finished his public humiliation but that was not his concern, springing Cristal was. All the rest of it was just noise.

He was sure the team at Guantanamo had done their best to get Boone to talk but they didn't have the life of his former lover, and the mother of his daughter in their hands. After sleeping on it, he was quite certain Daniel Boone was the father of Cristal's baby and there was an outside chance he could use that to get some cooperation.

Her life was riding on this meeting and that was why he had decided to inject himself directly into it. Normally an interrogation of this type would be left to others who were more expert at it but his personal connection to Cristal and the fact that he had sent her to find Daniel Boone made him decide that he owed it to her. Apart from that, the specter of a public execution of one of his ex-operatives demanded his personal attention even in the face of a loose nuke.

In addition, if there was any way he could get this guy to talk, he might let something slip that would help in the pursuit of Khalil, the bomb and his whole organization, although he realized that was really wishful thinking.

The CIA jet touched down at the Cuban base's only remaining air strip, Leeward Field just after 9:30 am. Deputy Director Bill Carter was choppered over the bay to Camp Justice at the old McCalla field which now housed the Guantanamo terrorist prison camp. Within minutes he was in Commander James Watkins office at the Commander's request.

"Mr. Deputy Director, so good of you to visit us. We don't get many visits from Washington types these days. I guess we're the black sheep of the family now.

"I believe you've been here only once before. Hope you get some good weather. How long are you staying and what is the purpose of your visit?"

Still standing and looking directly into the commander's eyes he said, "Commander as you know I have no requirement to tell you why I am here but let's be civil and cooperate with each other.

"Let me start by asking why you had me brought here instead of to the interrogation area? Your sergeant who picked me up at the chopper was quite insistent."

The commander moved behind his desk and sat down, "Sir, I appreciate candor so I agree, let's dispense with the niceties and I'll come directly to the point. I understand you are here to speak with one Daniel Boone."

The DD wondered how that had gotten out. Likely Phil Harris had phoned ahead to arrange an interrogation room and told them whom to put in it. "Yes, Daniel Boone, or whoever he is, is of some interest in an ongoing high-level investigation. Why? Is that a problem?"

After a long pause as the Commander sized up the DD, he said, "Essentially yes. It's actually a very big problem."

The Deputy Director said nothing but continued standing and staring down the Commander who seemed reluctant to go on. He finally sat down across the desk from him.

After a long pause the Commander continued, "My career and possibly yours could be on the line here."

Bill Carter had not been expecting threats. Cristal's kidnapping and how he handled it was one real threat to his career. Was this man sitting in front of him signaling yet another? He took a deep breath and said, "Go on."

"You see Mr. Deputy Director, we've had trouble identifying Mr. Daniel Boone. This is something I'm sure you're aware of. He had no traceable history before the six months leading up to his capture so we've always assumed the Daniel Boone name was a red herring."

The Deputy Director simply nodded.

"Well after a couple of years he got sloppy and his fingerprints have started to grow back. We just found out in the last month who he is and frankly, we've been trying to decide what to do with him. This is the part where our careers come into jeopardy. You see in a sense he's one of ours or maybe better put, one of yours."

Wow! The DD almost said out loud, "What do you mean?"

"His real name is Commander David Crowe of Her Majesty's Secret Service, MI6. In fact he is apparently a fairly senior field operative of a very close ally and a colleague in the Military Intelligence business.

"He was thought for some time to have been killed in a car bomb in the Sudan about four years ago. In fact, according to our joint terrorism database there was a 'Terminate with Extreme Prejudice' order out on him back then from his own organization.

"It appears that MI6 saw him as a corrupt agent who had gone rogue or maybe switched sides and they wanted him dead at any cost."

The Deputy Director lost all of his composure and sat forward in his chair, "Are you certain of this? We've had an MI6 agent in custody for almost three years and tortured him endlessly without him giving up this information?"

"I think you know how we feel about that term 'torture', but just between us, that would be correct. Now you see our dilemma. Your guys put him here but we've held him and done all manner of things to him over the past few years to get information out of him. So we're both up to our necks in this mess. I must tell you I'm sick to my stomach about this. You can be sure I've had little sleep since this came to light. We've rechecked everything several times. There's no mistake. We now know for sure who he is.

"We stopped the enhanced interrogation techniques as soon as we figured out whom we had and we've treated him civilly since then but God save me, I don't know what to do with him now.

"So your visit is very timely and I think you will agree that we both have a God damned ton of egg on our collective faces. If he's released or turned over to the Brits and talks we're in deep trouble on any number of issues."

Bill Carter, red in the face interrupted, "I'll say! Apart from false imprisonment or at least being accused of ignoring his rights as a British citizen, he would be the poster boy and key witness for the prosecution in a World Court torture trial in The Hague.

"My God this is insane. I'm trying hard to get my head around this. A senior MI6 field agent? Putting up with all of that torture? But for what? This can't get out and we need to deal with it pronto. Who else knows about this?"

"We have a compartmentalized program of Intel here so only my second-in-command knows we have finger prints on him now and whom they belong to.

"I've been trying to figure out a way to escalate this without being arrested or court-martialed myself and you're the first one I've told because you're in this too and I'm hoping you might be able to help. Even the subject does not know we've ID'd him."

"But why do you think he tolerated all of the waterboarding, sleep deprivation and other techniques. He could have saved himself at any point and been transferred to a British prison."

"We've had a month to speculate on that and the only thing we can surmise is that one, they train their agents pretty well on handling our enhanced interrogation techniques and two, he's more afraid of the Brits than us. I suspect when MI6 puts a hit on you, you're not going to make it to prison.

"There is also the thought that one day he might find a way to get free. There are rumors among the prisoners that our government will likely set most of them free at some point due to the political problems of maintaining this facility at Guantanamo and the likelihood that we could never convict them in a court for a host of evidence issues you're familiar with. Not to mention the legality of the way we interrogate people to get information out of them.

"As you know there has been an ongoing debate over military versus civil criminal courts in these cases. A non-military judge would probably throw many of these cases out of court for prosecutorial misconduct or any one of several other issues including the inevitable fights over classified Intel as evidence."

The Deputy Director interrupted, "So this is a very fortuitous and timely meeting. You and I are really in hot water here if this gets out."

"I was hoping you would see it that way. If this gets out I'll likely be court-martialed for dereliction of duty and spend the rest of my days in a military prison."

The DD sat back in his chair, "My God. I was not expecting this.

"This would make international news for weeks if not months. Washington would be hammered with this. This could affect the Presidency. This might be bigger than Abu Ghraib. A British spy held at Guantanamo for almost three years and tortured. How did this happen?"

"Well don't look at me. You guys were the ones who targeted him, captured him and put him here and he has done an excellent job up until now of hiding his real identity.

"Yeah, don't get me wrong. I'm not looking for someone to blame."

After a long pause the DD just said "WOW!"

After a moment he continued, "You know there just might be a silver lining in this. The good news is that I may have the beginnings of a solution here. To be very frank we're considering a prisoner swap with him. I can't say more right now but I may be taking him off your hands in the very near future. That is all contingent on what he tells me. I now have something I can use on him but we don't want to send a terrorist back into the field."

The Commander was intrigued, "Well I don't know how you would do that politically or legally but I'm open to any solution to this total screw up. I'll do anything to help you get him out of my hair."

"Leave it to me. I think I have a way to make this work. I'll say one thing, my interrogation notes are now completely useless. We are going to have a very different conversation in there today. This new information may work out in my favor. Now can I see the prisoner?"

At that, the DD's personal cell phone rang.

As he hit the answer button on his phone a voice screamed so loud both men could hear it, "You Jackass! You will release Daniel Boone or we will send you pieces of Ms. Cristal each day until you do. I do not need 48 hours either. Watch CNN tonight for the first installment. I think we'll start with an ear." The line went dead only to ring again immediately.

This time it was Phil Harris, "Very sorry sir but he threatened to kill her right there if I didn't forward the call. We tried to trace it but they're using an internet phone with either IP spoofing or shielding. There's no quick or easy way to trace that. It could be bouncing through multiple countries where we can't always track the IP relaying."

"OK Phil. I've got it. I'm working on a solution. I should be back to you within a couple of hours."

After hanging up on Harris, Carter, now a sickly shade of grey, turned to the Commander and said, "You didn't hear any of that and I'll see the prisoner now."

***

Nine thousand miles away in Somalia, late in the evening, Khalil al-Adel turned to one of his deputies and said, "I just found out that Mohammed left Pakistan on schedule. The devices are en route.

The Americans found Sadoum in the hospital but it looks like they have no other information on our plans so we're still a go for New York. I want everyone in place and double checked on their plans. This will make 9/11 look like a tea party."

The Prisoner

Daniel Boone aka Abu Nistal aka Commander David Crowe was waiting in the interrogation room looking unexpectedly comfortable. It was a bit of a surprise to the DD that like the other prisoners at Guantanamo he sported long relatively unkempt hair and a straggly beard, but the scruffy appearance and orange jump suit didn't hide the fact that he was a westerner.

"Good morning Daniel," opened the DD as he sat across from the prisoner who seemed mildly amused that a suit from Langley was visiting him.

Daniel simply nodded.

"I've been reading your file and I must say, you must be the world record holder in holding out under intense interrogation."

"Oh, that's what you call it." He smiled showing some nervousness for the first time.

Carter couldn't place the accent, "Actually, you've given us lots of information but to date we have not been able to make use of it so I suspect it has all been lies.

"You seem to know how to give us 'keep them busy' answers. As I understand it, we've been busy for about two years chasing down the leads you've coughed up. Sorry, no pun intended. But none of those leads seem to actually lead anywhere. Just to more questions in fact. A masterful exhibition I must say.

"Let me ask you a few non-threatening questions that I'm sure you'll feel can be answered without giving away too much."

Daniel just smiled.

The DD closed his notebook, "Being obviously a westerner, a westerner I must admit that has no past or roots that we can find, but being a westerner why are you fighting us. Are you a true Jihadist for Allah?"

"I have never been a Jihadist. I just hate the things some western governments have done to emerging nations. The polite word might be bullying. But other words like subversion, bribery, insurrection, sedition and many others might be more appropriate."

"Good enough. But why have you refused to cooperate with us in any way, like telling us who you are?"

"I have my reasons."

"Well I think that is about to change."

He paused for effect and then continued, "Before we leave this room today you're going to tell everything I want to know."

Daniel leaned back and stifled a laugh. The only way that was going to happen he figured was if the Yanks had some amazing new truth serum.

"And how do you propose to do that? Some new torture you're here to deliver. You're wearing the wrong clothes. Or is it some new drug that has shown promise? You do know that you need a willing participant if you're going to use hypnosis," he laughed.

"None of the above. Something much more effective. Something that will make you want to disclose everything I need."

Now the prisoner was starting to show real signs of unease.

"You see we now know who you are, so your deception is no longer required or useful and on top of that I have something I think you want."

Daniel was now showing some concern but apparently was not ready to yield to this trick as he saw it.

"You may have noticed that your treatment here has changed of late and I'm here to tell you why."

The DD paused as he sized up the prisoner. He had to play this just right. He had to get the prisoner to aid him in a host of matters.

"Happily as it turns out for both you and me, in the last month your fingerprints have started to re-appear."

Boone was now showing distinct signs of stress but he resisted the overpowering urge to look at his fingers.

"To the point where we now know that you are Commander David Crowe of Her Majesty's Secret Service, or do you prefer MI6?"

That was all it took, Crowe sat up straight in his chair red in the face. The secret he had kept for nearly three years, two of which through monstrous torture in this hell hole was out. He shuddered, had all that sacrifice been for nothing? The years and the unimaginable torture he had endured came rushing back and his heart was pounding. Had that all been for nothing? Had he gained nothing for his incredible sacrifices?

There was a long pause as he gained his self control and then he spoke in a distinctive British accent, "Good of you to drop by with such earth-shaking news, Deputy Director William Carter."

It was Carter's turn to be shocked, "Have we met?"

"You probably paid little attention to me back then but if you actually had my MI6 file you would know that about ten years ago I was stationed at Langley in analytics on an exchange program. You were an up-and-coming section head at the time.

"They give us US newspapers to read in here and I noticed your new title in an article where you were testifying to congress about a year ago.

"So the fact that you didn't know about my Langley days tells me you don't have my file and MI6 has not yet been informed of my resurrection. Am I right? This is very important to me."

"Let's take this one step at a time. First I need a lot of information from you which I expect you to give freely. In return I'll give you something I think you will value. You'll have to trust me on this one but your truthfulness will be amply rewarded."

Crowe thought about this for a time. Calculating that the game of deceit was up and that he could be handed over to MI6 at any moment and that he would never make it back to England alive, he realized his best option was to cooperate with the CIA and hopefully win them over to his side. He simply nodded agreement.

"OK. We know that MI6 wants you dead. Why?"

"Well as they say 'The gig is up' so my life is in your hands.

"You have no reason to take my word for it but here goes.

"There were two things I found intolerable in my old job. One was the hypocrisy of Britain and let me add, the US in supporting despots in the Balkans, the

Middle East and Africa and the underhanded way in which it was done in terms of the spin and manipulation of the press to make it look like we're always on the 'good side' of every conflict. I had seen it all up close and knew better.

"And two was the total corruption, repression and atrocities that were spawned from that support by said despots. These animals were raping, robbing and killing their own people, blaming it on others and we were supporting them.

"Add to this that I had just stumbled upon a massive scheme where someone in MI6 was using contractors across Africa to funnel massive additional funds from some mysterious source to some of the same very bad people and getting a kickback on every transaction.

"I had just about worked it out and I was closing in on the local culprits when I discovered that a Terminate order was out on me, and the two contractors I was after set me up and attempted to take me out.

"The person in MI6 running the scheme must have been high enough to make it look like I was the mastermind of the corruption scheme and also authorized to put out a Terminate order.

"I knew that they would not stop until I was gone so I made it look like the contractors and Commander David Crowe all expired in the car bomb they had set for me."

"Why did you not tell us this when you were captured?"

"You thought you had captured Daniel Boone and I had to assume that MI6's order to terminate David Crowe had made its way to the CIA. So it was a lot safer to remain as Daniel Boone until this moment where I have been discovered.

"If both the CIA and MI6 are out to kill you on sight, you had better find a hole to crawl into. Unfortunately for me, the hell hole I ended up in was this one.

"Believe me I was glad to hear that you were unaware of my file and likely had not yet contacted MI6. If I'm turned over to MI6, I won't make it back to Britain alive if whoever was running that scheme is still in business.

"It was much safer to remain as Daniel Boone and accept the horrendous torture you guys handed out, waiting for the day Guantanamo would have to be closed, than to identify myself and be killed in transit. Although I must say, that torture is vicious. There were days I actually thought of ending it all myself. Oh by the way, some of your people here are clearly sadists.

"So Mr. William Carter, my life is now in your hands. In some ways, this has worked out for me. At least someone has heard my side of the story before I have to deal with a bullet to the back of the head."

The Deputy Director stared him down and reflected on the man in front of him and the plausibility of his story as well as the tremendous courage this man had and the pain he had endured. There had to be less than a handful of men on the planet that could have had the determination, strength and personal conviction to take the course this man had chosen.

He had instant respect for the man and suspected intuitively that he in fact had nothing to do with the corruption London had accused him of. Yet to save himself he had to endure the most horrendous tortures the CIA, his own organization, had invented.

After a long stare at the man, where he became increasingly convinced he was getting the truth he said, "OK, let's assume I buy all of that. How did you survive the waterboarding, sleep deprivation, cold water treatment and whatever else they tried on you?"

"Simple but very painful. Your torture program does not initially search for the truth of the matter. It only searches for information. All I had to do was control the situation so that we were always in the information phase by coming up with plausible answers that were impossible, impractical or very hard to check out. If we had ever gotten to a point where they knew enough about a subject that they were zeroing in on the truth I could be easily trapped in lies and doomed. So in short, they took a pause every time I gave them something plausible and juicy to chase.

"One thing you have a lot of in here is time. Time to think up answers and complex scenarios. Most of the information your team got out of me sent them off on endless wild goose chases as you've just verified. I really have very little information that would be of use to you. You are after Al Qaeda and our operations had nothing to do with them. We were fighting for liberation against a corrupt government in Burundi who was guilty of unspeakable atrocities. We were only trying to stop the money flowing in to support them and stop them from killing and raping their own people."

"Not so fast," said the Deputy Director, "your second in command Jabir Habib is brother to Mustafa Habib who is a key deputy of Khalil-al Adel. The most wanted man in Al Qaeda. You were getting some of your funds directly from 'The Source'. You are a legitimate Jihadist by any definition."

The Deputy Director was sure the shock on Crowe's face was legitimate.

"We just missed picking up Jabir Habib when we got you. He is still on the loose and making trouble."

Crowe was red faced. "I want you to understand, I had no idea Jabir was related to Mustafa. Habib is a common name. I would never have teamed up with him if I knew Al Qaeda was in any way connected to them. At no time in my short stay with them was there any indication of such a connection."

"OK. Let's assume I believe that. Why did you pick the FLN to support? Why Burundi?"

Crowe paused for a minute, "Simple. That was one of the most corrupt regimes in Central Africa at the time and I had seen firsthand some of the atrocities committed by the government.

"They were slaughtering their own people for the most trivial of reasons. Allowing their troops to use rape as a weapon of war on the women and children. Stealing most of the humanitarian aid coming into the country and blaming it on the rebels.

"Add to that the fact that MI6 even after my pleading, had refused to station any resources there so I had no concerns about running into people who knew me. It seemed a good place to take a sabbatical, freedom fighting with people your government and mine had abandoned until the time was right for David Crowe to re-emerge.

"I had a few contacts in Burundi who knew me as an American business man. I think I pulled off the accent rather well," he said exaggerating his native British accent. "After re-establishing some former contacts I was eventually introduced to a rebel cell in the FLN run at that time by Jabir Habib.

"My plan was to help them out for a while until the David Crowe thing was off the front pages at MI6 and then figure out a way to get back in the game and find out who at MI6 had set me up. That was working right up to the point where I woke up one night with a room full of Navy Seals and a gun in my face."

"OK, let's assume I buy all of that, now it's my turn. We had picked up Intel that there was a westerner, probably a US citizen who had infiltrated an Al Qaeda cell in Burundi and was gaining power and influence. We were afraid of another US citizen gone native in Africa and becoming a recruiting tool for Al Qaeda as we've seen a few times now. In fact, Khalil himself grew up in the US and is often referred to as the American master Jihadist.

"We sent Cristal in to find you but we had no leads on where to look. Then we got Intel that it was actually you in Burundi and you were about to hit a cash train over a ravine somewhere nearby killing hundreds of innocents so we had to move."

David Crowe laughed out loud, "It was indeed a government train with loads of cash from God knows where and headed for the corrupt Bujumbura regime. We picked a ravine because we wanted to make it hard for anyone to follow us if we disabled the train on the bridge and no one was going to get hurt unless a crazy guard got rambunctious.

"We had an inside man on the train in the cash car and by 'hitting' the train we simply meant robbing it. You guys believe too much of the government propaganda that the rebels are out killing villagers. The rebels ARE the villagers."

Now it was the Deputy Director's turn to look embarrassed. "Still we had what we thought was an American Al Qaeda we had to get out of there."

"Well I am neither an American nor a terrorist and certainly not a Jihadist."

They both sat looking at each other for some time. How had this world gotten so completely turned upside down. There was a way to look at this that had them both on the same side fighting for the same thing, yet fate had positioned them squarely against each other.

After a long time Carter said simply, "They have Cristal. She was one of ours."

Crowe shivered and just stared at him as his eyes became misty. This was not what he had expected to come out of Carter's mouth. She was never far from his mind.

After a very long pause with the two men just staring into each other's eyes, David said, "I thought she might have been the one who set the trap on me. What do you mean 'They have her.'"

"I'm pretty sure I had a call this morning from Jabir Habib or one of his lieutenants. They are in the US we believe and are holding her in exchange for you. He is threatening to cut her up into pieces if we don't comply."

Crowe stared at him, "I'm a little surprised that Jabir could pull off something like that and there's no doubt he's serious.

"I'm honestly not sure what to think of her right now. You obviously sent her into Burundi to find me. I don't mind admitting that I fell for her hard but I guess that was her job. I must admit she was good at it. Now you confirm for me that she set me up for capture. I honestly don't know what to think of her."

"Well Jabir Habib seems to have figured it out as well and tracked her down and now they have her and he's not in a good mood. In fact it may be too late already to head off some of the torture."

Something in the way the DD was handling this made David think that this was a lot more personal to Bill Carter. Cristal had been close to this man and if you looked closely you could see it written all over him. "So what are you going to do? The US as I remember does not negotiate with terrorists."

"I think you know how that goes. We don't 'overtly' or directly negotiate with terrorists."

The Deputy Director sat forward staring at the floor between his feet. "I'm going to take a big risk and assume that we've been very honest with each other. I've been truthful and I think you have been too. I'm inclined to give into their wishes if you and I can strike a deal."

Crowe nodded his interest.

"We will keep this secret but I'll set up a transfer of you to my custody under some pretense. During the transfer, you will be allowed to escape and the swap with Cristal will be achieved but you must make sure Habib does not harm her or I swear by God I'll hunt you down myself and cut you up into little pieces and you know I can do it.

"Then you need to disappear and not get back into the Al Qaeda business. In return you will get your freedom and any help I can offer to find out who at MI6 set you up."

Crowe answered immediately, "How can I say no?

"But if you don't mind I don't want any inquiries going to MI6. There is a good chance the people who set me up are still there. If they find out I'm alive I'll have big problems to deal with."

91

The DD nodded as Crowe continued, "I must say, I had no idea when I woke up this morning that I would be looking at freedom from this house of horrors.

"We both have problems. You're stuck trying to explain torturing an MI6 agent for a couple of years and rescuing a kidnapped undercover agent by trading with Jihadists. Mine is staying alive long enough to clear my name and make someone in London pay. I think we have an agreement."

The DD hesitated and then continued, "There is one last thing I need you to do. As I said, we suspect it's Jabir Habib that has her and that they must still be in the US. Now that you know his Jihadist associations, I think you will agree that before he tries to get out of the US he will want to leave a rather big message behind.

"It's rare for one of these Jihadists to make it on to the mainland and he will want to take full advantage of it. Clearly you are very valuable to them because they've gone to enormous risk and expense to get her just to free you. But he will want to kill two birds with one stone and make us pay in some horrendous way. You need to stop any plans he has for an attack in the US."

Crowe smiled, "As they say in French 'Vous avez raison!' You're right! He'll want to leave his Jihadist mark on the US mainland for sure. He is very capable of it too. If I can stop it I will."

The Deputy Director lifted his phone and clicked on a speed dial. "Philip did the kidnappers leave any way to connect with them?"

"They left an e-mail where we can tell them to call us."

"Send the e-mail."

Bob Watson

Bert was first in the next morning and, after getting his coffee, logged into the database where they kept everything on their case load. Cristal Wiggins and Bob Watson were taking more of his time as she was now an official missing person with foul play a possibility given her husband's background of a faked death, double identity and his bizarre behavior.

As he had left the previous day, Colt had taken the action to pick up the banking records from the Wiggin's bank now that they had a subpoena.

There was nothing new in the database meaning no other law-enforcement organizations had inquired or left any info that might help in the case. He could see that her credit cards had not been used and her SUV was still missing.

Colt showed up a little breathless from running up the stairs, "Wait 'til you see this." He said as he ripped off his overcoat and slammed some papers on his desk.

"That jerk had a private account besides their joint account at the same bank. Their joint account has nothing of interest in it. Just the regular pay deposits, bills being paid etc. BUT about 2 months ago there was a deposit of $75,000 into his private account on a Tuesday and it was withdrawn over the next three days never to be returned. Guess which branch it was deposited and withdrawn from?"

Bert bristled, "I hate it when you play these guessing games."

Com'on Bert, "Vegas! The Luxor Hotel to be exact. My guess is he's back to his old gambling addiction. Looks like he borrowed some money from you know whom and lost it all in a binge on the strip. So my guess is he has a $75,000 bill to pay plus interest that his wife doesn't know about and he needs a way to get it.

And here is the clincher. Their insurance policies are also with the same bank. Each of them has a $250,000 life insurance policy with the other as the sole beneficiary. Not unusual for a couple who both work and have a sizeable mortgage but it does provide a solution to his gambling problem if the guys in Vegas are threatening him. And as you said yesterday, this does not bode well for the wife."

Just then the screen on Bert's desk beeped. He looked down and he still had the database on the Wiggins' case opened and there was a new entry.

"They found her SUV. Let's go!"

***

Cristal could tell something had gone wrong. While she didn't speak French or whatever language they were yelling at each other, there was no question her captors were very agitated by something. The only assumption was that they had finally after two days made contact with someone, demanded their ransom and it was not going well.

The door burst open and Habib came stomping into the room and headed for her with an open box cutter in his hand. His eyes were almost popping out of his red face and he was screaming something to the guard behind him.

He grabbed her hair yanking her up to a sitting position and then used his knee to pin her back down on the bed. With her arms and feet tied behind her there was nothing she could do.

"So now we go to plan B! That asshole at the CIA doesn't want to play ball so I'm going to send him your ear! You can thank him if you ever see him for his arrogance," he yelled.

As he threw her on her side and went for the ear she screamed, "I have Daniel's baby!"

Habib had just about started the slice when he stopped cold and jumped off her.

He stared at her in disbelief.

"The baby you saw me drop off at the daycare belongs to Daniel!" she screamed with tears in her eyes.

"I was pregnant when they caught him."

Habib, eyes almost popping out of his head, was staring at her as if he had been electrocuted. Could this be true?

Cristal was a little calmer now and through the tears said, "I don't think Daniel is going to be too happy when he finds out you're carving up the mother of his only child."

Habib finally came out of his stupor, "You wretched whore! You demon trash infidel! You would lie with a man who is not your husband? You gave him a bastard child? I should cut off your head right now for your blasphemy!" He yelled. He seemed close to openly crying with rage.

After a moment of thought and stomping around the room, he spat out, "How do I know this is true?"

"Do the math. My daughter is 2 years old. We took Daniel almost 3 years ago. We were in love before I found out who he was."

Just at that another guard appeared at the door and yelled something in French. Cristal could only pick out the term 'e-mail'.

Habib stood for a moment staring at her and then appeared to reluctantly close the box cutter and he headed for the door.

***

Phil Harris was back to the DD in under 5 minutes, "We posted the e-mail so the next call should be from them. We'll record it and trace it if we can."

"Phil, this is eyes only. I want any tracing or recording done directly by you or someone close to you but no one else at CIA can know of this. I'll explain later."

"Understood sir."

The call was transferred while Deputy Director Carter was still interviewing Commander David Crowe, "This is Deputy Director Carter."

"You son of a bitch. Have you come to your senses yet or do I cut off her ear?"

Carter hesitated. He was relieved to hear that he had probably reached him in time before Habib had gotten busy on Cristal and the tone of voice seemed to confirm the animal would have no problem acting on his threats.

"I think we can come to an agreement but only if she's unharmed, and only if we keep this all secret, so no more threats about CNN. Let me speak to her."

Habib hesitated. His plan was working. He was pretty confident she had no idea where she was and that the IP phone could not be traced. They had scanned her and her clothes for any electronic devices so he decided to comply.

He walked into the next room and directly up to her, "Here, speak to the Deputy Director of the CIA and tell him you're OK but nothing more or you will regret it."

He held the phone up to her ear and she said, "Hello!"

"Cristal is that you? Have they harmed you in any way?"

"Don't do it Mr. Carter. Don't do the swap!" she screamed as Habib slapped her across the face and pulled the phone away.

"She's unhurt … for the moment but you were almost too late. Now I want some proof you have Abu Nistal."

"He is right here with me now. Talk to him." He handed the phone to Crowe.

"Habib!"

"Nistal is it really you?"

"Yes Habib. You've done a great job. You really have the CIA scared you're going to kill one of their own."

"Yes, I have the bitch here that trapped you. The whore will bleed for what she has done. There are things she has done that we'll discuss when we're together that will make your blood boil and you will want to deal with her yourself but we can't discuss this on a phone call."

Cristal was still close enough that she could make out the two-way conversation.

Habib suddenly thought this might be a trick and said, "Nistal, what was the name of the person we thought was the best cook at our first camp?"

Commander David Crowe laughed, "His name was Dabir Hadi and as I remember we all had the runs for three days."

Jabir Habib laughed along with David, "Abu Nistal it's so good to hear your voice. We cannot wait to see you."

Crowe spoke again, "Habib do not harm her but hold her until we're together."

Carter grabbed the phone and put his hand over it, "That was not the deal. I want her swapped when you are released!"

David whispered, "Listen, There's no way they will let her go. They'll find a way to kill her at the swap or at least torture her unless I tell them to keep her safe for me. The only way is for me to get there and control the situation. Trust me. Besides, I want to see her face-to-face one more time. You have my word she will be unharmed."

Carter could hear Habib screaming something into the phone he had pinned to his chest. After a long moment seeing no options and still feeling uncomfortable with David's initiative, he spoke into the phone.

"All right. We will release Abu Nistal and he will release Cristal once he sees her. I have his word as a man of honor that he will keep this promise."

Habib saw an out here. HE had not promised to release her unharmed, Nistal had. They could still get their revenge on her. "OK, here is what I want you to do."

"No! We are giving up Abu Nistal before we see Cristal so we'll decide how it's done. You will still have Cristal as insurance.

"Call me in one hour and I'll tell you how we'll do it. And here is my word as an honest man. If she's hurt in any way I'll put the whole of the CIA on it and your entire family will be hunted down, slaughtered like animals and left to rot with pigs in a garbage dump." At that he hung up the phone before Habib could respond.

Jabir Habib was furious. He promised himself that before he left this godless country he would kill that blasphemous infidel.

He gave Cristal a wicked smile, "Wait until Abu Nistal finds out what you've done. You will wish you had never been born." He turned and stomped out of the room.

***

Cristal's white SUV was parked in a way that it could not easily been seen from the road. It had been moved off the road behind a row of trees and hedges about 5 miles from the day care center. The road was lightly traveled so it appeared that whoever had placed it there could have done so in broad daylight and not been noticed. The crime scene folks were already at the SUV having being called in by the local detachment. Colt recognized one of the techs.

"What do you have so far?"

"Well we're just getting started but we found a sponge on the back floor that smells like chloroform. No signs of blood anywhere though."

"So someone could have incapacitated the driver and hauled her away?"

"That would be one scenario."

Bert had been circling the SUV and had overheard the report. "What about fingerprints?"

"We're still looking. You would expect to find them on the steering wheel but for the most part they are all smudged. That would indicate that someone cleaned it up or the last driver wore gloves.

"To me it looks a lot more like a crime scene than someone who dumped their car and walked off. There is no sign of anyone being dragged anywhere so they were either mobile or more than one kidnapper carried the victim.

"You wouldn't park it here if you were walking off either. Too far away from everything. Most likely there was a second car to pick up the driver and anyone else in the car. Either there was a car following them or someone planned this and left a second car here for the swap. There's no sign that anyone walked off into the woods either.

"It's looking more like a kidnapping than someone trying to disappear, at least with the early evidence."

As Bert and Colt returned to their sedan they saw the first of the press arriving. There was no doubt they would piece it together and the Cristal Wiggins abduction would make it back to the top of the local news.

Bert spoke as Colt drove back to the station. "Let's get Wiggins aka Watson back in. This time we'll hold him on something.

"He'll have a lawyer this time so not sure if we'll get much more out of him but now that we have the car and the bank records I don't want him getting spooked and making a run for it like he did the last time in Wichita."

***

The news about the SUV was a local news bulletin so it was not hard to get Greg Wiggins back into the police station. Two hours after the find, they had him and his lawyer in an interrogation room.

"I see Mr. Wiggins that you have a lawyer with you this time," Bert said as he and Colt entered the interrogation room.

The lawyer spoke first, "I am James Dow. I'm Mr. Wiggins' lawyer and I want to know why he has been summoned here again?"

Colt spoke up looking directly at Wiggins, "We found your wife's car and we're processing it now. We would like to ask you a few questions in that regard in an effort to find your wife."

At that the door opened and a uniformed officer indicated he needed both detectives.

"We'll be back shortly," said Bert Wilson as they left the locked interrogation room.

As they stepped outside the uniformed officer said, "One of you better get upstairs fast. The chief is in a snit about this Wiggins kidnapping and he wants you there pronto."

Bert nodded and turned to Colt, "I'll handle this. I suspect the pressure is on and I want to keep ahead of the game. Get on to Wichita and see what warrants they have or can drum up quickly that we can use to hold this creep."

Two minutes later Bert was seated in front of a clearly upset Chief of police. "I told you guys to keep me in the loop. I have several press people on their way over here right now. They claim you guys found the missing woman's car and now I hear you have her

101

husband downstairs for the third or fourth time. Have you got anything on him?"

"OK, I apologize but we've been busy. We got his fingerprints the last time he was in here and guess what? He's not who he says he is. He is actually a guy named Bob Watson of Wichita who was declared dead a couple of years ago after running up some big gambling debts with the mob, staging his own death and abandoning a young wife and two little girls.

"Add to that what looks like a recent loss in Vegas of about $75,000 that he didn't have until he got there, likely more mob involvement and an insurance policy on his wife for $250,000. So it's starting to look like she's going to turn up dead and he plans to make off with the insurance money himself this time."

"OK all circumstantial but you have nothing to hold him on yet in our jurisdiction."

Colt had just arrived at the open door of the chief's office as he was speaking. "That just changed. Wichita wants us to arrest him and hold him for extradition to Kansas for a host of infractions including fraud on the $100,000 life insurance his wife collected. They promised us we would have the paperwork within the hour."

Ten minutes later the chief was being interviewed on camera in the main lobby of the building, "Chief, where are you on the Cristal Wiggins kidnapping?"

"While we don't comment on ongoing investigations I would like to remind you that this is an alleged kidnapping. Yes we've retrieved Mrs. Wiggin's car and we're processing it now but we have reached no conclusions on her whereabouts or what might have happened to her if anything."

"What about her husband? We saw him come in an hour ago and by my count this is at least the third time he has been in for questioning. Are you going to arrest him?"

The chief paused for a moment, "Mr. Wiggins will be arrested today on an unrelated matter. Apparently, Mr. Wiggins is actually Mr. Robert Watson of Wichita, Kansas. A man who was declared dead a few years ago and whose insurance policy was paid out.

"Kansas state police have asked us to arrest Mr. Watson on charges of insurance fraud and hold him for extradition."

There was a gasp from some of the reporters while others ran to report what they had so far.

The chief continued, "As to Mrs. Wiggins, we're still doing everything we can to locate her."

Bert Wilson exited the back of the news scrum and headed back to the interrogation room. He picked up Colt on the way and explained what had just happened, "I wish the chief had not done that but I guess he figured if we don't announce it Wichita is likely to so why not take the credit before they do."

As the two of them entered the interrogation room, the lawyer stood to complain about the delay and harassment of his client but Bert gently brushed him aside, "Mr. Robert Watson you are under arrest for insurance fraud and will be held for extradition to Kansas."

Greg Wiggins aka Bob Watson was shocked.

"You have the right to remain silent. Anything you say can and will be used against you in a court of law. You have the right to an attorney. If you can't afford one, one will be provided to you. Do you understand these rights?"

Watson was shaking and pale as he stood there nodding.

All the stunned lawyer could say was, "Who's Robert Watson?"

The Release

The call came through exactly an hour later while the DD was still with Crowe. They had come up with a plan that would work.

So far, only the two of them and Habib knew there was a plan to release Daniel Boone aka Abu Nistal and beyond that, only the Guantanamo base Commander and his second-in-command knew of the prisoner's real identity. They all wanted to keep it that way.

Deputy Director Carter took the call, "Are you ready to listen to the instructions for the release?"

Habib was excited that his plan was working, "Yes we are but we will not walk into a trap. We are not so stupid."

"I want Cristal back so there will be no traps and you will succeed if you follow my directions precisely."

Carter looked at his scribbled notes in front of him, "Obviously we don't know where you have Cristal and to ensure this escape happens properly I'll give you four choices of cities where we'll release Abu Nistal later today. Your choices are New York, Chicago, LA or Houston."

Habib thought this could be a trap to locate them so he thought carefully. He knew New York best and figured he could get in and out of New York the easiest. The population was so large that they couldn't possibly put roadblocks on every highway coming in or out. He could fly into any of the New York airports or even Philly and return by car. He said, "New York."

"OK, I will fly Abu Nistal to New York immediately. The cover story if we need it will be that he is to be tried in a civil court in that city. During the ride from the airport I'll give him this phone so you can communicate with him. We will give him a change of clothes and some money and drop him at Times Square. You can take it from there. I'll cover the story of his escape if need be.

"I'll have another phone with me that Abu Nistal will have the number for and you will confirm that you have him under your control. You will then release Cristal within twenty-four hours and you will call the same number to tell me where to find her. I have Nistal's word on this. Understood?"

Habib thought for a moment. They would obviously have the site staked out and a tracking bug on him but he had a plan for all of that.

He could bring a change of clothes and scan Daniel's body. He would fly into New York this afternoon and drive a rented car cross country off the main drags back to the Pittsburgh area where they were holding Cristal. David could wear something over his head in case they had facial recognition capability on New York streets.

There was no concern about meeting the 24-hour deadline, as she would not be returned alive. This would be perfect. Even if they bugged his phone he would replace it immediately and jumping on and off a few subways would clearly drop any tail they had on him. He finally answered, "This is acceptable. I want him at Times Square by 4 pm today."

"That works for us," said the DD and promptly hung up the phone.

***

Khalil was just finishing his morning prayers when one of his deputies came in looking a little excited.

"Master, we've heard some wonderful news from our brothers in Burundi that an action has been taken in the land of the Great Satan. Our brother Jabir Habib has penetrated their defenses and has captured one of their CIA operatives. He plans to trade her for our brother Abu Nistal. CNN has confirmed the abduction and our brothers in Burundi say Habib has been in contact with the CIA and is negotiating an exchange."

Khalil didn't show any emotion, "Al-hamdu lillāh. This is good. I know they felt Abu Nistal was very important to their operations. It would be a great embarrassment to the Americans if they had to release him. We did tell them to launch their own campaigns, but I would have preferred to have been informed of this operation before it started. The timing could be a problem for us.

"Jabir had some education in America so he's well prepared to break through their defenses. Ask our people to pay careful attention to any American media coverage of this action. I pray to Allah that our brother will strike a dagger into the heart of America before this operation is completed."

An hour later the same aid was back with a portable video system, "Master, CNN is again covering the abduction of the CIA operative. They don't know she's CIA but our brothers in Burundi confirm it. They say she was the agent who betrayed Abu Nistal and had him captured and sent to that torture chamber in Guantanamo. Here is the disgusting picture they published of the American whore."

Khalil glanced and then stared closely at the picture. "I think I've met this woman. But where did I see her?" He stared for another minute or so, "Yes, she was a US journalist I once met. I executed one of her group in front of her a long time ago. And she's the one our brothers say is a CIA spy?"

"That is right master. They are sure of it. They saw her with him many times. She disappeared from Burundi after his capture. She's the one who set him up."

"Keep watching the American news for any news on this and let me know immediately."

"Yes master."

***

Habib called the DD's number at exactly 4 pm, "Abu Nistal is that you?"

"Yes, my friend. I am free for the first time in nearly three years all due to you and I'm in the heart of the Great Satan. The fallen towers must be very close to here. Now what have you planned to get me out of here?"

"There is a MacDonald's near you. Go into it and go to the toilet and above the ceiling tile right over the toilet you'll find a new phone and some clothes. Change and call me as soon as you have it. Drop this phone in the toilet and speed dial 1 on the new phone to reach me."

It took Crowe only a few minutes to comply and he was back in touch with Habib, "What now?"

"Turn right as you exit MacDonald's, walk one block north and go to the closest subway station. Keep this line open. Do you see anyone following you?"

"No. the Deputy Director dropped me off and left and I see no signs of anyone following me."

Five minutes later, "OK, I'm at the subway station."

"Go down to the Yellow line and wait until the first train you see is about to leave and get on. It doesn't matter if it is a north or south train. Watch for anyone getting on after you. Get off after one station, look for anyone following you and get to a place where we can hear each other on the phone."

About ten minutes later, "OK I took the south-bound train and I didn't see anyone get on after I did and no one is following me."

"OK. Go back and take the north-bound train and watch for anyone following you. If you are clear, go two stations past the Times Square station and get off at the 57th street station and walk to the north end of the platform.

"You should see me but do not approach me. Follow at a safe distance watching for anyone following you. Follow me out, I have a car parked nearby.

"If you are followed, stay on the train for a few more stops and then get off and get to a place where we can talk and we'll plan a better way."

"OK. I hope to see you soon brother Habib."

Ten minutes later, after seeing no one was following him, they met and were hugging as they were seated in Habib's car. He was clearly nervous and still looking in all directions for a trap but there was none.

Abu Nistal feigned excitement, "My friend I have no idea how you did this. Do you know what a victory this is against the Americans? No one that I know of has ever swapped a Guantanamo prisoner with the CIA. How did you do it?"

Habib smiled, "Much planning. When the American whore disappeared right after you, I made the connection that she had set it up and she could only have been CIA to have that support, so I set it as my life's ambition to capture her and trade her for you. It took some time to find out where she went and then to plan this operation. I'm sorry we left you there so long. Our brothers will be more than glad to see you back in the lead of our cell."

"But before we move I must scan you for bugs." He reached into a bag in the back seat and brought out a modern electronic scanner and scanned David and the car just in case.

David said, "You told the Deputy Director you would call him and tell him you had me."

"That is not necessary. As you will see, our dealings with him are terminated. You will not let me release that CIA whore when you hear what she has done."

At this, David simply smiled.

Jabir Habib lifted his phone and hit one of his speed dials. "My brother we have succeeded. I have Abu Nistal with me. We will be with you soon. Tell our brothers in Burundi the good news. We will see them all in just a few days."

Before he put the car in drive, he handed Nistal a rather large cowboy hat from the bag in the back seat.

"I parked where there are no cameras but as we move through the city they may have facial recognition capability on some of the traffic or security cameras so if you would Nistal, please wear this and pull it down low over your face."

Commander David Crowe smiled and complied. Apparently, Habib believed that people with long hair and a scraggly beard looking like a terrorist and wearing a cowboy hat would not stand out in New York. As they started out and Crowe looked around he realized Habib might be right in this particular part of town. There were some interesting characters on the street.

Habib drove carefully out of downtown New York thinking that even the CIA could not follow him in this traffic and there was no evidence of helicopters. He reasoned drones would do no better because they would have lost Daniel in the subway and they had no idea what car he was driving. For the moment at least, he felt they were in the clear.

As they passed through the Lincoln Tunnel Habib said, "You promised to set the American whore free but I did not. When you hear from her lips what she has done you will beg me to slit her throat for you."

Crowe shivered at this thought wondering what the secret could be. He knew now she had set him up and he certainly wanted a piece of her or at least to confront her for her deceit and to see those lying eyes, the eyes that once had melted his heart.

He had fallen hard for her and at one point was thoroughly convinced that she felt the same. He had often wondered if she had been the one who had actually set the trap for him but until it was confirmed by Bill Carter that very morning, he had wanted to give her the benefit of the doubt.

How could she have done this to them? How could she have turned on him? But then again, that had been her assignment and plan from the beginning. There was no question in his mind now that she was a pro, trained well to do the job on him.

She had never loved him. Like a total sucker, he had fallen for the oldest trick in the book, simple seduction. He wanted to see her face-to-face and get some answers.

The only possible saving grace was that according to Carter, if he was to be believed, they didn't know his real identity at first and she thought she was capturing a ruthless terrorist about to kill hundreds. "Kill hundreds of innocents?" he still could not get that out of his head. These people actually thought he was capable of that?

If he could bring himself to believe that she didn't know who he was when they first met then that might have to be taken into account. But he was not inclined to believe that. After all Bill Carter had a strong motive to lie about what she knew and her behavior given he needed David's help to save her. Carter had also not been specific on when they found out his true identity and whether it was before or after he met Cristal.

Even if there was a slight possibility she hadn't planned it from the very beginning and there had been some love there, she hadn't trusted him enough to confront him with her concerns about the train job. Instead she'd done her job and betrayed him.

He came right back to the fact that she actually thought he was capable of killing hundreds of innocents to rob a train. Had he ever known her at all? Who was this woman? Was there EVER any love there on her part at all or was it total deceit from the very beginning? He couldn't decide yet but he had a nagging feeling that he was just being naïve and living in a dream world if he could not see what she really was. She was CIA after all.

Well that was water under the bridge. Soon he would see her face and watch her eyes as she answered his questions. He wondered if he would see any signs of remorse there. He thought not. If she was as good as he thought at her job then she would have rationalized her behavior as just doing what was needed to capture him. He decided he definitely want some time alone with her to get his questions answered.

He had made a commitment to Carter and he was going to keep it. He would make sure she got away safe but she would get a piece of his mind before that. She would understand his rage and condemnation before she was set free.

His focus returned to the present, "Where are we going?" he asked.

"I'm afraid it's about a six-hour drive back to the Pittsburgh area. We have friends there and there are enough Arab looking people in that region that we don't stand out as odd."

"How did you get into the US and find this place in Pittsburgh?"

He smiled with confidence, "We've been busy since you've been away. Our organization has been building up our network. When you worked with us in Africa you didn't know of our whole network. You took over the leadership of our cell from me but I never told you about our connections because you are an American. We didn't know how you would react to plans to hit American interests or even America directly. But I think now after you have been held by them for nearly three years, your attitude towards this government must be well established."

Nistal stared straight ahead and thought this through for a moment, "Yes you could say that. I had not lived in the US for a long time so I had no problem trying to undo their dirty work in Africa but three years of torture will change a man's mind. They are an out of control regime governing an empire by torture and intimidation in its death throes.

"Violence, prejudice, pornography, greed and corruption are their strengths. More now than ever. Ever since 9/11, Muslims have been vilified in this country. I'm not a Muslim but I think you know how I feel about injustice. That's what we were fighting in Burundi."

He needed to ensure Habib continued to see him on their side but this man beside him had linked him into a group that was actually Al Qaeda, bent on Jihad. How could he have missed the signs and linked up with these murderers?

When they were in Burundi the talk was only of freeing the people from their tyrannical government. Somehow he had missed all of the Jihadist rhetoric that seemed so obvious now. Although in his own defense Habib had just revealed that they held back on the western trashing when he was around.

Habib was all smiles and very proud of himself as he navigated the rush hour traffic on the outskirts of New York, which he reasoned was lighter than normal due to this being US Thanksgiving Day.

Lost in the thought of this most special of American holidays taken over by so much commercialism he said, "I think we're in agreement. Look around you. This could be a paradise. America has so much given to it but they have turned their back on God and slipped into the ways of Satan. Their consumerism and in particular their television is disgusting. They are a morally bankrupt and godless people now."

Crowe didn't want to get sucked into a debate about God but he needed to take this opportunity to gather as much current Intel as possible, "Tell me more about how you launched this campaign."

"As I said, since you've been away we've been building our network. I have a connection in Mexico that can get us into and out of the US. An amazing tunnel where we can come and go. We have friends on this side for transport who are committed to the cause and ask no questions.

"The interstate highway system is very safe if you do not exceed the speed limit and do not use their rest stops. Believe it or not, GPS machines now direct you to Halal restaurants and markets where we fit right in and can get food we can eat.

"We even have scouts and a few cells in some of America's major cities. The cell in Pittsburgh found us an abandoned building that they rented for storage. Again these people are dedicated to the cause and do not ask questions."

He was careful to be a polite driver in this mess of rush hour traffic. No need to draw unwanted attention he thought.

He continued. "I have a very small team of only three here with me to watch the CIA whore and help with logistics. The plan, that you will approve when you hear from her lips what she has done, is to behead her and leave her where she can be found but not before we're well on our way back to our exit point in Texas tomorrow. We'll leave videos for her old bosses at CNN. I'll gladly do the dirty work for you. I would have slit her throat already but I was sure you would want to confront her yourself."

David squirmed at the thought. While he had a real hate building for the heartless bitch that had seduced him, betrayed him and then sent him to Guantanamo for nearly three years, he didn't think she needed to die, especially a gruesome death like Habib had planned. Besides he had promised Bill Carter to set her free and he was committed to honoring that deal no matter what this secret was that she possessed.

But that meant taking on this terrorist gang himself. It was highly unlikely that the CIA could have followed them with the tricks Habib had used. He was on his own.

As to Habib, there was a lingering admiration of the man who had once fought at his side in Burundi but that had all changed now. Once he found out that they were actually Jihadis, and Habib had as much as admitted the fact, all bets were off. These guys were the enemy, had been all the time but he had not recognized them as such. If they had restricted themselves to freedom fighting in Burundi he could have rejoined them willingly but now their entire agenda was laid open and sides had been picked.

After nearly three years of confinement and torture, he was out of practice but now, according to Habib's headcount, he knew that he would have to dispense with four Jihadis if he was going to save Cristal, return her to Bill Carter and stop whatever other plan they had for Jihad in the US.

Then he had to figure out a way to make his own escape. He himself had no such network in the US and he wondered if he still had any friends alive and well in MI6 who would be both safe to connect to and could help him. His only hope was to free Cristal, stop the attack they had planned and then hope Bill Carter would give him some money and a way out of the country. That would be a start at least.

His mind was starting to gear up for the challenges of taking on this gang. Challenges he had not faced in a long time. Physically and mentally he had to be ready.

Crowe was curious, "Why did you risk so much to rescue me?"

Habib glanced at him and smiled, "Before you, we were a small cell doing very little to achieve small goals and the people of Burundi lived under the boot of that corrupt and Godless regime, who by the way are still in power.

"You took us to a point where we were starting to make a difference. We were really starting to hurt them. You knew all their political tricks and how their corruption was funded. Your leadership made all the difference. You set our goals much higher. Stopping the money was the key.

"Sadly after your capture, our plan for the train robbery fell through. When you disappeared we assumed something had gone wrong and we were afraid that they knew about the plan for the train and would be waiting for us.

"As soon as you disappeared our people lost that leadership and we fell back into our old style of thinking small. I'm sad to say that I am no substitute for your knowledge and leadership. You know things I do not. It will be wonderful to have you back leading us.

"You may be an infidel," he said laughing, "but you're a good one and Allah has sent you to us.

"As far as rescuing you. We would not have known what had happened to you if the Americans hadn't bragged about capturing the American Jihadi Daniel Boone in Burundi and sending him to Guantanamo. Not all of our people knew your American name but I did.

"It became my life's mission to both rescue you and penalize the Americans and I felt confident I could do it.

"I did some schooling in America and I felt that if I could get a small team into the country through

Mexico that I could track down that CIA whore and they would have to make a deal for her release.

"It's what Americans call a game of chicken. If they refused to negotiate and we were forced to torture her and use the media, our chances of getting you released were almost zero but the threat of publicly torturing a young pretty ex-CIA woman would be too much for the CIA and they would have to make a deal as long as it was not in the press. We had to make sure they took us seriously and as you can see, it worked.

"They've covered her disappearance in the media but they have not admitted she was CIA or might be part of a prisoner swap. As long as we kept it quiet and our connection to Jihad was not public, I felt we had a winning plan.

"So I am a very happy man today. Happy to say that my plan has worked so far. A happy man to see you too."

David was thinking that as usual Al Qaeda had underestimated their enemy. Bill Carter would always deal from strength and if Habib thought he had gotten away with something he was predictably mistaken. It had been fortunate for Carter that Commander David Crowe was willing to play ball but if it hadn't been that it would have been something else. Habib didn't have the chops to take on the mighty CIA.

"You've done a masterful job Habib. I know of no other freedom fighters who've ever been able to make the CIA drop to their knees like you have. You need to be very proud of your accomplishments and I can never repay you for rescuing me from that torture chamber."

Now that David thought of it, part of that last statement was actually true. He would still be at the hands of his torturers if Habib hadn't launched this rescue mission.

There seemed no reason to hold back so Commander David Crowe aka Daniel Boone to his business associates in Burundi and Abu Nistal, his nom de guerre for his terrorist friends explained in detail how his life in Guantanamo had unfolded and how he had not given the American's anything useful even under torture. He gave him just enough detail to make it all plausible but held back on some information that might be considered as classified such as how he had personally defeated their interrogation techniques, although he had to wonder if he had actually defeated them or possibly just prolonged them.

He finished with, "A long time ago I loved America and it was a law abiding country but now I see the damage that has been done to emerging nations around the world and how brutal they can be, violating their own laws and international laws on torturing prisoners. I'm anxious to get back to Burundi and make life difficult for those evil bastards."

After a long pause Crowe said, "I think you and I make a good team and once we've rebuilt our organization to the point where it can sustain itself I hope you will join me in moving our revolution to other African countries where more governments are oppressing their own people."

Jabir Habib simply smiled. Nistal was after all an American and it was not clear what his feelings might be on attacking the homeland directly as opposed to their nasty business overseas. He felt it better to keep his plan for a major attack in the US to himself for the moment.

His plan was to attack a major shopping center tomorrow, on Black Friday, American's biggest shopping day of the year. It was a masterful plan and so easy to implement.

Nistal didn't need to know any of this.

As far as Habib was concerned, the Trade Tower attack had shown the world that Americans could be made to over react in fear. They avoided planes for a long time, which hurt many industries but mostly the airlines. They implemented very restrictive rules for security at airports that were a major inconvenience for travelers and then of course they spent trillions reacting to the threat created by a few Muslim patriots.

Yet many Americans were not directly affected by air travel and many more didn't work in skyscrapers in the world's financial capital, so the impact while significant was limited and the fear in the mind of middle America was limited.

Still the success of the attack had been its financial toll on the country and it was massive. Trillions of dollars on defensive strategies like wars, common law-enforcement databases, TSA, Air Marshals, and Homeland Security.

But it was not as big as his own plan, he felt. A massive attack on a large mall in a secondary city would be different. Millions would avoid any mall thinking it could be the next target. Americans would see that they were not safe in their own little towns and cities doing what they normally did with their families, shopping at the mall.

Consumer spending would plummet. The damage to the US economy would be massive. Every mall in the US might instantly be a white elephant as shoppers wouldn't dare go near them for fear that more Jihadis were plotting an attack on them, wherever they lived in America, not just large cities.

Just like after 9/11 when nerves were on end and people saw terrorism everywhere, any small police action at a mall in America would be covered by the media as 'Breaking News' and made to relate somehow to another terrorist attack. The media could always be counted on to be the gasoline on top of the fire. They always blew things out of proportion with their Breaking News, panicked voices and exaggerated rhetoric.

After his example he hoped that other sleeper cells in the US and like minded individuals would take his model and repeat it. It would only take a couple of successful attacks like his to completely shut down US consumer spending and throw them into a depression.

This was not the Boston Marathon where courageous people would insist on running in the years following the attack. This was soccer moms with kids deciding to stay home rather than risk their family in one of thousands of enclosed areas that was so easy to target and could never afford the security of the Boston Marathon or a sky scraper in New York.

There might well be a solution downstream like a buffer zone near the buildings, barriers near entrances or online shopping but a few successful attacks over a couple of weeks would be enough to bankrupt the malls and consumer spending made up a giant portion of the US economy. A full fledged depression could be the only result he reasoned.

***

Habib's small American team had been handpicked. Of the three, two spoke English enough to get by, they were all totally committed to the cause, wanted to be part of the Abu Nistal rescue and wanted a chance to die as a martyr on the soil of the Great Satan in Holy Jihad.

Habib had not told them yet who would be the chosen one and they had no idea what an attack would look like but they were certain he had something big planned. He had promised that one of them would be known for millennia to come, as the one who had brought Jihad to Middle America and from what they could see this was Middle America that they found themselves in.

His call to his team in Pittsburgh was reason to celebrate. Their plan was working perfectly and they had passed the news back to their brothers in Burundi.

Besides monitoring the American CIA whore there was little else to do. Provisions were purchased by a short ride to a Halal market that actually carried some edible food reminiscent of central Africa but other than that, life was pretty boring so they tried to watch American TV which was even worse than they had been told.

Initially they had discussed whether watching American TV was an abomination. Later they all agreed it was part of their mission to understand the enemy, gather intelligence and watch for any mention of the kidnapping or the prisoner exchange.

Jerry Springer was an eye opener as was Honey Boo Boo and apparently adults watched obscene and blasphemous cartoons here. There was something called reality TV which was more disgusting than they could imagine. Apparently, all Americans were scum with no morals, no shame, and no thought of God.

They did stumble upon a few Christian broadcasts that seemed very polished but they had a hard time following the jargon and decided it was probably an abomination to watch Christian broadcasts anyways.

The TV selection was enormous and almost all of it seemed blasphemous to them. People half dressed and kissing each other on almost every channel. They discovered that there were even programs that had openly homosexual people on them.

They occasionally watched CNN, FOX News and the local Pittsburgh news channels to see if there was anything on the kidnapping or a Guantanamo prisoner escape or exchange. It was early evening when they saw the replay of the Chief-of-police's remarks on CNN that Greg Wiggins was really Bob Watson and had a wife and two little girls.

They had been told not to interact with Cristal Wiggins and to be extra careful as she probably had some combat training but they could not resist this one. The one with the best English approached her as the other two covered her with their weapons and looked on with glee.

"Do you miss your husband, Miss Cristal," he started.

She didn't answer but wondered what they were up to. Clearly something had entertained them. They seemed almost giddy.

"You might like to know that he's a big TV star now. He has been arrested by your government. Not for the kidnapping. No. He was arrested for faking his own death years ago and abandoning his real family in some place called Witchy something, in Kansas."

He didn't seem to be getting the shocked response he wanted so he pushed on, "He has two small girls. They are now showing the family on TV," he said laughing.

Suddenly his mood changed to disgust. "He is now a big star and you laid down with another woman's husband you wretched whore. You were not even legally married to him. It looks like you will lie down with any man who is not your husband but I would not touch you if I was paid, you dirty witch." He acted like he was going to slap her or kick her and then suddenly changed his mind remembering Habib's words to stay away from her even though she was probably helpless tied up the way she was.

Cristal was in fact shocked. Was this some kind of a trick? What did they have to achieve with making up this kind of story. They seemed pretty convinced the story was true. Maybe they had made a mistake. Then again, she had heard the sounds of a TV coming from the other room and they were probably watching the news for any reports on the kidnapping.

Could Greg actually have had a previous family? It was possible she had to admit.

She had never met another family member so he could be hiding an entire past. She knew little to nothing about him before they were married. Was it possible his whole life story was a lie?

Her dad had always thought there was something strange about 'the guy'.

That time at the Robert's when he had said he had never been to Palo Alto but had done a few years at Stanford had never come up again. She had overheard it and let it go but the idea that he might lie about something like that had always stayed in the back of her mind.

The Jihadi was not finished tormenting her, "You are the biggest whore I've ever heard of. You lie down with a man you are not married to and then go on to lie down with another man you are not married to who already has a wife. You are a devil. I should behead you myself for your blasphemy."

He could see she was not buying this completely. He sneered at her, "If you're interested his real name is Bob Watson. We will tape the news for you when it comes on again," he said now laughing.

"You should go on Jerry Springerstein or one of those other American programs where whores are exposed. You might become famous. Oh, I'm sorry. I just remembered. You are not getting out of here alive," he taunted.

"Jabir and Abu Nistal are on their way back here now and they will want to handle you themselves, otherwise I would kill you right now for what you have done," he said spitting at her and turning for the door.

He seemed to have had his say and said something in French to his two counterparts by the door that amused them as he left.

She sat there bound hand and foot wondering if this could be true. The more she thought of it the more she thought it plausible.

But that was not her immediate concern. Apparently, Habib was on his way back with Daniel Boone and she was most likely going to be executed when they returned. She kicked herself for being so easily found and captured.

Daniel was likely to enjoy doing her in. He must have known by now if not years ago that she had set him up.

Sadly, she actually thought she had loved him for a short time. Then the word came through that Daniel Boone was actually Abu Nistal, and she had overheard the conversation about hitting the train on the bridge.

How could she have fallen for a guy like that? How could she have misjudged him so badly? He was willing to kill possibly hundreds of innocents to get his hands on some money to finance his little revolution against the Burundi government. Sure they were corrupt despots, and she didn't understand why America was supporting them but killing innocents to finance your terrorism? How could she have misjudged him so badly she thought again?

She almost had to laugh although she felt more like crying. Apparently she had completely misjudged Greg Wiggins as well. Of all her skills and accomplishments apparently knowing her men was not one of them. Both had turned out to be villains. Her heart sank. Her two chances at a 'forever love' had turned out to be cruel tricks of fate, nightmares actually. Or was there something in her makeup that attracted her to these monsters?

She couldn't get over it and was starting to believe it was true. Greg had actually abandoned a wife and two small girls, but why? According to her captors, he had been arrested for just that so if they were telling the truth, the police must have had some solid evidence.

If he faked his death, the most likely reason was insurance fraud she thought. But why? Was he sending money to her? Did she know he was alive? She thought not. She had seen no evidence of him being pursued by his wife or him trying to connect with her and surely she would've seen something after a year of marriage.

Their bank accounts were joint and she would have noticed something if he was skimming money. Then again, he could always have had a separate account if he was supporting another family. Was there even more she did not know about him?

No, it was more likely he had left his wife for some reason and she thought he was dead.

But why not simply divorce her? And what about his girls? Greg was a good and loving step-father to Tiffany. Who leaves two children behind and doesn't try to contact them or take them with him and leave them to think he is dead?

She realized it had to be something urgent and something so dangerous that he had to disappear.

Was he an agent of some kind? That seemed unlikely as she was pretty sure he had no skill set for it. Then it hit her, some kind of death threat against him so he had to fake his own death. Maybe a very large debt, an illegal debt. Owed to unsavory characters like the mob. Probably gambling. That must be it.

There had been one or two occasions when they had been asked by friends to go to the track or even buy a lottery ticket and he had seemed like he was almost having a panic attack and had made ridiculous excuses to avoid any game of chance.

She had also noticed that he had very poor money management skills so she had handled most of the banking. Those were the signs of someone who had a serious gambling problem.

It actually made some sense and sadly she had to admit that it might be in character for him. It could be that he had run up large gambling debts. Debts that might be life-threatening if they were owed to the wrong people. Debts that only a life insurance policy might be able to solve. She could see where that might be the logic of it all in Greg's mind.

For the moment she could not be sure but this seemed like the most plausible answer.

It was starting to look like he had tried to start a new life with her and Tiffany which had worked up until now. But now the question was, did he ever stop loving his real wife and what did that mean for her own bogus marriage. Clearly she was not legally married to whoever they had said his real name was. He seemed to love her but maybe he still loved his first wife too, and maybe he loved her more if she was his first love.

If this was all true then he had lied countless times to her to maintain his cover story and there was no way to piece that back together. The man she thought she knew for a little over a year was not the man she had married and how did you rescue a relationship with all that hanging over your head. Even if you felt you wanted to.

No, her captors had not made this up. There was no reason for them to do that and they seemed gleeful in their discovery.

Greg Wiggins and Cristal Wiggins were no more. They were through. She was now sure of that. She had to believe what she had just been told. The pieces fit together too well and she had no desire to try to 'work things out' with a man with so many damning secrets.

It suddenly occurred to her that she didn't feel a great sense of loss. What did that mean about their marriage?

Maybe her dad was right when he had warned her about it being a 'rebound' thing.

Then a truly disturbing thought came to mind. She had never entertained the idea of having a child with Greg. He had never brought the subject up but more importantly, it had never entered her mind. He was handsome and charming and all but for some reason she had never had that 'nesting' feeling with regards to him. What did that say about her feelings for him?

In all honesty, she had to admit that their marriage had been one of convenience. She had needed a distraction from the pain of her good friend Tiffany's murder and the betrayal she felt when she found out Daniel was a terrorist and then found out she was pregnant by him. It was convenient for Greg as well. He was on the run and had needed a new life.

Their short mirage of a family life was over. Greg and Cristal were truly finished. There would be no question of custody of Tiffany either, given he was not even her biological father and had lied to get into the marriage.

Knowing her mom and dad she was sure Tiffany was safe with them until she could get back for her. That was if she could.

Right now, there were soon to be five terrorists standing in front of her who wanted her to die a painful death. She was going to have to figure out a way to get out of this alive before she could even think about going back to little Tiffany or confronting Greg.

She suspected there would be a face-to-face with Daniel and she hoped that they would be alone. That might be her chance. Disarm him and use him as a hostage. If they were willing to go to these lengths to launch a dangerous rescue mission into the US for him then they wouldn't want their plan to fall apart at the last moment by causing his death. He would make an ideal hostage.

She would have her face-to-face with him, get a question or two answered and then disarm him and take control of the situation. All of this contingent on convincing him to untie her somehow. As a terrorist he probably had some combat training and she would have to be prepared for that too.

It would be him or her. She would have to be prepared to take him out if need be. That was just the way it had to be. She would have to bury any deep-seated fondness she had had for him when she once again saw that handsome face in front of her. She would have to be resolute. It was likely he would not make it out of this alive and if he did, he was headed back to Guantanamo anyway.

Then there was the CIA. Surely Bill Carter had them under surveillance and a team would storm the building just after they arrived.

But what if the CIA had lost track of them?

These terrorists were no dummies. They probably had some skills at losing surveillance. That was the real nightmare scenario, her still tied up and alone facing five terrorists who wanted to decapitate her. Her only hope was that none of them realized her combat skills. Even Daniel had never seen her in action.

She could not figure out how the swap had been bungled so badly. You don't give up one prisoner before you have the other in your hands. The CIA was just not that stupid or at least Bill Carter wasn't. What was he thinking or had something gone wrong at the swap? What the hell had happened at that swap?

She had expected Jabir Habib to take her with him when he went to the meeting but now she was told he was already on his way back with Boone so the supposed swap had happened already.

Apparently Habib had never intended a swap. Something had gone very wrong for them to release Daniel without getting her in return. And as far as she knew, Jabir had gone to the exchange by himself, all the other Jihadis were still here. One man against the entire CIA? None of this made any sense.

Whatever had happened, if these Jihadis were telling the truth and Jabir was on his way back with Daniel, she had to prepare for the worst. They could have screwed up the swap or lost track of them or both. If either of those scenarios were true, she needed to be ready to take them on by herself hoping against hope that it would only be for a short time until Carter's team swarmed the building.

Daniel was the key. She started to run through scenarios of how she would disarm him and take him hostage and then make her escape or find a way to kill them all.

She had to hope he would have a weapon when he faced her, otherwise she would have to kill him or at least incapacitate him quietly and then rush the outer room banking on the element of surprise. She had seen the next room when she had used the toilet and thankfully it was a small room and she could probably get to each of them before they had time to get weapons on her.

First priority was Daniel and second was getting the best weapon they had. She had seen at least two AK-47's. Any one of those would do the trick. She knew the weapon well and if she could get her hands on one, she would have a chance.

As she had been led to the bathroom one time she had noticed clips of ammunition on the table in the next room. Good to know but it would be unlikely that she would get a chance to reload if she got hold of a weapon. She would just have to hope it had enough in the magazine to do the job. Ammunition would have to be used sparingly.

She would have to be alert and on top of her game. Her martial arts skills and the element of surprise would be a major advantage but she was rusty for sure and she really needed that element of surprise on her side with this number of targets.

All they needed to take her down was one lucky shot coming from a direction she was not focused on. Her primary focus was going to have to be situational awareness. Where was everyone at all times, who either had the guns or were within reach of them and whom did she have to handle first. The numbers were at the outside of her comfort level in a situation like this even with the element of surprise that she hoped to gain.

Her confidence was building and needed to, but the fact she had to face was that right now, she was still tied hand and foot to the bed and immobile.

If she couldn't get Daniel alone and find a way to get him to untie her hands, all the planning was moot.

A Meeting

Greg Wiggins had only been in custody about three hours when the FBI showed up at Bert Wilson's desk.

The tall thin pair of FBI agents, badges hanging out of their breast pockets, stared down sneering at Bert seated in his cubical, "We have an order here to take possession of the prisoner Bob Watson. Thank you for picking him up but I think you know you should've called us and we should have been involved before this hit the press.

"Most kidnappers cross state boundaries to throw off the locals and then kidnapping is a federal offense. You guys know that. And interstate insurance fraud is federal for sure. What made you clowns think you could hold on to this one?"

Bert smiled an oversized smile, "Good afternoon gentlemen. So good of you to visit us down here in the boonies where the real police work gets done.

"You should've called. I could have had lunch ready for you all. Then again I could have saved you the need to get yourselves dirty by visiting us down here in the trenches.

"I'm afraid you're about an hour too late. Mr. Watson is on his way to Wichita. You'll have to take this up with the other *'clowns'* down there. Have a good day."

They stood there for a moment, red faced and trying to think of some way to counter this nonsense. They finally turned and marched back towards the door.

Some of the other cops on the floor had overheard the encounter and snickered audibly as the two grumbling FBI agents walked by.

Colt waited until they were gone and broke out laughing, "Wow, I had no idea you were such a charmer. Is that why you accelerated the transfer to Wichita?"

"Yeah, I figured these monkeys would be here pretty soon and I just felt like bustin' their balls. I've had to deal with their type before and I knew they would come in here and dump on us. I could have pointed out that the information was all on the database if they only chose to look at it. Besides, I don't think we're going to get anything more out of Greg Higgins or Bobby Watson so may as well let Kansas have him and his lawyer said they were not going to contest the extradition. I don't think Greg Wiggins likes me and he wanted out of here fast. Also if he made bail here then he could hide evidence. This way we can take our time searching his home and car.

"But here's a shock for you. I'm starting to think the CIA tip from that call was a real call. He is dumb but not that dumb to offer such a weak distraction. Either someone did their homework and was just pestering him or maybe that call was really from a former CIA secretary. The wife did spend years in Africa if you remember and speaks the local language. There could be some CIA connection to this thing after all.

"Besides, that chloroform sponge in the car surprised me. If Greg was the guilty party why did he wait until she was in the car to attack her? He could have incapacitated her while she was asleep or any other number of ways. That sponge in the back seat screams unknown assailant to me. Whoever it was wanted her alive too or maybe Wiggins is that smart, killed her and put the sponge in the car to make it look like a kidnapping.

"Her best chance if she was kidnapped for being a CIA spook is if they rescue her but we'll never know. If the CIA thing is real, we'll find nothing leading to her disappearance, the case will go cold, the CIA will never admit anything and one day somewhere down the road the baby will disappear.

"Mark my words, watch the baby. All of this assuming she's not already dead."

***

Khalil was awakened early in the morning by one of his lieutenants, "Al-hamdu lillāh. Master, wonderful news. Our brother Jabir Habib has succeeded in America on their very Thanksgiving Day. Our brothers in Burundi relayed the message that he has Abu Nistal and they have not given up the CIA whore yet so they will kill her."

"This is truly wonderful news. What do we know about how the transfer was made? How were they able to hold on to the woman?"

"I don't know master. I only know that Jabir Habib negotiated it that way. They said there's a promise to release her within 24 hours."

Khalil was instantly on alert, "What have the Americans said about the escape. It must be on the news."

"Nothing master. They have said nothing. The Americans said they wanted to keep it secret so they're not seen negotiating with terrorists. There has been no word of any escape on the news channels we monitor. They wouldn't say anything until they get the woman back, no?"

Khalil stood and walked to the tiny window in his borrowed room, "Something is wrong. They would not have negotiated a deal where he goes free before they have her. They know she would not be returned. If they've not announced an escaped terrorist then they are not afraid of him. They could also have them under surveillance and will strike when Jabir leads them to her and his team."

He paced back and forth in front of the small window, "Surely they could not have been certain to be able to track Jabir. He would have had a good plan to lose them and they would have been expecting that. So if they've released him and not gotten her in the swap the only answer is that Daniel Boone must have made a deal to save her. The only reason I can see for the Americans yielding to Jabir's deal, agreeing to releasing him before her and not announcing an escape is that Boone is working for the Americans. His plan is to set her free and probably kill or capture our brothers. There can be no other explanation for this.

"Jabir Habib should have seen this. The Americans want us to think that they won't announce an escaped terrorist because they don't want to panic their citizens but if they truly feared him it would be on every TV channel. It could not be otherwise. There would be a country-wide manhunt and their TV screens would be covered with pictures of the American Daniel Boone. It is clear and indisputable, they do not fear him!

"No, I don't believe what we are being told by Jabir's people. They have been betrayed. I'm afraid I see only treachery here. I never trusted this American when he worked with Jabir in Burundi. I'm convinced now that he's either a spy or a traitor.

"Boone has set it up so Jabir and his group will be caught or killed.

"How could Jabir not have seen this. He is too taken by this American who helped him in Burundi. I don't know what they told him to make him think this would work but there's no way the Americans especially the CIA would let this unfold this way.

"He cannot see the deceit and he's blinded by his own success against the Americans and his respect for this Daniel Boone who has turned on him.

"We must take immediate action. Get a message to our brothers in America. I have issued a fatwa on both Daniel Boone also known as Abu Nistal and the CIA woman because they are both spies and treacherous enemies of Islam. Explain to them that the Americans have not announced his escape because they don't fear him. That he has made a deal with the Americans and he must be killed immediately with the woman, Insha'Allah."

***

It was late in the evening when Jabir Habib and Abu Nistal finally arrived at the Jihadi hideout just outside of Pittsburgh. Out of respect for his former leader, Habib had yielded to Nistal request to have some one-on-one time with Cristal on the condition that he ask her about the BIG secret she had kept from him.

Exhaustion had gotten the better of her and she was starting to doze off as he entered the room. Immediately she was awake and sat up as best she could as he approached. He seemed thinner and his beard and hair were long and straggly. He had a relatively deep tan which she attributed to Guantanamo and he definitely looked all the part a Jihadist.

He took a chair from the corner, placed it in front of her bed and sat down heavily. Disappointed, she noticed immediately that he was unarmed. She might have to kill him quietly and then rush the other room after all, to get her hands on a weapon.

It had been three years since they saw each other and each simply stared at the other with overpowering contempt.

Under the full beard and long hair, she recognized the face of the man she once thought she loved. Handsome and charming but in reality a monster who had played her and used her. A terrorist, Jihadi and a butcher of innocents.

Her look showed the fury she felt and she wanted to spit in his face before he could get a chance to kill her.

He looked like he knew how to handle himself. He had apparently kept fit in captivity. It was not going to be trivial to incapacitate this man. It might be safer to simply go for a quick death blow.

Pretty as she was even in this captive state, suddenly the contempt he felt for her was unbounded. Now that he saw her, his emotions started to boil. He was shocked by the rage he felt. It was something he had never experienced before and yet even in this wretched captured state wearing oversized men's clothes and uncombed hair she was beautiful. This made everything worse. A treacherous witch if ever there was one. No matter what emotion she instilled in him it peaked. When he had loved her it was all consuming and now he desperately wanted to strangle her until there was no breath coming out of this witch, she had such a powerful grasp on him.

How could she have thought so little of their relationship that she could find it in herself to betray him? But then again Carter had sent her to find him. She had played him from the beginning. It was her despicable job to con him. He could see it in her eyes. The eyes he had thought of so many nights in

Guantanamo. Beautiful eyes that once had seemed to be a window into and equally beautiful heart.

Now he saw clearly that they were the eyes of a liar. Her professed love for him had all been lies. She had been sent there to capture him and did it by seducing him. He felt like such a fool. He could see it all clearly now in her eyes. How many other men targeted by the CIA had been victim to those very eyes. Even seeing her now he found it hard to believe that he could be tricked so easily and by the oldest trick in the book, seduction.

Here was the woman who was responsible for nearly three years of horrendous torture at the hands of the sadists in Guantanamo. Memories of the helplessness he felt while brutes held him down and poured water over his face came flooding back. He felt instantly nauseous at the thought.

He wondered if she had any idea or had ever thought of the helplessness and hopelessness he had had to tolerate at the hands of those monsters in Cuba. His blood was boiling and his heart was pounding with hatred. Suddenly his commitment to Bill Carter seemed in jeopardy. His only thought was to reach forward and strange the life out of this bitch.

She spoke first, "You have me at a disadvantage. If there's any humanity left in you then you will untie my hands at least. I've been bound like this for days and I can't feel my hands anymore."

That voice! That heart melting voice.

He wanted to slap her or worse but as he started to calm down he realized he was not that kind of man. Even if she was a CIA enforcer, he was not going to throw the first punch at a woman. He sized her up and something in him detested seeing her bound like an animal. Even though he saw her as the enemy, she had a powerful hold on him and he had made a promise to Carter. The deep seated gentleman in him thought that no woman should be bound like this. He could see the pain in her eyes behind the rage and a quick look showed that the hands and feet were showing the results of extended restriction and immobility. He was likely going to need her anyways when it came time to handle Habib's team although what good was a woman going to be in a man's fight.

He motioned for her to turn around and he untied her hands leaving her feet bound. He had no time to duck as the fist came around and caught him square on the jaw, but he was quick enough to grab the second hand that went for his throat. He got control of the first hand too. She tried to use her knee but she was still bound and made a clumsy attempt at going for his groin. He could tell she was strong for her size and apparently had some hand-to-hand combat skills.

In a flash he let go of one hand, slapped her across the face and regained control of her free arm before she could react.

Now that they were locked in a sitting grasp she started to try a flip of sorts but with her feet anchored both realized instantly that none of her moves were going to work. He was too strong and the element of surprise had been lost.

"You almost broke my jaw you bitch. So that's how it's going to be," he growled.

"You son of a bitch," she snarled, "How could I ever have thought I could love a monster like you? I loved you and you turned out to be a vicious Jihadi bastard trying to kill hundreds of innocents. You played me you heartless creep. None of your charms were real. All of that crap back then was total lies. Have you no shame, you animal? Why don't you just kill me and get it over with you vicious bastard."

She detected an immediate change in his face. Surprisingly it looked more like shock than hostility but it was quickly replaced by something full of malice.

"Don't even go there you callous bitch. You can drop the act now. You were sent in there to seduce me and capture me. You are the worst kind of whore. You had no feelings for me at all. How many other men did the CIA call you in to seduce and trap? I know all about you now. It was all an act so drop it right now.

"I don't know why you didn't just kill me there and then. I had no information the CIA wanted. Do you understand that there was nothing I could tell them to get them to stop the torture. I had nothing they wanted. Did you ever think of what you had done by sending me to that torture house? I was being endlessly tortured for almost three years while you were sipping your martinis. What kind of a heartless animal can do that to a person?

"Believe me, you have no idea what waterboarding is like. Even if you've been prepared for it. I wish I had a bucket right here, right now to give you a taste of your own medicine.

"What did you do? Sit at home and laugh at this? Did they give you a medal for catching a big terrorist? I could kill you with my bare hands for what you did to me. But the hardest to take, the worst torture was your betrayal. You planned it all from the beginning and I fell for it like a total sucker. That was the toughest part of all. Worse than any physical or psychological torture was the betrayal."

Somehow in his anger he had dropped his American accent and a British lilt was obvious to her.

She was furious, "What are you talking about. I had no idea who you were until we had been together for at least two weeks. Then your real character shone through you animal. You were not the man I thought you were at all."

He shook her, "You expect me to believe that. Why do you keep up with this story. Bill Carter told me only this morning that you went in there to get me."

"Bill Carter? Why would he tell you anything? We went in there not knowing who Abu Nistal was. I found out just before I heard you were going to kill all of those people. Women and children. But that didn't matter to you. You just wanted the money to fund your Al Qaeda friends and your private little war. That's what you people do, right? You kill innocents. That's why you're a terrorist."

Now it was his turn to be shocked, "Kill all of those people? I wasn't going to kill anyone. 'Hit the train' meant rob it you moron. We had an inside man. No one was going to get hurt. Even Bill believes me on that one."

He kept talking about 'Bill' like they were old buddies or something but she wasn't about to buy that story.

Something here was not going as planned. She needed to find out more, "Why did Bill release you? We never negotiate with terrorists. Abu Nistal was a big catch. What the hell is going on?" she almost yelled.

He motioned to her to keep her voice down. He stared at her for a very long time. If she really had not known who he was when they had fallen in love was it possible the love at least in the beginning had been real? "If what you say is true. If you found out who I was and

142

what I was planning after we made love then why didn't you ask me to explain?"

"Are you kidding me, have a sane conversation with a known Jihadi? Would you ask someone ready to kill hundreds of innocents for an explanation?

"Our Intel was that you would kill anyone in your way. You're a terrorist, a Jihadist, one of Al Qaeda's top field men. Nothing like the man I thought I loved."

He thought this over for a moment. "If I release your arms will you hear me out?"

There was something in his tone and that British accent. She decided to postpone her attempt at incapacitating him until she got all the info she could get. Still time was limited but if it got her hands released that was a step in the right direction. She nodded acceptance.

He released her hands and sat back into a safer position.

"To answer your earlier question about what the hell is going on here let me start with this morning. Deputy Director William Carter shows up in Guantanamo this morning and tells me that they've finally ID'd me and he needs my help. First let me introduce myself formally. My real name is Commander David Crowe of Her Majesty's MI6 Secret Service," he said in full British accent.

Her mouth unintentionally dropped open and her eyes widened.

"I had bolted from my previous job when I uncovered a major conspiracy, but I was set up by someone in MI6 to take the fall. MI6 had a Terminate order on me so I had to disappear. I started my own little war as you call it, in Burundi where they were particularly brutal to their own people. At that time, I had no idea Habib was tied to Al Qaeda.

"Anyways Bill Carter released me on the promise that I would rescue you from these barbarians and stop a major Jihadi attack they are planning before they leave. Until this moment, I believed you had never loved me and had set me up for three years of the most unspeakable torture, which I'm still inclined to believe. But because of my deal with Carter, my plan was to slap you silly before I let you go.

He continued, "So, I'm still not convinced you're telling me the truth. If your story is true then you were a heartless bitch for setting me up and not trusting in our relationship."

Her heart jumped into her mouth at his accusation, but she was not quite ready to feel guilty and to buy any of this. She was staring at him and not knowing where to start. This was the guy they had gone after. They caught the right guy. They knew he led the cell in Burundi. He was not denying that. He HAD been caught by her discussing 'hitting' a passenger train.

"Why should I believe any of this?" she asked.

"Whether you believe me or not, if you want to get out of here alive you had better cooperate with me. The way I see it you have no other options."

He saw she was not quite there yet, "OK. One; have you ever known the US to barter with terrorists and especially to release one for the 'Promise' of reciprocity. Two; why would I tell you all of this if I was just going to kill you. Three; we need to get you out of here and stop that attack. The rest of this reunion or whatever this is can wait!" he sneered.

She wasn't ready for this. It could be some sort of cruel trick.

Then David remembered, "Oh yeah, one question. Habib says you have some big secret to tell me that will cause me to cut your head off. I'm really starting to hope he's wrong. What is this big secret?"

Apparently Habib had not told him. "OK, in the vein of true confessions, yes I set you up for capture before you could kill hundreds ... we thought. After that I was so broken I left the CIA. Now for the big surprise. I had your baby. We have a two-year old daughter but I'll burn in hell before you ever get near her."

His face went pale and his jaw visibly dropped. He stared at her for a long time and finally said, "I have a two-year old daughter?"

"Yes. And that is not all. Six months after she was born I married ... or at least I thought I married a man in Cincinnati."

"What do you mean you thought you married ...?"

"Turns out that through investigating this kidnapping the cops have found out that he was previously married under another name and faked his own death. Apparently, I was never married to him.

"Before you ask, I loved him enough to marry him but nothing like what we had and as of now I never want to see that bastard again, or you for that matter. But why am I telling you this?" she said as she started to mist up. "It could all have been so different if you hadn't turned out to be such a creep. You asshole!"

"Wow, I have a daughter. You got married. You're not married. This is all a lot to absorb."

She had started to calm down and get back to her current predicament, "OK ... David, right?"

"Yeah it's David."

"OK David. Assume for a moment that I believe enough of what you just told me so that we can call a truce. Just for the moment. Anything that will help me get out of here is fine by me. What do we do now. Your Jihadi friends want to kill me tonight and you say they are planning a big hit in the US. What's your plan?

***

Of the team, only Habib had known Abu Nistal before his capture. After the initial excitement and celebration at seeing the first part of their mission succeed, the team were a little surprised that Habib had allowed their new arrival to spend some one-on-one time with the hostage.

"I didn't tell him of her treachery," he informed them in French.

"I think it's better if he finds out that he has a child with her directly from the whore's mouth. If he kills her right now with his own hands then he has earned that right and it's Allah's will. Insha'Allah"

His second-in-command spoke first, "We have a problem. While you were in New York today, we received a communication relayed from master Khalil al-Adel himself. The message says he's sure that Abu Nistal is also CIA and he wants you to kill both of them. He says the US has not announced an escaped terrorist therefore they are not afraid of him and he must be CIA."

"What are you talking about," he almost yelled. "He has been held and tortured by the Americans for almost three years. He can't be CIA and not only that we've just launched the greatest operation in our cell's history to penetrate America and bring the CIA to their knees. This cannot be true. It cannot be true that Nistal

146

is CIA. He worked with us and led our cell in Burundi. It's not possible. They have not announced an escape because we still have the woman."

"Habib, please remember that we only have his word that he was tortured by the Americans. Master Khalil must have information we do not have. He has declared a fatwa on the two of them," he pleaded.

"A fatwa? He has no right to issue a fatwa. He is not a religious man and he's certainly no expert on Islamic law. Besides Nistal has done nothing to offend Allah.

"Why would Khalil wait until now to unveil this 'information'? Is it because we've succeeded where he has failed? Is he worried we will get too much credit for our bold action? He has been unable to penetrate US defenses and is embarrassed by all of his own failures.

"Look around you. Our little team has done what his whole organization has not.

"No, this is wrong. He is not CIA. Khalil is wrong. Whatever information he thinks he has is wrong. I've trusted Nistal and he has never let me down. You can even see in his eyes that he has been tortured. Look at his body. He has lost so much weight. Khalil does not know what he is talking about.

"I'm determined. I won't allow our plans to be derailed by someone thousands of miles away who does not know what we see in front of us. We will proceed with our initial plan and we must put it into action right now. We can't wait or change plans at the last moment. That is my decision and I'm still the leader of this operation. I'll deal with Khalil once we are clear of here."

He turned to the youngest of the three, "Aaban Abboud you my son are the most honored one. I've

watched you closely and you are a most devout Muslim and the chosen soldier who will deliver a stake into the heart of America through holy martyrdom, Insha'Allah!
"

Aaban smiled as the other two looked on a little shocked and disappointed that they had not been chosen.

"You must prepare yourself tonight. I called our contact from the car and he will pick you up very soon. In the morning you will destroy Middle America. Our friends have hijacked a large propane delivery truck and armed it. It is a massive bomb on wheels. Tomorrow at noon you will follow the GPS in the truck until you arrive at one of the biggest American Shopping Malls where thousands of people will be gathered on America's biggest shopping day.

"Believe it or not they call it Black Friday but Aaban, you will go down in history as the devout Muslim who changed the meaning of Black Friday for all Americans. The infidels will know that their heresy, blasphemy, their aggression towards Islam and their disrespect for Allah cannot continue.

"When you arrive at the Mall look closely for the main entrance, it will be shown to you on a map by our friends. Drive as fast as you can through the glass entrance, there will be nothing to stop you. Do not detonate the truck too early. We've planned it so that you can drive right into the center of the mall.

"When you've penetrated as deeply as you can and are surrounded by infidels then detonate the bomb. Thousands of infidels will be incinerated and you will be in heaven with Allah, Insha'Allah.

"The American economy will fail. It will make 9/11 look like a joke. You will be a hero throughout the

Muslim world forever. You will join Allah in heaven where he is waiting for you with all of your rewards and your family will share in all of the praises of your martyrdom. Allahu Akbar."

In unison the others repeated, " Allahu Akbar."

The young Arab was beaming. He loved the plan. He could see himself already, driving a large truck through the entryway while reciting his prayers. He would be in heaven within seconds, "Thank you brother Habib. I'm honored to give my life in Holy Jihad and defense of Islam."

The others hugged him and congratulated him. His ride arrived as promised a few minutes later and he was gone.

***

David Crowe and Cristal Serpe sat staring at each other, both wondering if it was all true and if so, how such a potentially tragic misreading of circumstances had changed their lives so drastically.

She thought of how things could have been different if David was in fact an MI6 agent on the run and not the monster she had imagined.

He was wondering what it all meant if she had not targeted him initially but only after the CIA had tied him to Abu Nistal. What if she was telling the truth about thinking he was going to kill innocents?

Both looked at each other with new eyes but both were still confused and cautious. This seeming new reality could all be a mirage. There was a lot of evidence to support their initial understanding of what had happened. Both realized at that moment that they had better not get ahead of themselves.

David spoke first, "We need to get you untied but leave the ropes on you so they think you're still bound. Let me do the talking. I know their mentality best."

Just as he finished her ropes the door opened and three of them walked in. Habib led and the two guards had their AK-47's. Both David and Cristal immediately wondered where the fourth was. A loose Jihadi in the other room with a potential third AK-47 was a major threat.

Habib approached David with a smile, "Well brother Nistal, did the whore admit her betrayal to you?"

"Yes she did. I want her killed for her treachery but there's no sin on the head of the baby girl she gave birth to. I would like to see her before we leave and make some arrangements for her care."

"That will be impossible I'm afraid. We are on a tight schedule and must head back towards Texas in the morning before certain other events make travel more difficult."

Both guards with their fingers on the triggers of their AK-47's stepped forward until they were right behind and beside Habib. One whispered in his ear in French, not knowing David was fluent, "Brother Habib I'm afraid I can't allow this. We must obey Khalil's fatwa and execute the two of them now!"

Before Jabir Habib could react, David swung into action reaching behind Habib he grabbing the barrel of the AK-47 and whipped it upwards causing the guard to depress the trigger as it exploded in rapid succession nearly cutting Habib in half and spraying blood and guts over Cristal and the other guard.

As he spun the big guard toward the ground, he caught a glimpse of the other guard swinging towards him but didn't see Cristal's roundhouse kick to his

150

temple dropping him and disarming him before he was half way through his turn toward David.

David's lethal chop to the throat of the big guard served to make him release his grip on the gun and instinctively grab for his wounded neck.

David had just enough time in one swift movement to get control of the AK-47, put two rounds in the chest of the downed Jihadi and swing around to see Cristal put two slugs of her own in the chest of the half conscious second guard. All three of the Jihadis seem to breathe their last breath together seconds later.

A blood-drenched Cristal and David stood over the bodies, adrenalin pumping and ears ringing as they maintained a bead on the now lifeless corpses on the floor.

Suddenly they found themselves aiming their AK-47's at each other.

There was a long pause as they stared into each other's eyes.

"You go first," he said.

"You're an escaped terrorist from Guantanamo and I'm taking you back. The US cannot be seen to be negotiating with terrorists."

David laughed and pointed his gun at the floor, "Bill Carter might disagree with you. Put that gun down. We have a job to do. I told him I would get you back alive and he wants me to stop that attack. We have a missing Jihadi and we have work to do."

After a long pause she reluctantly pointed her gun at the floor. He had saved her life but she still saw him as a terrorist. There was no getting past the things he had done in Burundi before they met and she only had his word on the rest.

David got her attention as he bent over Jabir Habib rifling through his pockets, "When we were driving back from New York Habib made a call. He said they were ready to go and to send transport for Abboud. I am guessing he's the missing Jihadi and the lucky martyr. He must have left already and the plan is still a go to launch some kind of attack.

"Habib just said we have to be out of here in the morning so this thing, whatever it is, is going down tomorrow. I'm guessing he wanted to be well out of Pittsburgh and on his way to Texas before road blocks got set up."

He turned over Habib's body and found his cell phone. Luckily it seemed undamaged except for all the blood. He wiped it off and hit redial.

The call was picked up quickly and David Crowe doing his best Habib impression in French said quickly, "Abboud is on his way. Is everything ready?"

"Yes, the propane truck has been … Habib, what is the password?"

David pointed the AK-47 to the ceiling and shot a short burst and screamed.

Just before he hung up, he heard on the other end the contact yelling "Habib, Habib, what is going on."

"What is this?" Cristal asked.

"I'll explain. Let's get Bill Carter on the phone pronto. We need his help to stop this thing. Do you remember his number?"

"No but I can get him. I remember my old security code which may still be active."

She took the sticky, bloody phone from David and dialed a Langley, Virginia number. She was happy to see that her code still worked and she asked to be patched through to Deputy Director William Carter's phone. Philip Harris picked up.

"I need to talk to the Deputy Director right away," she said.

"You used an old code to get through to me, who is this?"

"I'm Cristal Serpe and if you're this close to Bill Carter then you've been read into this operation."

"Cristal so good to hear from you. I'll patch you through right away."

The line clicked, then rang and was picked up quickly, "Hello?"

"Mr. Deputy Director, this is Cristal. I'm alive and well as is someone else here. Can you verify his identity."

"Cristal it's so great to hear from you. Yes, Commander David Crowe is who he says he is and he and I have a deal to free you and stop a terrorist attack. Does that do it for you?"

"Yes, at least for now. I'm going to need some explanations but we need to address something else first. Let me put you on speaker."

"Bill. This is David. Three of the terrorist including Habib are dead. You may have preferred them alive but we had no options.

"We are somewhere southeast of Pittsburgh in an abandoned building. One of the terrorists left before our encounter and we have no idea where he's going or who he's with but it looks like he's the suicide bomber. They apparently have people in Pittsburgh helping them and transport to and from the Texas Mexico border. We just discovered that some kind of a propane truck bomb will be used sometime tomorrow because Habib said we had to be out of here before the strike."

Bill Carter breathed a sigh of relief. A propane truck in Pittsburgh for tomorrow made it less likely that the dirty bomb had yet to make its way to the US. "Do you know anything more about the terrorists, names, descriptions, targets?"

"The remaining Jihadi who I expect will be the martyr is a young Arab and we only have one of his names, Abboud. Get your team to home in on this phone signal to find this place. We are not using any relays.

"Abboud left here within the last twenty minutes, we think to prepare for the attack. Tomorrow is your Black Friday so I'm assuming it may have something to do with shopping. If I were you I would put full attention on a recently stolen or purchased propane truck and come up with a strategy to isolate it, find it, destroy it or whatever it is you guys do."

The DD interrupted, "I'm sending a team in to find you two and we'll get on this right away."

David stopped him, "On that, because of what happened here a moment ago there may be a gang of Jihadis on their way over here now to check things out. We don't plan on waiting around for them. I have Habib's car so Cristal and I are out of here.

"You need to get a fast team in here to stake out this joint and capture anyone who shows up. If no one shows up overnight you might want to get rid of these bodies before the locals and press get on to it. I think you need to get working on that propane truck. We'll call back later. We have some things to sort out here."

The DD interrupted, "OK, you do what you need to do but remember confidentiality. We want to keep this out of the press and Cristal, at this time we don't want it disclosed that you were once CIA and that David has been released from Guantanamo so please keep this quiet. I don't even want the local cops or the FBI in on this partly because David must remain deceased.'

Cristal's frown indicated to David that she was going to need an explanation on the 'deceased' thing.

The DD finished with, "So do what you need to do and call in at some point," and at that he hung up.

David turned to Cristal, "You handled yourself pretty well for a retired mother of a two year old. Apparently wet work is not foreign to you."

She mustered a half smile, "Torture and three years of incarceration does not seem to have hurt your skills either."

He looked around at the mess and then at themselves. "We're not very presentable. Too much blood on us. What say we clean up as best we can, find a motel and have a real tête-à-tête?"

They went through the pockets of the dead terrorists and found enough money to get them started and found the keys to the car outside.

They cleaned up quickly as best they could in the little toilet and Cristal did the best she could with the oversized men's clothes to look a bit more presentable.

They were both anxious to get on the road before another gang of Jihadis showed up to find out what all the fuss was about.

The Bomber

It was near midnight on a hectic Thanksgiving Day by the time Deputy Director William Carter made it back to his office at Langley from his New York Operations Center where he had remained after releasing David. One urgent call had brought in all the key members of the team and then some.

The CIA Red Alert had kept many at their desks for long shifts but people had to sleep even if they were only getting eight hours off. There would be no more sleep tonight.

Some of the new arrivals had apparently had a great Thanksgiving dinner and had imbibed to a greater or lesser degree. Coffees brought in for all started to bring them up to the right level of focus.

There was a threat to the mainland that was imminent and the CIA went into high gear. The posting on the Homeland Security database had triggered reactions all across the US especially the Pittsburgh area. The CIA retained the lead at the moment as there were international terrorists involved and they had been tracking the threat and had a better idea of what to look for having had files on some of the principals.

The Homeland Security level was now set to a localized Red alert level due to the fact that they now had a specific threat; an attack in the Pittsburgh area with a propane truck on Black Friday.

As Carter entered the large Ops center at Langley, the team came to order with everyone instantly paying attention, "OK, Philip has briefed you on what we know so far from our confidential source. It looks like it will be a propane truck and tomorrow," He looked at his watch, "I mean today. This is Black Friday so a shopping target might be in order. We also believe it is within driving distance of Pittsburgh. Has analytics anything to say?"

The department head of analysis shuffled some papers, "There are quite a few major malls in the area. But the only real important one is the Monroeville Mall, biggest in the area and a likely target for Jihadists. You could probably drive a propane truck right through the glass entryway."

An aerial shot of the mall and a floor plan flashed up on one of the large screens at the front of the room.

Carter interrupted, "An attack there would likely shut down every mall in America, and on Black Friday of all things.

"As far as we know there's a single bomber so it is unlikely it will be one of those coordinated attacks on several targets at the same time. I'm thinking it will be a soft target but just to be safe, get out a list of all likely targets we have in the Pittsburgh and surrounding area especially other malls, airports, nuclear facilities, water treatment, etc.

"Unfortunately we have no specific target at this time so we can't alert the public which would only panic them but I want to be able to hit the send button to all media outlets the moment we have anything specific.

"As to the Monroeville Mall, I want double-teamed snipers, invisible to shoppers, on every side of the roof of that mall before it opens this morning. Work with the Pittsburgh PD and their SWAT team. Their orders are shoot to kill on any high-speed approaching propane truck. I want the driver dead and the engine and tires disabled so make sure they have the weapons to penetrate the engine block to do that. No checking

157

for clearance either. Weapons released and they need to execute before that thing gets too close to the mall. A full propane truck could do a lot of damage even if it's a couple of hundred feet from the building. If it's allowed to go off the shock wave alone could knock out walls and bring down part of the building never mind blowing out windows.

"I hope to hell there are no legitimate deliveries of propane to the mall today. For that matter, we're not sure it is the Mall. Someone get on a phone book for Pittsburgh and see if anyone has legit trucks out there today. It's a holiday so they may all be shut down. If there are any propane trucks scheduled to go out, tell them to stay home today, even emergency deliveries. Police orders.

"Now let's talk about pursuit. OPS, I want all the drone assets we can get into the area on station by daybreak, armed and unarmed. Alert the FAA that there will be drones in the area. Get NORAD to talk to FAA to clear the airspace and altitudes they need. I don't care if it shuts down the main airport. Use the appropriate National Security flags to get their undivided attention.

"As the drones come on site we'll task them from here so get an open line to their control center up and ready and with full redundancies.

"And everyone. This MUST be kept out of the press. Everyone drawn into this must understand that. If we're successful in stopping this attack, but word gets out of the details, then the terrorists may have won and malls across America will be affected.

"We'll decide later what if anything we need to do to prevent this kind of attack in the future. For now, let's make sure any news of this does not get out.

"I want this war room staffed with all resources until this is resolved and use the usual prioritization and escalation protocol to get things done. Our first job is to get a detailed photo of any stolen propane truck and feed it to the drone handlers. We'll want their video feeds on our boards as well.

"Let's cover all approaches to the main targets we identify.

"Alert local and state law-enforcement that we may have a truck bomber that will have to be stopped by extreme force but not to guess at who the bad guys are. We don't want any stray propane trucks being shot at. Hopefully we'll be the ones telling them which one to go after so we also need open lines to their dispatchers.

"As usual see either me or my point man, Carole Glass with any developments or questions. Now get to work and find that propane truck."

Just as they were about to break up a junior female staffer who had been afraid to speak up said loudly, "Have any of you every shopped on Black Friday?"

There was instant silence in the room as everyone turned and stared at her.

"I mean I don't know if any of you actually do that stuff and I wouldn't say anything but I just heard us all getting ready for a threat tomorrow morning when the stores open."

"For the last couple of years, Black Friday actual starts the night before. That's where I was when I got the urgent call to come in here. It's a mad house out there. Most of the big box stores and malls opened a couple of hours ago and many more will open, or did open at Midnight and more at 5 am. We are already in Black Friday. The stores are mobbed."

Everyone turned and looked at Bill Carter who was thunderstruck, "She's absolutely right. We're in it already. They could hit us at any minute. And given the terrorists have local support in Pittsburg, they know about the stores too.

"Take everything I said and move the time frame up to NOW! Get everyone we need out of bed. Now please, let's get this truck before they get us."

As they all returned to their stations, the Deputy Director called Phil Harris aside, "I know it's still controversial but my understanding is that the NSA is still keeping all phone records in the US. We may not have time to track them down but I want a team on any call in or out of that phone that David and Cristal recovered. If we have time it may lead us to that sleeper cell or maybe even the bomber and his handlers. Get on to the NSA pronto and get their team going. You have the number they called from earlier. Point NSA to the Homeland Security alert to get them to call their teams in from their Thanksgiving evenings."

***

On his way back from New York, William Carter had given orders to get a Pittsburgh SWAT team to the abandoned building where David and Cristal had been. Even though it was nearing midnight a stealthy group of 10 SWAT team members were on station within twenty minutes and were just settling in for a long night when a car approached.

The commander of the team was in a perfect spot to see two suspects exit the car carrying what looked like AK-47's. If he let them reach the door they could barricade themselves so he gave the 'take down' command and all hell broke loose.

Orders to drop weapons were being screamed from every direction and with powerful lights in their faces and multiple red dots on their bodies the two Jihadis soon complied and were in custody before they could figure out what was happening.

***

The car Habib had rented had a built in GPS and David soon found a motel within a short drive. He wanted to stay close to the scene in case something came up.

Cristal was still too covered in blood to go into the rental office so after renting a room, he ushered her into a standard motel type of room on the ground floor with two double beds.

"I rented only one room because I didn't want to stand out asking for two and you were in no condition to walk in there looking like that. I don't think we want to attract any attention while those Jihadis are still around.

All she said was, "I need to call my mother."

"OK but use the room phone in case someone is monitoring Habib's cell. And ask her how my daughter is doing," he teased.

A few seconds later Cristal was talking to an extremely emotional woman who quickly put her on speaker so her father could participate. "OK, calm down. I'm fine and unhurt. I was taken against my will but it had nothing to do with Greg. How is Tiffany. Do you have her?"

"Of course we do and she's doing fine. But she really misses her mommy and keeps asking for you."

Cristal choked up at this. Part of her wanted to jump in the car and head straight for home. But instinct told her this was not over and there was still danger ahead.

"Is it true what I've been told is on TV about Greg?"

Her father jumped in. "Yes. They're reporting that he faked his own death and has a wife and family in Wichita. His real name is Bob Watson. I always knew he was trouble! He's either in custody or on his way to Wichita now but Cristal, where are you and what's happening?"

"Mom and dad I wish I could tell you more but you're just going to have to be patient. I don't know yet when I'll be home because there is something I absolutely must do first. Some of the people that took me might still be out there and I have to take care of it or they may follow me home. I have professional help in this but this is important, you must not talk to the local police or the FBI about this. I can't explain but I can tell you that I'm in no danger right now." She had a feeling that might not be quite true.

Her dad needed more, "Are you CIA like Greg claimed?"

"Listen, I'll tell you all about it soon but for now just let me say that I'm OK.

"Trust me, I'm not doing anything that is morally or legally wrong and I need you to look after Tiffany for a little while longer. I love you both." And she hung up.

She hated treating her parents so abruptly but they weren't ready for the whole story and it would likely just put them in jeopardy and make them even more anxious if they knew the total dimensions of what had happened.

As much as she wanted to grab the keys and head for home, she knew this thing was not over and many lives were at stake. Maybe after tomorrow she would be able to return.

Whether she liked it or not, she felt she had just been drafted back into the CIA. There was nothing she could do personally about the bomb right now but there were terrorists on the loose in this vicinity and after tonight, some of them wanted her hide. And they knew where she lived.

David walked out of the bathroom wearing only a towel. She was shocked. He had quickly removed the beard she had always known him to wear. She was emotionally confused and pretended not to notice him, instead playing with the phone she had just used.

Her stomach was churning and her mind racing over this man. It was only about an hour ago she had convinced herself to put any feelings for him aside and use him as a hostage, killing him if need be. Now this hunk of a man was quickly walking her back to three years ago when they had had a torrid love affair and might have been deeply in love.

She decided to go with her heart and just let go for the moment, "Wow! I like. I forgot motels have free razors. You must have beaten the hell out of that one taking off that scruffy beard. I've never seen you without a beard. Now all you need is a haircut."

"Well I had a trimmed beard in Burundi because I was in hiding and it helped a bit with the disguise.

"That motivation remained in Guantanamo and added to their story line that I was a western Jihadi but to be honest I've always hated the beard. I feel like a new man."

"I approve. You did look pretty masculine and virile in Burundi but I like this much better. British accent and a clean face, who knew?"

163

David smiled and mocked a muscular pose for Vogue, "Listen, what's this about you are not going home right away?"

"Well first there's that bomb and I think we need to resolve a few things between us.

"Also, I don't want to put my family in harm's way. That Pittsburgh cell and that Abboud character have my home address which means Al Qaeda has my home address. So I would like to figure out if we are in any jeopardy before I return.

"But before that, even though you saved my life tonight, I have about a thousand questions for you. Like, why did you move so fast to disarm them tonight? You gave me no warning."

David looked deep into the eyes of the woman he had once loved. Here she was just out of harm's way and he was about to put her back into it. He hesitated and then spoke, "The big guard either didn't know or forgot that I'm fluent in French and when he came up behind Habib he said words to the effect that he was not going to allow me to go free because Khalil had ordered a fatwa on both you and me. With the three of them standing there off guard and about to change my status from rescued leader to target of a hit, I had to move."

Her face went pale, "A fatwa? But why you too?"

"I don't know but when a kill order comes from him it does not go away so we're both marked. In my case they must have figured out I'm not who I say I am. But why would he want you dead too?"

Cristal looked puzzled, "I don't know. Maybe in sympathy with Jabir Habib? You know I saw Khalil once up close. He murdered my best friend Tiffany in front of me and threatened me with the same if I didn't leave Muslim territory. Add to that we just killed three Jihadis and if he didn't have a reason before I'm sure he has now."

Then she thought, "Wait a minute. He would likely have seen my picture on TV. I'm certain either the TV station, Greg or the cops would have provided a picture of me and he could have put two and two together figuring out what Habib concluded, that if I was the one who set you up, then I must be CIA. The only CIA agent who can identify him!

"So now I have to live with that axe hanging over my head. He wants me dead because I may be the only person in the west who can ID him.

"We know now that they have at least one sleeper cell in the US so I am not safe."

David smiled, "Me neither. I have a long shot chance of clearing my name with MI6 with Bill Carter's help but that won't help to get Khalil's Al Qaeda organization off my back."

Cristal interrupted, "Now that we're free and I still don't trust you I need some answers."

"Fire away."

"If you're really MI6 and you really endured almost 3 years of torture, why didn't you just come clean about your identity and why were you hiding in Burundi in the first place?"

David spent the next few minutes recounting his fear of not surviving a trip to jail in the UK, his training on handling torture and his hopes of one day being freed. He elaborated on why he had to go into hiding in the first place and how and why he had kept his identity secret. Then he had slipped up and allowed his fingerprints to recover to the point where they made him and he wrapped up with a summary of his incredible visit from Bill Carter.

Cristal was starting to see the pieces come together. "OK, but what about the mayhem you created in Burundi."

"What mayhem? Your Intel was a little off the mark back then. The government was doing most of the killing and blaming it on the rebels. I had only been leading that cell for a few months when you appeared.

"I was doing two things at the time. Cruising the hotels where westerners gathered looking for the network that was propping up those tyrants in Bujumbura. There was some legitimate US and British money flowing in there to the government but my investigation across central Africa had shown that there was some secret organization sneaking millions from overseas into the pockets of those despots for what I could not figure out.

"Some corrupt piece of MI6 was supporting that and had set me up as the supposed leader and if I could uncover the links I could kill two birds with one stone. Clear my name and shut it down.

"The rest of the week when I was not wearing a business suit I was helping the FLN to disrupt weapons distributions and money flows to try to slow down the crap the government was perpetrating on its own people. Yeah we had operations that killed a few bad guys, smugglers, rogue Army types and government enforcers but I can sleep at night knowing we were helping the people free themselves from those tyrants. I only wish I could have done more.

"I don't know how I missed it but I swear I had no idea Habib's organization was getting some of its funding from Al Qaeda and no idea they were Jihadists at heart. Either they had converted to freedom fighters for Burundi at the time or more likely, they didn't trust me being an American, or so they thought, to let me in on their ultimate aspirations of turning Burundi into an Islamic state with Sharia laws.

"Earlier today Habib as much as said they kept me in the dark because I was an American and for one thing they didn't disclose their entire network to me. Still I feel like an idiot for not recognizing who they truly were."

Cristal sized him up one more time, "Wow. I have to say that is a pretty convincing story. Not that I believe it all but given Bill Carter is your new BFF I'm willing to delay killing you or returning you to Guantanamo in handcuffs for a while."

"Gee thanks," was all he could say with a smile. And then, "What's a BFF?"

She smiled and said, "Later."

Cristal rose from the bed and circled the room, "But he still wants us dead, Khalil has issued a fatwa on us."

"Yeah, and as we know he has operatives in the US. Right here in Pittsburgh as well."

Cristal thought for a second, "You know Africa and I know Africa. I see only one option to change things in our favor. We get him before he gets us. That won't solve the whole problem but it will be a good start."

David was shocked, "What are you talking about. The entire Western World has been after this guy for at least the last ten years. They haven't been able to find him never mind hit him. You just said they don't even know what he looks like. Before I went away, MI6 did not know how he moved around or even how he communicated. Given he's still on the loose I suspect no one is any closer to finding him."

"Yeah but we have three advantages. One, I've seen him. He was in disguise but I think I could recognize him. I'll never forget those eyes. He has eyes like a shark. They seem dead and lifeless.

"Two, we're highly motivated by self preservation and I swore revenge about five years ago when he stoned my best friend Tiffany to death right in front of me. You have no idea how horrible and barbaric a stoning is. I get sick every time the images come to mind.

Tiffany was a beautiful and completely innocent victim. I named our darling little girl after her.

Our little extracurricular activities of tonight seem to have snapped me out of my malaise. I feel a lot stronger suddenly. With this latest attack on me, I think I'm finally ready to go after him.

"And three, we have Habib's phone and I'll bet his brother Mustafa's phone number is in there and he's a key deputy of Khalil."

David smiled, "I can see you have this all worked out. If there was ever any chance we could pull this off it would mean we would need a lot of resources and lots of help and I think I know who might be willing to help us."

"Deputy Director William Carter," she smiled.

"That will be a neat trick for him to pull off," David continued, "especially given the fact that I suspect he has just launched a US-wide manhunt for an escaped terrorist known as Daniel Boone. How else is he going to explain my disappearance from Guantanamo. He can delay with some story surrounding you but that can't go on for long. So him supporting me in particular on any operation might be a non-starter."

Cristal smiled, "Well that is all for tomorrow. Tonight he has to find a propane tanker. So now I have another question for you and after tonight I want a truthful answer. Did you ever care for me at all? Be straight with me while I'm still mulling over the idea of killing you. Was it all charm and nothing else?"

David's attitude changed instantaneously, "Wow that was my question for you! But being a gentleman I'll go first.

"Actually, your question is impossible to answer. If I say yes I loved you from the start you will say I'm just charming you again and trying to save my skin. But given that I had to put my life in jeopardy to save yours tonight I think you would have to admit that I've proven my motives when I say ... I loved you from the very first moment I laid eyes on you. I have to admit it was lust for a few minutes, after all you're a hell of a looker. Five foot five or so," he said, sizing her up, "longish auburn hair, blue eyes, killer figure even after a baby," he teased. "I even loved your voice when we first spoke in the creepy little hotel bar in Bujumbura. It was your voice again tonight that snapped me out of a rage I had never felt before.

"Back in Burundi, I was shocked to find out you were the CNN producer and not the on-air talent with your looks and intelligence but I guess knowing what I know now, that would not have been a good job for an undercover CIA agent."

She smiled and nodded, "I constantly fought with them over that. They desperately wanted me on the other side of the camera. I told them I was too shy and would freeze on camera although all the time I wanted to give it a shot."

He smiled, "Yeah, I can see that. No, even with your faked shyness I have to admit that I loved you from the start, more than I thought I could ever love any woman and sadly there were a few other women in the earlier years. I was not a saint. You basically knocked me for a loop. I had never felt that way about anyone and never thought I could. You were a complete shock to my system. I know it's a cliché but you took my breath away.

"And even though I was pretty sure you had betrayed me which made it all the more painful, I was never able to draw myself to hate you. As you saw earlier this evening, there were moments when the thought of you infuriated me, but even as they tried to drown me daily with that waterboarding, I couldn't get you out of my mind. In a good way!" he added. "That's my definition of true love.

"I just want you to think of this. You had me hook line and sinker. I couldn't think of anything but you back in Burundi. I was one love sick puppy and then in a moment you turned on me, I'm in a torture chamber and you're gone.

"Losing you was the ultimate torture."

The look on her face said it all. He realized he had better stop. In her world it had been painful he was now convinced but at least she had always been able to fall back on the thought that she had done the right thing, he was a monster killing innocents.

Now he could see that she was starting to realize that it had all been a terrible mistake and the steps she had taken had doomed their love. If she had truly loved him at some point, as he now was beginning to accept then the pain of being the agent of his demise must now be unbearable.

He gave her a few moments to gather herself. She looked all around the room trying to stem the tears. He averted his eyes but he knew she was having trouble catching her breath so as not to sob out loud.

He waited a long time until she seemed to have regained some of her composure.

"Now it's your turn. Did you ever really love me or was it all just an act to trap me and how could you marry another?"

She finally smiled, wiped away a few tears and returned from the waves of guilt to the matter at hand. In a cracking voice she said, "I thought you were a cocky American business man when we first met. You know, the quintessential ugly American traveler who is arrogant, thinks the world owes him and is insensitive to any other culture. Thinks everyone in the world should speak English and make the same shitty coffee he's used to.

"I was in no mood for romance at the time. Tiffany's murder was still weighing heavy on me. I think they were trying to get me back in the saddle by sending me into Burundi looking for Daniel Boone.

"I needed some contacts in Burundi to track down Abu Nistal and you looked like a good one, so my first interest in you was definitely not romantic. That quickly changed and your charms won me over. I soon saw you as the closest thing to the perfect man; handsome, quietly powerful and strong, charming, worldly. I was hooked before I realized it. After my first false impressions, I was shocked to find that there was actually a type of quiet confidence, strength and empathy about you that was intoxicating.

"I was heartbroken and ready to kill you on the spot when I found out you were Abu Nistal. I felt betrayed and used by a monster that had already and was about to kill hundreds.

"There is no question I was conflicted but what options did I have. We knew who you were and we had what we thought was solid Intel that you were guilty of all kinds of atrocities and about to do your worst. I had to call in the extraction team.

"After they got you and I disappeared back to the US, I was a total mess. Tiffany brutally murdered in front of me, losing you, you turning out to be a Jihadi and then I found out I was pregnant. I was borderline suicidal when I talked Carter into letting me retire to a shitty little producer job in sleepy Cincinnati.

"Only the birth of my daughter brought me back from the edge. My God she changed my life and saved me. I owe her everything.

Still the last couple of years I've been walking around in a trance. My professional TV work was mediocre at best and pretty boring and I even married a hunky health club guy who turned out to be a fake and a jerk.

"It may be the adrenalin from earlier tonight but much more likely hearing your side of the story, but at this moment I feel more alert and alive than I have in years. Shockingly and suddenly I feel like me for the first time since I last saw you."

She wiped away a few tears again, "As to you, I must say I do like your new found English accent and your clean face, adds a bit to the mystique. New man indeed.

"And to address my motives, I don't know if you will believe this just yet but when you untied me this evening I could easily have killed you instead of punching you. Something held me back. And that was

172

not a real punch. I can usually break an inch of oak with the right punch and I could easily have killed you. You should know that I had made up my mind to use you to effect my escape and kill you if it came to that."

She smiled as he rubbed his jaw, "So trust me when I say that I fell for you hard and I was a broken woman when I had to set you up. I could not believe I had been such a bad judge of character and it was awfully hard trapping you. As I said, I damned near had a full-blown depression when I found out I was pregnant by you and I had just sentenced my baby's daddy to unbelievable torture. But what could I do at that point.

"In all fairness I was out of my mind with anger in those days having decided you had deceived me and you were a despicable terrorist."

Suddenly she became very melancholy and with a cracking voice she said, "And now to find out that it was all a mistake. My mistake. I sent you to that horrible place. I caused us to lose those years. My only solace has been that I have a little angel who has your eyes." At that the tears really started to flow and she couldn't stop the sobbing.

Still crying she said, "I even had to lie to my parents about the baby's father. They think you were a US Marine who I met at an embassy, married quickly and then you were killed almost immediately in action in Afghanistan.

Gaining some composure she continued, "As to Greg Wiggins, he was a health club instructor with a great body, a bright smile and at that time I was probably still depressed and I needed a distraction.

"Now that I know more about the man I see where I was just looking for a diversion. I loved you then and I'm afraid to say that I love you even more now. I just hope to hell that you're not playing me for some sick reason."

David took her gently by the shoulders, "I'm not playing you. I love you, I always have. But how could you believe that I could plan to kill hundreds of innocents. That's what I can't get my head around. You really thought I was capable of that?"

"Listen, looking back I guess my hormones might have been rushing out of control. You said you were going to 'hit' the train over a ravine and I had no time to process the whole idea and so I had to act quickly. Killing innocents is what terrorists do, right?

"HQ had just told me they were sure you were the lead terrorist and all the atrocities of that poor country were on your head. I had to act. There was no time to confront you alone. By the way, if I had confronted you it would have been with a loaded gun and one false move back then and we wouldn't be having this conversation."

David could see the honesty and pain in her eyes.

She started to sob again thinking of the terrible mistakes that had doomed their love. Thinking of the years of torture she had committed him to. How she had been the agent of her lover's fall into a hell hole for three long years. Thinking of the years that could have been so different if their love had survived Burundi. Thinking of him sharing in her pregnancy and seeing Tiffany born. Thinking of raising their daughter together. It was all too unbearable.

Finally between sobs she blurted out, "I'm sorry. I'm so so sorry."

He stepped towards her but she indicated she needed space for a moment.

After a long time and using up about half the box of tissues by the bed she regained her composure, wiped the tears and said, "Anyways, I for one want to put all of that in the past. Now that we're here, and you're not a terrorist, a clean-shaven British spy trumps an American business man with a well-trimmed beard any day of the week."

David smiled, "Well that answers one more important question."

"What's that?"

"One bed or two?"

They showered long and sensually together and then made love. He was gentle and she was red hot. He wanted her badly and she devoured him. The best sex in both of their lives.

He had been deprived of a woman for nearly three years and not just any woman, this woman. The most beautiful and amazing creature on the planet.

She had no idea what she had been doing for the past few years but whatever it was it had not been love making. Not like this and with a man that only a few hours earlier she had committed to kill. She thought the irony was amazing.

As they lay there in each other's arms he whispered, "I guess that's what they call 'make-up sex'."

She giggled and punched him hard in the arm.

Just before they dosed off she heard him whisper, "I have a little girl."

The Mall

The two Jihadis captured at the Pittsburgh hideout were flown immediately to Langley and sent into interrogation. It was a pretty good bet that they knew something about the planned attack on Black Friday but given it was now three am on that very day, there was little hope they could be forced to cough up anything useful in time. But the CIA's best interrogation team gave it a try.

Upstairs, the CIA HQ team was fast at work and got their first break right away. A large propane truck had been stolen the day before just outside of Pittsburgh and because of its potential as a weapon, it had been entered into the Homeland Security database.

There was always the possibility that this was a coincidence and this was not the truck they needed to find but the decision was made that if it was found anywhere near a known target, wouldn't stop or displayed any aggressive behavior it would be taken out.

They had all the details including the VIN number so within minutes they had a photo of what the truck must look like Photoshopped with the paint job of AmeriGas, the propane distributor. They also had its license plate or at least the one it had when it was stolen. The bulletin that had gone out to law-enforcement was updated with the photo and license.

A notice also went to all local media around Pittsburgh that the police wanted to talk to a person as a material witness in a federal case and he was driving an AmeriGas propane truck. If it was spotted, people were to call 911. The focus was clearly on the person and not the truck so as to avoid any panic. The picture and the license were included.

By 4 am thankfully, three of the six available drones had arrived on station and were circling Pittsburgh at high altitude using their night vision systems looking for the suspect propane truck. Three others would arrive between 8 and 10 am from McGuire AFB in New Jersey after having weapons loaded and making the cross country trip.

The Director of the CIA had called to say the President had authorized this use of drones for surveillance and possible attack within the borders of the United States, a step that could be seen as unconstitutional given the Posse Comitatus Act which restricted the Federal government from using the military on homeland targets. This would not be the first time since 9/11 that the restrictions had been bent, circumvented or simply ignored by a Commander-in-Chief.

The morning dragged on and everyone was terrified that the truck was already on its way to the target and that any moment they would hear of a massive explosion and hundreds of deaths.

With all of the coverage it was surprising that no one had spotted the truck. The bet was that the truck was hidden somewhere and would only appear shortly before the attack so every effort was made to spread resources around to try to get full coverage of the area. If the truck was hidden near its target, it might be out in the open for only minutes before the attack.

The tension was unbearable and after many hours of being on edge and no sleep, tempers were frayed. People were running around trying to get one more pair of eyes out there on the Pittsburgh streets and the surrounding municipalities looking for the truck. Nearly a dozen people in Langley and more at drone control were scanning the live videos from the drones trying to pick up a propane truck on the streets of Pittsburgh and the surrounding area.

The only good news seemed to be that all the propane companies in the general vicinity were either closed down for the long weekend or had recalled their few trucks at the behest of the police, so any truck on the road would likely be their target.

The later it got the more Bill Carter wonder if they should be widening the search area as by now the attackers had had time enough to travel further. Still the most likely targets were within their current search area.

Just after 10:30 the big break came. A report came in that a local Police car assigned to the area near the Monroeville Mall was tailing the wanted vehicle. The Duty Officer in the war room started barking orders, "Get his position and get the closest drone over there now!"

Coordinates were relayed quickly to drone control. The drone's vision systems were so sophisticated they had the truck on the video feed in under two minutes and long before the drone had arrived in the vicinity of the truck. Even from this distance they could see it was the right type of truck and seemed to have the AmeriGas paint job.

The D.O. called out, "Do we have positive ID on the truck?"

One of the operators yelled back, "It fits the description and the police have confirmed the license. He says it appears to be headed for the Monroeville Mall. They are about two miles away from it now."

The D.O. in the control room yelled, "Get me the cop's audio."

Within seconds he was signaled to go ahead, "Officer we see you on video trailing a propane truck on a secondary road south of the Monroeville Mall and you are about 50 yards behind."

"Yeah that's me. It has the tags we were given in the alert. I followed him on to Patton St. coming up behind the Monroeville Mall. I'd say we were less than two miles from the entrance. Hey, I think I've been spotted. He's speeding up. Now he's doing 50 in a 40 zone. What do you want me to do? Should I shoot out his tires?"

The control room duty officer said, "Nevada do you have weapons on him yet?"

"Yeah, we've got him."

From the video, the CIA officer on duty could see the truck was heading into a wooded section of the suburban road, half a mile from a sharp turn where both sides of the road were tree-lined with no houses nearby.

He could also see the status of two drones closing on the site and one of them confirmed that it already had 'Missile Lock' displayed even though it was three miles away to the south and at ten thousand feet. He yelled into the mic. "Officer stop now! Break off pursuit and take cover.

"Nevada, take him. Try to time it for the curve."

The second drone was approaching from the southwest now and continued to display 'Missile Lock' on the truck. One of the screens in the control room shortly showed the release of the newest hellfire missile which was very small, fast and left virtually no vapor trail. They all watched its onboard camera tracking the truck.

The wide shot from the other drone showed the Police car breaking hard and pulling off to the side of the road. Seconds later the missile struck with a blinding flash vaporizing the truck and most of the trees close by. The long shot showed a shockwave radiating outwards for a hundred yards, wiping out most everything in its path which was mostly trees and an enormous red and orange mushroom cloud climbing quickly over the quiet suburb of Pittsburgh.

Cheers went up in the control room and people were jumping up and down and hugging each other.

At the Mall, all the stores had Black Friday specials and were mobbed. The biggest issue for the police was fights in the parking lot breaking out over parking spaces and fights in some stores that were running out of their best deals.

All the snipers having a bird's eye view, had heard the orders over their headsets and could barely see the missile from the invisible drone and then the explosion more than a mile away. The shockwave and the really loud boom came about 5 seconds later and they assumed they were off the hook.

Moments later as they were still high fiving each other they were told to stand down, pack their weapons and make discrete exits.

The fire department arrived and they were dousing a small forest fire that surrounded a twenty foot wide crater in the road. Trees were down or damaged for quite a radius but the fire department soon had the flames extinguished.

The press arrived shortly thereafter and interviewed a local cop who seemed to know what was going on.

Minutes later a TV crew were set up and he was interviewed live on the local news channel, "As I said earlier I had just turned on to this road when I saw this propane truck flying past me. I don't know what the guy was doing. Maybe he had a heart attack or something but there was no way he was going to make that sharp corner at that speed. I was just about to turn around and chase him when all hell broke loose. The truck flipped on its side and boom. The shock wave nearly blew my car off the road. I've never seen a fireball that big. There's nothing left of the truck."

The CIA team in the control room saw the live broadcast and decided to take up a collection for the cop. He was a legitimate hero, had found the truck in time and had done exactly as instructed right down to the cover story.

***

The CIA Director and his deputy Bill Carter were sitting at their places as the Senators and Members of the Joint Oversight Committee filed in to the closed hearing.

Because it was the day after Thanksgiving and most were in their home states, not all were present but they had a quorum in the hastily organized meeting. When they were all seated, the Director asked his deputy Bill Carter to proceed.

"Ladies and gentlemen I'm obliged to keep you informed of any major terrorist activity so here I am. A couple of days ago it became apparent to us that a retired CIA agent had been kidnapped here in the US by Al Qaeda agents.

"The ransom demand was for a swap of a prisoner at Guantanamo. I personally released the prisoner in New York yesterday for reasons I will soon explain."

Several Members of the committee were startled and started scribbling notes.

"The kidnapped CIA agent has been rescued.

"Between the kidnapped agent and the released prisoner they broke up the cell involved in the kidnapping and some of their support in an Al Qaeda sleeper cell here in the US and more importantly they directed us to an imminent Jihadi attack in the Pittsburgh area that was to have been executed a few hours ago.

"We tracked a stolen propane truck and eliminated it with a drone strike less than two miles from its target which was the Monroeville Mall near Pittsburgh during Black Friday shopping, which would likely have killed hundreds and jeopardized all retail sales in malls across America and our economy for months if not years.

"If you have been watching the news then you will have seen that our cover story of an out-of-control propane truck having had an accident is holding.

"Before you pepper me with questions. The person released from Guantanamo was actually a western intelligence agent and for his safety, I do not wish to release his name or any other details about him at this time. Suffice it to say that he was at Guantanamo and we are one prisoner short there now.

"I'm sure you will join me in congratulating the men and women of the CIA, our Armed Forces, the Pittsburgh Police and Pennsylvania State Police for a job well done."

There was a long pause as the Director looked up and down the line of lawmakers across the table to his right and left. He finally spoke, "Bill is there anything else we need to know on this matter at this time."

"Not on this matter but let me turn to other developments. A known bomb maker in Pakistan recently died of radiation poisoning. That's all we know but we're taking the position that a bomb or dirty bomb may be available to Al Qaeda and we're doing everything to drive this to ground. Of course I'll keep you informed of any developments."

Deputy Director William Carter could sense the shock in the room.

After some thought and a long pause the Chairman of the committee said, "Sir, you have our complete confidence. Clearly this is the most important threat you've brought to us since I would say the 9/11 attacks. We will assume the administration and the Joint Chiefs are being briefed on these matters daily in your NATSEC briefings."

The Director nodded.

"Is there anything else we need to know on these matters at this time?"

"No, Sir."

"Well on the other matter of earlier today please express to your team and the supporting organizations, our deep-felt gratitude in the manner you and our law-enforcement community have handled this and I declare this meeting adjourned."

On the way back in the car the DD updated Carole Glass his lead on these matters, on what had just happened, "I think that was unprecedented. They didn't even ask me one question. The whole meeting was over in about three minutes. I think they all know just how bad this could have been and they are every grateful but there's no question they're very concerned about the bomb and everyone in Washington is going to want to be briefed constantly on any developments."

Carole was puzzled, "Why do you think they didn't ask more about David Crowe? Were they not curious as to what a western intelligence officer was doing at Guantanamo, who he is and where he is now?"

"If I had to guess I would say that the Director is doing his secret behind-the-scenes briefings with each of them. That meeting was a formality and had to happen or they could be accused of not doing their oversight job but even in a secret, closed door briefing, they want some things to stay out of the minutes."

Carole smiled, "Nice job boss."

A New Threat

Evening was falling in their latest hideout in the south end of Mogadishu when Khalil Al-Adel welcomed Muhammad Basoum in the traditional way kissing him three times on the cheeks, "My friend you've done a great service for Allah. Al-hamdu lillāh! How was your trip?"

"I must admit master, I was very nervous. As you know the seas remain very busy with the westerners looking for pirates. We came across no less than three large warships but our work to disguise the ship and our heading seemed to offer them no reason to board us. I was afraid we would be found out with the coast in sight."

"The package. How is the package?"

"Sadoum gave us two packages for transport. They are both well screened as you will see. They are both contained in a large box made of lead and each is wrapped in lead. I used the device you gave me and it shows no signs of radiation so I think the Americans will not detect it. He warned me not to open it at any time before we delivered it."

Khalil put his arm around his trusted lieutenant, "I'm honored to tell you that our brother Sadoum martyred himself to provide this to us, Allahu Akbar.

Sadoum seem surprised.

"He unlike you had to work with the materials and has now given his life for that work. Just after you left, he was taken to the hospital where our brothers tell me an American agent discovered him but not before he had died a glorious martyr's death.

"We must assume the Americans know someone has this material but they don't know who, where they are and what our plans are. Your trip from Pakistan to our shores proves that.

"Your work is done for now. We have work to do here before we launch our attack. You will be called on once more when transportation to the land of Satan is required. You will be our eyes and ears on that trip. Now take some rest while you can."

After dismissing Mohammed, Khalil sent information that he needed his weapons expert immediately. Allah willing, Al Qaeda had a special Christmas present for New York City this year.

***

Cristal and David both woke late in each other's arms and snuggled for only a moment both relishing the difference twenty four hours had made in their lives.

The snuggling soon turned to caressing and again they made love which if anything was even better being less urgent and rushed than the previous night.

As they finally rose, their attention soon moved to the propane truck on its way to kill hundreds of innocent Americans.

The local TV only said the police wanted to interview the driver of a propane truck, so the attack had not happened yet.

There was nothing they could do themselves to track down the tanker so it was with great relief that they saw the breaking news not long after that a propane tanker had missed a curve and exploded with tremendous force. There was no doubt in their minds that headquarters had been successful in intercepting the attack. There was speculation that the driver had been

186

the one the police were looking for and had possibly tried to outrun a cop car which had caused the accident. But the police had refused comment on that speculation.

They finally allowed themselves to breath. Cristal had washed the man's shirt and it had dried overnight. They went out stopping first to pick up some new clothes for both of them, change and then go out for lunch. It had been a long time since either had eaten and they were famished.

It was as if the three years had disappeared, they were deeply in love and all of the nastiness was pushed to the back of their minds for the moment. Each had to pinch themselves from time to time and wonder if it was all real.

Just in the last day she had narrowly escaped a vicious death at the hands of Jihadists and he was free after years of torture in Guantanamo.

Even though they had made love the previous night and again this morning, the cold hard light of day still had them both wondering if they really knew the person across the table. It was all new again for them.

She now knew him as a British MI6 operative and not an American businessman or much worse, a terrorist.

He now saw her as a CIA operative as capable as himself and not a simple civilian from the US who was a CNN producer or worse, a CIA seduction weapon and betrayer of their love.

The change was too much for both of them to absorb so quickly.

Neither of them seemed to pay attention to what they had ordered to eat and most of the meal was spent staring into each other's eyes in silence and just appreciating the moment.

Like two star crossed teenagers, they held hands across the table in the tiny diner and ate with one hand not wanting to let go for a minute.

Cristal thought of it as three lost years, years of almost walking around in a trance. Apart from missing David for all that time she didn't get a lot of fulfillment out of her job at the TV station after handling international news for CNN but much more than that, she actually missed the intrigue and danger from the CIA work.

And David. She had sentenced him to the most unspeakable torture. She found she couldn't think about it for even a second without welling up. She had no real idea of what he had been through but she had to believe it was unbearable.

The US had from time to time denied that it still used 'enhanced interrogation techniques' in the US but Guantanamo was not in the US and it was always a lower level person doing the talking. The higher ups and the oversight committees either knew the truth or knew which questions not to ask. Any denials had been carefully worded.

She had no firsthand knowledge of waterboarding, sleep deprivation or the other techniques but she knew they were designed to break even the strongest of men. Looking at the handsome man across from her she could still see some of it in his eyes and his weight loss. He had aged some but he was still south of forty and very handsome.

From time to time during lunch, the visions of David being tortured returned and the total cost of the last three years and her sense of guilt overwhelmed her. She kept thinking, "Why didn't I trust him?"

Maybe even worse than that in some way was the fact that she had kept his daughter from him too. Tiny Tiffany thought that jerk Wiggins was actually her daddy.

He caught her wiping a tear occasionally and the odd quivering lip but then her beautiful smile soon returned. He knew it had to be massively unbearable and heartbreaking for her.

For him it was much more positive. In the last thirty-six hours it was like he had won the lottery. The palpable relief from being free, rescued from that outrageous trauma for so long and the excitement of reconnecting with his gorgeous Cristal. Eliminating Habib's gang and stopping the truck bomb, well that was just icing on the cake. Bill Carter owed him big time.

He paused for a moment to remember the last three years. Aside from the torture, he had been without a woman as well for that long but much more than that it had been the lack of any meaningful human contact.

The guards at Guantanamo had made sure the prisoners could not communicate with each other which left them by themselves all day, every day unless they were being interrogated. The guards that brought food had been instructed to avoid any interaction with the prisoners which was part of the protocol for breaking them mentally and spiritually. He had tried speaking to them but they had ignored him.

For David losing Cristal and the total boredom of confinement was the real torture. Having led a very active and exciting life up until the moment he was caught and then to be put in such isolation was mind

189

bending. He was surprised he had been able to keep it together that long. He credited his strategy of keeping active mentally with saving himself from insanity. He had spent many long hours cooking up the stories he would reluctantly tell them under torture. Stories that had to be plausible and tie in with information he knew they had from his MI6 days, yet stories that would take a long time to check out and could not be falsified. Great material for a book he laughingly thought to himself. A book he would never be allowed to publish.

He was overjoyed and relieved that it was all behind him and he had this wonderful, gorgeous woman all to himself right across the table. He could not get over his luck. Everywhere she went she turned heads.

The one painful memory that brought back rage was one interrogator in particular. A complete sadist who showed subtle but unmistakable signs of liking his work.

He had done most of the waterboarding and while others seemed to go about it in a somewhat professional manner if there was such a thing, this guy had taken a disliking to David or maybe it was everyone under his boot and had clearly enjoyed dishing out torture. It was going to take a long time for that rage to dissipate. Maybe the gorgeous creature across the table from him was the key.

They made it back to the motel room by one thirty and figured it was time to check in with the boss. Cristal made the call and was patched right through to his office where he was just trying to get a much needed nap after a day of flying back and forth to Guantanamo, New York and Langley and then spending the entire night and morning managing the team to clean up the Pittsburg hideout and break up the terrorist attack followed by his quick briefing of the Oversight Committee.

"Cristal, you'll have to excuse me. It has been a pretty hectic 36 hours. For you too I know, but we were at it all night, on you know what."

She paused. "According to the TV a propane truck blew up. Is that the good news we were expecting?"

On the other end he smiled as he blinked his eyes open, "Yup. We obviously could not have done it without you two. We also captured two you know what who appeared at the abandoned building last night and we're hopeful they will lead us to their friends in the Pittsburgh area. Where are you by the way?"

"David and I have resolved our differences," she smiled at him sitting across from her on the bed, "And we're still in the Pittsburgh area. You need to know that I've spoken to my parents and told them only that I'm safe. I know about Greg too but what is important now is something David has. Let me put you on speaker."

The Deputy Director spoke first, "David, my congratulations and thanks for sticking to your word."

"Thanks, but just to repeat, before all hell broke loose in that abandoned building last night, I found out that a certain man in the south has issued a directive against both myself and Cristal. They tried to take us out last night and that's when the fun started. But as you know, neither one of us is safe now, especially if there are still some of his friends in Pittsburgh that we have really pissed off."

The Deputy Director paused, "OK we have already gone way too far on an unsecured line. There are things we must discuss. Give me a second."

They waited sitting across from each other on the two double beds in the cheap motel room. Finally the Deputy Director spoke, "I want to keep you both out of sight for now so I won't be sending anyone to you. Cristal I want you to go immediately to the Pittsburgh airport. Go to American's lost luggage counter and retrieve luggage in your name. You'll have cash and a secure phone and anything else we can dump in there in the short time we have. Call me back on that phone."

"Done." Was all she said and they hung up.

***

Within an hour they were back with a small travelling bag that held $5000 in cash, two disposable phones that they assumed had encryption chips in them, a tiny laptop and two 9mm hand guns and holsters with substantial ammunition. Cristal immediately hit speed dial 1 on the phone and was patched through to Deputy Director William Carter's office. Again, she put the phone on speaker.

The Deputy Director started, "First thing is some legal stuff. I'm going to deputize the two of you retroactive to yesterday so that you have legal coverage to work as law enforcement officers for anything you've done or may do in support of the CIA. We can dispense with the oaths. You both know your responsibilities and restrictions under the oaths."

"That said, where were we?"

Cristal jumped in, "I can't go home until I do something about this fatwa. They know where I live. I don't think this death order is an actual fatwa as Khalil is not a Mufti but it carries the same weight for anyone in Al Qaeda, Al-Shabaab or any of their other friends."

They had the DD's attention, "What can I do to help you?"

David answered, "Well this may sound bizarre but the only solution we see is to go after Khalil and at least take the head off the snake. I know there are intelligence networks all over the world that want to get him but we're highly motivated and have the skills to give it a shot. In addition, we may have a lead we can follow and one thing no one else has. Cristal has seen this guy up close and can see through his disguises."

Cristal whispered, "Stop selling. I'm not sure I can do that."

The DD rolled this over in his head. It was a real long shot but these two might just have a chance and he needed everyone looking for Khalil, "Say more."

David spoke first, "Before we get too far on this, I would like to know my status. Am I an escaped terrorist with the entirety of the US law-enforcement structure after me?"

Bill Carter laughed, "I can see where that would concern you. No, the cover story is that Daniel Boone has been transferred into the custody of the CIA and is being interrogated at a secret location. The Oversight committee knows only that you're on our side so there are no APB's out on you. No one is looking for you. At least no one on our side."

"That's good to hear."

The Deputy Director continued, "Now what is this about a lead on Khalil?"

Cristal spoke, "We still have Habib's phone. We don't know how they got messages back and forth but as you know part of it is constantly changing e-mail addresses and spoofed IP's. Now we have something else. We feel confident that one of the numbers on the phone is Mustafa Habib, Jabir's brother. Maybe you can confirm it but at least back three years ago CIA's Intel was that the brothers were close and Mustafa was a key Khalil lieutenant."

"Let me look into that. Their organization is pretty secretive but we have some rumors that Mustafa is actually second-in-command and one of Khalil's most trusted associates. I want that number if you can confirm which one it is from the phone."

"Not going to happen." David butted in. Cristal was a little surprised. "I'm sorry Bill but I've had enough trouble with intelligence organizations to fill a lifetime. I'm not going after Khalil with secret back-up teams breathing down my neck. That's one sure way to get MI6 back on my tail. If we go after him it's Cristal and me alone. We're more effective that way. We will need your help from time to time but you can't know where we are and what we're doing and you can't put back-up teams in there."

The DD thought about this for a while. Clearly, the CIA, MI6 and the very competent intelligence services of several friendly nations had been unable to lay a hand on Khalil so maybe it was time for a different approach.

"OK, let's say I go along with this for the moment. You are motivated, have the needed skills and have potentially a lead to finding him, and Cristal can ID him. I'll help you in any way I can and we won't put tails on you. But, and there is a BIG BUT in this arrangement. I am going to approve Top Secret Status for both of you here and now and what I'm about to say will up the ante on this a thousand fold." Shivers ran down Cristal's back and David was clearly attentive. "We think Khalil has a bomb in play and I think you know what I mean by a bomb.

"About a week ago we found a known bomb maker in Waziristan who had just died of a massive

194

overdose of radiation. While he's not part of Khalil's direct organization, we assess that only Khalil has the means to finance and use such a weapon. This would take a very wide network and lots of resources to pull it off. For all we know there could be an atomic weapon sitting in New York today but it could also be a dirty bomb and is en route to the US or Israel or one of the major cities in Europe. But if I were Khalil, I would want it to be New York.

"We think he's under a lot of pressure to take the fight back on to US soil. So your little vendetta just got escalated into a major operation. You can imagine that we have every resource here and overseas as well as everything our allies can muster against this threat so I can't guarantee that you won't run into another team like Seal Team 6, the SAS, Mossad or even JTF2. All I can promise is that I won't put them on your tail. You'll have to be careful distinguishing the good guys from the bad because this is an all-hands-on-deck operation.

"Now what can I do to support you two?"

Cristal spoke first, "Before we even get to that. This is an unusual request but if it gets out that I'm alive and the bad guys put two and two together they may try to get to my daughter and parents as leverage or revenge."

"Say no more." The Deputy Director started, "I'll put someone on it right away. If they are willing to move we'll take care of them and if not we'll have 24/7 coverage on them."

"They don't know about my CIA connections so for the moment I would prefer the invisible shield around them."

"Done. What else?"

David spoke, "We'll need more money, a full ID run-up, credit cards, passports, some standard security gadgets and drops of weapons and money at airports we'll identify later. Use Jack and Belinda Foster for the ID's. Come to think of it, I see a laptop here so I'll send you everything we need in an e-mail. I'll use this smart phone to send you current photos for passports, drivers' licenses and the like. We'll need an appropriate cover story, just the minimum for now, place of birth, Parents' names, schools, etc. Make it simple please."

David paused as he assumed the DD was scribbling notes to himself, "On a personal note let me say that I think I'm being rather magnanimous about this given that you pricks water boarded me incessantly for years. I'll be looking for a significant apology when this is all over."

There was an uneasy silence on the other end of the phone. Cristal broke the awkward moment, "We also need anything and everything you have on this bomb. And the whole file on Khalil. We need to be out of here like yesterday so we'll send you the e-mail tonight and we're going to need the whole package by noon tomorrow. The airport looked like a good drop so let's use it again."

"Well, good luck to you both. Your operation is a long shot and a dangerous one but you never know, your op may be our best chance at stopping this attack. Getting Khalil would be icing on the cake."

At that they signed off.

Cristal stared at David, "Belinda?"

"You always looked like a Belinda to me," he chuckled.

Weaponization

It had been a long two days and CIA Deputy Director Bill Carter was just thinking of going home to his wife, last night's uneaten Thanksgiving dinner and to finally paying a visit to his own bed when his right hand, Carole Glass, also looking pretty tired, knocked on his door.

She came in holding some papers and stood in front of his desk, "I have good news and bad news. First the bad news. It looks like we really have a weapon in play. The good news is that it's potentially a dirty bomb not a nuclear explosive device."

"Give me the whole story."

She sat down in the chair facing his desk, "The team in Pakistan has collected much more evidence. We've confirmed as best we can that it was in fact Sadoum Al-Binal who died in the hospital of radiation poisoning.

"The drones you ordered did the job. One of them equipped with highly sensitive gamma ray detectors got a hit in a tenement building in Kalibari, a suburb of the city of Peshawar, not far from the hospital where Sadoum died. We sent a team in and found his bomb making workshop and early reports are that it's highly radioactive with at least Cesium-137 and Cobalt-60 present."

The Deputy Director sighed, "At least it's not uranium or plutonium."

"Yeah, small mercies. The most common source for these isotopes is in either hospital radiation equipment or more likely mining and pipeline operations

197

where they're used in quite a few places including x-raying welds, pipe joints and the like.

"This means it didn't necessarily come from Kazakhstan or Iran but could have come from anywhere including both Pakistan itself and Afghanistan. We have no idea how much of this stuff they have. They could have been collecting it for years without anyone noticing. But here is the really scary part of it. The Cobalt-60 has been weaponized."

"What do you mean weaponized."

"Usually Cobalt-60 is found as a chunk of bluish metal which is only dangerous if you handle it or are really close to it but Sadoum did himself in by grinding it into a fine powder and likely inhaling some of it. We found traces of the radioactive Cobalt-60 powder in the workshop.

"This is hard to believe but it looks like he chopped up the soft metal and ground it up with a blender and then a small mortar and pestle in his kitchen. We are analyzing what he left behind but the experts tell me that it would be tough to grind this stuff enough using that method to make it into an aerosol. But it does appear that some of it was ground up fine enough that he inhaled it himself.

"We have to assume that he was able to grind it finely at least to some extent, so we could be looking at something like that anthrax attack of decades ago. People get a letter and the action of opening the letter releases this stuff into the air and then they breathe it in. Both Cesium-137 and Cobalt-60 give off significant gamma rays so you don't even have to inhale it and get the beta particles into your lungs but you're pretty much cooked if you do."

The DD trying to stay awake blinked hard and stared at her across his desk, "Great! If they have it shielded properly they could transport it anywhere. You haven't mentioned targets or transportation so I assume there was no documentation at the site."

"None. It's likely he was just the bomb maker and didn't know what the targets were. It could be any of a number of targets with the US and Israel at the top of the list but we're acting as if we have hard evidence it's on its way here."

The DD leaned back in his chair to stretch his aching back, "Hell if they try that Anthrax method of putting it in letters they could mail it from wherever they are now."

"Actually the guys tell me that's not likely. The terrorists know that it would be picked up at the major postal or courier gateways if it was in a letter unless it was a letter that weighed ten pounds with all the lead shielding and that would get special screening too. No, not letters through the mail. They could always send packages but we think it's more likely they will bring it in to the US in whatever quantity they have and re-package it or use it in some other capacity from here.

"If it's to be used in a letter format, all major government mail goes through an off-site screening center that would catch it so it might have to be a hand delivered because not every government building has radiation detectors. That's if the targets were federal government. It could be state or local government, clergy, celebrities or any other high profile target. Think of Mickey Mouse or Sleeping Beauty at Disneyworld getting hit and the damage that could do.

"At least it's unlikely that it would be a mass attack because they would need a massive amount of this stuff to make a real bad dirty bomb for air dispersal and both the type of materials, the assumed quantity and the weaponization we've seen so far would make that unlikely. It's much more likely that any device they build will be used against individual targets. We think they are going after people that will make a splash, not populations."

The Deputy Director interrupted, "We just saw them go after a soft target in Pittsburgh so make sure we're looking at all possibilities like dumping this stuff in a fountain at a mall."

Carole Glass nodded and continued "Oh yeah, Cesium-137 by the way is water soluble so think about contaminated mall fountains as you suggest, water bottles or coffee if they could get into a building with it. Maybe swimming pools."

"Why Cesium and Cobalt?" the DD asked. "They are pretty tame for weapons of mass destruction aren't they? Why not polonium or plutonium or something much more dangerous than these isotopes?"

"Easy. Unless you're KGB or the CIA, you're not likely to get an opportunity to steal those kinds of materials. Remember, they've been trying that path for years and so far, we've been able to thwart them. Those isotopes are highly controlled and so far, we've done a good job of keeping a lid on the real dangerous stuff even out of Pakistan, Chechnya, North Korea and Iran.

"Cesium and Cobalt are much easier to get your hands on as they are used in lots of industrial applications. They are not as spectacular but used right they can still be a major headache."

The Deputy Director thought for a moment, "Do we have any way of tracking or investigating lost or stolen Cesium and Cobalt?"

"Not really. There have been very few thefts or losses reported around the world but the big issue is that we can have no confidence that losses are reported at all in that part of the world.

"Hell, around 2001 in Thailand some Cobalt-60 was actually found in an uncontrolled metal recycling scheme and killed 3 workers and injured over 1800 so this stuff is not as highly controlled everywhere in the world as you might think and it can be dangerous.

"Corruption is so rampant in that part of the world that they could easily buy someone off in Pakistan or Afghanistan to intercept shipment reports or change the records or whatever.

"For that reason there's really no way of knowing how much of this stuff could be in play. All we know from Sadoum's kitchen is that both radioactive Cesium and Cobalt were in his possession at one time.

"They have half lives of between seven and thirty years but it's almost impossible to get any reading that would be helpful on quantity. He had enough to kill himself by handling it. Did he spill a gram out of 10 grams or a gram out of 100 kilos in his kitchen? We have no way to know."

Both the DD and his Ops Manger were drained from the past thirty-six hours and they were starting to show it. He wanted to draw this to a conclusion quickly, "OK, keep me informed if we find out anything more and keep every channel we have focused on this pursuit. Make sure the key staff gets briefed on this. Do we have any leads at all on where the stuff is and who has it?"

"Absolutely no leads on either of those. All we have is a dead bomb maker and his workshop. We don't know whom he was working for or whom he transferred the material to, when they did it or where it's headed. As I said, we just have to assume it's headed here.

"We've expanded the drone program in Pakistan and we've commissioned additional drones and other Air Force detection systems to cover the shores of Pakistan, the gulf and the coast of Somalia just in case our guess is right on Khalil but if this is a small amount of material, well shielded, we'll be unlikely to pick it up unless we're right on top of it. All we can do is keep trying."

"OK, keep up the mediocre work," he joked with a smile. "But before you go I need to bring you up to date on the Cristal Wiggins thing. This is interesting and related to Khalil."

He spent the next thirty minutes briefing her on everything that had happened in the last thirty six hours. She knew part of it due to the hunt for the propane tanker but was shocked to hear the total story of Abu Nistal/Daniel Boone/Commander David Crowe. He made sure she knew it was eyes only as both David and Cristal were in jeopardy from sources that he didn't want to go into 'at this time'.

"The oversight committee is fully briefed on this now; at least to the level I just gave you. Sorry I had no time to bring you up to speed earlier on this but now we have one more team going after Khalil and the bomb."

He stretched again, "Listen Carole, neither one of us is in top form after the last two days so get home and get some sleep. I'm going to do the same."

She nodded and left.

***

By noon the following day, David and Cristal having everything they had asked for and more, took a short trip to buy some better clothes and luggage and had decided to start their pursuit in Germany where David had some reliable contacts. Germany was also a good hub for any travel into Africa.

After rehearsing their cover stories, Cristal took some time to dye her hair blonde. She liked the results.

In a short call from Phil Harris earlier, she had learned that photos of her in a bikini had been all over the TV and web and were still getting lots of hits so additional work on a disguise was definitely called for.

As to her passport photo, she was just going to have to wing it with an explanation of trying a new color until they could get new documents.

As she exited the bathroom David mocked a heart attack, "Wow! Let's keep this up. I get to sleep with a different movie star every night. I love the new do."

She mocked a swipe at him and smiled as she dressed for their trip. Tiffany was never far from her mind but there was no way she could go home with this threat hanging over her family. She was just going to have to tough it out.

She made a second very short call to her parents explaining that her absence was likely to be longer than she wanted but necessary. While they were worried, she had their trust and they told her not to worry about Tiffany.

They took a quick flight from Pittsburgh to JFK. So far, her new disguise including a large pair of shades seemed to be working. A few heads turned but it was all men and that was natural she figured. She had to admit, the blonde thing worked for her and wondered why she had never tried it before.

After waiting an hour for their connection, they proceeded to the gate and were in line for boarding Lufthansa Business Class for Frankfurt.

Neither of them took notice of a man who was showing great interest in them from across the room. He moved to a newsstand where he was partially covered so he could watch them. After a few minutes he lifted his phone and dialed a London number, "Jack, it's Harry. I'm at JFK just waiting for my London flight and you won't believe whom I'm watching boarding Business Class Lufthansa for Frankfurt."

"Don't play games with me. It's late over here."

"None other than David Crowe."

Jack Hammond was just about to go to bed in his condo near the city center in London but this news snapped him wide awake. "That's impossible. He died in a car bomb four years ago."

"I know. We were certain we had gotten rid of him but I'm quite sure this is him, unless he has a twin brother. He looks more than four years older and has lost some weight but I'd know that face and gait anywhere.

"At a minimum I would get someone to the Frankfurt airport to get a picture of him. I don't have the right equipment here and I don't want to walk up to him with my iPhone. If he spots me, he'll bolt for sure, right after he kills me. We were not best buddies back then but there's no question he would recognize me.

"I think you know what this means. Our little group is in a heap of trouble with him walking around."

Jack Hammond was thinking fast, "This makes no sense. I'm inclined to go with the twin idea or a total doppelganger. Where the hell has he been for four years and what is he doing marching bald-faced through JFK?"

"You got me. Oh, by the way he has a girl with him but I've never seen her before. Nice looking blonde though."

"OK, thanks for the call. I'll get someone to the Frankfurt airport for their arrival. Zoom in with your smart phone even if it's bad and get me something I can send to Frankfurt so they'll know what to look for.

"If you're right this is a hell of a find. You know the drill. This is for us only. No one else is to know of this. No one. I'll bring in the others if needed.

"You'll get a tidy bonus in your next expense check. We'll handle everything from this end. He's already dead, right?"

Hammond hung up the phone and sat there thinking that it couldn't be Commander David Crowe. They even had some DNA from the site of the car bomb although that could always have been a plant.

He thought to himself, "I won't be getting much sleep until this is cleared up. If it's Crowe we had better make him disappear fast, one more time."

The Plan

Sitting in a large comfortable chair in one of his safe houses in Mogadishu, Khalil anxiously awaited news from his deputy Mustafa as he enjoyed his morning tea. This particular safe house belonged to an important supporter in Mogadishu and was rather comfortable with lots of amenities including its own electrical generator.

Mustafa came in almost breathless, "All is in order. Basoum did a wonderful job. The package is now in our staging area near the docks and it looks good. We have many kilos of both weapons. I had no idea we had been collecting this material for so long and kept it secret. Our brothers in Pakistan have excelled in acquiring this. Our weapons expert says it will be more than enough to achieve our goals.

"We are carefully getting it into our transport package to be ready for the ship and it seems to be on schedule too."

Khalil shifted in his seat, "This cost our brother Sadoum his life. We have to warn the others to take precautions. Apparently, this material is at least as deadly as we thought. Sadoum took precautions but it was not enough.

"As to the amounts we have, I know something of these matters from my engineering education and the dilution issues are the tricky part in this attack. When you next see the weapons expert tell him I want to see the dilution tables and assumptions he is making for each attack. The total amount is not as important as the dilution assumptions. Too diluted and it will not work.

"I think we have been both good and lucky delivering the material this far. Allah has clearly blessed our plan. But we cannot lose focus. If there are any leaks in the package, the Americans will pick it up with their satellites.

"Also, please make sure we have total security on that staging site. If word gets out about what we have there are others in this city that would want it for themselves. We are at high risk of discovery until we deliver this weapon. Make sure our inner circle is only aware of the parts of our plan that they need to do their job. If there's any doubt, or if someone asks too many questions, don't hesitate. Take them out.

"This operation is the biggest in our history and will do amazing things to hurt America and re-establish us as an active threat for major operations."

He shook his finger for emphasis. "We are now closer than ever to striking the heart of the Great Satan. Let's have no mistakes. Allahu Akbar! "

Mustafa looked concerned, "Have you heard anything about my brother in America?"

Khalil hesitated, "I received some news this very morning. Our brothers in Burundi are very concerned. They think something went wrong at the hideout and they sent two brothers to check it out but even they did not return. At first they were afraid to approach the hideout again, but when they did gain entry, there was no sign of brother Jabir's team, Abu Nistal, the woman, or the two others they had sent to investigate. We have to assume the CIA followed them and has all of them. It would appear the operation was a complete failure."

He hesitated and then continued, "Also they had planned an attack on a major shopping center with a propane truck before they left and it was intercepted.

The US media is reporting it as a vehicle accident but our people in Pittsburgh say they had a car following about a half a mile behind with a back-up detonator. They say just before the explosion there was a Police car following the truck and it pulled off just as the truck was hit by an almost invisible missile.

"There has been nothing in the media about a missile or a drone. It appears that somehow the plan was uncovered and the American's blew up the truck before it reached its destination. No one was hurt except the driver who thankfully died a martyr's death defending Islam. Al-hamdu lillāh!

"We have to assume that the CIA has Jabir and his team and the CIA may have gotten the plans for the attack from them. Or that they were betrayed and they are all dead. We can only pray to Allah that Jabir died as a martyr for our cause."

Mustafa was clearly distressed and emotional about the news of his younger brother, "Allahu Akbar . That is my wish and my hope master Khalil. There was no greater patriot for our cause than my younger brother. He gave everything he had. He did what no one else has been able to do by getting a team into the US and bringing the CIA to their knees. We will hope that he's enjoying the fruits of martyrdom in heaven with Allah and our glorious prophet."

Khalil continued, "If he was betrayed it was by that American Abu Nistal, the man he trusted and sacrificed everything to rescue. I know now that he was in a relationship with the woman Jabir kidnapped and that she was CIA."

He continued, "I also know the US has said nothing about his release from Guantanamo. Can you think of any reason they would not want to warn everyone of an escaped terrorist on American soil?

Unless they were not afraid of him because he was working for them and he's likely back with them now.

"He is American. Either he was always CIA or maybe they got to him and converted him. As I remember Jabir said he was never actually committed to the cause of Jihad. He had his own agenda for going after the Burundi government."

Mustafa was furious, "If this is true. If Abu Nistal has betrayed my brother and killed him or had him captured by the CIA in America and held for torture, I'll hunt him down and kill him like a dog myself."

"Mustafa. I must ask you one very important question. Did your brother know anything of our plans for the attack on America."

Mustafa blushed under his full beard, "As far as I know, I'm the only one from our group that has ever been in direct contact with him and I would NEVER discuss an ongoing operation with anyone outside of our inner circle without your permission. No, even if the CIA have captured him, I'm confident he knows nothing of our plans."

Still Khalil was nervous but he needed Mustafa focused. Now was not the time to elaborate on his fears.

***

The Cristal Wiggins case had gone cold right after they had turned her polygamist husband over to the Kansas State police. Nothing was moving and the biggest surprise for Detective Bert Wilson was the parents. It had been a few days and not a peep out of them.

They had given a short interview at their front door to a WKRC reporter but had limited their comments to the feeling that there had always been something off about Greg Wiggins who they now knew was actually Robert 'Bobby' Watson and headed for trial in Wichita.

"I agree." said Detective Colt Baker, "It's odd we haven't heard anything from them. You'd think they'd be pestering us daily. Why don't we pay them a visit and see what they have to say?"

They arrived at the modest bungalow just before noon and were invited in by a shy and sixtyish Mary Serpe.

As they headed toward the tiny living room Frank Serpe entered, "Good morning gentlemen. Good to see you again. Do you have anything new on Cristal?"

Both cops picked up on the cheerful greeting and the seeming diminished concern. Not what they would expect from a man whose daughter had been missing for almost a week.

The mother was even worse. She seemed so disinterested in the conversation that she headed for the kitchen.

Colt started, "No I'm afraid we have no news and we're running out of leads. We were hoping you may have thought of something that might help us locate Cristal."

"I'm afraid not gentlemen," he smiled unconsciously, "we have no idea what has happened to her."

Again the casual and almost cheerful attitude. Bert was getting a bad feeling about this. They were hiding something, "Do you still think Greg had something to do with her disappearance?"

"Well one can't be sure. I told you I don't trust the man but he does not appear to me to be the kind of person that would have done harm to Cristal."

That was all Bert needed. He had seen enough. Something dramatic had changed and they were hiding it. "Mr. Serpe do you know something you're not telling us? If Cristal is safe and this has been something other than a kidnapping then we need to know now."

Frank Serpe blushed and was obviously embarrassed and feeling cornered. He seemed to physically take a step backwards, "All I can tell you is that we don't know where Cristal is and I'm more sure than ever she was kidnapped." He realized immediately that he might have worded that poorly.

Bert Wilson decided to get a little more aggressive and leaned forward, "What has changed in your view of Greg's involvement but convinced you that it was a kidnapping? I must remind you that this is an official police inquiry and if you know something and are concealing it you could be charged with felony obstruction in a police investigation."

Frank Serpe continued to blush and now looked fearful, "There is nothing I can tell you. I just feel that it must have been a kidnapping."

Colt took over, "Mr. Serpe when we met last week in front of their house you seemed convinced Greg might be behind all of this and you were staking out the house yourself. Now you seem to dismiss him as a suspect in her disappearance yet you seem sure it was a kidnapping. What's changed?"

"I'm sorry gentlemen. This has been very hard on us. We're still in the dark as to what has happened to our daughter and we hope you'll find out for us." He looked like he wanted to run from the room. He paused for a long time staring both of the cops down and looking completely guilty, "You said I could be charged with obstruction. Do I need a lawyer?"

Bert backed off. No point in giving the distraught father a heart attack.

Whatever they knew they wouldn't or couldn't say for one reason or another and they didn't look like the type to do any harm to their daughter themselves.

"I don't think you need a lawyer at this time but Mr. Serpe if you know anything it's in your best interests to tell us. You have my number. We'll show ourselves out."

As they walked back to the car Colt said, "The plot thickens. What the hell was that all about? They don't seem concerned about where their daughter is?"

Bert looked across the car as he opened the door, "That's because they've spoken to her."

"What?"

As they got in the car Bert Wilson continued, "They've spoken to her. That's why the lack of urgency or fear for her. Did you notice the wife disappeared right away? Who does that when your daughter has been kidnapped? This will turn out to be something she did on her own or possibly they have had a ransom call that said to keep the cops out of it but I highly doubt that. We would have sensed a really different vibe if that was the case. As I said before I'm more inclined to put some credence into Bob Watson's CIA story. We might be getting the runaround from our friends in Langley."

Just as Bert was putting the car in drive, Colt noticed something and motioned to Bert. "There's a car around the corner within sight of the Serpe's front door with two men sitting in it. Let's go check out those two."

They drove completely around the block and pulled up behind the suspects' car. The car with Virginia plates and the people in it screamed feds. With Colt on the passenger's side, Bert approached the driver's window with his service revolver unclipped, "Good morning gentlemen. I'm detective Wilson and this is detective Baker of the Cincinnati PD. Can we see some ID please."

Both occupants carefully handed over Virginia driver's licenses, "Now can I ask you what brings you to Cincinnati and why you're parked here?"

"Sorry, can't say. All I can tell you is that we are brothers in law-enforcement and we're here on a stake out."

"What agency?"

They smiled at each other, "A Federal one and it would not be a good idea to pursue that. If you really think we're bad guys then take us in and be prepared to be more than embarrassed."

Bert thought for a second and then asked," Whom are you staking out?"

"Sorry, can't say."

He was pretty sure they were feds but he wanted to have a little fun with them and make sure they understood the local guys were no pushovers, "What is the Federal Criminal code for resisting an officer in the performance of his duties?"

The driver smiled. "Good one. That would be 18-7-111, Title 18 chapter 7, section 111."

Bert smiled back as he handed them back their documents, "Have a good day gentlemen."

Back in the car Colt said, "WOW! You were right. There is a lot more to this than meets the eye. They had to be secret service or CIA or FBI. I hate playing in a game when the game is 'hide the ball'".

Bert sneered, "Yeah!"

They arrived back at their desks and Colt noticed a call from Harry Cote, Cristal's boss at WKRC. He put the phone on speaker and had Harry on the phone within a minute.

"Detective Baker, thank you for getting back to me so quickly."

"Before we start Mr. Cote, I have you on speaker and Detective Bert Wilson is with me here. He is the lead detective on the Cristal Wiggins disappearance."

"Good. Well gentlemen this may be nothing, after all Cristal's name has been in the news lately but there was a guy in here this morning asking about her. He seemed to be Middle Eastern or Arab or something but anyways he was asking weird questions like did we know her maiden name or where her parents lived. The receptionist didn't give him anything but alerted me. We didn't get the plate number but she's pretty sure the car had Pennsylvania plates. Does that mean anything to you?"

The two cops look at each other puzzled. Bert spoke, "I'm glad you called us with this. You never know. It doesn't tie to anything we're investigating right now but every lead helps. If that is all you have let me ask you to contact us immediately if he returns."

"Sure. Will do. But com'on guys you must have something for me. We've had no news for a few days now on Cristal and she's loved by everyone at the station, so even if it's not newsworthy but better if it is, what do you have for me?"

"Sorry, absolutely nothing has changed. We have very few leads but we're following every one of them. We'll let you know if we find out anything." And at that they hung up.

Bert had heard enough, "I'm calling the CIA myself this time."

Within fifteen minutes, he had gotten as high as he could in the CIA and was surprised that his attempts at escalation had actually worked because now he was waiting for a high level manager.

"Detective Wilson, I am Carole Glass, Deputy Director Bill Carter's Operations Manager, how can I help you?"

"Well let me say my old cop's nose tells me we're getting the runaround from you folks.

"As I'm sure you are aware we're investigating the Cristal Wiggins aka Cristal Serpe disappearance and several leads point back to you.

"Now we have some Middle Eastern types from Pennsylvania trying to track her or her parents down. That and other items ties in with evidence we have that Cristal once worked for you folks.

"Also we met with her parents today and they seem to know something that they won't share with us. They seem a lot less concerned with her absence.

"We also ran into what I think were a couple of your guys staking out their house. What can you tell me? Am I chasing my tail on this disappearance."

There was a longer than normal pause at the other end of the line which spoke volumes, "Look detective. I would love to cooperate with you completely on this but frankly it's way above your pay grade. I'll deny anything we discuss here but I want your word first that this call is not being recorded."

"We do record some calls but this one is not being recorded. So what can you tell me?"

"What I'm willing to tell you and you alone is that we're aware of the allegations that she worked for us. We continue to publicly deny that. We've made our own inquiries and we believe Cristal Wiggins was in fact kidnapped and not by Greg Wiggins.

"We have reason to believe she is no longer under the control of her kidnappers and may have contacted her parents to let them know she's free, but we don't know where she is at this moment and her parents are likely telling the truth that they don't know either.

"The information about people from Pennsylvania is news to us and important so if you hear anything more on that front please let me know. That's all I can tell you and as I said, I'll have to deny this conversation ever happened. Have a good day," and she hung up.

Bert Wilson turned to Colt Baker and said, "She's CIA. She's free of her kidnappers. Wiggins was not involved. They don't want us finding her or talking to her. The Pennsylvania connection is probably the kidnappers trying to find her again. The CIA is protecting the parents and the baby and watching for the bad guys and we're not going to get anything more out of the CIA. Watch the baby. Either she comes back and claims the baby or the baby disappears and she has been back."

"So what do we do? What do we tell the boss and the press?"

"We're following up any leads and right now we don't have any. If anyone pushes we'll say Greg Wiggins aka Bob Watson might know where she is and he's not talking. Hopefully one day we'll find out what all of this was about but I'm not spending another second on this.

Colt stiffened, "Hey wasn't there a Red alert in Pittsburgh the other day for a guy in a propane truck and then a propane truck blew up and now we have Pennsylvania plates that might be kidnappers looking for the family? This could all be related."

"Wow! You really gotta' get a hold on that imagination. What are you some kind of conspiracy freak now? Watch the baby. That's all we can do."

Frankfurt

Neither David nor Cristal got much sleep on the red eye to Frankfurt and were yawning and stretching like the other travelers as they waited for their luggage just after 8 am local time.

As they exited the 'Nothing to Declare' aisle after immigration, David waited while Cristal stepped into the ladies' room near the exit. When she returned her carry-on bag was a little heavier with the two 9mm guns and ammo she had picked up from the drop.

For the second time in the last nine hours, they missed the attention they had garnered from a stranger. This time he was at the back of the crowd who were all waiting for friends and relatives on the JFK flight.

With his high-powered camera casually resting on some baggage carts he had about a dozen great pictures of them. While the woman was in the ladies room, the four best shots were soon traveling over the internet to the personal account of Jack Hammond of MI6 in London.

Hammond heard the computer incoming mail beep and knew what to expect. "My god, that's him," he said to himself sipping his morning coffee at home. "But who is the blonde?"

Her face was too familiar. He had seen that face somewhere in the last few days but something had changed. "It's the hair," he smiled to himself. He had seen that face on top of a wonderful bikini a couple of days ago on TV. A mother of a young baby had been kidnapped somewhere in the US and CNN's noon time feed from the US had played it to an international audience. Was Crowe now in the kidnapping business?

He thought not. The woman, Cristal something as he remembered, looked too comfortable.

He had no time to waste or take appropriate precautions so he lifted his private smart phone and quickly dialed a number only he in MI6 knew, "Kurt, does your guy still have them in sight?"

"Yes. I just spoke to him. They have a long walk to the exit."

"OK, he needs to follow them and report back when they get to wherever they are going. Get him some back-up right now. Code name for this operation is 'Frankfurt' and you deal only with me or anyone I send to you with this operation identifier, understood? I want to know something more about them before we take them. Don't lose them!"

"Yes, Herr Hammond."

Jack hung up, looked at his watch, he'd have to get to the office soon but first he had to figure out what to do with Crowe and the girl. Before he made them disappear he wanted to know more about who she was. It was possible they had a tail or she was someone who could not be made to disappear easily or cleanly.

There was always the possibility of reopening the Terminate order on David but that meant involving more of MI6 and reopening the issues around how he was fingered as the leader of the corruption in the first place. Especially given his reported death hadn't put a dent in the corruption in Africa. Better to take this one step at a time he figured.

Kurt Willems relayed the message to his man at the airport.

He didn't get too many of these assignments from Kurt and he wanted to be thorough.

He rushed to catch up with them and then stayed at a discrete distance. Following them through the airport, he had to duck into an alcove while the woman apparently needed to visit the toilet again. That seemed odd to him but he put it down to too much booze on the plane.

The male subject made a U-turn and came right past him to rest his luggage on a bench so he kept on walking until he found a spot where he could wait.

As was her habit in certain public places, Cristal had made the toilet break to check for tails and as she returned she spotted him immediately. He was focused on David and averted his attention when he caught her out of the corner of his eye.

He was pretty sure she had not made him so he busied himself looking for something in his coat pockets as Cristal headed for David.

With her back to the watcher, she whispered to David that they had a tail and they hatched a plan to confront him.

David had retrieved his weapon from Cristal's carry-on and now took his luggage and rounded a corner into a vacant hallway marked 'Scheingründe' which he knew to mean 'Authorized Personnel'. It seemed to zigzag leading to an employee area.

Cristal made like she was busy looking for something in her luggage but out of the corner of her eye she noticed the confusion on the part of the watcher. He finally decided he had to keep David under surveillance and glancing around the corner, followed him.

Cristal quickly and quietly caught up with him and stuck a silenced gun against his spine. Their plan to interrogate him backfired when the man turned suddenly with his hand in his pocket. Cristal had no choice but to take him out with a 9mm slug under the rib cage and into to the heart dropping him where he stood. David was at her side in a second.

"There was nothing else I could do. He was going to take me out," she whispered as she pulled his hand out of his pocket and a small gun appeared. They dragged him around a corner so they could not be seen from the concourse. Cristal checked and was happy to see there was no visible blood on her clothes and there were no security cameras in this area.

David whispered as he started rifling through the man's pockets. "Looks professional and German so he's not likely a Jihadi. Hope to hell he's not one of the good guys." He found a tiny camera with a powerful digital zoom and a wallet.

Cristal shivered at the thought of killing one of their own and silently took out her iPhone, pulled up a special app and pressed the man's fingers one at a time on the screen.

David was looking through the camera he had found, "Shit, he got about a dozen snaps of us and mailed four of them to an obscure and probably disposable mail address. Someone knows we're here."

He stood with the man's wallet going through it, "Gerald Hendrickson. German driver's license, credit cards in the same name. We need to get out of here. I'll take the wallet and the camera."

Cristal nodded and was first to move headed for her luggage which sat unmolested on the bench where she had left it. It had all happened so fast that security had not yet had an opportunity to identify it as abandoned. They wasted no time getting their rental car and headed to the Westin Grand in central Frankfurt.

En route Cristal, still concerned she might have killed a friendly foreign agent, sent the fingerprints to Phil Harris with a cover note explaining the confrontation at the airport.

They checked into their hotel and both quickly showered and jumped into bed to try to make up for the lost sleep on the plane.

Cristal's phone woke them both. The time on the bedside alarm said 13:15 and she could see it was Bill Carter on the phone. She realized it had to be early morning for him. She put him on speaker.

The DD jumped right into it, "Well you picked up an interesting tail. Gerald Hendrickson is actually only one of the names we have on record for those prints. To allay your fears he is not one of the good guys. He is a mercenary; retired German intelligence officer who we believe has gone private and working for some shady characters. He is for hire for anyone needing some dirty work done so I've no doubt he would have done you in if you had not reacted. One big question left outstanding is how he found you."

"Yeah, I've been wondering about that myself," said David.

The DD continued, "We'll leave that for later. We have some information that he may be working for a very secretive organization we jokingly call the BSB around here, the Bean Stalk Boys."

Cristal finally offered a smile, "What on earth are they?"

"Well for some time we've been trying to run down a theory that some of the big Agra companies have a dirty tricks division. A well-funded organization that will use any means to further their goals. There is some evidence that a couple of these monstrous Agra firms have formed a cartel and fund this BSB group to do their dirty work.

"We have investigations ongoing into BGG, Carstares and Maestro just to mention a few, but so far nothing that connects them to anything.

"We think that the BSB are probably based out of some place with no US extradition. You might be surprised to find out that there are still quite a few safe havens for people breaking US laws. Hell even France, Germany and Japan to name only a couple will still never extradite their own nationals.

"Anyways, BSB, if they actually exist as an organization, is probably made up of ex. Special Forces types around the world including lots of local ex-heavyweights like Herr Hendrickson. Apart from using these guys for dirty tricks, assassinations, orchestrating unrest and the like, we've thought for some time that this cartel has been funneling money to bad actors. Sometimes to both sides of the political spectrum to make sure they are in charge with today's regimes and those of tomorrow. Could be related to what David was working on back in the day."

David spoke, "What is their purpose behind this?"

"Well, Africa in particular is an emerging breadbasket for the world, a serious growth area for these Agra companies and as you both know, politically unstable.

"Here is just one scenario for you. They corrupt some African government with money and threats. They get loads of influence and leverage over them, convince them to rapidly expand their agricultural expropriations or zoning, land clearing and mandating the cartel's clearing outfits, seeds, fertilizers, processing plants etc. Get them to legalize lots of things favorable to them such as GMO's, that's Genetically Modified Organisms for the uninitiated. Get them to eliminate or bypass laws that require labeling food as containing GMO's and ship these products to countries in Europe and America where GMO labeling is either mandated or GMO's are outright banned. This is a multi-billion dollar business.

"GMO's are great for the cartel because they increase yields, kill off pests, are weed-resistant, etc. but little is known about the long term effects of genetically modifying what we eat. We've been doing it to many products for years but some people and some states in particular are very concerned about them. Lots of scientists and doctors think that is overkill but the other side thinks they are being naïve.

"Problem is that it's worth billions to these big Agra companies and it doesn't even have to be GMO's. Cornering the market on fertilizers, seeds, herbicides etc. is worth billions alone.

"Agra is monstrously big. After all of the consolidation over the last few decades, a couple of companies control most of the basic food industries right through land ownership, production, processing, distributing and marketing.

"The US alone spends almost $2 trillion a year on food or about 12% of our GDP. They are one of the largest industries on the planet and it's increasingly controlled by a few so the incentive and the power are there to go the extra mile to ensure their profit stream and executive bonuses and Africa is really fertile ground in more ways than one."

He continued, "I'm no Agra expert but our people tell me these guys can quintuple their profits if they can get away with what they want and remember Africa also has some of the lowest labor costs and poorest working conditions of anywhere on the planet so it's a goldmine for them.

"That means they have lots of incentive to try to manipulate corrupt regimes and we think they have the muscle with the BSB to pull it off. If the money doesn't do the job they send in the muscle."

"Now some of these regimes play ball and some are more reluctant. So this supposed cartel through their enforcers, stirs up trouble for them and funds the opposition, just to keep the current regime on its toes and you never know when the other side might get into power somehow.

"Often they need a little muscle to make it work or some civil unrest and for others simply some personal financing or what normal people would call bribery. The old stick and carrot approach. The BSB are the enforcers and the security team to ensure that all of their plans come off without a hitch.

"So David, in my mind there's a good chance that there's a connection to your MI6 problems especially seeing as we think Gerald Hendrickson is part of the BSB. A rogue MI6 operation working with BSB could be behind the attempt on your life back then and looks like with your problems at the airport they are back on your tail."

David had been listening intently, "You may be right. And it would have to be big as you said. What I was chasing was millions sneaking through the door and supporting some of these corrupt regimes. I first stumbled upon it when I realized that if you tracked all of the advertised funding from NGO's, World Bank, and various Foreign Aid donations, there was still millions appearing out of nowhere and being used mostly to suppress opposition and line the pockets of the corrupt leaders."

Bill Carter broke in, "Well we don't know enough about this shady cartel or their BSB enforcers but believe me, they can afford a program like this. Their profits are massive.

"We suspect they've built in layers of plausible deniability and we have not been able to pin anything on these companies but I suspect the BSB is highly motivated and someone like you would have been and may be again, a big threat in their eyes."

David had been playing with the camera he took off the attacker, "The more I think about it the more I think this might be the people who were after me in Africa. Somehow they got tipped off we were arriving in Frankfurt and we now know that this guy mailed a couple of pictures of us to a dummy mail address. So whoever it is knows we're here and they've likely ID'd me at least."

The DD spoke, "Well it would appear you may now have two threats to deal with. Not only have you a fatwa on you but you may have the BSB out to get you too. I would have my head on a swivel but then again the two of you have had a wealth of field experience and you showed this morning and a couple of nights ago that you haven't lost your touch. You're leaving a trail of dead bad guys wherever you go. Keep this up and there won't be any bad guys left.

"Joking aside, I would be really careful. What is your next move?"

This time Cristal spoke, "David has contacts here in Germany. I have some contacts in Sudan, South Sudan, and Burundi that might come in handy. We need to meet a few people here first and see where they can lead us. We also need to crawl through that file you sent us on Khalil so let's plan on talking tomorrow to see where we are."

"OK, but just remember there's a potential dirty bomb in play. We now know that they have some quantity of both Cobalt-60 and Cesium-137. Both emit gamma rays and beta particles. What we don't know is how much of it they have and when and where to expect it to appear so time is of the essence.

"One last thing. I didn't mention this before but we picked up two Jihadis when they came to check out that hideout they had Cristal stashed in. If we get anything out of the interrogation of them we'll let you know. So far nothing useful. At least we now know there's a sleeper cell in Pittsburgh that was not previously on our radar and we hope to round them up at least. So the benefits of your night of excitement just keep rolling in. God speed."

They spent the rest of the afternoon alternating between munching on a few room service goodies, cat naps and reviewing the Khalil files. As evening fell they decided it was time to get a real meal.

They found a local Brauhaus that looked like a good place to disappear. David immediately noticed the Köbes with Kranz. As they found a seat near the back he explained to Cristal. "If you haven't been in one of these places you might like this. The waitress over there is known as a Köbes. She carries around those tall thin beer glasses of their local brew in a Kranz like a milkman delivering milk in the old days. Every time you're near finished a glass or two she takes away the empties, gives you full cold ones and marks it on the beer mat until you put the beer mat on top of your glass. As to food, my German is rusty but the house specials are usually good."

David had the Haxen mit Kraut enjoying the pork leg immensely and Cristal tried the Bratkartoffeln mit Spiegelei which David said was like home fries with fried eggs on top and a salad on the side. With all the travel she was not excited about trying some of the heavier German food tonight.

Checking they could not be overheard David spoke softly first, "I've been thinking about that material we reviewed this afternoon. We know he's a master of disguise. He seems to have access to professional forged documents and there was some indication that aside from being the master planner behind many of the terrorist attacks around the globe, he might also be their top salesman."

"Yeah, I saw that too. He seems to fancy himself as the fund-raiser-in-chief. What are you getting at?"

The Kobes arrived again and David paused looked around again to ensure no one was paying undue attention or within listening range.

The tiny Brauhaus was not very busy and the few people there seemed relaxed and uninterested in David and Cristal especially the large Labrador Retriever sleepily sprawled across the floor where people had to step over him in the center of the room, something both David and Cristal realized was unremarkable for these small eateries in Europe.

As the Kobes moved on David returned to his thought, "I suspect Khalil travels more than is generally thought. I know Langley thinks he's hunkered down in Mogadishu for the most part but I think he's so arrogant that he meets with his funding sources to press the flesh as it were. And given his confidence in disguises and forged documents, I'll bet he has traveled to high risk destinations where he has no established security set up. Maybe our respective intelligence agencies have been looking in the wrong places. He may not be hiding in Mogadishu all the time."

Cristal was enjoying her 'light' meal, "Say more."

"The files say they have long suspected that he receives money from Islamic organizations and other sympathizers all over the globe. But how does he do that? We've gotten pretty good at intercepting wire transfers, freezing bank accounts and even intercepting some of their Hawal money networks so he might be forced to meet with these funders directly and accept payment in some other fashion. Shipments of diamonds or suitcases full of cash, who knows but the point is this, assume he has to meet Imam X from a western country like France, the UK or even the States. Where are they going to meet?"

He took another bite of his meal as Cristal thought this over.

He continued. "There are too many eyes on these funders in their own countries or for them to get away with a trip to say Tunisia, Yemen, Somalia, Afghanistan, or Pakistan. But not so much interest if they visit Fiji, Barbados, Singapore, Tokyo and the like.

"What if he's everywhere we're not looking? Remember, to some extent Bin Laden hid in plain sight, in a sizeable city. What if Khalil is even more confident and arrogant, enough to pull off visits to major international cities or even resorts to meet his funders where they would feel safe and not scrutinized as much as if say they travelled to an Islamic country."

Cristal smiled, "What you say makes a lot of sense but it's simply speculation. There is no way to know if he actually does this high-wire act, laughing in the faces of everyone looking for him. Seems risky but it could be in character for him."

She continued as David focused on his meal, "But how would you track him down if he was making these trips. All of his travel would be out of Mogadishu and I can see where Al Shabaab would have no trouble getting him in and out of there if they still have an entente of sorts. That's if his real base is Somalia and we can't even verify that."

David again checked the room before responding. He kept thinking of Bill Carter's advice to keep his head on a swivel. There were bad guys around and there was no telling what their capabilities were for tracking them down. "Yeah, that's just it. We know so little about Khalil except that the Intel says he moves all the time and never sleeps in the same place two nights in a row. I now suspect he moves a lot more than just inside the city. Some of that movement could be international.

"Hell, with his skills, resources and confidence he might even have entered the US at some point. Flew right into JFK wearing a disguise and carrying papers that made him look like a rich businessman from Dubai or Riyadh. No one knows what he looks like anyways. I'm not saying he did that but I wouldn't bet against it.

"And knowing now what I know about his personality profile I would not put it past him to be bragging to his funders that he can go anywhere with impunity. Remember he grew up in Detroit and probably has a very passable American accent. I think this guy is a true chameleon, a showman and a dare devil besides being a ruthless killer.

"As far as his funders go, he wouldn't want to meet them on their own turf in case they were being watched but he could meet them somewhere neutral like Oslo, Toronto, Mexico City or Bermuda for all we know."

Cristal nodded, "Well hitting him outside of Somalia would be preferable. Mogadishu is likely a mess and he probably has people all over the place watching for him and the two of us will stick out like sore thumbs down there but that presents some big problems. Getting his travel plans and then finding him when he gets there."

"Yeah, that won't be easy. We would need some really specific Intel."

Cristal finished her beer put the beer mat on top of her glass and said, "Let's get back to the hotel, I told Bill we would talk tomorrow but I want to run these ideas past the DD tonight and get his thoughts, it's only mid afternoon in Virginia."

Movement

Even with all of his disguises and security, moving around inside Mogadishu in the daytime was risky for Khalil. He was keenly aware that the intelligence services of all the major western nations surely had undercover operatives everywhere and thought he was in Mogadishu. He didn't trust Al Shabaab for security but relied instead on a small number of close associates who would give their lives for him and the cause that he represented.

It was difficult to near impossible for foreigners to operate in the city and all of the local fighting age men were mostly government military and paramilitary types or Al-Shabaab. Any new faces would raise suspicions making it hard for them to infiltrate the city but the bounty on his head made him suspicious of everyone.

Clearly the intelligence agencies had to have some well positioned spies in Mogadishu and they were likely locals or at least they would fit in well with the local population so he couldn't take any chances.

He always played it safe and today he had a full contingent of his men checking out his path in front of him and lookouts behind as he approached the old port. To any onlooker none of this would stand out as they had become expert at stealth.

At all times he knew who surrounded him and what their jobs were but neither he nor his sizeable team stood out from the normal hustle and bustle of this old part of town. Their varying disguises, hidden weapons and staggered arrival times made it impossible to see them as all working together and his disguise he felt, was close to flawless.

He was used to sleeping in a different bed every night but the boredom of waiting for things to happen had gotten to him and he wanted to see the progress up close. As he approached the old port on the high rampart above he headed straight for his lieutenant waiting for him, scanning the ships below.

After a moment of taking in the scene he asked, "Is that her over there with the red paint?"

"Yes master. The one on the right in the dry dock. They are almost finished working on her and she'll be back in the water tomorrow."

"What is the story we're using to cover the work?"

"She needed scraping and painting before the big trip. She hasn't been out of the water in about 5 years so that should not look suspicious."

"And the additions for the package?"

"They have finished the moorings already. The workers think they are simply ring mounts fastened under the bulbous bow as a new requirement of the Panama Canal as tow points. Doesn't make much sense but it's good enough for them so that they don't ask questions."

Khalil looked satisfied, "So we're on schedule?"

"I would say we're right on schedule. It may be just as bad to be too early as too late. I assume whatever the package is will be ready in the next few days?"

Khalil smiled, "Insha'Allah. I would love to visit them and praise them for the work they are doing but that would be too risky. They need all the privacy they can get. We can't risk their security."

***

The DD had been in a meeting and it took some time for him to return Cristal's call. It was near midnight in Frankfurt when the encrypted call was set up but Cristal and David were still pretty much on Pittsburgh time.

Bill Carter immediately took over the call, "We got some good Intel out of the two that showed up at the hideout in Pittsburgh after you left. Some of it could be misdirection but these two didn't seem to be very well trained or even as committed to the cause as some other Jihadists we've captured so there's a good chance what we got is real. Besides we're using some new techniques on them including drugs that seem to be working."

Cristal and David were listening intently as he continued, "Firstly Khalil is definitely behind their group at the top. So he has connections to the Pittsburgh group who seem to have dispersed and we're looking for more of them now.

"Secondly, you won't believe this. After praising Khalil for his brave leadership, they let it slip that they have been told that he has actually attended the execution of some of Al Qaeda's attacks. At least the ones that he has managed directly. Now this is a rumor but it's something to think about."

He continued, "We think we've confirmed that Cristal's kidnapping was carried out by the Burundi group with help from Pittsburgh, but you two already knew that. Khalil would typically not get involved in something that small himself. Sorry Cristal, you were just not a big enough fish. But the point is he apparently is bold enough and confident enough to travel internationally and show up in countries where he has attacks planned."

Cristal motioned to David that she would take it, "That seems to tie to an idea we've been discussing and

234

the reason I called. After reviewing your file on him and what we know of him we think he might make funding visits too. With your information added to this, I think we have a picture of him visiting his funders in person in neutral countries and bragging about his exploits and his personal involvement in the attacks. It would also boost the morale of his troops so we tend to agree with what you found out in the interrogation. This terrorist is so bold and arrogant and confident in his disguises and paperwork that he virtually laughs in our faces by attending some of these attacks and we think he does not limit his travels to just sites where he has attacks planned."

The Deputy Director cut in, "That's a great piece of work and it all ties out in terms at least of a theory. Now all we have to do is figure out a way to strategize on this premise. If it's true, how do we catch him when he's on the move?

"But I saved the best for last. The two we captured were held in isolation so we told them that the attack on the mall was successful. After a moment of pride and celebration, one of them blurted out, 'Well if you liked that, wait 'til Christmas.' He quickly caught himself right after that.

"Still, with the information we got out of them, we're pretty sure they have no idea what the target is but looks like Khalil's big show and by that I mean the bomb, is going to be around Christmas. And from what we just discussed it would seem imperative for Khalil to be there to witness or drive that attack if he dared to enter the US."

David spoke, "I think you're on to something. If we have Khalil's profile right then he would want badly to be there. This will be his masterpiece, the culmination of all his rhetoric and threats. There's no question that if he has the guts to do it he'll be there but again we have no idea what he looks like or what papers he may be travelling on so there is no point in warning any of our border stations. Besides, he might use the tunnel Jabir Habib spoke of and all we know is that it's in Texas just like so many other drug smuggling tunnels that you can't find today. You can't dig up the entire Texas-Mexico border.

David continued, "So we have less than four weeks to find either the bomb, the target, Khalil or all of them together. That sounds like a lot of time but it will go by quickly if we have no leads on where to look."

Deputy Director Carter sighed, "Yeah, this info we have today is a major breakthrough but actually it gets us no closer to stopping the damned thing. We need to find something that points us in the right direction.

"Listen I have to run into another meeting right now. I'll get some kind of advice to the ICE folks and Texas law enforcement but it is unlikely to do any good.

"You two get going and see what you can dig up. Just be warned that just about the whole of the CIA will be on this job so forget about being given elbow room. None available on this matter. Talk to you soon." And he signed off.

Cristal looked at David. "I work better on a full night's sleep so no more hanky-panky like the other night. At least not tonight."

David simply laughed and nodded.

They were both dead tired from the lack of sleep on the flight over and so they were asleep almost as quickly as they hit the pillow.

***

David had asked Bill Carter to give them some standard security gadgets before they left the US and he had been pleased to find one item disguised as a very small handheld GPS device that golfers use. He had set the tiny proximity alarm on the hotel room door which was now signaling his iPhone with a low volume beep and strobe that someone was standing at the door.

As he put his hand over Cristal's mouth to wake her quietly he noticed the clock on the end table read 2:13. Hand signals ablaze, both were out of the bed naked, weapons in hand and stationed strategically just as the concussion of the door being blown hit. As the dust and smoke started to clear two men with silenced automatic weapons stepped through the door firing in the direction of the bed. They were dispatched instantly with single shots to the head from directions they were not expecting in the darkened room.

The smoke and shock from the blast had set off the hotel's fire alarms and within seconds the halls were filling with frightened guests trying to make their escape. David and Cristal took just enough time to grab the essentials, throw on some clothes and catch the last of the fleeing guests who had also dressed before exiting.

Bolting down three flights of stairs, they made it to a side street exit and quickly mixed with the rest of the crowd, all the time looking for the back-up team that would surely be watching for them.

David motioned towards an all-night coffee shop on an adjacent side street and with eyes darting all over the scene, they quietly made their way into the shop and headed for a rear table where they could survey the scene and gather their thoughts.

A few other guests of the hotel who probably had been through hotel alarms before, straggled into the coffee shop behind them for some heat and engaged the owner who wanted to know what was happening. Most of them were in pajamas and not looking like any threat to the two.

David spoke first, "Pretty clear that was gang number two. The BSB gang. Mercenaries for sure and pros. They were definitely not Jihadis. Looked to me like more locals like the guy at the airport. They were taking no chances and they were quick. Didn't take them long to find us either, even with the changes in ID at the hotel so we'll have to be careful. Either they got really lucky with pictures or they needed specialized resources and access to government systems to track us down that fast so I suspect MI6 is actively involved already."

Looking around he continued, "There has to be a back-up team around here somewhere who are probably figuring out right about now that things didn't go as planned so we'd better not hang around."

They exited through a side entrance away from the hotel and left their rental car where it was.

They grabbed a taxi a block away at a taxi stand and David told him to take them to The Hotel Tabitha on Elbe Strasse, a hotel David had once used for a similar purpose. The standard three series Mercedes cab whisked them through the near empty German streets and they were there within minutes.

David paid the driver and waited until he disappeared around the corner. Then he motioned to Cristal to follow him across the street to the equally tiny pension, the Hotel Aba.

As they approached the hotel he said "Sorry, nothing like your regular fare but this will do for tonight. I've stayed here before and taxi drivers can be found and bribed so I think we'll choose this one and keep an eye open for any visitors across the street at the Tabitha. An extra twenty Euros and the desk clerk here won't ask for our passports and of course with all the clubs around," he winked, "he will not question our lack of luggage either."

She simply smiled back at him.

They picked a room where they could see the street and settled in to the sparse accommodations which didn't provide nearly enough sound insulation from the rather loud late night festivities going on in the local bars.

Cristal spoke first, "You must have really pissed these guys off because they are pulling out all the stops to get to you before you can do whatever it is they think you're going to do. We've dispatched three of them in under twenty-four hours so they are rather upset at you, as you Brits would say."

David smiled, "I guess the issue is that I'm supposed to be dead and me turning up alive does a couple of things. One, it is unexplainable with the narrative they produced four years ago. Two, I might get back in the business of trying to gum up the works for them and three, they know I'll be trying to figure out who set me up so yeah, I would say that gives them good incentives to see that I do not remain breathing for long."

Cristal continued, "At least we got the important stuff and anything with ID on it out of that hotel room but I need to get some clothes and toiletries when the stores open."

"Yeah, we'll take care of that in the morning. I can see where we're going to need some pretty convincing disguises. We're in Europe and they are big on surveillance so most of the airports we might use are covered with cameras and facial recognition software was widespread even before they put me away.

"Given tonight's excitement I would rather make our stay in Germany a short one so here is the plan. I know a guy who can get me hooked up with some new ID's. I'm not comfortable with the packages Bill Carter is giving us after tonight. They may have a mole or someone who can get to these background setups we're getting. That could explain them waiting for us at the Frankfurt airport.

"Also, I don't think those two at the Westin just got lucky with a couple of photographs although in retrospect, the Westin was probably not the place we should have chosen to 'hide' as it were."

He took one more glance out the window at the hotel across the street and then sat down on the bed next to Cristal, "Here's the story I propose for Somalia. You are an auditor for an NGO doing performance and financial reviews on the NGO's operations in Africa. We'll pick a big one that operates widely so you won't be expected to be familiar with any of their in-country team. We can probably find one in Mogadishu that has played ball with the CIA before.

"I'll be a UN investigator doing needs assessments and reviews of UN operations in African countries. We'll travel separately when possible, never arriving or departing together and stay in different hotel rooms, adjoining if we can work that out. That should give us some freedom to move around and figure out the lay of the land. But again, disguises while we travel through areas possibly under surveillance will be critical. I think we may need several disguises in case they lock on to us. I want them to lose us as fast as they find us.

"That guy at the airport knew what to look for so I am guessing they have a picture of us together and you likely with blonde hair from somewhere in the US so I might have been either Pittsburgh or JFK airports but most likely the latter. Either those two tonight had that picture or more likely one of the four Hendrickson sent off. Either way disguises will definitely be needed, especially your hair."

Cristal nodded agreement as he continued, "Given we have a short fuse on this thing I think we have to be out of here quickly. As soon as we can get these ID's set up, we go straight to Somalia. We have to start there. It's the best guess of the experts as to where Khalil is based.

"We may not be able to get through his defensive screens there but we have to figure out his movements if we're going to get him and we must find that bomb. We'll start with whatever the local CIA team has in Mogadishu."

Cristal nodded, "You know I've been thinking. We are both out of practice and we should not have been caught so easily tonight. I'm not anxious for another close call and I am still fighting jet lag although I have to admit my adrenaline is now pumping and I don't think I can sleep right away. It's just after three. What say we do three on, three off for tonight and keep an eye on that hotel? I'll take the first shift."

"I'm with ya babe," he chuckled. "I think my life has been a bit more stressful than yours these past few years. Knowing you're likely to be waterboarded at any time of the day or night is designed to screw up your sleep cycle and tonight's fun was almost as intense as that. But I have found through necessity a way to compartmentalize stress so I can turn on sleep when needed.

"At least I felt some sense of control tonight with a gun in my hand. I'll freshen up and I bet you I'll be asleep before you can count to ten." He looked at his watch, "Wake me around six."

True to his word he was out like a light in mere seconds after he returned from the shower and Cristal was left to stand guard.

The night was peaceful as the noise level of the clubs slowly diminished and no cars showed up with assassins across the street. She had been to Germany only a few times in her career but she loved what she saw.

Germans knew how to have a good time. The food was great, especially any kind of pork. And it was not unusual for bars to clear out very late. But tonight was not a partying night for her and David. Her sentry duties gave Cristal time to put the last few days into perspective.

She had been kidnapped by Jihadis, threatened with amputations with a box cutter and then with decapitation, lost a husband to his first wife and presumably jail, re-discovered a lover, personally killed three men on two different continents and watched three other men die at the hands of the lover whom she had been prepared to kill, the handsome man who was sound asleep and breathing softly right in front of her.

Somehow, the previous week of producing news segments on Cincinnati's preparations for Thanksgiving, Christmas and the approaching winter stood in stark juxtaposition with her renewed career of international mayhem. Still her boss Harry Cote back at WKRC 12 and the rest of the gang were all very sweet people and they must be worried about her.

If only they knew the real Cristal and what she had been through in the last couple of days.

She reluctantly woke David a few minutes before six as the adrenalin had worn off, the jetlag was really hurting and she was struggling to keep awake.

The rest of the early morning passed without incident. He let her sleep until ten and then they made their way to a small nearby café and had a rather late, typical German breakfast of crusty rolls, cold cuts, cheese, hard boiled eggs and some delicious yet strong coffee.

Langley was six hours behind them so they got some shopping in for essentials and then they waited until 1 pm to call in to the DD when they got back to the room and had a better chance of not being overheard. He had just arrived at his office in Langley when he took the call. She held the receiver and David listened in on an earphone.

After her review of the previous night and the plans for infiltrating Mogadishu, Carter jumped in, "Well obviously I'm very happy to see that the two of you can still handle yourselves. I must say that I was aware of some of this because Interpol is looking for you."

Cristal blurted out, "Already?"

"Yeah. Apparently there was an explosion and some kind of shootout in a downtown hotel with lots of blood and shell casing left behind but no bodies and no evidence of the two guests Blanche and Will Burton from Chicago. And guess what? A quick check found that these two do not really exist but they have pictures of them from the passports you gave copies of to the desk clerk so apparently you might be spies and you might be dead but Interpol would really like to find you. Just read it in the morning briefing book. At least they have not connected you to Herr Hendrickson at the airport. I'm sure your faces are all over those airport security cameras and eventually they'll connect you both to the hotel pictures and figure you two as suspects at the airport."

"Wow that was fast on the hotel encounter," said David.

"Yeah they really hop to it when there's a chance of terrorism but even then I think this was too fast. Either the Germans are really efficient or someone is telling them to put a full court press on the investigation.

"The good news David is that the passport photo does not look too much like your file photo of four years ago so unless someone is looking specifically for you, the rest of MI6 is probably unlikely to ID you from your current passport photo. But whoever the threat is at MI6, he's likely connected to these attacks and as our theory goes, in cahoots with the BSB.

David suspected something, "How do you know what my passport photo looked like four years ago."

"You didn't think I was going to take your word on everything did you? We pulled what we have locally on your MI6 file to check a few things out so don't worry, we didn't flag MI6 on your resurrection.

"Anyway, I can see from the GPS locators in your phones that the Aba is your current hiding place. Good choice, I've used those small hotels myself in the distant past. A couple of Euros will buy some silence and anyone looking for you won't be able to hand out pictures in every tiny pension in the city. Interpol has not raised the alarm to the point that they are spreading your picture around. But they'll step up their search if they connect you to the airport so I would not hang around there too long.

"At the same time, someone else clearly IS likely to be using your photos.

"Now about them tracking you down. I'm pretty convinced there was no leak on this end. That pack of ID's was secret and only a couple of my direct reports knew whom they were for. We have kept this as 'eyes only' so I think you just got unlucky. Besides no one on this end has any issue with you so it's hard to see a leak here.

"I'll bet someone gave out pictures to staff at a few of the big hotels they thought you might use and bingo, some bellhop or concierge made a hundred Euros for making a call. You might want to spool up the disguises from here on in and any ID's we give you will have to be a little deeper than the last to keep folks like Interpol at bay.

"As to your plan for Somalia, I like it. We have a couple of sharp guys down there and we have good contacts in a couple of NGO's. Let me do some checking and see who has a set up that would work with your plan.

"I suggest you rely on me alone for this and dump David's connections. I know David you feel some loyalty and comfort with your own contacts but remember, they are pretty old, untested of late and of questionable loyalty. They could be working for the guys who are after you. After all, these guys didn't sit around waiting for you for four years. There is a limited market for their talents and it's quite possible they have alliances with people you would not like to meet. At least in dealing with me you only have one source of potential betrayal and not more if you contact these guys.

"Back on the subject of ID's, our contacts with the UN are not as universally cooperative as some of the NGO's but I think I can get you an ID that will work in most places you might want to go as a UN assessment officer. They are so bureaucratic over there that if someone reported an imposter it might take them weeks to do anything about it."

David spoke into Cristal's iPhone, "I understand the logic and I concur. We'll use your ID's but please double check the chain of command and look for anyone who might be ex. MI6 on your team. I still can't figure out how they knew we were arriving in Frankfurt. It had to be someone leaking something or they had a stroke of amazing luck and someone spotted Cristal and me at JFK getting on the plane to Frankfurt.

"Last night was definitely contractors of the type MI6 would use and not Jihadis. Besides I see no way the Jihadi network could have tracked us to Frankfurt. If we do run into any of them, it will be because we confronted them on their pitch.

"One last thing you need to look into. London has best-in-class video surveillance and facial recognition software. You may want to check if they have access to or may have hacked into the security cameras at JFK."

The DD frowned, "Now there's an ugly thought. I agree with your analysis of the situation so I'll do what I need to do on this end. Stay safe and we'll try to expedite the ID's in the next day or two but we want to make sure it's tied out completely with the NGO and the UN. We may only have one crack at your operation so we need to be quick but we need to be thorough as well.

"Somalia is not a place to enter half prepared. You're headed into a nasty place where everyone is suspicious of new arrivals so we don't want your cover blown the minute you get there. If you get killed on day one in Mogadishu we've just lost one of our better shots at getting him or the bomb or both. No disrespect intended.

"Remember we have other teams on this as well but so far no additional leads over the fact that it is nuclear material and Christmas is likely the target timeframe. Time is not our friend. If we do get anything, we'll make sure you know. "

At that he signed off and two were left staring at each other. Cristal was the first to speak, "Nice to know he doesn't want us to get killed.

She grabbed David's hand, "Well it looks like we're cooling our heels today and while I'm anxious to get on the case I for one am feeling much more rested now and I have the rest of the day off," she smiled and winked at him.

That was all the encouragement he needed and he jumped on her pushing her back on the not so comfortable cheap hotel bed.

Again it was love making like she had not experienced in years. Each time it felt new and better than the last and they took their time to enjoy each other. As they both lay there sated and the afternoon grew older she was thinking that if it wasn't for the urgency of their mission, this would seem almost like an amazing lover's secret getaway.

It was late afternoon and Cristal had fallen into a deep sleep when David rose, dressed and headed out on his own. The DD had been right about minimizing the number of people who knew of their whereabouts. The age and loyalty of some of his old contacts were suspect but there was one man he just had to see and he had been David's main reason for picking Frankfurt as a staging area.

Before leaving the hotel he checked the phone book in the lobby and found one of his friend's aliases still listed at the same address. He walked two blocks checking constantly for tails and then hailed a taxi. Fifteen minutes later he was dropped off two blocks from his old friend's flat. He advanced and doubled back twice but there were no signs of a tail.

He only had to wait a few minutes for someone to exit the locked building so that he could enter without ringing. Now he stood outside the penthouse door listening for any sounds from within. At that, the door opened and Franz Becker said, "If you really think you can sneak up on me like that then you don't have much respect for my security."

David smiled and entered as Franz followed him into the familiar living room, "David Crowe. Now there's a name I never thought I would ever say again. They killed you about four years ago but apparently you didn't get the memo."

Franz poured them both a glass from his collection of premium single malt scotches he was renowned for. David took the seat he had been so familiar with in years gone by, "Yeah for a long time they thought I was dead too but apparently I've awoken some old enemies and they've had a couple of cracks at me already. Oh, don't worry. I took the regular precautions coming here. I was not followed."

As Franz sat he handed the scotch to David, "I must say it's an unusual pleasure to see you still breathing but then again you were always more business than social so what brings you to my door."

"Well first let me compliment you on this scotch. I have been away from it for a while but this is first rate. What is it?"

"I would gladly tell you but I have been told recently that I am pronouncing the name incorrectly so it will have to remain a mystery. I will only tell you that I bought it at an outrageous price at an auction in Scotland, so enjoy it."

"Well OK then. So down to business. Let me tell you that anything you hear about me through your MI6 contacts is rubbish. That stuff four years ago was all a setup from within. Someone high up was running their own crooked Ops and I was getting too close. Lots of money changing hands."

David took a sip of the excellent scotch and looked Franz square in the eye. "My old friend, we did a lot of work together back then. If you have any respect for me you will tell me straight up if I can trust you. Should I have any reason to doubt your loyalty? In other words, in my absence have you formed any alliances that might be of a threatening nature to me?"

Franz smiled as he put his glass down on the modern glass end-table that separated them, "David if that had been the case and knowing your capabilities I would have shot through the door instead of welcoming you in. To answer you directly, I currently have no dealings with MI6 or anyone else that has you on their radar screen. Until a moment ago, I'm sure most of the world thought you were dead, I certainly did.

"I have operations with others that might come looking for you but your name has not and will not come up from me in any of those dealings. Satisfied?"

David smiled, "I thought I would be able to count on you. So let me get to the reason for my visit. I'm on a special assignment from the DD at the CIA."

Franz stiffened and raised his glass in a mocked salute, "You know I've not always been on the same side as the CIA David so I have the same question for you. Can I trust you?"

"Believe me Franz, you're not implicated in anything I'm doing. As far as I know, the CIA has no interest in you and no one knows I'm talking to you so I have no reason to put you in jeopardy and besides I need your willing assistance.

"Franz the reason I've come to you is that there's a bomb in play. Probably a dirty bomb and almost certainly headed for the US for a Christmas attack. As you might expect Al Qaeda is probably at the center of this and it is likely Khalil himself who is driving it. I need to get into Somalia with another agent, female, and get as close as I can to Khalil's organization to find this bomb."

Franz stared at him dead pan, took another sip of his drink and said, "Wow, all the way to the top after four years since I thought you had died in a car bomb. Impressive. A bomb, the DD of the CIA, the head of Al Qaeda, diving into the worst rats' nest on the planet and chasing the hardest guy to find on the planet as well. As they say in France 'Bonne chance mon ami!'

"I don't give you much chance of success, but of course I'll help in any way I can. How can I assist you?"

"I need to know everything you have on Khalil. I need you to review our plans and I need your help getting in there if that is something you can still do."

David went on to tell him of the NGO and UN cover story plans and ID's, and then waited for Franz to do his dump.

"Let me start with Khalil. Everything you have heard about him is true. He is intelligent, some might say insanely brilliant with some of his schemes. Most have him pegged as the most dangerous and sick man on the planet.

"He speaks at least Arabic, English and French. He is pathologically brutal, charismatic, a master of disguise and no one has a recent photo of him. The last one I saw was a poorly focused picture with him in the background almost 20 years ago when he was living in Detroit and going to Engineering school at some state college. Since about that time, it would seem that he has been very careful not to be photographed. The fact that he was doing well in Engineering school gives you some idea of his education and intelligence.

"The story is that he was four when his father took the family to Detroit from Yemen. He has two younger sisters, the youngest born in the US and he had an older brother whom he idolized.

"The father apparently was an old-time fundamental Islamist who today would likely be a Jihadist. He wanted a more stable life for his children than the nonsense that was going on in Sana'a and the rest of Yemen at the time but the culture change in the US was too much for him. By all accounts, the emigration turned out to be a bad move for the family.

"They say he raved all the time about the scum, infidels, bullies, and whores, in the US and was very loud about it. He saw America as lacking culture, dignity and morals. Of course, he was appalled at the women with their scanty clothes especially in the summer and what was on the TV every day was blasphemous as far as he was concerned. I'm sure he'd be shocked at what he saw in Germany today as well.

"Anyways, I've heard that he had a big effect on his son who learned English quickly but lived an insulated life under his father's roof and in a mostly Islamic enclave in Detroit where I'm told they promoted and enforced Sharia law under the very noses of the police."

He took another sip of the scotch, "When Khalil was about 20 and half-way through college his father and older brother were murdered in an apparent road rage incident in Detroit. No one knows the whole story about how the incident started but the end of it was that a man jumped out of his car at a red light, shot them both in the face as they sat in their car and disappeared.

"He eventually turned himself in and pleaded guilty to manslaughter saying they had threatened him first. He was a white American and he got probation.

"The defense and the press played it up that the immigrant, Khalil's father, had started the whole thing and was to blame for his own fate. Lots of stories came out about his racism and radical Islamist tendencies including the fact that one mosque had asked him to leave because he was a bad influence on the others.

"You have to understand this was shortly after 9/11 and Khalil was never able to get past what he saw as the injustice of America to his father and his beloved older brother.

"Add to that the teachings his father had subjected him to as he grew up and before graduation Khalil was off to Yemen at first, that being his place of birth, to join the Jihad.

"Initially he was a trophy jihadist. The latest American Jihadist who had turned on the Great Satan. His western engineering education, internet expertise and public profile helped him gain a reputation inside the organization and he moved quickly up the ladder.

"Oh by the way, the guy who killed his father was mysteriously murdered a couple of years later. The police immediately thought of Khalil because of all the noise he had made in the press around about the time of the trial but they could never find any evidence he was actually in the country at the time. If you ask me there's no doubt it was either him or someone close to him that did it.

"Whether he loved his father and his strict ways is not clear but he certainly bought the dogma of fundamental Islam and he definitely idolized his older brother who looks like an innocent victim in the road rage incident. So he started out with a deep seated hatred for America.

"No one knows much about him from then until now. All we know is that he has demonstrated he is a vicious Jihadist who seems invisible and is one of the most insanely dangerous people on the planet. He has personally done horrendous things to torture hostages, filmed himself doing decapitations and as we all know he's thought to be responsible for the majority of terrorist attacks in the world these days. Hundreds if not thousands of innocents have paid for his raging Jihad."

David spoke, "I knew some of that but thanks for filing in the blanks. Do you know anything about him that is more current."

"Well the western agencies seem to be convinced that he spends a lot of his time in Mogadishu where he likely has a significant security setup. Like some other terrorist leaders of the recent past he rarely sleeps in the same bed two nights in a row. He is possibly the best master of disguise in the business. There is a story that he picked up one of his own lieutenants at the airport driving a taxi. He was in disguise and the lieutenant didn't make him until they arrived at their destination and Khalil surprised him. There are more stories like that but the bottom line is that he could be anyone. No one knows what to look for. If and when they catch him or kill him we will all be waiting for the DNA test because as of today, that will be the only way to ID him."

David sat forward in his chair, "There is a rumor that he travels outside of Somali frequently. Maybe to funding sources or even to witness or participate in attacks."

"I've heard no such rumor about funding trips but it would not surprise me. Occasionally you'll hear rumors that he was there when this or that attack took place but I've heard of no reliable sightings of him in that regard. With his ability to disguise himself, it's quite possible he was there but impossible to verify.

"As I said, in times gone by before he was at the top of the most wanted list he set the gold standard for personal brutality. The guy must be criminally insane for the things he did in the name of his God. But of late he seems more interested in not being caught so he tends to direct things from afar.

"Like a lot of these big mouthed terrorists I don't think you will see him personally wearing a suicide vest. They tend to leave that for the younger more gullible ones. But yes, I can see him in the background at attacks just to be able to claim he was there.

"There is a general consensus that he has access to excellent forged paperwork. My sources think it might be one of his lieutenants and rumored to be his successor Mustafa Habib, who has a network that provides the forged docs.

"So yes it's quite possible that he travels internationally with impunity but it could all be bluster as well. No one really knows and that's his greatest talent. Remaining unknown and unknowable. If the intelligence community ever actually tracked him down they wouldn't know if it was him. Hell they may have had him in custody already and not known it. You may be too young to remember the stories about Carlos the Jackal, but Khalil is today's version of that very phantom."

Franz got up and went to the window, looking down from his penthouse window for any signs of trouble, "Now as to your plan for using an NGO and the UN as cover let me tell you that the terrorists think they are all spies. Al Qaeda is pretty sure that is how the CIA and MI6 and others get their agents into hostile countries.

"Them and the international press who they think are all spies too, and some of them are. So the good news is that it works but the warning is that they are on the lookout and the paperwork better be good. They will do what they can to check out any false ID's so you better have a real address and a real wife and kids somewhere who will verify that you work for said NGO."

He came back and sat across from David, "As to transport, I think I can help there. You don't want to fly directly into Mogadishu. Enter through Kenya. Nairobi International. Too much attention and too many spies looking for anything odd at the International Airport in Mogadishu.

"I would suggest flying a small plane into Wanlaway airstrip which is about 50 miles north of Mogadishu and driving into town with someone I will provide who can get you through any checkpoints either by saying the right words or paying the right bribes. I have done it myself and my guy is good. The whole area is still a checkerboard of zones controlled by government forces or Al Shabaab or even some of the old warlords so you absolutely need my guide and good docs.

"At the moment no one is trying to kill NGO staff or UN assessors but kidnapping is not out of the question. My guy can avoid most of the pitfalls but be on your guard. If you do have to confront anyone, hide the bodies and don't let them get tied back to you or it will be a lot longer than four years before we see each other again."

Before leaving David and Franz exchanged secure and anonymous e-mail addresses where they could communicate the details of the Somalia insertion. Franz offered to front all the costs if David would deposit money within a day in a numbered account he would provide in the e-mail. He promised to have the details to him for the travel within a few hours.

When he got back to the hotel, he gave Cristal a big hug and a long kiss. He knew he had some explaining to do.

"I know the DD doesn't want me to use my old contacts but there was one I just had to connect with and now I have a safe way into Somalia and a local contact down there who sounds like he may be a big help. One thing my friend insisted on was comprehensive IDs. Our IDs must bear some pretty deep scrutiny so we need the whole package."

Cristal nodded, "I had the same thought when we were so easily found before, so I sent Bill Carter a secure e-mail and reminded him we needed the full workup, back stories, the lot."

David smiled, "Good, well I'm starving let's go see what Germany has to offer tonight. After that I'll take you shopping for some new clothes and luggage."

***

Jack Hammond was really on edge waiting for news from Germany. Crowe had killed one man at the airport. The agent had been instructed to follow the pair so Hammond would have time to find out more about the woman and set up a proper hit. Somehow Kurt's man had ended up tangling with Crowe and lost his life so now David was aware someone was after him.

He had been expecting an update from Kurt in Frankfurt but there had been nothing so far. He had just reached his office at MI6 when his private line rang, "Hello."

"Sir did you receive your copy of the Daily Mirror today?"

"How did you get this number. This is a government office. Remove this number from your database immediately," and he hung up.

A few minutes later he left his office telling his assistant that he needed a caffeine fix and would be back in fifteen. Hurrying downstairs and out on to the street, he entered the Vauxhall Tube station next to MI6 Headquarters and headed for the corner shop on the upper level.

Taking out his disposable phone he had modified with encryption, he dialed a German number he had memorized, "That was a bit risky calling me at the office. What news do you have for me? Did you find them?" He said looking around to ensure he could not be overheard.

Kurt Willems had a slight German accent, "Yeah, we found them. They got my two best men last night and then disappeared. That makes three in one day and I've lost track of the targets. You are going to have to help me track them down and I'm running short of resources now so you had better come up with some reinforcements and a contingency plan because I'm not tangling with this pair myself."

He had been afraid of this. He had seen the Interpol report of two American's being involved in a shootout at the Westin in Frankfurt but he had hoped Kurt would be delivering good news that they had taken care of them.

Furious, Hammond thought for a moment, "Let me get back to you. I may have to bring the organization in on this before he does any damage. You'll be paid ten percent of what we agreed just to cover your costs and because I want to maintain our relationship unless of course you can finish the assignment. You need to know that I'm not happy about this. I need people who can deliver as promised."

Kurt himself was now furious, "Yeah, well you didn't tell me this guy would be a pro. He wiped out most of my goddamned German team. I'll continue to try to complete the mission but I would be more effective if you could use some of your resources to track him."

"We'll see." Was all he said, hung up and looked around again to see if he had drawn any attention. He was pleased to see that the hall was filled with busy commuters rushing to their jobs and paying no attention to him.

"Shit." He thought to himself. "I don't need this."

He didn't want to raise the alarm in MI6 that a rogue agent who was supposed to have been disposed of four years ago was on the loose again. He didn't need this grief or the risk that certain things might lead back to him.

He had known Crowe, but not well for several years at MI6 and they were not overly friendly. He always thought Commander David Crowe threw his weight around a little too much, as if field agents were the cream of the crop in MI6 and the only people that mattered.

Crowe had become a real problem four years ago when Hammond realized he was asking all the wrong questions and closing in on his secret little organization. He thought then that the matter was resolved and his team had taken care of him.

He knew Crowe could handle himself but he had always thought his team in the Sudan had just gotten sloppy and taken themselves out along with him but clearly Crowe had turned the tables on them and escaped that attempt and now had escaped three trained assassins in Frankfurt. This guy was more than a handful and he had to be taken care of fast.

His greatest fear was that Crowe would show up at MI6 or get to one of his old contacts and convince them that he was innocent. If he could be successful at that then it might start an internal investigation of why he was targeted in the first place and were there any other potential culprits for the corruption that had been uncovered. Eventually it would lead to Hammond's own desk. That was not going to happen.

As it stood now, he was relatively certain that Crowe had not figured out who was at the top of the scheme, but still, he had to be eliminated before this whole thing unraveled.

Not long after Crowe's reported death, Hammond had replaced his two dead contractors and reconstituted his network. Their scheme was back in full force with new players and a different Ops strategy assisting the 'gang' of international enforcers.

Whom the 'gang' was enforcing for had never been disclosed and he was not about to get too nosey. They were only referred to by his contact as 'the cartel'.

His role was to facilitate and complement the limited number of contractors the 'gang' had of their own. There were only a few internal to MI6 on the team but they had a fairly broad network of mercenaries such as Kurt Willems' organization, at their disposal.

Hammond knew he was really only a middleman and a resource who sometimes did the cartel's dirty work under the direction of his contact and other times directed some of the network as he was doing now with Kurt. The important point was that he was becoming a rather rich partner in schemes that he only knew parts of.

Still others inside MI6 had some inkling that something was still amiss, possibly corruption similar to what David Crowe seemingly had pulled off four years ago.

But if he was dead, why was there still a comparable level of corruption and could MI6 still be involved?

Apart from shielding his 'off-the-books' organization from current inquiries about corruption there was no question he had to eliminate Crowe, who would certainly be interested in hunting down Hammond's team and eliminating all of them.

Bringing MI6 into the hunt for Crowe now might be asking for too many problems so he decided he would have to stay within his own tiny network for the moment but be ready to spring some new fictitious story on MI6 if things got further out of hand. He was going to have to find a way to support Kurt in picking up the trail of Crowe again. What he needed was a dim-witted pawn and he had a feeling he knew just the 'boy' for the job.

Somalia

Khalil was becoming impatient with Mustafa. For the last few days, all he could seem to focus on was his brother and the two CIA types that had trapped his brother and must have escaped from Pittsburgh. There was still no news on Mustafa's brother or the others who were certainly either dead or being tortured by the CIA.

Khalil didn't really care what had happened to Abu Nistal or the woman. He wanted them dead but they were not his current priority. Now Mustafa was demanding more of Khalil's time on the matter.

"Master, I need your help to find these two CIA criminals. They have completely disappeared and Allah demands retribution."

"Who are you to say what Allah demands? I remind you that we have a very important mission to complete. This will be bigger than 9/11 and I need your full attention on the planning and execution of our objectives.

"These two will eventually surface and I guarantee you we'll settle your vendetta against them at the proper time BUT Mustafa, Hear me! All our network, all of our people, all Islam is depending on us to strike the devil at his heart. You must put aside this obsession with Abu Nistal or Daniel Boone or whatever his name is and his CIA whore for the good of the cause.

"Have you forgotten our mission? Do you no longer see the infidels and the Great Satan to be our primary focus? They have attacked Islam for generations. Their crusades once swept the land just as they are doing again. They have infiltrated and gained power in every Islamic land. They must be driven out. Their customs, their laws and their godlessness are abhorrent to all good Muslims. Their international media and their blasphemous films are spreading a plague throughout the world.

"They twist the minds of our youth with their phony promise of democracy, their rule of manmade laws and all their other platitudes. All the time stealing and rigging elections, with no regard for the religious leadership who represents God's will and God's laws. They write laws that can be easily twisted to benefit only the chosen few in their schemes."

Mustafa hesitated for only a moment and then realized it was futile to push what was surely more important to him than Khalil. He finally nodded, "Yes master. You are of course right. You have my complete attention."

"Fine, now here is what I want you to do. It's much easier for you to move around than me. I want you to go to the port and see our people. Tell me first hand if the ship is in the water, being loaded and ready to sail. It's very important that it does not sail before we have the weapons loaded. I'm told they are nearing completion of the weapons' packaging and loading, so they should be ready to install tonight or tomorrow night under cover of darkness.

"The ship must not leave before we are completed and it cannot be delayed if it is to get to its target a few days before December 25th so that our people can retrieve the weapons and deploy them in time. The timing on this is all critical so there can be no mistakes. Bribe whomever you must or use any other means to make sure that ship leaves at the right time. Insha'Allah.

"Now Mustafa, no one else knows this but I must attend this attack myself. I've promised our friends who support us that I will be personally directing this attack. It's too big and complex to be left to people who've never executed an attack before. They don't want to spend all of this money and effort, putting themselves at risk, without some personal guaranty of success. They don't want another Times Square bomber, shoe bomber, underwear bomber or the disaster of those non-exploding Philadelphia train bombs last year.

"Also, if we're to leverage this for future support I want to be able to say to our supporters that I personally oversaw the planning and execution of this attack.

"I'll be leaving for the US soon at great risk to myself. It will take me some time to travel there through other countries so that my passage cannot be tracked back to Somalia. I'll fly to New York from Istanbul just before the attack so the weapons must be delivered just before I get there. Timing is critical. The boat must leave so that it has enough time to compensate for any bad weather en route."

"Master, are you sure you want to take that risk. If you're caught you could destroy not only this operation but our entire network. Think of the public relations disaster if you're caught."

"I've taken precautions. I won't be taken alive and if I should be martyred I'm leaving written instructions that you are to be my replacement."

Mustafa almost blushed at this last remark. He knew most considered him to be the number two in the organization but to have it said out loud and by the master himself was new. Suddenly he thought of the tremendous responsibility if it was ever to come to pass that he was the leader of their worldwide organization.

"Don't worry master, I'll stay on this operation and ensure that ship gets loaded properly and sails on time. And I'll follow its every progress as much as possible without jeopardizing our communication paths. You have nothing to worry about.

"Please master Khalil, spend your time double checking all of your plans for New York and be careful. We need you leading this organization. It is through your steadfast leadership that we've accomplished so much."

At that he rose and hurried out of the small bedroom Khalil had seconded from another of their supporters.

***

Cristal and David finished dinner and did a quick swing through a nearby shopping district to collect what they needed in luggage, wardrobe and disguises. It was late when they finally got back to their econo hotel. Both circled the block in opposite directions watching for anything suspicious but it looked like they had yet to be discovered.

David explained to the desk clerk with the aid of fifty Euros that they didn't like their room and asked for another also facing the street. In an abundance of caution and just in case their room had been discovered and bugged, they moved their possessions to the new room. Realizing the hotel was mostly vacant and the soundproofing between rooms acceptable, they made their check-in call to the DD.

Cristal started, "How are the ID's coming?"

"We should have them to you late tonight our time or more likely early morning your time. If there are any issues and I'm not available, contact Phil Harris. He's my go-to guy on this file and he has been doing most of the leg work so he's completely up to date on what we've been doing. Other than Phil, there are only one or two others that have any detail on this operation.

"I've tied out both of your cover stories. David, as agreed you're a UN needs assessment official doing a tour of all UN affiliated NGO's which ties you to Cristal. Cristal you're an internal auditor for Oxfam America on loan to Oxfam International to look at the effectiveness of their operations in Mogadishu. Both organizations have operations in the same building in Mogadishu and the leaders of those organizations will assist you and not get in your way.

"They've been amply rewarded and are American patriots who only know you're on an important assignment which has implications for the safety of America.

"Now about transportation and a local contact."

David interrupted, "Ah Bill, I know we agreed to use your folks but I do have one very trustworthy person in Frankfurt and that is why I chose this as a staging area. I've met with him and checked him out and have confidence in him.

"He will provide us a contact to pick us up at an airstrip north of Mogadishu and show us around the city as well as help us where he can to start our search. He knows the ropes and can get us around any obstacles. We just need a plane to Nairobi and then my friend has chartered a small plane to get us to the airstrip.

"According to him, entering through the Mogadishu International airport could be problematic as various groups would have people there and possibly even looking for us. "

There was a long pause on the other end of the phone and then the DD spoke, "So I guess I can cancel the airlift off the carrier to the nuclear sub and the insertion team from Seal Team 6."

Cristal and David stared incredulously at each other.

Cristal finally broke the silence, "Are you serious?"

"Damned right I am. We are talking about a dirty bomb headed to the US in the next few weeks. But come to think of it, I like your plan better. It's probably faster and easier on the logistics and I like simple.

David interrupted, "And I'll bet you it's cheaper too. I'll need $25,000 wired into a numbered account when I get it to cover the private plane and some other logistics."

The DD smiled, "A lot cheaper than a carrier, a couple of Ospreys a nuclear sub and international transport for a Seal team for sure."

"Ok, then it's settled, you two get out of Dodge and on your way as quick as you can right after you get the care package which by the way will be in locker A12 at the main Zugbahnhof just to the east of you."

David whispered, "Train station" to Cristal.

She whispered back, "I knew that!"

The DD was still talking, "The key will be dropped off by an agent and held at the front desk of the Aba as soon as everything is in place. The agent does not know who you are or what you're doing. Make sure when you get it that the tamper proof envelope has not been opened.

"Got to go now, I have dozens of operations on the go to try to track down this bomb. I still think you guys might be the dark horse that pulls it off though.

Remember Phil Harris. Just call this number. He'll pick up if I'm not available."

He signed off and the two were left in a silent room STILL waiting for pieces to be delivered to start their operation.

"I hate this,' said David. We're supposed to be finding a bomb in Somalia and instead we're cooling our heels in Frankfurt. This is taking too long. This is no way to run an operation. We've got to get out of here!"

Cristal nodded agreement but neither of them could think of a way to speed up the insertion without messing it up.

**

Jack Hammond at MI6 had decided what to do. He called in one of his newest, sharpest, youngest and most gullible analysts and closed the door.

"OK James, I am seconding you into an important mission. You and I are now on a two-man mission called 'Lunch Break'.

James smiled.

Hammond cut him off, "I'm not joking, Lunch Break.

"As you may have heard rumors, there is substantial corruption still going on with international funding in Africa. There is some thinking it might have ties to MI6 and you and I are going to start an internal investigation ourselves. This is Eyes Only for you and me. There may be an internal mole and it could be you!"

James looked terrified and started to protest but Hammond cut him off again, smiling, "I'm quite sure it's not you or I wouldn't have put you on my team. But if anything goes south or you're caught in any of the tasks

I give you or if you divulge any of this, you WILL be seen to be assisting an internal mole and I'll ensure you are tried for treason. Do I make myself clear?"

The young analyst was visibly shaken as he nodded his head. Half of him was thinking 'big break' working with a heavyweight in the organization while the other half was thinking of failure or trial for treason.

"OK, here's a picture of two people photographed in New York two days ago. And here are a couple of additional pictures as they arrived in Frankfurt. We have reason to believe they are currently still in Frankfurt. We also have reason to believe that they are pros if you know what I mean. I need you to get every surveillance video you can get your hands on which shows places we normally look for these types; security lineups at the airport, Embassy entrances, known agents' abodes, weapons handlers, known friendly banks, forgers, informants, contractors, etc.

"Start the search as of midnight night before last. Find them for me and don't go home until you have. Do you understand the task?"

"Yes sir. I'll do my best but understand I can only look at some of these sources at double or triple speed if I'm going to ID someone. So six hours of video from the airport security lines will take me two or three hours to view. Some other sources will be much faster. I could use some help."

"Understood but no help. This has to be kept between the two of us because of the potential mole I mentioned.

"Do your best. I have others working on other angles. It's very important that we find one or both of these characters. They've murdered multiple friends of the organization in the last forty-eight hours. Now you see the urgency.

"So as not to be interrupted I want you to use my servers and workstations in here so transfer anything you need and get working. I've already approved access for you to all video available to us from Frankfurt."

James was staring at the pictures from the airport and thinking these two didn't look particularly dangerous when he realized Jack Hammond seemed to be waiting for an answer, "Got it. Where will you be sir?"

"I'll be in and out and if I need a desk I'll use your cubical. Call my cell if you need me. Remember don't answer questions from anyone about this. Just say you're doing something critical and 'eyes only' for me."

It was mid afternoon by now and Jack Hammond decided to work from home while James did his work.

It seemed like only a couple of hours later when James rang, "Sir I have your guy on a video. We have him on a hidden camera entering a building at about 5 pm local time today at the residence of a known operator and Intel source that we have under persistent surveillance, Franz Becker."

Hammond knew Becker and the hair went up on the back of Hammond's neck, "Thank you James. That's all I needed. Take the rest of the day off." He looked at his watch and it was already 7:30 pm. "Remember, eyes only. You've done a good job. Go back to your normal posting in the morning. Good night."

Five minutes later Hammond was down the street two city blocks and lifted his disposable encrypted phone to call Kurt Willems in Frankfurt.

He skipped the pleasantries and went directly to the point, "Do you know Franz Becker?"

"Yes. I don't know him well but I know of him and I know where he lives."

"Get over there, he had a visitor a few hours ago. The one you're looking for. Find out where he is and where he's going and don't leave any loose ends." He hung up briskly and headed home.

***

From the street Kurt could tell immediately that Franz was not home as the all glass penthouse was in complete darkness. He reasoned the man was out for a late dinner and decided that the best way to get to him would be to ambush him in his own hallway as his apartment likely had a sophisticated security system.

He didn't have to wait long. Having entered the building as another resident left, he was hiding just off the elevator in a portico for an electrical room. Fifteen minutes later as the elevator doors opened on the penthouse level, he had a silenced gun behind Franz's ear before the man knew there was anyone there, "Why don't you invite me in for a drink."

Franz half turned slowly and ID'd his assailant. A man he had not seen in a few years but a pro who could handle himself. A struggle in the hallway with him holding the gun was out of the question.

"I could use an after dinner drink," he said calmly moving forward towards the door with keys in hand.

As they entered, Kurt frisked Franz and made sure to place him in a dining room chair in the middle of the floor far away from any potential hiding places for weapons. Keeping his weapon fixed on Franz's chest he pulled out another chair and sat about four feet away facing the man, "So you had a visit from an old colleague earlier this evening."

Franz hesitated and seeing no point in denying it said, "Yes it was a pleasant surprise to see David."

"Good I appreciate dealing with a professional. There is no point in lying when I already know he was here. Now for the tough part. Where is he now?"

"I don't know. We didn't discuss where he was staying in Frankfurt. We only exchanged e-mail addresses so I don't even know how to contact him apart from e-mail."

"Now that's a problem for you and me. You see I need to find him and I know that threatening you or hurting you will take time and might not do the job so there is only one somewhat distasteful path left open to me. Does your daughter Nicola still live at 425 de l'Eglise in Paris?"

Kurt Willems had done his homework. Few people even knew Franz had a daughter for this very reason. This one did.

Franz stiffened as the much larger Kurt continued, "Now I don't want to go to Paris to pay her a visit and I don't think you want me going there either so just tell me how I can find David Crowe."

Franz swallowed hard. It was most likely over for him because he could always warn David by e-mail if he was left alive. This was the kind of end he had always thought might come his way. Just not tonight. He wondered if the bullet would hurt.

If this Kurt Willems, who Franz barely knew, was what he seemed, an old hangover from the cold war days, and got what he was looking for then there would be no reason to draw Nicola into this. After staring Kurt down for what seemed like forever and eliminating all other scenarios to save himself, he spoke, "As I said I don't know where he is but his plan is to travel to Somalia through Nairobi in the next few days. That is all I can give you so please promise me you will leave Nicola alone."

Kurt returned the stare looking for any sign of deceit. What he saw there was simple fear for his daughter and resignation to his fate.

He wondered if there were any other questions he needed to ask and finally decided he likely had all this man knew about David.

He said, "As one professional to another, thank you," as the silenced gun came up quickly and put a small hole in Franz's forehead and brain matter all over the back of the white leather couch and glass tables ten feet away in the living room.

It had been swift and except for the expectation, painless he assumed. Professionalism was to be honored. Franz had known there was no reason to lie and every reason to protect his daughter. Kurt waited until there was no pulse, walked over to the tiny wet bar and poured himself a premium single malt scotch from Franz's impressive collection. He had to hand it to the guy, the rumors had been true, it was an impressive collection, some of which Kurt had never seen before.

Minutes later he sat in his car one block away and looked up a number he had not used recently, "It's Kurt. I have a job for you. Regular rate plus premium. I'm sending you by e-mail pictures of two people who will arrive in the next few days. You need to meet every plane arriving by connection from Frankfurt. You know what to do."

***

It was early evening when Mustafa found Khalil in yet another safe house. This was a new one they had never used before.

"Master I have great news. The ship sailed last evening and everything is in order. Allahu Akbar."

Khalil looked him over and then responded, " Alhamdu lillāh. That is truly wonderful news. We are on schedule to deliver a message to the Great Satan on one of their most important religious holidays when our targets will be full of infidels, Insha'Allah."

Yet Mustafa could sense that there was something bothering him, "Are you worried about something, master?"

Khalil hesitated, "You've done a wonderful job managing this operation and your part in it's now complete so I feel we can now discuss a distressing matter."

Mustafa was wary, "Go on master."

"You didn't tell me about your brother's operation in America. I had no warning from you of either the kidnapping or the bombing attempt of the shopping mall."

"Master, to be clear I knew something of the kidnapping plot but I didn't know about the bombing."

Khalil motioned to him to sit down, "Still every campaign we fail at emboldens our enemies and not only that, this blatant and poorly thought out operation in America has undoubtedly raised their threat level just when we're planning our biggest operation ever. Jabir's initiatives have made it much more risky to launch this operation and jeopardized its success. The Americans will be on high alert going into their Christmas. I cannot fathom why you would hide this from me."

Mustafa was visibly blushing behind his full beard, "Master there was no attempt at deceiving or hiding information from you. You and I were very preoccupied with acquiring the weapon and I saw my brother's mission as one localized to the Burundi group.

"You will remember that before and after Daniel Boone, their small group was very ineffective. Abu Nistal's leadership made them one of our strongest cells. They achieved much a few years ago when they had Abu Nistal leading them. I'm still shocked that he has turned out to be a traitor.

"It was predictable that they would want to rescue him and it was a very bold campaign to get the Americans to release a prisoner from Guantanamo. Something no one else has attempted and now we know it can be done. We had told them to run their own operations as well.

"I knew little of their plan but what I did know looked achievable. They had an excellent insertion and escape plan and we can still use that hole in their defenses.

"If the whole plan had worked, and remember the prisoner swap worked, we could publicize it as a direct and successful attack on Guantanamo. If the Americans refused to make a deal then he would have killed a CIA agent on US soil and broadcasted it to the world."

Khalil interrupted, "You say it worked but you forget that they still have not announced a terrorist on the loose even though we believe the two are free. They released another CIA agent. That is why there has been no announcement. And yet now we have the worst of both worlds. We have lost four of the best of our Burundi cell and two from our Pittsburgh cell.

"Insha'Allah they are all dead martyrs but if any of them are in CIA custody then we have jeopardized much. I only heard about the operation once it was launched in America and not from you."

Mustafa was floored, "How did you know of this operation then?"

"I have always had my own undercover contacts in America, especially in the Pittsburgh cell. One of our missing fighters is my cousin. We grew up together as young men in Detroit. He was the one who provided some of the inside information and made contacts for our upcoming attack.

"Luckily he only knew the date of the attack and not the target or the weapon. So if he has been caught, the Americans likely know a major attack is coming on Christmas.

"Now you see why I'm so upset. I would never have approved this operation or his involvement if I had known they would also try a bombing. The prisoner swap likely would not have raised the threat level because they had to keep it secret."

Mustafa was thunderstruck. His silence may have jeopardized the entire operation.

Khalil spoke again, "So you see my good friend, your silence has a major cost to us. I've grown to rely on your professionalism and council. We will mark this one up as an unforeseen complication but please Mustafa do not let me down again."

Mustafa was speechless. He had never been spoken to in this tone of voice from Khalil. Clearly the master was angry and likely nervous about his upcoming trip. After a long pause, he gently bowed to the master and left quietly.

***

By the next morning David and Cristal had retrieved the 'care package' from the train station locker and were familiarizing themselves with their cover stories. She was Virginia Cummings of Oxfam America out of Washington and he was Victor Brookes of UN HQ in New York.

"Cristal laughed as she read the info packet. So now you are who? Is it Victor Brookes or David Crowe or Daniel Boone or Abu Nistal?"

David smiled, "Well it depends on whom I am with. With you I'm David Crowe. But when you think of it this is a unique opportunity. Which of these four men would you like to sleep with tonight, Cherie?" he said, mocking a French accent.

She laughed and went back to studying her new identity.

They had picked the most direct route. Their trip would take them out of Frankfurt early the next morning through Amsterdam to Nairobi and then a small private jet in the evening into Somalia.

As a habit David had left the TV on without sound watching the local news channel as he checked all of his varied e-mail addresses and true to form there was the e-mail with the Somali contact and private plane details from Franz mailed shortly after they had parted.

As he read it, his eyes were drawn to the TV across the room where the name Franz Becker was crawling across the screen. He grabbed the remote and turned up the sound just in time to catch a few words in German and pictures of medics removing a body from a familiar building.

Cristal had seen the quick move on his part and put two and two together, "Let me guess. He was your contact in Frankfurt."

David hit mute on the TV which had now moved on to other news and turn slowly to her, "Yes. An old acquaintance.

"Best guess is that his house was under some kind of surveillance that I didn't see and they got to him. The good news is that he didn't know where we were hiding in Frankfurt. The bad news is that he knew where we were going. They may even have the itinerary from his computer so we'll have to be alert.

"They must have had something on him to threaten him and get him to talk. Sadly, the only threat he posed to them was telling me that they were back on my tail. Now we know anyways."

He thought for a second and then continued, "Even if they don't have our itinerary, we have to assume he had to tell them something and they know where we're going and we won't be driving there so they'll have the airports staked out. They can't stake out every airport for every connection but for sure there will be a team at Frankfurt and Nairobi. Our flight is one of the shortest available tomorrow morning. It's just under 12 hours through Schiphol so I think we'll be OK in Amsterdam but we need to be in full disguise in the public areas of the other airports. Our cover stories and passports don't allow for elaborate disguises so we'll have to wing that part of it somehow."

They set about building a plan to get to Somalia without getting picked up by the inevitable BSB gang on the lookout for them.

***

Jack Hammond was furious. MI6 was all abuzz with the fact that a frequent MI6 informant had been taken out in Frankfurt. It was apparently all over the German news. If David Crowe was still in the area and had seen the reports then he too would know they were on to him again. He gave his assistant the regular ruse and headed off to the tube station.

"What were you thinking you mindless idiot. Did I not say do not leave any loose ends?"

"I didn't." was all Kurt Willems could come up with.

"You didn't think the police would find the body and put it on the news. You should have ensured he could not be found. Now Crowe probably knows we're on to him."

"Well he's not in Frankfurt for long and I know where he is going and I have already set up intercepts at Frankfurt and Nairobi. So I'm still on track to eliminate the two of them."

Hammond thought about this for a moment. Why was he going to Nairobi? Before he could ask he got the answer.

"They're on their way to Somalia. God knows why. But I'll get them before they get there."

Somalia? Was he working for the Americans and going after the head of Al Qaeda? But why? Then he remembered that David's mission wasn't his primary concern right now. Still furious with this numb skull of a contractor he said, "Please tell me you at least got the computer out of that penthouse before you left."

"You never asked for his computer."

"Wonderful! Listen, I'll tell you two things. They are likely to be disguised now that you have telegraphed our pursuit and two, please show me that you're not the biggest idiot on the planet and get this guy before he gets to Somalia where we have zero chance of getting him." At that, he hung up and headed back to the office furious.

Five minutes later James was in his office.

"James I'm afraid we have a problem."

"Yes I know. That Franz guy I found last night was killed."

"Yes. Apparently, those two we were tracking got to him before we did. I really wanted to save him but we were too late. You didn't tell anyone did you?"

"Me? What? You're asking me if I told anyone about this Franz guy? Of course not. I'm not a field person. I don't even know the man. Whom would I tell? I dropped everything like you told me," said James visibly shaking from the accusation.

"OK. Now listen carefully James. Because you found that assassin guy through Franz and he's now dead, you may be considered an accessory to a murder before the fact or at least a co-conspirator and Britain still maintains extradition rights with Germany. You and I both know you didn't do anything wrong but it's imperative that you NEVER mention any of what we did yesterday to ANYONE, EVER. We are the only two who know about this and you have to take this to the grave if you want to remain a free man. Do I make myself clear?"

James looked like he was about to cry, "Yes, Never to Anyone. Thank you, sir."

Jack waved him out of his office and he was gone.

***

David and Cristal left it late to get to the airport. There was no sense in hanging around longer than necessary for someone to recognize them. Still with her niqab covering her hair and a pair of dark shades and loose fitting Arab style clothes and David's overweight Scotsman's disguise with full beard, longish wig, slouching posture and jaggy bunnet they would be hard to pick out traveling apart.

Although David had never seen Kurt Willems, he spotted him immediately as he entered the concourse. The big man was on an upper level, standing hard up against a pillar, sans luggage and highly focused on the entry for KLM flights. David reasoned he would be here all day moving to different positions as varying flights from different airlines were scheduled that could connect through to Nairobi.

While not making anything close to eye contact he was pretty sure that his heavyweight disguise had worked as the hit man made no move when David walked under him on the lower level.

David assumed Cristal presented as big a challenge with her disguise.

There was something about Kurt Willem's look and demeanor that made David think he was likely the local ring leader. The man in charge of the three people they had dispatched since landing in Frankfurt just over three days ago and given that his team was small and he was doing his own surveillance then he was likely the guy who had killed his friend Franz Becker.

In the old days, that would have been enough for him to circle upstairs behind the man and take him out but for the moment any action like that was not on the critical path to finding the bomb and could only serve to complicate matters. He made a mental note to find out who the guy was and take care of him at some point.

Out of the corner of his eye he saw the man look away and he took the opportunity to get a really good look at him and freeze his face in memory.

Being a short hop within the EU and both of them carrying Schengen Visas they made it through the fast security check and used the facilities beyond the check point to change into clothes that better fit their cover stories which would be needed at passport check exiting The Netherlands and immigration in Kenya. Because Germany and The Netherlands were both EU, detailed passport checks might only happen on boarding the plane so getting out of the disguises was critical.

Both flights were uneventful but just for safety David and Cristal sat far apart whether on the planes or in the waiting area at Schiphol.

The changing appearance process was reversed in the restrooms after they exited immigration to collect their luggage in Nairobi at the Jomo Kenyatta International Airport.

After collecting their bags and wearing their disguises they picked up their waiting weapons, this time from the men's room and they headed separately for the same exit.

Again it was Cristal who noticed the assassin at a newsstand taking a keen interest in David who was about ten people ahead of her. It was clear to her that he had ID'd David so things looked like they were about to get busy. She felt in her pocket for her weapon so she could retrieve it quickly.

Surprisingly, he made no effort to follow David. As she drew closer, she was shocked to see what seemed to be a tiny smile go across his face and it seemed to her a nod of appreciation in David's direction.

As she caught up with David at the taxi stand she watched the exit and whispered what she had seen.

"Yeah I saw him too. I forget his full name. Jason something. I think he used to be and maybe still is CIA. Surprised your paths never crossed when you worked in Africa. Maybe Bill Carter sent him or maybe the BSB or the MI6 connection hired him by mistake. Either way I'm pretty sure he's on our side and I noticed he didn't attempt to follow us."

"Apparently my disguise is not as good as I expected at least with someone who has seen me before."

As David entered the taxi, he handed the surprised driver sixty dollars American and directed him to the cargo terminal for the private plane they were expecting. The trip was only a short hop on the airport grounds so the taxi driver was very happy to get a major fare and get back in line at the arrivals area.

Everything was in order and the tiny private jet had them airborne in minutes. As they crossed the Somali border the jet dropped down to a perilous altitude. "We are not landing at an official airport with customs and immigration so it's best not to announce our presence," the pilot explained.

The flight was just long enough for them to struggle out of their disguises in the tight confines of the tiny plane and then catch a few winks.

The pilot woke them when he was on final approach. They had no idea how he did it but they were on a seeming invisible and uneven runway before they even knew they were close to an airport or what turned out to be actually a poorly maintained and abandoned airstrip with no landing lights. GPS navigation and lots of programmable technology in the cockpit came to

Cristal's mind. Given how dark this area was she was sure he had been on total automation until seconds before he hit the nearly invisible runway.

The pilot drew the plane to a halt and made a one eighty turn on the old runway and taxied back towards a mid point, "I have to get out of here quickly. This is not an official airport and most pilots would not try it especially at night but I've made this run a few times. This area was recently under the control of Al Shabaab who would love to capture this plane so please grab your things and get out of here quickly. I see a car waiting for you just off the runway about a thousand feet ahead. Thank you for flying Air Nighthawk," he joked.

"Please call our regular number when you want to make a fast escape." He smiled.

Thankfully the one car on the airstrip was in fact their contact.

Anis Cadey looked like a local taxi driver which they found out later was his actual job. His English was better than expected, "I've been told by my good friend in Frankfurt that I'm to take you to your hotel and drive you around Mogadishu as you need. I'm also to offer any assistance I can provide but I'm not allowed to ask you too many questions."

David decided not to tell him what had happened to his good friend in Frankfurt. No point in complicating things.

David glanced at Cristal as they endured the bumpy ride into Mogadishu, "Ah, there's no big question of secrecy Mr. Cadey."

"Call me Anis. All foreigners do."

"OK. We are just very security conscious so my friend here didn't want to enter through the normal airport given everything we've read about Mogadishu. This is our first time here," he lied, "and my friend wanted to be careful. As you may know we're here to check on progress with our two organizations. The UN and Oxfam, to see if we can find ways to improve services to the good people of Somalia."

Anis was not buying any of this. There was no way to tell if any of that was true but UN and NGO types usually didn't come into the country on private jets in the dead of night at abandoned and unlit airstrips. He decided to keep up the small talk and mind his own business. People who asked too many questions these days had a habit of getting into trouble.

"We are always pleased to welcome people like you to our country. We really need the help. But if you follow my directions and stay out of trouble areas around here you should find it rather safe these days. Kidnapping is still a problem so do not travel out of your hotel or office without security just in case."

The rest of the ride passed in total silence. They had been led to believe there would be multiple checkpoints but somehow, with a little zigging and zagging Anis, who probably scoped out the checkpoints on his way to the landing strip had apparently avoided them all and about an hour later, they were at their hotel.

The Jazeera Palace Hotel was where most foreigners stayed and was relatively safe with its truck bomb barriers all around it. They had not had a terrorist attack on the hotel for a number of years but the signs were there that the hotel was not letting down their guard either. Armed guards were everywhere around the perimeter and very much in view.

Both were exhausted and after verifying the phone number to call Anis if they needed him, they hit the sack around 1 am local time. It had been a long day.

The morning light came quickly it seemed and they got their first daylight view of their surroundings. David had been in Mogadishu once before but this was the first time for Cristal and she was moderately shocked by the lack of color.

It seemed everything in view from their second floor room was the color of sand. The buildings, the roads, even the people all seemed to be sand colored with the pattern only disturbed with the odd brightly clothed local in the morning light.

The monotony of the compound was only broken by a few obviously transplanted palm trees near the front of the hotel. Sand colored rubble was everywhere from buildings that looked like they had taken direct mortar hits. Mogadishu was taking a long time to shake off its recent wars. It looked nothing like the photos she had seen of its former self before the civil wars of the nineties.

As planned, they had found adjoining rooms and resolved to depart and arrive separately with shuttles from their respective organizations which always included security.

As they had arrived on a local holiday, they spent the day acclimatizing to the heat and breaking Anis's rule of wandering off the hotel campus to get a feel for the place. Cristal wore the niqab in the morning but retired it once the sun was fully overhead. She was not accustomed to the heat having left Pittsburg at Thanksgiving to arrive in this furnace a few days later. Ditching the black niqab head covering was essential if she didn't want to pass out.

Both carried concealed loaded weapons, stayed to the shadows and tried not to stand out too much which was impossible with her blonde hair now exposed. The main market was the most interesting and they saw other foreigners there indicating this was a rather safe part of town. They browsed the market for a while and bought a few knickknacks but the heat was building fast and they decided to get back to the air-conditioned hotel.

They noticed all manner of nationalities as they passed through the hotel lobby and at dinner both sat at separate tables.

The international buffet food was passable with the highlights actually being some local fare unlike the poor attempts at western food. Cristal suspected the spaghetti with meat sauce actually had goat as the meat which gave it a very unfamiliar taste.

Their waiter who spoke English told them to stay away from the cambuulo even though it was probably the most popular dinner dish in Mogadishu but, as he explained, it was known to give serious gas problems.

By the end of the day, they reasoned they had drunk tea five or six times and every one of them was a bit different.

After dinner, they met secretly in David's room to plan the following day. Both were growing anxious that time was flying by and they still had not even started their pursuit of Khalil and his bomb. They resolved to step up the pace from zero to intense once they got to the office.

They turned in early and were up and ready to meet the folks at their new offices in the morning.

After a quick and satisfying breakfast of local fare including sampling Canjeero and Polenta, Cristal was first out and caught the secure shuttle to the building in downtown Mogadishu where she met her contact at Oxfam, Boris Nugent.

He greeted her as if they had met before for the benefit of those within earshot and then took her into his office.

"Look, I know very little about your trip but I know I shouldn't ask too many questions. Anyone who arrives with the instructions we received for you is working for someone other than Oxfam and it's my job to turn a blind eye to your activities. But understand if you bring any trouble to our organization or if Oxfam International gets involved and finds out you're here, the deal is off. No amount of under the table benefits is enough for us to risk our mission here or my life for that matter. Do we understand each other?"

Cristal smiled. She had expected something like this, "Understood. All I need is a desk and a phone to make it look all legit. I'll be in and out at irregular times and my cover story is that I'm doing an operations audit of some of your programs. You haven't been made aware of which programs and that your advice to everyone if asked is to keep out of my way if they don't want to be considered to be interfering with an important HQ audit. Most people tend to avoid auditors anyways.

"Just have someone bring me files that you pick from time to time to make it look like I'm actually auditing something."

Boris nodded and said, "Can you at least tell me how long you'll be here?"

"No but I suspect it will be less than two weeks. I want to get back to my family before Christmas," she lied.

He made a very overt deal of directing her to an office in the corner with an elaborate welcome.

Minutes later she noticed an off-and-on stream of people entering his office with side glances at her, ostensibly looking for information on the newcomer. Normal office politics she reasoned. "As long as he keeps to the script," she thought to herself.

The CIA had a skeleton team in Somalia and it took only about an hour before a young man looking like a local homeless person showed up at her desk. After introducing himself in a mid-west accent as Rick Sawyer, her CIA contact, she followed him to a cafeteria on the second floor of the building where they could find a place to talk.

"How did you get into the building dressed like that," she asked.

"They all know me here. I'm here often. My cover is that I'm a courier and I actually put in a few hours a day doing just that. It's a great cover. No one pays attention to me, I can go anywhere and I overhear and see lots. I think you will agree that I fit right in and I'm told I have mastered the local accent too."

He proceeded to bring her up to speed on what the local guys had been up to, which amounted to lots of chasing leads and getting nowhere.

She noticed David entering the small cafeteria with another man. She was surprised to see that David's guest was none other than Anis Cadey, the taxi driver from the other night. Rick followed her gaze, spotted Cadey, explained that his cover could be in jeopardy and excused himself quickly as he exited the back stairway.

David had left the hotel slightly behind Cristal and taken a second secure shuttle to the same building, different floor.

His introduction to his desk had been a similar affair but his CIA contact had shown up earlier. Norm

Lulham had explained that Rick Sawyer and he were the two local CIA guys.

As they exchanged info to get each other up to speed, David quickly found out that Anis Cadey was known to the CIA as an infrequent informant and had a good track record of providing accurate tips. He didn't know that Rick and Norm were CIA though, just curious day workers like himself.

Norm had come bearing gifts. They had just received new Intel that Mustafa might be using yet another alias from time to time and after comparing notes on Anis Cadey, David made a quick phone call, an offer of some money and now Cadey was seated with him in the cafeteria.

Norm Lulham had exited saying he didn't want Cadey to make the connection between David and himself.

Conscious of the short timeframe they had David had decided not to get too cute with Cadey. "Anis, good of you to come back so quickly. Here is the money I promised," he said as he passed an envelope under the table. "I won't pretend to be only a UN auditor of programs in Somalia if you will promise not to ask too many questions. Our mutual friend in Frankfurt said you were a man who could keep matters private."

Money in hand and checked, Anis nodded agreement.

"Some people I know here say you're a man who gets around quite a bit in Mogadishu and if there's something happening you'll know about it."

"In some ways they are right. I do travel a lot, have many rides, have many friends and some people talk a lot."

"OK, I have a name here. I want to know if you have heard of this name before."

"OK"

"The name is Tariq Aziz. And not the famous one from Iraq."

Anis looked happy, "I know this man. I can't say I know him well but last summer I gave him a ride from your very hotel to the International airport. He is some kind of consultant and travels much of the time. I think he is not from here and does not have an address in Mogadishu as I think he was staying at the hotel."

David was at once excited and then less so when he realized he would not be getting an address. "Can you tell me anything else about him?"

Cadey thought for a second, "I know only two things about this man. One, he is a football fanatic. He told me himself. Football has been off and on in Mogadishu but this year we have a full schedule. I do not know which team he supports but the way he spoke about it, he never misses a game.

"The other thing I know is that he breaks Allah's laws by betting. When I drove him, he gave me a very good tip which is unusual in this country so he must be a very rich businessman.

"I told one of my friends about his generosity, another taxi driver at the airport, and he said he had picked him up once at a meeting hall in town and dropped him at the airport and he bragged about just winning a lot of money in that building.

"This is something most Muslims would not do but it has become pardonable with rich people if it is kept very secret.

"He got the impression that it was not the first time this man had gambled. My friend didn't get a big tip like me."

David pressed on, "This is all very interesting Anis but it's important that I find this man. Is there anything you can tell me that would help me find him?"

Anis thought for a moment, "I'm sorry, he looked plain to me and I don't even know if he lives in Somalia. It was many months ago. There was something about his accent that made me think he was not Somali but that is all I know. I only know his name because he ordered the taxi under that name and I gave him my number after he gave me that large tip.

"It's always good to remember the names of people who tip well Mr. Victor Brookes," he smiled.

David could see that he was at a dead end so he handed over an additional twenty US dollars which put an even bigger smile on Anis's face, "Now I don't want anyone hearing of my interest in this man, understood?"

"Yes"

Anis rose, said goodbye and was gone in a flash.

David had noticed Cristal across the cafeteria and joined her to brief her on what he had learned. They compared notes on their two CIA contacts who they agreed seemed to fit in rather well to the local populace. Both were Americans but somehow had completely blended in and adopted the look and sound of the locals.

David had a cell phone number for Norm and ten minutes later the four of them were gathered in a small third floor unused office at the back of the building away from prying eyes and ears.

"This is what worries me." said Norm Lulham. "When we do get any kind of a lead on these guys the information we're able to dig up is usually useless. So now we know Mustafa at least twice in the last year has used the alias Tariq Aziz and that version of him gambles, loves football and sometimes tips big. Big deal. What do we do with that. That and a dime will buy you a cup of coffee." He smiled at the two new arrivals, "It actually still costs about a dime here."

Rick smiled and nodded agreement, "And it's good coffee too. You'll get used to it."

***

At that very moment, less than two miles away in Mogadishu, Khalil was making final touches to his disguise for the first leg of his trip to America. He had planned a very circuitous routing so he would not stand out at any international crossings.

He had also planned his trip to meet with a couple of people who funneled money to Al Qaeda to reassure them, pump them for more money and personally brief them to stay tuned to their TV's on Christmas.

Mustafa entered Khalil's room in yet another safe house and took a double take at the man he saw staring into the mirror.

Only the posture told him it was Khalil, "That is amazing master. I would never have recognized you myself but you look just like the old passport photo you gave me last week. Here are the final set of documents you need. Swiss passport, driver's license, Visa card and a few other relevant cards to your cover story. I've arranged other documents for you at your stops as you travel. If you change your appearance you will need additional photos but that is all arranged."

For some reason, even through the disguise he could see Khalil was not himself. Something was worrying him or upsetting him, "Is there a problem master?"

Khalil looked at him through the mirror, "As I told you my cousin was my main contact in the US. Our family relationship was kept a secret for security reasons but I suspect the Americans were always on the hunt for him because they must have known of our relationship from their investigations in Detroit.

"Luckily he knows very little of our plans and nothing of our whereabouts, communications, organization and people. We wanted to keep it that way. But I have to assume he was not martyred and has instead been captured by the CIA. With their torture programs we must assume that they now know we have something major planned for their Christmas. Abdul didn't know of the weapon or the target but the Americans know about the bomb factory in Kalibari so we should expect much higher level security at the targets we've picked."

Mustafa had been holding his breath waiting to hear again that his brother Jabir had jeopardized their biggest attack on America. They had put several years into the planning of this operation and on one level it was starting to unravel. As Khalil suggested, they had to assume the Americans knew something radioactive was going to be deployed on Christmas Day. There was no suggestion that they knew it was New York or what the precise target would be.

Khalil continued, "Because our Burundi brothers planned to use the Pittsburgh cell for support I blame myself for this mess. I should never have let them proceed. The prisoner swap was one thing but the bombing attempt has cost us dearly. As you know Abdul was one of the two they sent to the hideout to see what had happened and he was never seen after that. Now I no longer have my cousin as my contact and my relay for confidential messages in the US and to feed me any relevant news.

"So in a way I am walking into this blind. We can only hope none of the conditions we need for the attack have changed.

"Our people in New York who will execute the attack only know small elements of the attack. Each of them reports things are on track but we can't afford any more failures.

"I want you Mustafa, to take every possible action to ensure our security on this operation. You will be in charge when I'm gone. My ability to communicate within our network for the next few weeks will be severely limited. Now please help me with these bags and let's get to the airport."

***

After four very long days of jumping between airline departures in the Frankfurt airport from early morning to late at night, Kurt Willems was exhausted and more than disappointed that he hadn't spotted Crowe and his woman and even more irate when he heard from Jason Fletcher that he missed them in Nairobi as well.

He was now beginning to think that the old fart Franz Becker had lied to him before he put a bullet between his eyes. He had second thoughts about actually visiting the bastard's daughter in Paris and then dropped the idea as it would achieve nothing except put him in jeopardy of being caught in another murder.

The call to Jack Hammond at MI6 was going to be a bitch. This had been a catastrophe all round. He had earned only ten percent of his normal fee, put nearly a week of his own time into it, killed a man and been chastised for the way he handled it, and lost most of his German team. Hammond had never told him why they wanted the pair killed but he had half a mind to do it for free if he ever ran into this David Crowe.

Minutes after Jason Fletcher in Nairobi had delivered the bad news to Kurt in Frankfurt he put a call in to Phil Harris at CIA HQ, "So Phil, tell the DD that I think Kurt has given up on trying to find David and Cristal. Sorry, I still have no idea who was pulling Kurt's chain but they were pretty anxious to get the two of them.

"I must say Crowe hasn't lost his touch. I almost missed him in that ridiculous getup he had on at the Nairobi airport. If we hadn't discussed the targets Kurt gave me I might have been obligated to kill them even though I knew David from an earlier life. I didn't know he was on our side before you told me. Why didn't you tell David and the woman I had been hired to kill them?"

"The DD wanted to keep them on their toes and apparently it worked as both of them picked you out at the airport. Anyways, thanks for all your help Jason. Looks like your networking in Africa is paying off with the fact that Kurt picked you as his Kenyan assassin. I didn't know before we spoke that you knew and could recognize David. Where were you all the years we were trying to ID him in Guantanamo?"

"Yeah I knew him briefly when he did his exchange in Langley but hey, they don't send me pictures of prisoners to ID. Maybe they should start."

"Well it worked out well this time, and thanks for the dump from your phone. We're backtracking your calls with Kurt now. We may be able to figure out who his contact is from this end if he spoke to them just before or after any of your calls. Stay safe."

***

It was another hot day in Mogadishu as Cristal and David returned independently to the hotel early in the afternoon and found the place to be almost abandoned which meant less chance of them being overheard in their call to HQ. David swept his room and then hers for planted listening devices.

The DD was not available so it was Phil Harris they got on the secure line. In lowered, almost whispered voices they reported they had made contact with the local CIA skeleton team, settled into their cover stories and revealed what they had learned from Anis about Tariq Aziz aka Mustafa Habib.

David continued, "On another front we were hoping to get something out of that phone number we got from Jabir Habib's phone but there were only two Somali numbers in his call list and we were hopeful one of them was his brother Mustafa.

"We had your guys here hack into the cell towers to triangulate both numbers but even before we got that far we discovered that both numbers are no longer active and guess what, the local phone company does not keep records for local or incoming cell calls from phones on their own network. Everything is prepaid unless it's an outgoing call from an off-network phone and apparently Jabir Habib was never in Somalia with that phone, so another dead end there."

David finished the report, "So all we have so far are some personal characteristics of one of Mustafa Habib's cover ID's which would not seem to be very useful. We could have passed him or Khalil on the street today and we wouldn't have known them."

Phil was sympathetic, "Well it's a start. You never know when some small piece of information is going to break a case for you.

"On our end we also have something that probably means nothing but it's interesting. One of the Jihadists from the Pittsburgh cell who we grabbed when they came to investigate that night has given us all the info we've passed to you so far like the fact that the US is the target and Christmas is the timing.

"Turns out that his real name is Abdul Abadi, a Yemeni National and landed immigrant in the US. We've been trying to find this guy for a long time because he is a first cousin of Khalil and was almost like a little brother to him in Detroit when they were growing up.

"We've had suspicions for years that he too was radicalized by Khalil's father about the same time but we had no idea whether he was still in the US or abroad. Incidentally, we're now looking at him as a possible suspect in the death of the man who murdered Khalil's father and brother.

"He fell off the grid about the same time as Khalil. So we have a family member in custody. He's particularly susceptible to some of our newest drugs. He also spilled the beans on the Pittsburgh cell but they had cleared out before we raided all of their known meeting places and homes. The bad news is that he seems to know almost nothing beyond the timing. There is no indication he even knows what the weapon is and we're pretty sure he doesn't know anything about the exact target.

"In the vein of useless information, under hallucinogenic drugs we found out that Khalil used to love burritos when he was younger and found American food too bland so he used lots of pepper on almost everything.

"He loved Young and the Restless on TV too. Never missed an episode and loved the billionaire character, Victor Newman. How's that? For all we know he still watches it in Arabic in Somalia. That stuff makes it all over the world.

"Lots of trivia type info and none of it helpful. At least in any obvious sense given the limits of what we know about Khalil and this operation. You might start watching for a terrorist who refuses to miss an episode of Y&R," he joked.

"Back on the cousin, there's a theory here that he was a major conduit for Khalil in the US given the family relationship and now that we have him out of service we may have put a wrinkle into their communications. But that's all speculation."

It was Cristal's turn, "As you said, you never know when one of these trivial points is going to pay off. Now, remember I'm the only one who has seen Khalil. It was years ago and he was undoubtedly in disguise but I will not and cannot forget his eyes.

"Tomorrow your guys here are going to collect all of the mug shots they can find for me to look at just in case we've had him or the Somali's have had him in custody and didn't know it."

They agreed to speak again once Cristal had seen all of the mug shots. A couple of days into their investigation in Mogadishu and they were no further ahead. Time was running out.

Setup

It had been a miserably hot and humid day when Anis returned home about an hour later than normal. His tiny ramshackle apartment where he, his wife and their eight-year old son lived, at least had a window fan which was a real comfort as long as the electricity didn't go out, which it frequently did.

He could tell from the moment he walked through the door that something was wrong by the look on his wife's face. As he turned and looked into his tiny living room, he was horrified to see two very mean looking men sitting on his couch with their son squashed between them. He had never seen these men before.

"Come in and join us," said one of them who looked like he hadn't washed in a week.

As he sat in a straight-backed chair facing them, the other one, the bigger and more presentable of the two spoke, "A few nights ago you picked up people from a jet that landed late at Wanlaway airstrip. We need to know who they were and where they went and what they are doing here."

Anis started to sweat profusely and had trouble finding his breath. After a long pause where he convinced himself he loved his family more than his promise to remain quiet he spoke up,

"I do not know their whole names. His name is Victor and her name is Virginia. They are both westerners but I cannot tell what nationality. I do not know where they came from. I dropped them at the Jazeera Palace Hotel. I saw them both in the same building where the UN and Oxfam have their offices so

I think they work for one or both of them. That is all I know about them."

He was focused on the bigger of the two who had started the questioning. His questioner smiled, seeming pleased with Anis's efforts to cooperate.

He patted Anis's son on the head and then turned back to Anis, "You also went to that building yesterday. Did you meet with one of them?"

This really alarmed Anis. They knew much more than they were letting on. Clearly they had someone following him or them and he understood implicitly that any lie he spoke might result in terrible consequences for his family.

He sat up straight in his chair, "Yes, that's what I said. I saw them both at that building. The man, Victor called me and asked me if I knew a man named Tariq Aziz. I told him I remembered the name from someone I took to the airport a long time ago and that he gave me a big tip. That is all I know and I told him so."

"Did this man ask any other questions about Mr. Aziz?"

"I told him another taxi driver had taken him from a hall downtown to the airport too but he didn't get a big tip."

The big one stared Anis down for a long time and based on his own knowledge of the situation figured he had gotten everything out of this man who was clearly very worried for his family.

"You understand Mr. Cadey that these people are outsiders and could be a grave danger to our country. Here is what we're going to do. Your son here is going to visit some of our friends for a few days. He will be cared for properly and treated as a guest. We are not in the habit of hurting innocents.

"You will make contact with this Victor once more and this is what you will tell him. You will tell him that Mr. Tariq Aziz has engaged you to take him to the airport this coming Sunday at 10 pm. You are to pick him up in the driveway behind 3451 Wadada Wadnaha. If he wants to see or meet Mr. Aziz, this will be his only chance. We will take it from there and we'll find out what this Victor wants. Do you understand?"

"Yes, tell Victor that Mr. Aziz will be at 3451 Wadada Wadnaha at 10 pm this coming Sunday. What will happen to my son?"

By now, the young boy was whimpering at the prospect of leaving with these two strange men and pleading with his eyes to his mother who still stood by the door, arms crossed across her waist, tears running down her face.

"Your son will be taken care of in the proper way. We will make sure he says his prayers. If you comply with everything he will be returned to you unharmed Sunday night. And then you will go about your business and forget about us, Mr. Aziz, Victor, our visit, everything. Understood?"

"Yes."

The two men rose each with a firm hand on the boy's arms. Anis bent and hugged his son and whispered in his ear, "Please be brave and go with these men. Everything will be fine and I'll see you in a few days."

They were gone and Anis stood there consoling his wife who was frantic.

Fifteen minutes later, from their well-guarded apartment using a secure line, the bigger of the two kidnappers briefed Mustafa on their evening, "The taxi driver was very cooperative and I think we got everything out of him. He does not know much. The two spies may not know who you are but they are likely CIA and they are looking for Tariq Aziz. There was no mention of Mustafa Habib so they may not have made the connection but that alias is no longer safe."

"Go on", said Mustafa.

"They are staying in that bunker of a hotel, the Jazeera Palace near the airport. They are the first ones with some new information and are trying to find you so I think we have no choice but to eliminate them quickly. When we see them, we can assess if they are the ones from Pittsburgh as you suspect but all we know is that they are the man and woman that your source says flew into Wanlaway a few nights ago.

"The woman's hair is the wrong color but western women color their hair. The taxi driver only knew their first names Victor and Virginia but there's no way to know if that is made up. We've set a trap for Sunday and we have some insurance that the taxi driver will not warn them. I would suggest Tariq Aziz disappear forever. I don't know how they got that name but clearly the infidels are looking for him. We'll know much more on Sunday when we capture them and try to get everything out of them."

Mustafa was insistent, "They cannot be freed. After you have interrogated them, kill them and dump the bodies where they won't be found."

***

Three days in Mogadishu, and time was flying by. They had reviewed all of the leads the local CIA team had and Cristal had continued to look over mug shots they were getting from their own files, the Mogadishu police, government files and even a file that was shared with them from AMISOM, the controversial and sometimes violent African Union force that was assisting the official government.

None of the pictures seemed to remind her of Khalil. All of the pictures were blurring in her mind and she realized how hard it was for a westerner to pick out the subtle differences in Arab faces. Almost all of the men in the target age group had full beards making it even harder. It was starting to seem that there were only about ten typical face types and everyone was a minor change on the theme.

Then David received a surprise call from Anis who had urgent news to share with them. They met once again in the second floor cafeteria. This time David was wearing a wire so they could replay his discussion in case there was anything hidden or subtle.

Anis was thirty minutes late for the meeting and looked pretty shaken up. As he sat down in the second floor cafeteria with David he said, "I received a call from Mr. Tariq Aziz last night. He is planning a trip on Sunday and wants me to pick him up to take him to the airport at 10 pm at an address on Wadada Wadnaha. That's a main road not too far from your hotel."

David immediately smelled a rat, "Why do you think he called you?"

Anis realized he had not rehearsed this enough and he hesitated, "Maybe he liked my taxi. He did give me a large tip and not to my friend. I had given him my number on a piece of paper when I met him before."

"Will he be travelling alone?"

"He did not say. I was just told to pull around the back of the building to pick him up at 10 pm. I think it's the same place my friend picked him up. There may be some gambling going on there."

"What's the address?"

"3451 Wadada Wadnaha, not far from the big Bakaara Market."

"OK Anis you've done well." He said as he handed him fifty dollars American. That brought a wide smile to Anis's face and he seemed to relax just a bit. "If anything changes or if you hear anything else on this matter call me first, OK?"

"I'll do exactly that Mr. Victor."

David rose and walked him to the door. Minutes later, he was in the vacant office on the third floor going over the tape with Cristal and the two local CIA guys.

"Clearly it's a setup," said Norm Lulham, the more senior of the two CIA agents, "It always amazes me how amateurish some of their attacks are. You would wonder how they are ever successful as a terrorist organization. Khalil is not behind this or it would be so sophisticated we would not see him coming. This is a lower level security team for sure."

David nodded, "One question is how did they find us? Either Anis went straight to them or someone found out he was helping us and they have something over him. Maybe they are threatening him or a family member is in jeopardy. Either way we can't trust Anis anymore. He's been flipped."

Everyone agreed.

Lulham took over again "Now to their plan. That area is a dicey part of town at the best of times but ten at night and behind the building? We should have had this Anis watched as soon as he entered the picture but we're pretty short of resources here. I'm bringing in a drone and we're watching that building on Wadada Wadnaha from here on in.

"I'm pretty sure I know which building it is too. It could actually be a good cover for a private poker game but it's dead at night over there and generally an Al Shabaab zone. Perfect for an ambush. We can't just waltz up there and inspect the building either and on top of that setting up top cover would not be realistic even if you did believe that Mustafa was going to show his face."

David nodded, "I agree. Sure looks like a setup to me. I trust Anis to some degree but as I said, it would not be hard to imagine that they have a relative in peril if he does not do their bidding. He sure looked nervous."

Cristal nodded, "I think you're right. What resources DO you have to cover us?"

The big agent, Norm Lulham was shocked, "You're not thinking of going?" he said rather than asked. "This is Mogadishu NOT Frankfurt. This would be a suicide mission even if it wasn't Mogadishu. We have no idea how many they'll be and where they are.

"There is no chance that Mustafa is going to show. The only people there will be his hit squad. They'll likely grab you, torture you for information, kill you and dump you in the desert. No. No way any of us are walking into this. We'd need twenty men and half of them snipers to do any kind of a meeting like this and even then, on their grounds? No way!"

He paused as the others looked like they were coming around to the reality of the situation. No matter what their skills and technology, the deck was completely stacked against them on this one.

Lulham continued, "Here's the plan I propose. We get to Anis's cab before Sunday and load'er up with a

GPS tracker or two, bugs, and maybe even a wifi camera hidden in an air vent on the dash. He won't notice it unless he gets it detailed which would never happen here."

"I have an electronic switch which will render them all inert until we need them so even a scanner won't pick them up.

"We watch the building from a high altitude drone starting now. We monitor Anis' arrival from a safe distance where we can find good cover and they won't find us and if against all odds Mustafa or Tariq Aziz or anyone else actually shows we take them at a point of our choosing before he makes it to the airport. I know just the place to take down a car near the airport if we need to.

"That's a plan that keeps you out of danger and achieves our purpose and by the way, stands a much better chance of success than you hiding in a cab or driving up there yourself."

Cristal and David looked at each other and nodded. Cristal spoke first, "Your plan makes sense given how our options and resources are limited here. It's not like we can send in a SWAT team in downtown Mogadishu. What can we do to help?"

This time Rick Sawyer, the younger of the two CIA guys spoke, "Keep your heads down. They just told us with this setup that they know you're here now.

"They almost certainly know your cover names, your hotel, your cover stories and there's also a chance they know your real identities. You did kill Mustafa's brother and that was after Khalil ordered your fatwa. Unless they get really ambitious you're safe enough in this building and in your hotel. We'll double security and change routes on your trips between the two but any other wandering around the city is out. Keep your eyes open for a tail. You will almost certainly have one if you don't already but they are unlikely to move on you unless they are sure to catch you off guard and that would require some knowledge of where you're going to be."

"If they have you figured as CIA they will be nervous about taking you on given the training they assume you've had so they'll wait for a chance when they have insurmountable odds and everything is in their favor before they will move on you."

Norm Lulham spoke, "Rick's right.

"Now for Sunday night we'll want David on the road and lose the tail so they think you're headed for the ambush. The more we can make them follow through the more we'll learn about them."

The plans were set and the next three days went by painfully slowly. Neither David nor Cristal made any progress on tracking down Khalil or his organization.

David spent his time revisiting all of the old tips and interviews the CIA team had and Cristal continued to look at any mug shots that trickled in but nothing. Headquarters in Langley reported no luck on the search for the bomb either.

Langley's theory was that the port might be important if they had smuggled the radioactive material in that way or planned to ship it out by sea but the CIA's 24/7 surveillance of the port by drones had picked up nothing unusual.

David and Cristal really wanted to get out, just drive around and look for signs of something. They didn't know what. All of the CIA's file on Khalil and known associates, operations, etc. had been gone over multiple times but nothing new was jumping out at them.

Sunday night arrived and all was in place to monitor the meeting. David took a taxi around a couple of streets, paid the guy to show him his 'losing a tail' moves, made sure he was not followed and ended up back at the hotel. By 9:45 he was in the back of a crowded and beat up van with Cristal and the CIA team close to the target but well around the block.

A tiny wifi camera buried in what looked like a piece of rubble had been added to the alleyway that led to the back of the target address. They could monitor it, the drone and the camera in Anis's car as well as the bugs in the car. They tracked Anis' car with the planted GPS transceivers as he left his home and approached the meeting place.

He arrived five minutes early. After he turned into the area behind the building all they had was the video from inside the taxi, a grainy wide angled infra-red image from the drone and audio from two separate bugs in the front and back of the taxi.

He had been there about ten minutes when they could hear him addressing someone approaching the car. The grainy drone image picked up a body approaching the taxi from behind on the driver's side. In slang Arabic Anis said, "Why do you have a gun? Is Mr. Aziz ready to go to the airport?"

The voice out of camera range said, "Are you alone?"

Anis was heard and seen to say "Yes."

"Did you deliver the message we gave you?"

"Yes I did. Right after you gave it to me. He understood completely."

"Did he say he would be here?"

"No but he was very interested. He might be around here somewhere. You should look out front for him. Is Mr. Aziz coming or can I leave now?"

A radio was heard to crackle to life and they heard, "Is there anything happening out front?"

A voice replied, "No sign of anyone here, just the taxi. Should we wait?"

"No. He would have been here by now. It looks like he did not take the bait.

"Anis it looks like you didn't do your job."

"I did exactly as you told me. What else could I have done."

A shot rang out as the side of Anis' head exploded and his dying body slumped in front of the hidden dash cam.

All four in the van jumped at the loud shot. None of them had predicted Anis would be killed. Surely he could have been of more use to them.

"Mohammed, come back here and get rid of this car and the body. I couldn't let him leave and warn them. He may be working for them. At least now they'll know to get out if we cannot get to them."

The four agents in the van one block away gasped as the realization set in that not only was it a trap but they had just witnessed the execution of the only man who had tried to help them.

David said, "Let me off around the corner, I'm going to kill those bastards."

"I'm coming with you," blurted out Cristal.

Lulham spoke first, "I understand the sentiment but keep your eye on the prize. This is not our mission. Our mission is much more important than tangling with this scum and we don't need to introduce complications like having the local authorities chasing us."

David calmed down and simply stared out the window at nothing. Cristal seemed despondent.

After a moment or two of each of them looking at each other Cristal with tears in her eyes was the only one to speak, "Some days I hate this damned job."

No Guard

They were back in the office the next morning and still very shook up about Anis.

David was particularly pissed, "We didn't even get a look at those monsters that just off'd an innocent guy. I wish we had stuck around and at least got a picture of them leaving the building."

"Too dangerous," said Norm Lulham, "Remember, keep your eye on the prize. We're running out of time. We need to keep focused."

David pounded his fist on the table and left the room.

He headed for the men's room near the back stairwell. Toilet paper was strung across the door apparently in a makeshift sign indicating it was out of order. He quickly ran down the back stairwell to the second floor cafeteria level and found the same thing. Down one more flight and bingo, no paper strung across the door.

Just as he pushed the door open he noticed the guard at the back door was missing from his post at a small desk. Before he could put two and two together, he had a gun in his face. There was no option that wouldn't get his face blown off.

A second man hidden inside the men's room quickly tied his hands behind his back with duct tape and covered his mouth with it too.

The other one then searched him and seemed very happy to have found a new gun to play with. It looked like a better one than his.

The two of them manhandled him out into the hallway and out the back door and into a waiting beat up van which immediately sped off.

It was ten minutes before Cristal thought to ask Rick to go check on him, "Tell him we need a plan and to stop sulking if that's what he's doing."

Rick was soon back and out of breath, "Can't find him anywhere and the guard is missing from the ground floor entrance at the back."

"Shit" was all Cristal said as she ran out of the room and headed for the UN manager's office with the two CIA guys in tow.

They briefed him and Rick finished with, "They must have known we were on the third floor because they had blocked off the other two bathrooms. What do you think happened with the guard?

The UN guy was looking pretty scared, "I told you guys that if any trouble came our way because of you folks we would have to throw you out. I don't know what you're up to and I don't want to know but I want you guys to clear out of here now!

"As to the guard, I got a call late yesterday from the security firm saying that we would have a new guy here this morning. I saw him when I came in the back way and said hi so don't ask me who he was or what happened to him but you can be sure I'm going to do a full security audit."

Norm Lulham spoke, "This could be one of two things and we might get a ransom demand." Looking at the UN manager, he said, "If you get a call from the kidnappers call me on my cell immediately."

Back in their room at the rear of the building on the third floor the team regrouped. Norm Lulham took the lead, "Worst case scenario is that these are the same guys as last night and David is in big trouble but I am a little surprised they didn't wait to get both of you together. If it is them there will be no ransom note.

"The more likely scenario is that this is a bunch of jokers from Al Shabaab who are just looking for a pay day. If it is them then we will definitely get a ransom call to the UN Director."

The call came in two excruciating hours later but not to the UN. It came in to Boris Nugent who the outside world thought was Cristal's boss in Mogadishu. He had heard of the kidnapping which was now all over the building and he called Cristal's cell. She was back in the third floor conference room with the two CIA guys when the call came in.

She put Boris on speaker so the two agents could hear.

Boris filled her in, "They apparently don't know his name but they know he's important, they think he works for me and they want $100,000 US by 9 pm tonight. They gave me a GPS point where you're to drop off the money in a duffle bag. They said he will be released somewhere in town in the morning if we comply.

"Victoria I warned you about bringing trouble to our doors."

"Listen Boris, if they don't know his name then they were not after him in particular. They don't even know he's attached to the UN and not Oxfam. Think about it. That trap was set for any man walking into the men's room. The idea was to funnel anyone to the restroom on the main floor. Pretty much all men in this building are foreigners working for big organizations and worthy of a ransom. The only thing you have to

313

worry about is the security of this building. Talk to your buddy upstairs at the UN and fix the security problem and they won't be back. I'll take care of the ransom. You just look after the security." She said as she hung up quickly.

Norm Lulham had been listening and responded, "You may be right but we're not out of the woods. Yes, if that had been Khalil's gang they would likely have done more to target David and you and there'd be no ransom demand. So it's likely Al Shabaab or someone else and they don't know who they've got.

"But the problem is these guys have been known to sell hostages. If it's Al Shabaab as we suspect, they'll take the money and then get more when they sell him to Khalil or one of the other old warlords who will do the same but there's a high likelihood he will eventually end up in Khalil's hands and they know who David is."

Cristal realized his argument was sound, "OK, so what do we do?"

Agent Rick Sawyer spoke, "Listen, I know these guys. They won't sell him until they have the money in their hands in case we need proof of life. Let's check out the GPS coordinates. I'll bet it's out in the desert where they can see anyone trying to observe them or follow them.

"I'll get Nairobi to get the money in a duffle bag and fly it into that airstrip near the village of Wanlaway this afternoon.

"We bug the duffle bag and bring in a drone by tonight with night vision and follow them to their hideout and pray that is where they have David. We'll take them down and get David."

All agreed that was the only plan they had. Rick got the GPS coordinates from Boris and sure enough they led to a place well out in the open desert.

By 9 pm Norm and Cristal had dropped off the bag and they headed back to town and took up a central location waiting for word from Rick on where to go as he was monitoring all the telemetry from their old van.

Rick had live streaming video from the drone of the bag sitting by itself in the desert.

Almost an hour went by before he radioed Cristal and Norm.

"They just picked up the bag, two of them. They looked inside and seemed pretty happy. They are now headed in the general direction of Mogadishu. They haven't found the GPS transceiver in the bag because it's still working."

Drone control on the USS Carl Vinson just off the coast was doing an excellent job of following the van.

Rick kept Cristal and Norm updated on the movements of the kidnapper's equally beat up pickup as it approached Mogadishu and then took a circuitous route through town apparently looking for a tail.

All the time he had Cristal and Norm on a parallel course about two blocks away.

Finally, he radioed that the pickup had pulled to a stop in front of a building, "You won't believe it. We were here last night. They are almost across the street from where Khalil's guys killed Anis. These bad guys all seem to like this part of town.

"OK they both got out and they have the bag and they are entering the front door. There's a sentry on the roof facing the front of the building covering them.

"I know this building. I've delivered stuff there before. There is a back alley. I can see you on the drone now. Go ahead one block and look for an alleyway on your right."

About ten seconds later, "That's it. You want the third building on the left. There is a back stairwell. Watch out for sentries. The guy on the roof is sitting down at the front of the building. Park out of sight of the roof of that building in the alleyway."

Cristal and Norm parked before the building they wanted and crept up to the back door. It was not locked and they were in without opposition and creeping up the stairs as quietly as possible.

"In their ear-pieces they heard Rick, "The GPS transmitter sown into the bag says it has increased in altitude by 23 feet. They're on the third floor."

Just as Cristal came quietly around the corner heading up to the third floor, she spotted a sleepy sentry sitting with his AK-47 on his lap. Before he could react, she put two silenced rounds in his chest and finished off with one to his head. She grabbed the body before it could roll down the stairs.

They made their way on to the third floor and could see a dim light coming from under the door of a room about 20 yards in front of them. The door was slightly ajar.

"The bag is about mid building, front side, third floor," came the direction from Rick in their earpieces. That tied to the door with the light.

Both agents crept towards the door watching for any additional sentries. There was the low sound of a radio playing Arab music coming from the room. Cristal signaled she was going in first.

Squatting low she very delicately eased the door open with gun at the ready. Thankfully the door made no noise and then she came upon a scene she had not expected.

"It's about time you showed up," said a smiling Commander David Crowe sitting on a duffle bag. "I thought you were going to make me rot here.

In the dim light, she could see three bodies all either dead or near death on the left side of the room.

Norm came in and they all stood there smiling at each other.

Cristal laughed, "Looks like you didn't need our help at all."

"Well, when they came back with the bag I figured my time was up. I was expecting them to trade me to Khalil instead of releasing me so I had to act.

"My hands have been free for a couple of hours. Duct tape in this heat and humidity is not a good restraining device.

"As soon as they turned their backs to examine the money, I jumped all three of the scrawny bastards. As you can see I didn't even have to use their guns which would have brought some others I suspect. I also retrieved my gun from the skinny runt on the bottom. I thought you might be here soon and you might know where the sentries are.

"These guys are clearly in the wrong business. Not a single one of them had any hand to hand combat training. Honestly, I hardly broke a sweat taking care of three of them at the same time. You have to wonder how they are every successful at this but I guess most of their victims are no better prepared."

In Cristal's ear she heard Rick, "What's going on?"

"We have him and the money. Four bad guys down and one still on the roof, right?"

"Yeah, he looks sleepy. You should be able to get back out the way you came in with no problems."

Cristal said, "Too bad this is a dry town, a little celebration seems in order."

"Oh, I think I might have a little something hidden back at the office that might suit the occasion," said Norm.

Rick passed on the results of the night's work to the Carl Vinson and they recalled the drone.

Twenty minutes later they all met up at the offices and shared a bottle of scotch Norm had hidden in the ceiling tiles.

Finally David spoke, "Sorry for all the trouble guys I must have been a little off my game when I walked into that trap.

"I might have been able to break free earlier but I knew pretty quick they didn't know who I was and they were probably Al Shabaab and I was hoping to get some Intel out of them but then when they returned with the money I thought it would be only minutes before the good guys showed up and I wanted to save you a little work."

They all smiled sarcastically.

"But at the end of the day I'm afraid all we've done is wasted a day chasing my silly ass and we're no closer to getting any Intel on Khalil. We better kick it up a notch in the morning."

***

Another day had passed and the team was still pretty broken up about Anis. The GPS signal from the taxi indicated Khalil's gang had simply driven his taxi out into the desert and abandoned it. The camera and bugs had been out of range so there was nothing of any use.

They knew they were running out of time and Headquarters was reporting no successes from anywhere else on the planet in terms of tracking the potential dirty bomb likely headed for the US for Christmas.

Cristal was at her desk in the Oxfam office pretending to go over some inventory reports but she was really spending her time becoming anxious over the lack of progress when the young Somali girl she had been working with came up to her, "I don't know if you noticed this. It's not part of something we fund but just to show you what we're dealing with. Maybe you can get something done from Headquarters Miss Victoria.

"Part of the money donated to the new government by the World Bank was for the police; new cars, new uniforms, and some weapons but look at this inventory. About six months ago, they shipped an additional fifteen new police uniforms to the central distribution center here in Mogadishu but only ten ever appeared in the inventory. This is what we deal with all the time. That central warehouse is totally corrupt. Whatever we send in there gets pilfered. We're wasting our time here. They just steal everything we bring in. As managers representing an international charity we should be demanding they clean that place up. We must be losing millions in relief supplies out of that one warehouse."

Cristal had been only half listening to her but the message finally hit her, "Let me see that report." The girl showed it to her and pointed to the discrepancies.

"Excuse me, I'll be right back," she said as she rose and briskly walked out the door.

A few quick phone calls and twenty minutes later she had David and the two CIA agents in their vacant office meeting place, "So six months ago five police uniforms disappear from the central distribution warehouse. Who would want police uniforms?"

Norm Lulham spoke first, "Al Shabaab of course. To infiltrate government forces, stage suicide attacks, or kidnap the opposition."

Cristal nodded, "And have there been any reported cases of these types of activities in the last year using police uniforms as a cover?"

"No."

"That's what I thought. I'm betting if you check all the police reports or attacks there have been none that used stolen police uniforms."

Lulham spoke again, "Maybe they are waiting for the right opportunity."

Cristal smiled as David and Rick Sawyer started to see where she was going, "Who else would want to steal police uniforms? I'll tell you. Someone who wanted to move freely around town without being questioned. What's more, the police have weapons and a brand new fleet of Toyota Land Cruisers. They must have 50 of them. How hard would it be to spoof a Police car?"

Rick smiled, "I don't know but that one should be pretty easy to check out. I'll bet you there can't be more than five Land Cruisers that are in the hands of individual citizens. I'm going to check the records for the last 2 years. I can get them from Somalia's equivalent of the DMV, imports logs or Toyota shipping records. Chances are some part of this was done legit and then they painted it like a Police car. I like this theory. It would be perfect." He dashed off to start the work.

David smiled at Cristal, "Nice work. I like it too. A perfect way to hide in plain sight. Find a place to stash the car at night. Maybe a body shop or something where it wouldn't arouse suspicion and use it only when needed.

"With the re-establishment and growth of the police force it is likely that most of the police don't know each other or at least a new person would not stick out.

"Khalil and his lieutenants could move around town with impunity, and fully armed too. They've got forged document capability so they probably have Police ID's as well. And it would explain why the stolen police uniforms have never appeared. Good work."

It took until the following mid day for Rick to track down all the information he needed and then he disappeared from the office for an hour. When he returned he called the group together in their regular tiny office in the UN section of the building.

He had a big smile on his face as he started, "There was only one Land Cruiser outside of the police department's acquisition to come into Somalia in the last two years. No one here can afford that kind of vehicle and if they could the Land Cruiser would not be high on the acquisition list.

"Anyways, I tracked it down to a name and address in Mogadishu and I went there in the last hour. The man bearing that name at that address has no idea what a Land Cruiser is never mind ordering one. By the look of the place, he couldn't afford to top it up with gas even if he did have one.

"So, that means we have an unaccounted for Land Cruiser, same model as the police use by the way, and five missing police uniforms. I'm convinced this is a good lead that we have to drive to ground."

"But how?" Norm Lulham asked.

The four of them just stared at each other.

David spoke first, "First of all, Rick, get all the license plate numbers for the legit Police cars. I don't know how we find it and I'm pretty sure they would not be stupid enough to park it where they sleep so it might be an indirect lead to where they are. They likely have someone driving it who can pick it up and drop it off somewhere far from their hideouts. Someone who is good at picking up a tail.

"We'll need that drone back to look for it. But there's a high probability that if we find it, Khalil won't be in it. We can't storm every building it goes to and I'm not sure we're going to identify Khalil from a drone getting in or out of that Land Cruiser. We are certainly not going to get a close up of his eyes for Cristal to look at. But if we do find it, we can bug it.

After a moment of thought, David continued, "No this won't work. The biggest problem is that this is likely to take too long. We need some other method of finding that Land Cruiser and determining if it does belong to Khalil. We could have drones flying around for weeks waiting to reacquire it if it's hidden from sight. We need a break of some kind."

Rick had an idea, "If we do find it and he's not with it we may have a real opportunity. If I'm not mistaken that SUV comes with a built in GPS and these days they all keep trip records.

"Even if the GPS has been disabled, most of those new Toyotas have a black box type chip like aircraft do. I remember some years ago it was used in a court case to show the driver of a car that claimed his car had

322

accelerated uncontrollably actually was applying pressure to the accelerator at the time.

"The guys in Langley might have something that if we can find that car, can dump either or both of those devices' data so we can see where it has been. From that we might get some of his safe houses and the place where the bomb is if it's here in Mogadishu."

David turned to agent Lulham, "See if Langley has such a device or can make one and get it here quick. I know at least the GPS's all have Bluetooth so they can likely hack it. Let's hope the chips also have some remote networking capability that Langley can hack into.

"I know Cristal's theory of the Police car is a bit of a long shot and we don't know if we can find the car but we're running out of time. Christmas is about ten days away and we still have no idea of the actual target or where the bomb is now."

Cristal had been listening to all of this and hadn't said a word. David picked up on this, "What's going on in your head?"

"I was just thinking that someone, probably Khalil's gang just killed our cab driver when they tried to set us up. They won't have given up. That hotel is like a fortress but a cop car with a couple of police could drive right up to the front door and go directly to our rooms. We need to be really careful with any involvement with the police. I can't memorize fifty license plate numbers but we need to be looking over our shoulder at all times. I'm afraid that any cop who approaches me now is a dead man."

Rick spoke up, "Don't take this the wrong way but if you're right and he has the ability to spoof the police, that is an amazing tool to remain invisible in Mogadishu and it would have to be used judiciously or if discovered he could lose that cover. You may not be a big enough target for him to risk it all."

Cristal smiled, "You may be right and I hope to hell you are."

Lulham got on to Langley about the electronic device within the hour. As it turned out Langley had all the pieces. A device that could break into any WIFI, Bluetooth or other communications protocol, and the codes required to get both the GPS and the Black Box chip to broadcast their data.

The only problem was that there was no time to make a miniaturized version. The concept would require several different electronic boxes and together they were a little bulky and they had to provide a decent power supply as well, but working late into the night they assembled a backpack that would do the job. It was on its way to Nairobi on the CIA's fastest jet.

They used the same private jet out of Nairobi because he knew the tricks to get in and out of Wanlaway. Agent Rick Sawyer used a contact of his and got to the airstrip and back in a few hours with no problems.

It was Friday morning one week until Christmas and now all they had to do was find the damned Police car. One out of fifty or so Police cars that would likely not often be on the road. They were in their usual conference room once more trying to brainstorm or will themselves to come up with a way to move ahead with the investigation.

Cristal spoke, "So where would that Toyota be and how do we find it."

David answered, "You know if we're only a week away from Christmas then I'm going to bet that Khalil has already left if he is headed for the US as we suspect.

324

To avoid US travel checks he needs a circuitous route to make sure his path from Somalia is not obvious. He'll be travelling under different names but his luggage has to transfer between planes and stop-overs too. I'll bet he left early and is winding his way toward the US.

"The same is probably true for the bomb. It's either already in the US or en route, I would suspect. Could be entering through Canada but more likely Mexico using that tunnel. I can think of a couple of ways they could get it into the US but I'll bet it's en route now.

"But the thing we have to concentrate on is that the information on where it's going and where Khalil is, is probably right here in Mogadishu. We can't chase after either Khalil or the bomb until we get a lead on where to look. And that Toyota is our only lead on getting inside his operations.

"Assuming we're right with Cristal's deductions, we need to find that Land Cruiser and find out where it has been. That's the only path we have. And if and when we do find it we have to get lucky and have it point us to something that will help us in tracking Khalil or the bomb."

Rick Sawyer took over, "You're right. It sounds like a long shot, but it's all we have. So where do we start?"

David turned to Cristal, "Com'on bright eyes, you came up with the last theory, where do we start."

She smiled but he could see the nervousness on her face this was really serious now, one week away from the potential deaths of hundreds or thousands of Americans.

"Well, if you're right and Khalil is gone, he would have left someone in charge here and from what we

325

know, Mustafa is head of Ops so he's the man and he probably has the keys to the Land Cruiser. He might take the opportunity to use the car while the boss is away. So what do we know about him to track him down?"

David spoke, "We don't know much. We know he's head of Ops. We know he had a brother in the Burundi cell who is now dead. We know he used an alias of Tariq Aziz at least twice. We think he's a gambler, big tipper and a soccer nut."

Agent Rick Sawyer almost jumped out of his seat, "That's it! He's going to the game on Sunday. The boss is out of town and the biggest game of the year is this Sunday. You must have seen the banners all over town. Banadir vs. Elman for the 1st Division title right here in Mogadishu at the Banadir stadium. As in the past Al Shabaab will likely cut the TV feed to embarrass the government so if you're a football nut you have to be there. The Police car will be a perfect cover because there will be lots of them there."

The older agent, Norm Lulham spoke up, "He's right. If he's a football nut he will be there for sure. Football is like a religion to these people and this is the biggest game of the year not only in Mogadishu but in all of Somalia. There is no way he could miss it and with Khalil likely out of town he can use the Police car and uniforms for himself and a couple of bodyguards who can carry AK-47's in the open. I'll bet he's as security conscious as Khalil and would be worried about going to the game in the open. Being cops they don't even need tickets. If I was him I'd use the cop car."

Cristal was worried, "This is all well and good but we have a weapon of mass destruction in play and we are seriously running out of time. We can't wait until Sunday when we have only five days left before

Christmas. He might not even show up at the game or if he does he might not use the Police car. What can we do now?"

The younger agent Rick, spoke up, "I have all the license tags of the Land Cruiser Police cars, their radio ID's, their patrol routes, the names of the cops assigned to them, etc."

David spoke, "Say more."

"Well we can try to cross reference all of this data with the visual from the drone. We can stream the drone video to Langley and get them to put a dozen analysts on it looking for Police cars that don't transmit, or Police cars off known patrol routes, or Police cars that park in a strange building overnight, who knows but it's a start."

Cristal was still not convinced, "I wish there was more we could do. This whole Police car angle is just a theory. Yes we'll be at the football match on Sunday and yes we'll stream video to Langley but these are all Hail Mary passes. Is there anything we've overlooked in trying to track down the leadership of Al Qaeda here in Somalia or finding that damned bomb?"

"That's why we're brainstorming," said David.

"We've tried all the obvious stuff," he continued. "We've been here for more than two weeks and all we have to show for it is two gangs trying to kidnap or kill us and a dead taxi driver. You've done all the mug shots multiple times. We've gone through every lead the local guys have. We tried to drop money on every contact we have and nothing.

"Khalil has a VERY tight organization. They must run on a skeleton crew here because they leave no footprints. We still have no idea how he communicates with the outside world. We are pretty sure he's no longer in town and the bomb is probably in America already.

"It's been almost a month since they found that dead bomb maker and he could have shipped the damned thing weeks before he died. Five weeks is enough time to get that thing anywhere in the world. If they did a great job of screening it they could have flown it into the US a month ago. Yes these are all Hail Mary passes but let's at least do that."

Everyone in the tiny room was exhausted and suffering from crippling stress given the stakes. Finally, they all agreed to do at least as much as Rick had proposed.

The CIA's team working off the US Carl Vinson was cycling high-altitude, stealth drones in and out of Mogadishu so that they had 24/7 coverage. The weather was great making visibility for the drones a non-issue.

CIA in Mogadishu sent HQ all the information they could get on the Police cars and live video was streaming to Langley within twelve hours and a team of twenty analysts was tasking the drones to check out and identify each Police car.

It was a long shot but it was the best one they had to work with at the moment. None of the CIA's other operations around the globe had anything to offer. There had been no signs of Khalil or the bomb.

The only radiation detector that had been set off was at the High Gate crossing from Quebec into Vermont by a man who had just finished a radiological cancer treatment.

Langley was starting to panic. They were days away from a high confidence attack but they had no actionable intelligence. There was no way they could raise the US threat level publicly because they could not tell anyone what to look for or what to do.

There was nothing in it to alarm the public. Yes, they'd catch hell once it got out that they knew an attack was imminent because the American people didn't understand that a non-specific alarm was almost worse than no alarm.

They had learned the hard way that getting three hundred million people enraged about an unidentified attack was more politically costly and physically dangerous than admitting after the fact that you had 'some' knowledge of an impending attack but no way to warn anyone that might be affected.

It also caused people to do crazy things and some people would die for a host of reasons including heart attacks brought on by the stress or being shot by people who thought they were terrorists.

Saturday seemed like a totally wasted day. They could think of nothing new to do to move the ball ahead. The USS Carl Vinson was busy keeping all of their drones cycling in and out of Mogadishu, analyzing video and passing it on to Langley. Cristal had stared at the sky a few times but she figured the drones they were using were so high they were invisible from the ground and certainly too quiet to be heard. Apparently, they had low radar signatures as well so the control tower at the International airport probably had no idea they were there. AWACS planes off the Vinson were keeping the drones well away from any other traffic.

Langley had all hands on deck supporting all of the various groups in the field running down any lead they could find. Financial transactions, boarding manifests, border crossings, anything that might turn up a lead in finding either the attack team or the bomb.

While the national threat level had not been specifically lifted, border guards were no longer spot checking but were searching the trunks of every car that entered the US because they had been given a non-specific escalation order from HQ to look for any weapons coming into the country. Lineups at all border crossings were growing and at one of the busiest times of the year, the week leading up to Christmas. Their nuclear detectors were all set to their highest setting but nothing had alarmed.

Because Cristal and David knew they were being hunted they decided to stay in the bunker style hotel all day, keep the curtains drawn in case of snipers and watch for cops. Cristal reasoned that as the Christmas deadline approached, Al Qaeda would be busy with the upcoming attack on the US and less interested in them for the moment.

Sunday morning arrived and it was an unusually hot and humid day even for Mogadishu. The normal high for the day was 88 F but by 10 am they were already into the high 80's. The football game at 1 pm would be brutal even for Somalies whether they were in the stands or on the field. Temperatures would peak in April but Sunday seemed like April had arrived in December.

The gang of four was in the back of their familiar beat up CIA van loaded with surveillance equipment including parabolic sound receivers, cameras, and high-speed video links to Langley and the drone's images being fed from the USS Carl Vinson forty miles off shore.

The undersized parking lot at Banadir stadium in central Mogadishu filled up quickly although most spectators arrived on foot or small dilapidated pickups with added railings which were used as buses.

Earlier they had seen nine Police cars arrive at various stages, most were the newer Land Cruisers but all had license plates on the list of legitimate cop cars.

The sounds from the stadium told them that the two top teams, both from the city, had taken to the field for the 1St Division playoff game. They had seen scalpers selling tickets near the entrance to the actual stadium but they were quickly disappearing so as not to miss any of the game themselves.

The national anthem played and a few minutes later the parking lot seemed deserted. Still no sign of a rogue Police car. Cristal was getting concerned that her Hail Mary was a bust. All she could think of was the dozens to hundreds of people in Langley, the USS Carl Vinson, the Pentagon, Homeland Security and potentially even the Situation Room in the Whitehouse gathered around screens hoping she had been right.

As she straightened her back and pulled away from the screens showing all of the cameras around the truck agent Rick Sawyer said quietly into his mike, "Here he comes. This has to be him."

One of the cameras finally caught the approaching Police car. It passed within thirty feet of their partially hidden parking position. Their own vehicle simply looked like another beat up van that could not find a space in the parking lot but they were strategically parked where they could watch both the parking entrance and also get a good look at the area near the stadium where emergency vehicles parked.

The subject Toyota Land Cruiser was moving too quickly to see who was inside but it looked like multiple players. As it passed on its way into the stadium parking David almost yelled, 'Eureka'.

Cristal said into her mike, "Langley did you get that?"

The Duty Officer at the other end broadcasted to everyone, "We have a rogue vehicle in play. This vehicle is not on the Mogadishu police roster."

Almost one hundred people on two continents had the hair on the back of their necks stand up.

David was out of the car with the backpack before anyone could stop him. Even though this was the plan he moved so fast he caught them off guard. In full disguise as a local peasant with a dirty backpack he entered the Stadium parking lot with his eyes glued on the receding Police car.

He zigzagged his way through the parked cars keeping low enough to be covered but not crouching enough to raise the suspicion of anyone who might see him although with the game in full swing it was unlikely anyone would be in the parking lot. He tried to remain in the Toyota's blind spot in case the driver was watching for any tails.

The team in the car, the aircraft carrier and HQ all had his back. They were all scanning the available camera shots watching for any danger to David.

The police SUV finally came to a stop near the stadium and parked at the end of the line of the nine other Police cars in an area reserved for emergency vehicles. Two ambulances were also in the line. The team in the van had been watching them and they all appeared empty. Apparently even the emergency personnel all wanted to be in the stadium at the game.

Three men got out of the suspect vehicle.

In the CIA van Norm Lulham had his high-powered digital camera on full auto and they were getting about four shots per second, trying to get close-ups of all three men. Within about 4 seconds he had great close-ups of all their faces as they milled around the Police van checking to see if anyone was watching them.

One seemed to be giving orders and from about eighty yards away David memorized the face. He imagined he could see some family resemblance to Jabir Habib. This HAD to be the older brother Mustafa, just as the team had predicted. All three had AK-47's, not unusual for police in Mogadishu. The one who must have been Mustafa and one of the guards turned and headed for the stadium entrance.

In Langley Bill Carter winced as the drone images and the van feed showed one bodyguard remaining with the Police car.

He immediately picked up a headset and indicated to the operator that he wanted to be patched in directly to David,

"David, this is Bill Carter. Even if this is Mustafa and his bodyguards, we have to get the data and get out of there without being detected. Any challenge to them in Mogadishu will get back to Khalil and we'll likely lose any chance of getting the bomb.

"We'll have Mustafa under surveillance from now on and we'll take them all when the time is right. Just find a way to bypass this guy and get that data."

Carter put his hand over his mike and looked around for his top tech guy. "How long to dump that data?"

The guy looked panicked but chose his words carefully, "It's a guess but I'd say up to thirty seconds depending on how much data there is. But he MUST wait for the green light indicating it's complete or it might be useless."

"David you need to get right up next to that van undetected for about thirty seconds but don't leave before you see the green light that the transfer has completed or it could be useless. And try to affix that passive GPS chip where they won't find it under the SUV."

Cristal turned to Rick, "I saw the instructions to plant that device but what is a passive GPS device."

It has virtually no electronic signature. It's inert almost all of the time until we send it a signal from a drone and then in a couple of nanoseconds it reports its position. Happens so fast no bug detector will pick it up even if they are sweeping for bugs right at that second".

Their attention switched back to David's progress. Two rows back from the stadium entrance and looking through the windshields of two vehicles to stay concealed David Crowe gritted his teeth. These guys were not asking for much. When he left cover he had to make it across a two lane driveway and get to cover beside the cop car. The distance suddenly seemed enormous. He'd be in the open with absolutely no cover for at least ten seconds and this guy had an AK-47 against David's nine millimeter. The CIA van was too far back to give him any kind of fire cover if needed and any drone strike would take out him as well as the SUV and the guard so he was on his own.

We wished now that one of the people in the CIA van had a sniper rifle trained on this guy, but no such luck.

Right now the guy was on the driver's side of the SUV which was the wrong side for David's approach. David needed to reposition under cover if he was going to have any chance to approach the vehicle from the other side undetected.

Just then there was a massive cheer in the stadium seeming to indicate that someone had scored. The guard turned franticly and ran across the front of the car trying to find a space in the stands where he could see the field. Now he was on his radio still looking for a peek at the field as David made his move. He sprinted from his cover and across the two lanes sliding like a baseball player into home plate on the opposite side of the car but exactly where the guard had been standing. The noise of his slide was heavily outweighed by the deafening noise from the crowd.

He pushed the backpack up against the driver's door and hit the execute switch. Time passed very slowly as he waited for the green light. He was suddenly aware that at least one hundred people had one of two or three different camera views of his predicament but none of them could offer any assistance.

In his ear he heard Cristal's voice, "The guard is easing back toward the car. You need to get out of there."

He could now hear the guard more clearly on his radio. He grabbed his gun and laid on the ground ready to fire. Suddenly he worried that the damned bag would beep or ring or something when it completed. A quick look at the light and it was still off. He hoped the batteries were fresh on the light.

Suddenly he saw the foot of the guard near the front of the vehicle and he was making his way back around to the driver's side. He rolled over just fitting under the car and dragging the bag with him pressing it against the floorboards of the Toyota in the hope that it was still collecting data. He got the passive GPS bug out of his pocket and stuck it above one of the frame members where it would never be seen.

Finally the light turned green.

Cristal whispered in his ear, "Nice move. The guard is still there and still on the radio." Which was more information than David needed given he was about three feet away from the man's feet. He could make out that the guard was talking to his counterpart in Arabic who was trying to explain how the goal had happened. His excitement indicated that his team had scored.

David rolled quietly to the other side of the car and got on to his knees to take a guarded peak at the man through the car windows which like most newer vehicles in town, had tinted glass because of the sun.

To his relief the guard had his back to him and was still engaged in an excited conversation over the score. David wasted no time and keeping low, trotted and then ran hard directly away from the guard on the other side of the car. To keep his cover of the Toyota between him and the guard, he had to run in a diagonal to the first line of parked cars putting him in the open for nearly twenty terrifying seconds with his back to a man with a high-powered automatic weapon, but it worked.

After catching his breath and ensuring the guard had not moved or raised an alarm, he made his way carefully through the parking lot always watching the guard in case he turned and saw him. He was back at the van in about two minutes and he could hear all sorts of cheering over his headset.

Inside the car, agent Rick Sawyer wasted no time plugging a network cable into the backpack, clicking a few keys on his laptop and within seconds, all of the data was streaming to Langley.

They were back to the hotel before they got the first word from Langley.

Phil Harris made the call, "You did it guys. Looks like we captured about three months of data from both the GPS and the Black Box chip. We'll be working on this 24/7 trying to plot where they've been and see if we can tie it time wise to any drone surveillance we have.

"The good news is that the drones we've been using for the last two months on our regular survey of Mogadishu have the latest hi-res video cameras so they are often wide shots that we can zoom in on and we always record everything.

"We'll get back to you pronto if there's anything we need you to do. And oh by the way, we have a second drone en route to follow that Toyota 24/7 now. We just ping'ed the passive GPS chip and it's working fine too. We won't let them get out of our sight."

The Mogadishu team spent the rest of the afternoon speculating on whether the data would tell them anything. They all agreed it would be interesting to know where the Toyota had been. It might tell them their major safe houses but as to the bomb, how would they interpret any data that helped in that regard?

It was two in the morning local time when they were all awoken in their separate rooms for a conference call. Phil Harris led the call, "For the benefit of those who were just sleeping in Mogadishu let me bring you up to date. The data is great. We have at least twelve targets that may be safe houses and of course we've identified the place they hide the Toyota when it's not in use.

"There are also several trips to a warehouse near the port which we now speculate is where they could have weaponized the device. There are also regular visits to a point above the port of Mogadishu but the vehicle always parked where there were no buildings so we've been able to synchronize those sessions with our drone coverage and it looks like at least two different individuals, dressed as police of course, seemed interested in something in the port.

"The good news is that overlaying several drone videos we were able to triangulate and we think we know what ship they were looking at. It was in dry-dock for a while last month. The bad news is that ship is gone and it didn't turn up on any of the recent drone scans so we don't know where it is, or where it's headed.

"What we do know is that it was painted mostly red, it came out of that dry-dock in late November and disappeared around December 1st which gives it plenty of time to reach either Europe or more importantly the US.

"We have no way from here to get the name of the ship so we need you to get us the name, it's possible destination and anything else you can find out. We are sending you by secure e-mail pictures that are relevant so you can find the dry-dock and see if you can get info on its registration, who owns it, and where it's headed."

The senior CIA guy in Mogadishu on the phone from his apartment took over, "This is Norm Lulham. We have contacts in the port. It will be 7:30 local time before we can do this without raising alarms. I don't see any other way to do any of this overnight without setting off major alarms and possibly getting arrested. Will that work?"

Phil Harris looked around the room filled with section heads and analysts. He got a bunch of nods and

338

some shrugs, "OK proceed as fast as possible. Call us the minute you have ANYTHING new.

As dawn broke agent Rick Sawyer was at the dock and looking for some of his normal contacts. A dock foreman he knew as Faraj was the first one he saw. Within minutes he had determined that Faraj was very familiar with the rather old red ship and had worked on loading it. It was registered out of Panama with a registered name of 'Arab Nights' and sailed for Tunisia through the Suez Canal with a mixed load of livestock, canned tuna, charcoal and bananas. These were all normal exports for this shipping company and with the exception that it had been in dry-dock for ten days for a scheduled scraping and painting, it had been a regular turnaround and destination.

He was back at the UN building in the vacant office with the others and on the phone with Langley giving them the full report of his investigation within the hour which made it the middle of the night this time for the Virginia gang.

Bill Carter joined the operations people in the control room from his office to hear the report. He had decided to stay close overnight expecting developments.

They were all hoping they had not reached a dead end because nothing seemed unusual with this ship. Within minutes an analyst rushed into the room in Langley with a CIA report, "The ship arrived in Sfax, Tunisia on schedule and off loaded all of its cargo BUT the ship was sold in Tunisia to a new company we've never heard of and it sailed to pick up a load in Rotterdam, Netherlands. We're checking on that now."

A second analyst rushed in with new information, "It should have arrived in the Netherlands about a week ago but there has been no sign of the ship. Finally a ship named Arab Nights has not made port in any international seaport we have access to. Unless it was sailing around the world to China it should have landed somewhere by now. It has just disappeared."

For a moment everyone froze knowing the implications. The pieces seemed to be fitting together. It was now a high probability that this ship had a nuclear device on board and was headed for the US.

Phil Harris was Duty Officer overnight and after getting a nod from Bill Carter spoke first addressing all of the operators in the control room, "Now that we have a name for the ship, we go to a Homeland Red Alert. Get everything we have into the Homeland Security system but no public announcements. Wake the rest of our team and get them in here.

"Pull the registration file. We must have a picture of Arab Nights or a ship of the same design. Make sure it's showing a red hull in the picture and get it out to every US port big or small on the east coast, Coast Guard, the Navy, Air Force, Drone management, and anyone else you can think of. We need all satellite data to see if we can track it from Tunisia. Get the Pentagon working on it now. We have to find this ship."

Alarms went out all over Washington and several military bases. Satellite images were being pulled up to try to track a needle in a haystack out of Tunisia about two weeks earlier. The Coast guard called up all of their assets on the east coast looking for a red ship, about three hundred feet long named Arab Nights.

They left the line open with Mogadishu in case anything broke immediately. While they waited Rick Sawyer took the opportunity to speak directly to the DD whom he had never met.

"Deputy Director Carter, this is agent Rick Sawyer in Mogadishu, I just want to say that every intelligence organization in the world has been trying to find a crack in Khalil's operation for years. In the last two weeks, actually the last 48 hours, Cristal and David have done what no one else, including Norm and me, have been able to do. They've cracked his operation wide open. It has been a pleasure to work with two pros like this."

Cristal was blushing as she broke in, all the time wondering who exactly was all on the conference call in Langley, "Sorry but that is wrong. It was our Mogadishu team here that came up with the lead that Mustafa might be using Tariq Aziz as an alias. That is the thread that unraveled this thing."

Bill Carter had heard enough, "OK folks. Calm down. We are all very aware of the excellent work that has gone down in your neck of the woods recently but at the risk of bursting your bubble, we have no evidence yet that any of this is leading to the bomb we're after. Yes, we're pretty sure we have Mustafa on a string but Khalil is still out there and there are a lot of ifs on whether this ship has anything to do with the bomb. Let's keep focused. We may be no closer to finding the bomb or Khalil and we have only a few days left to make that happen.

"I will personally handout the pats on the back if we get this thing and so let's just remember the stakes and keep focused on finding this damned thing. This is no time for celebrations."

Cristal could see the red on Rick's face as he stared at the floor. She reached over and patted him on the back with a smile which he returned.

Every resource on the east coast had been pressed into action looking for Arab Nights approaching the coast of the US. Port records were electronically searched and there had been no sign of the ship. Time was slipping by and they were getting no results. The team in Mogadishu could only sit and wait to find out if there was anything else they needed to do to support the hunt.

There was only one thing anyone could do now, find that ship. It was the key to the attack but it had simply vanished. Satellites had been tasked to search the North Atlantic and came up with several possible targets but none of them panned out as the Arab Nights.

On the morning of the second day Somali time during their scheduled early morning, late evening Langley conference call with all parties they had their answer and it was the worst they could have imagined. An analyst came rushing into the operations room out of breath, "We found it. Someone finally recognized the picture which was not really a good facsimile and we did some fast checking. It landed in New Jersey three days ago, within sight of Manhattan empty and ready for a load of relief supplies for Africa."

Phil Harris was furious, "How did we not pick it earlier when we searched the database?"

She blushed, "Because we did an exact search for Arab Nights and they renamed it at sea. It's now marked as 'Arab Delight' and it was accepted into port because they had forwarded paperwork en route as required showing they were empty and had a contract to pick up a load. We have not checked yet if they actually re-registered it or just painted the new name on it. No word yet on whether the port authority checked the background and registration of the ship when it arrived. They normally do a quick walk through of any arriving empty ship checking for contraband or cargo trying to avoid import duties. It was empty and probably had believable paperwork anyways. Apparently the picture we posted was not as close to the actual ship as we thought."

Phil was red faced, "Get every resource we have in New York on that ship and strip it. We need to find the bomb or traces of it to ensure we're on the right path. Find every person that was on board and get them in for questioning and be careful, one of them might be Khalil."

The DD took over, "Cristal and David are you still on the line?"

"Yeah, we're here Bill," said Cristal.

"Work with logistics and get to New York the fastest way possible. There's nothing left to do in Mogadishu. Take a fighter jet if you have to. You two have broken this wide open but we're in more jeopardy than ever. We need you here. Understood?"

"Yes."

Minutes later as they were trying to figure out the best way to get to New York fast, they received a call from the commander of the USS Carl Vinson. "Our buddies in the Air Force have a B1 bomber based in Diego Garcia in the Indian Ocean that could use a flight home. That's your fastest way and they have two empty weapons officer seats on board. They have permission to land at Arba Minch in Ethiopia. If you can get to Wanlaway airstrip by nine thirty, we'll have an Osprey fake an emergency landing and shuttle you up to Arba Minch. We'll have you in the New York area by mid afternoon today their time."

Cristal looked at her watch. It was almost 8:30. It would be tight but after getting a nod from the others she agreed and hung up.

Rick Sawyer said, "I'll get you a fast taxi and pay him well. You'll have to leave from here now. It will take you about an hour to get up there and that Osprey is not going to want to sit on the runway for long after an illegal landing. It's armed but we don't want to start a war. Better to get out of there before anyone knows about it. Wish I was the one getting a supersonic ride on a B-1B Lancer though."

The plan went well. Neither had time to return to the hotel but the CIA team had offered to clean the rooms out and ship everything back in diplomatic bags through the Australian embassy who was one of the few western countries with an embassy in Mogadishu and had assisted with delicate transfers in the past, like importing an illegal bottle of scotch.

They kept in touch with the Carl Vinson by cell phone on the way to Wanlaway airstrip. The US didn't have landing rights or even fly-over rights with Somalia so the Osprey was standing off the coast and timed its big loop over the northwest of the city so he landed at Wanlaway just as they approached. They lifted off in less than five minutes.

On board they were told there were no worries about the Somali Air Force which was still trying to re-launch itself after all of the wars and changes in leadership. The only possible threat would come from AMISOM, the African led mission helping the Somali Government but they had been notified of a humanitarian flight into Wanlaway with no details. An International complaint would be launched at the UN and IATA but that was the least of their problems now.

As they arrived in Arba Minch, they saw the big B-1B Lancer, looking like a space vehicle, sitting just off the runway ready to go. The Osprey with its vertical landing capability set down not far behind the big jet on a taxiway. They were strapped in military style at the vacant weapons stations complete with helmets in under 5 minutes and the big supersonic bird taxied out on to the runway.

As they made their hard turn at the end of the runway the pilot said, "Hang on, this runway is only nine thousand feet long which is minimal for this bird in this heat. We have a light fuel load and no payload so we're going to punch this thing hard."

The revving of the big engines and then the afterburners kicking in was bone shattering as he let go of the brakes and jumped into his takeoff roll. What seemed like about 20 seconds later he pulled the nose up just a bit and they lifted off as the end of the runway passed below them. After a few seconds where they figured he was building airspeed, he nosed up to about forty degrees and climbed quickly.

To Cristal this seemed like what a ride on the old Space Shuttle must have been like, noisy, bone rattling and climbing faster and faster.

Somewhere over Africa, they caught up with their first refueler.

So here they were, no passports and jetting at over a thousand miles an hour at very high altitude, breaking international rules of air traffic corridors at sixty thousand feet to make it to New York quickly.

The big supersonic bomber slowed and descended only when it was time to catch another refueler and then they were supersonic and over 10 miles high again. In their helmets they could hear the odd communication between the pilots and an unseen AWACS plane or two helping them avoid any traffic or any strict no fly zones.

It would be a long day so both of them tried to catch some sleep on the way over. The ride was smooth at this altitude but the adrenalin was really pumping and sleep was hard to come by.

They landed at McGuire Air Force base in New Jersey and were choppered the fifty miles up to New

York where they debarked at Battery Park and were shuttled to CIA New York HQ a few blocks away.

Bill Carter, Phil Harris and some of the team from Langley had transferred up and were there waiting for them. The control room at the CIA's HQ in New York was abuzz with activity.

Bill Carter opened with, "Wow you too must be tired, seven hour time change and about ten thousand miles under your belt.

"Here is what we know. The ship arrived almost three days ago. It's actually parked less than a mile and a half from here just on the other side of the Hudson. We came up with nothing searching the ship and so far the crew members we've been able to find and interview seem clueless to any shenanigans.

"Earlier this morning we had divers in the water and they found an unusual attachment on the hull under the bulbous bow. By the scraping it looks like something was mounted there and is now gone. So it's likely no one save possibly the captain, whom we have not found yet, knew anything about the bomb. But the attachment which is very unique and seems to have no other purpose has convinced us that this was the way they got the bomb here.

"We have no way of telling who took it from the hull or where they took it. Security cameras in the area show nothing so Khalil's divers must have entered the water somewhere nearby, they probably knew what areas had security cameras and avoided them.

"Because we are assuming nuclear materials, they are all very heavy and even relatively small amounts would be tough for a diver to haul around by himself so this thing was really well planned. They must have had floatation devices or a tow cable or something to get it away from the ship and loaded onto something. This took a lot of planning and maybe even custom tools so we had better not underestimate these people.

"We now have high confidence a dirty bomb has arrived in New York and will be exploded day after tomorrow. So we have to assume the target is here in New York but we're still no closer to intercepting it.

"We've checked and it's impossible to evacuate New York City, Eastern New Jersey, lower Connecticut, Long Island and all of the surrounding areas and we would cause complete panic, gridlock and deaths if we announce anything.

"We have meteorologists working on a forecast for winds on Christmas Day in case of an airburst bomb of nuclear material and so far it looks like lower Connecticut could be in the prime downwind hazard area if something is released in Manhattan.

"All law-enforcement have been given enough information that they know to watch for anything suspicious but we could not give them details or it would have leaked and gone viral.

"We'll be crucified for not saying anything to the public but that's where we find ourselves. We need to warn the public but there's nothing to say that would help them to know what to do or how to prepare themselves.

"After five weeks of intense work we've gotten so close but not even close if you know what I mean. I'm open to any ideas on how to track this thing down."

Everyone had been listening and the room fell silent. All of the worker bees were waiting for some direction.

***

At that very moment, a Turkish businessman impeccably dressed and with a completely normal B-1 visa was clearing through US Customs and Immigration at JFK airport.

"Mr. Berkant, what is the nature of your visit to New York?"

A Smiling Khalil al-Adel said in perfect English with an American accent, "It's a mixture of business and pleasure. I have meetings with potential distributors in the city and I have plans to take in a few shows with some friends."

"What is the nature of your business?"

"Fashion exports. America is a growing market for us."

"How long will you be with us?"

"Not certain but should be between a week and ten days."

"Your declaration form says you have nothing to declare. No Christmas presents?"

"No, I have a few friends here in New York but I'm paying for the Broadway shows as their Christmas Present."

"Well Mr. Berkant, welcome to America. Have a wonderful stay in New York and enjoy the excitement of our holiday season."

"Oh, I expect lots of excitement. Thank you."

A driver with a sign for Mr. Berkant was waiting for him after baggage claim and after exchanging the proper pass phrases, they were out of the airport in under fifteen minutes.

As they pulled away from the short term parking and he felt it safe to talk the driver said, " Al-hamdu

348

lillāh, it is so good to meet you master and to see that you've arrived safely. I was very worried you would not see my sign so I positioned myself so you could not miss me. I had no idea who I was looking for and I must say you look nothing like what I expected, and I mean that in a good way.

"Everything is in order just as you instructed. I received the package this very morning just as you said and Insha'Allah we'll be successful in our jihad."

Khalil was always nervous at this point in an operation. New people made him nervous even if he had checked this one out constantly since picking him six months ago with the aid of a sympathetic Imam.

He was turning out to be the talkative type. He sincerely hoped he had followed instructions and kept all of the plans strictly to himself. Besides this native New Yorker and himself, only Mustafa back in Mogadishu knew the exact target, the weapon and the timing.

Khalil looked out the window in the fading sunlight. Here he was in New York. Behind enemy lines as it were. The most wanted man in the world and he had just marched through their lines of security.

It had been over fifteen years since he had been in the US and except for the newer cars, everything seemed familiar. Still he had to stay as alert as he ever had been in his life. He was running the risk of handing the Americans a major victory if he was somehow discovered.

The driver couldn't help himself. There was so much to say and he had never dreamed he would be teamed with the master himself when he joined the jihadist movement in Brooklyn.

Khalil was easily the most wanted man in the world and here he was in his car driving in New York and teaming up with him for Jihad in America. This was unbelievable. It actually hurt that he could tell no one of this life changing moment. Only the Imam at his mosque knew of his connection to the master and even he didn't know of the master's trip or the impending attack.

He had been preparing himself for three months and now the attack was upon them. The plan was for him to leave the US with master Khalil after the attack and join him at Jihad Central in Somalia where he expected to be greeted as a hero by the only people who knew of their plans and be able to appreciate their amazing achievement. But by then it would all be public and known around the world.

He felt he was talking too much but he had so much to tell the master, "Our planning has gone even better than you instructed master. Because I'm the newest member of the organization, I was forced to work on their Christmas Day. I didn't even have to volunteer for it or swap days with someone. I have a company truck and the keys for the gates we need."

"Hakim you've done well. Insha'Allah we'll indeed have a most glorious day for Islam."

"Master as you instructed, I've abandoned my apartment and we have a room with two beds at a small secure motel that is convenient for our purposes. It's not fitting for a man of your stature but as you said, the Jihad must put security first. We only need to retrieve my company truck when we're ready. As instructed I have uniforms and weapons at the motel but I'm talking too much. You must be tired."

"I do not allow myself to feel fatigue. I am filled with the energy of our impending Jihad Hakim. Do not worry about me. This is not the first Jihad operation I've run. If you have done your job properly we'll be successful, Insha'Allah."

JFK

Two hours after Khalil's arrival a long-term baggage handler in Terminal 2 at JFK opened his lunch box in the baggage handling area for incoming baggage and released thousands of insects. Five minutes later he walked through the terminal and from time to time pulled a string in his pocket that released more bed bugs from a bag at his ankle. One of the insects crawled back up his leg and bit him but he carried on.

This process was repeated by others at the remaining five passenger terminals in the complex.

It was soon clear to airport management that someone had orchestrated a vandalism attack on their airport. Every terminal it seemed was reporting a sudden infestation of some kind of insect. An orchestrated attack that didn't require a SWAT team but one that required an exterminator. Someone joked that they needed a different kind of 'swat' team but no one was laughing. This was a really serious imposition and there would be hell to pay if security and the cops could figure out who did it.

Someone soon identified the bugs as bed bugs which was bound to strike fear into anyone passing through the airport as they had been known to spread quickly when transported to homes or hotels on luggage or clothing. The US had had a serious infestation a few years earlier and no one wanted to repeat that disaster.

There were constant calls streaming in from several of the terminals that people were reporting bugs on their luggage. Some of them familiar with the insects knew they were bed bugs. And this at one of the busiest times of the year, the day before Christmas Eve. Panic was spreading, the news of this would be in the press in no time and something had to be done quickly. Security was positioned at all exits and asked to inform people to check their luggage as they left the terminals.

The chief administrator's assistant came up with a business card of 'Bed, Bug and Beyond' a company that had serendipitously been by earlier in the week and claimed it had fumigated half of New York for bed bugs a few years earlier.

They were engaged immediately and planned to fumigate all of the terminals overnight but the chemicals they would use would be hazardous so the terminals would have to be shut down after the last flights and all electrical devices powered down for at least four hours until the air was safe. The airport was requested to divert any aircraft that might violate the four hour rule and a few flights were redirected to Newark which had to keep its international arrivals staff on duty to accommodate the last arriving international flights.

Teams of three or four exterminators showed up at each terminal around midnight with full Hazmat suits. Each team waited for the last flight, then made sure all employees were out of the building before they went around unplugging all of TSA's detection equipment.

Then using what appeared at first glance to be blackened pump-up type garden sprayers, went about their business. They specifically hit areas that were away from the TSA checkpoints and areas that would be hard to get to and clean. They sprayed elevator shafts, between the steps on escalators, baggage carts, food outlet cupboards, newspaper stands and doors leading to airways.

The operation didn't go completely smoothly. The syrupy solution of water, corn starch, magnetized iron filings and ground up Cobalt-60 would often jam up the sprayer nozzles which had to be adjusted from time to time but in all cases the job was done within two hours and they were on their way long before their deadline. Other exterminators made sure they got a good dose of the stuff on key external equipment including refueling hoses, airplane tugs, shipping containers, baggage conveyors, maintenance tools, bathrooms, and even the landing gear of a few parked planes.

Airport Security assigned to the internal parts of the airport had been convinced to remain for the four hours in their own building on the airport grounds for their safety. They monitored progress of the workers on their bank of monitors.

The Cobalt-60 was magnetized and easily found its way into every nook and cranny of elevator shafts and the like. The iron filings which were also magnetized and had been radioactively contaminated by the Cobalt-60, now served to dilute the total solution yet spread the effects much further.

Late night airport management became aware that the exterminators had left without saying goodbye and calls to their number went unanswered. Unworried about this as it was now 3 am on Christmas Eve, they were still sure they would get a massive invoice for the emergency call late at night.

All passenger terminals reopened for regular business on December 24th at 4:30 am. The first passengers arrived closer to 5 am and started setting off nuclear alarms at every TSA checkpoint.

Homeland Security was immediately informed. All terminals were closed, all flights cancelled, and all approach roads were blocked. All employees, staff, flight crews and civilians in the terminals were screened at TSA gates and carefully led out of the building if they were unaffected but those who set of the alarms were detained.

Not only were they all irate about the detention, it was clear to everyone that they had been exposed to radioactivity and panic was breaking out in every terminal. Security was ordered to stay in the buildings and secure the infected people but some security guards on the basis of the rumors that the buildings were contaminated, ignored their orders out of fear and headed for their cars.

The Deputy Director had been asleep for only about an hour when he received an emergency text. The beeping phone sounded really loud in his make-shift bunk in the CIA HQ. It was from the Ops center at 5:10 am. The text simply said, 'They Hit JFK !!! '

He was upstairs at the control center in under five minutes. The duty manager had already alerted the Nuclear Incident Response Team and NIRT had first responders covering New York State scrambled and en route to JFK within the hour.

As the whole team filtered in, the DD gathered those available, got the team at Langley on the video link and asked for a SITREP. The duty manager complied, "All we know is that some kind of insect infestation was reported in all passenger terminals at JFK yesterday evening. The airport administration assumed some kind of organized vandalism or protest and called in exterminators who had to clear the buildings of all personnel. Apparently they were wearing some kind of Hazmat outfits and went about fumigating the buildings. They were alone in the terminals for up to four hours. Security watched them on monitors but saw nothing suspicious.

"Then this morning as soon as the buildings were reopened and as passengers started filtering through the TSA checkpoints, not all of them but a large number of them set of radiation alarms. The administration made the connection to the fumigation and shut down the entire complex right around 5 am. Right now it looks like they hit every terminal but we're not sure yet and we don't know what they used, where it is in the buildings and whether the people that became contaminated are in any health peril with the radiation they picked up.

"Needless to say the company that did the spraying is not answering the phone and their address according to Google Maps is bogus."

Bill Cater was furious, "So you're telling me the entire JFK is shut down until further notice the day before Christmas and they may have killed a bunch of people? Where are the people that were contaminated?"

"The good news is that it was early and the buildings were almost empty. There were only about forty five of them and another dozen or so employees that set off the alarms. TSA protocol is to detain anyone who sets off an alarm. Everyone in the buildings was tested and released if they were clean although I just got off the phone with JFK administration and they think some security guards are AWOL and they are trying to find them and get them tested now, before they fire them.

"The head TSA guy over there was on the ball and got anyone infected onto buses, officially detained as per the law establishing the TSA and sent them to Jamaica Hospital Medical Center near the airport which as part of New York's Emergency Management Protocol, is set up to isolate contaminated individuals in case of a nuclear, biological or chemical incident. By the way, we're sure the three buses are contaminated as well.

"We have no report yet from the hospital on their condition but no reports of deaths yet either, although radiation poisoning does not always kill you in the first few hours."

Bill Carter took over, "I want a report ASAP on how those people are doing.

"Now back to the site. This will be massive. The first impact beyond the people infected is that this is totally unforecasted unlike weather events where they can plan around some of the disruption. This will screw up the whole airline business for everyone traveling for Christmas for at least half of the country not to mention probably a couple of billion dollars worth of aircraft which are now out of commission and probably parked at JFK for the foreseeable future.

"Is there any chance this is an industrial accident of some kind? The chemicals they used were slightly radioactive? Enough to set off alarms?"

The controller answered, "We had that thought too but so far what we've heard from the NIRT hotline is 'no way'. This had to be much more serious and intentional to set off all those alarms. We'll know more when their team gets on site."

Cristal spoke up, "Is this what anyone thought was meant by a dirty bomb?"

She and the DD could tell by the looks in the room that no one had thought of this scenario or anything like it.

David spoke up, "How much of this stuff did they need to contaminate, what, six passenger terminals at JFK?"

The duty officer answered that one, "We have no way of knowing how much of these nuclear materials they had yet. All we know right now is that there were at least twenty five guys carrying garden sprayers and they may have had additional sprayers or reloaded and it was enough to set off more than a dozen alarms, infect about fifty people and shut down a major airport. We warned the other airports in the region to look out for a similar attack but they've reported nothing so far."

There was a long pause in the room as the DD looked around to see who was present. Apart from David and Cristal and Phil Harris, Carole Glass his deputy and Bob Boutet his Khalil expert had flown up to NY with him and then there was Hank Morrison, head of the CIA in New York and about ten people who made up the New York Operations Center. More bodies were on their way in to relieve the night shift.

The DD spoke slowly, "Well we blew it guys. This one is signed sealed and delivered and the bad guys are all gone. We had our first tip that there was a dirty bomb in play nearly five weeks ago. These guys we're after are good. This is some of the most sophisticated planning we've seen from them so far. Somehow they found a couple dozen jihadists in New York or brought them here to contaminate that airport. My guess is they probably hit some planes too if they were able to get to them and that could be mega millions more.

"We have no idea yet of the total damage but it will be in the tens to hundreds of millions to the airlines if planes were infected, maybe millions to tens of millions for all we know to clean up JFK. Millions or more in healthcare for the survivors. As time goes by and we understand more of this attack I'm sure we'll find more ugly surprises. They had to have thought this one out pretty carefully to cause the maximum damage.

"They've probably closed that airport for the foreseeable future. I think there were thousands of flights a day out of JFK so how are we going to accommodate the overflow at other centers. They were all running near capacity already. The economic impact of that alone will be monstrous.

"It may be weeks before we have a handle on the total hit to our economy. We speculated that the economy was their target in Pittsburgh but no one could have seen this strategy played out. I really thought they would go for a bigger head count.

"Heads will roll for this. Probably mine first, for not intercepting this attack, for not warning people we knew something for five weeks was going to happen and for not catching the terrorists.

"I know we all did our best but it was not good enough this time. I appreciate your dedication but sometimes the other guys get one past us. You heard it before but it's true, they only have to be right once, we have to be right one hundred percent of the time to stop them.

"So expect to see me and the Director in endless hearings in Washington over this one. All I can promise you is that I'll represent you well and do my best to convince the American people that you did an outstanding job of coming very close to intercepting these animals."

Cristal could see by the faces in the room and on the video link with Langley that beyond this being a career ending event for some or all of them, everyone felt for this man. He had done everything he could but his career for certain was at a very tragic and embarrassing end. America would indeed demand accountability and a public flogging for the man at the center of it all.

An hour ago the chase was still on but now it was all too late. Actually, it had been too late about twelve hours earlier when men entered JFK with containers full of radioactive material.

The American people would never know or appreciate the intelligence and dedication of this man and the operation he had run.

The DD sighed, straightened himself and said, "But with all that said our job is not finished. We believe the leader of this organization, Khalil Al-Adel is likely in New York now and trying to get out as quickly and quietly as possible.

"This company that did the extermination could not have gathered all that equipment like hazmat suits and thousands of bed bugs without leaving some trails. And there still may be some story and trail behind the purchase and renaming of that ship parked at a Jersey dock. So let's get back to work.

"I want the New York team focused on the exterminators, the people in the hospital and the investigation and cleanup of JFK.

"David, Cristal and my team here from Langley will take the lead on Khalil. Langley needs to take on the ship and support the two teams here if anything breaks."

"Let's get back to work," he turned to Hank Morrison, head of the NY team and said, "Please keep me updated on the people infected and progress with NIRT at JFK. I don't want to be left out of anything. As soon as possible I want an assessment of the damage for the Director and the President."

He then turned to Carole Glass, "I have a dirty job for you. If this is not in the press yet, it will be any minute and there will be a shit storm. You are my point man on that. Call the Director. Get him out of bed if you have to. Brief him. Tell him to brief the President. You get on the call too if he needs you. Try to get the Chief-of-staff and the Whitehouse Press Secretary on that call too. The more I think of it the more I want you on that call. You never know what the Director might add of his own accord. Tell him for the press that it's an active crime scene and all questions should wait until we have the facts.

"The Director should offer to do a press conference with Homeland Security in a few hours with or without the President and get our press relations on it so that he has a speech with the latest info but keep it restrictive and conservative. Facts will come to light over the next few hours and days that may make any premature statements look ridiculous. You vet the press release and run blocking on the press. Get one of Hank's people up to speed to handle the New York Press.

"We still have important work to do and I want to spend all my time on that so after you make those calls head back to Langley and be our point man there."

This was a big assignment for Carole who was relatively new at her job but she had come up through the ranks and had seen big events before. The only difference was that she was to be the face of this one for a while and this was the BIGGEST of events to affect the CIA in years. She simply nodded and rushed off to call the Director.

Bill Carter watched her rush off and thought to himself that it was likely no one would ever know how people like Carole and the rest of his team stepped up when the time came and did outstanding work for the American people. But that would all be lost in the very public career ending execution some of them would be facing at the hands of politicians and the press in the coming weeks and months. But this was not the time to lament the situation they found themselves in.

He motioned to Harris and Boutet to follow him with David and Cristal into another conference room.

As they grabbed chairs he said, "OK guys. How do we find Khalil. If we can catch him and string him up by his nuts maybe, just maybe we can salvage something out of this."

Boutet being the agency's man on Khalil started, "Well here is what we know or speculate. We know that he's a master of disguise and has access to great forged paperwork. Our theory and it's a theory only, is that he is here in New York and participated somehow in the attack on JFK. He has likely been in town for only a day or two because he doesn't want to hang around too long and give us a chance to catch him.

"He may have already left given that the attack happened last night. He has support here so it's unlikely that he rented a car and is driving around by himself. He won't be flying back out of JFK any time soon so he'll likely try to get out through Dulles, Philly, or Chicago headed Europe way but that's not certain.

"I would think he would not go through Montreal or Toronto because he would have to face one more immigration interrogation and the borders will soon be on the lookout for an escaping terrorist."

An aid popped his head in the doorway after knocking, "Mr. Morrison says you might want to turn on CNN."

Cristal reached over and turned on the TV on the wall.

Everyone recognized the familiar face of Wolf Blitzer, "To repeat our Breaking News early on this Christmas Eve morning, CNN has learned that terrorists struck with a nuclear device at JFK Airport this morning. It was likely a dirty bomb of some sort and our sources say that several if not all of the terminals are now radioactively contaminated and unusable.

"All flights have been cancelled on this Christmas Eve and travelers are scrambling to find ways to get where they need to be for Christmas. Just a moment. We have more on this story."

He touched his earpiece and then accepted a paper from someone just off camera, reviewed it quickly and pressed his earpiece more firmly into his ear, "Yes we're hearing that many early morning passengers were contaminated when they arrived at the airport this morning. We don't know how many passengers or if any of them are dead but the hospital now reports it is treating dozens of victims for radiation exposure and burns from Cobalt-60 which has been found on all of the travelers and some of the airport staff. Jane Menendez is at Jamaica Medical Center near JFK, Jane what can you tell us?"

Jane looked like she had fallen out of bed, snow flurries were whipping her hair around as she tried to stand up straight, slightly caught off guard, to do her national spot out front of the hospital.

"As you just said Wolf, we cannot get an accurate headcount of the people admitted here to this hospital or their condition however early reports are that there was at least three buses of victims and that they were all ambulatory. That is to say that they all walked into the hospital from the buses that were sent for them. As far as we know no one was carried in on a stretcher or gurney which I think you will agree is a good sign. And yes, early reports from the hospital lab is that they all had varying amounts of Cobol-60 on them.'

Wolf interrupted, "I think you meant to say Cobalt-60 Jane which is a radioactive isotope of Cobalt. COBOL is a computer language. Thanks Jane, we'll get back to you when you have more information."

Cristal turned off the TV, "We live in strange times. The whole world knows it's Cobalt-60 before we do."

The Deputy Director lifted the phone and pressed zero, "Please find Jim Morrison and have him join us in conference B."

Jim was there in thirty seconds, "I know CNN is reporting an AP report that it was Cobalt-60. That's what the hospital is saying. We have not heard from NIRT on site yet but I will get on to them this minute to give us a reading of the type of material and an estimate of quantity and lethality."

Bill Carter forced a smile at the room, "See I didn't even have to ask."

Jim Morrison disappeared with his new task.

Bill Carter resumed his thoughts, "So how do we find him?"

Cristal answered, "We've had a theory that he attends some of his attacks. Last night would have been a perfect opportunity for him to brag that he did it himself. I say we pull all JFK security footage and look for the guy in the video that acts like the leader."

David interceded, "Yeah but he knows there are cameras in there and he wants to stay anonymous. So unless we find one where he's giving the camera the bird, I don't think he would be careless enough to get caught on video even if he's in a great disguise. But we have to review the videos anyways. I suggest we get the New York team to look for any signs of a leader or leaders at the same time."

The DD looked pensive, "When do you think he got here and how would he disguise himself to enter the US?"

Cristal spoke first, "I agree with Bob. I don't think he would want to be in the country for long so my guess would be that he arrived in the last few days."

David interjected, "If it was me, I would be well-dressed as a senior looking business traveler. First class cabin material. They get away with charm and confidence and are rarely stopped by immigration. You know, the profile that never gets checked for drugs or is asked to open his luggage. He could have come with a woman but I don't think that is his style."

The DD's man on Khalil, Bob Boutet spoke up, "I agree with both assessments and I too do not see him travelling with a woman. Doesn't seem to be his way of doing things. He's a loner.

"Apart from doubling the chances of being stopped or caught, there's some evidence he's a real chauvinist. I like David's idea of a senior, well dressed businessman, probably from a friendly Arab place like Jordan, Kuwait, Dubai, or Bahrain."

The DD turned to Phil Harris, "Get a watch out to all border agents in the tri-state area for an Arab businessman possibly wearing a disguise who entered in the last week. Fill in any details we have such as age, height, etc."

Phil left the room immediately just as Hank came back and joined the group.

The DD continued, "Who would be supporting him here. Clearly this company of 30-odd people spreading bugs and radioactive material at JFK is at least part of it. There's even a chance that thirty homeless guys were given jobs and they don't even know what they were doing as long as someone was directing them.

"Still there had to be a leader or leaders based here to do some of the leg work like finding the staff and retrieving that package from the hull of the ship. He would be Khalil's contact here and they must have been together if Khalil attended the attack. How do we track those guys."

Hank Morrison spoke up, "As you know we have a watch list of potential jihadists based in New York. Most of them haven't perpetrated any crimes that we know of but various sources have fingered them as potential trouble makers. Ever since the first warning of a dirty bomb we have had all of the top ones under surveillance but frankly we've seen no suspicious activity from any of them."

The DD asked, "Would suspicious include anyone picking someone up at the airport, train or bus stations or getting unexpected visitors?"

"Yeah, all of the above and more. Nothing doing on that front. Although I have to admit right away we have no idea yet who was behind that fumigation set up. That was completely out of left field and they did a great job of keeping it quiet with that many people involved. Had to be local and I'm guessing it won't take more than a few days to figure out who it was. You can't have that many people in on an operation like that and all of that equipment and keep a lid on it forever."

Boutet spoke up, "Yeah but as we all know, Khalil will likely be long gone in a few days if he has not already left."

Most of the rest of the day was spent going over the stake-out reports of the surveillance on the suspected Jihadists and brain storming any ideas on how to find Khalil. The New York team was still reviewing the security tapes they had received from JFK but all the exterminators wore Hazmat outfits making it impossible to identify anyone. They had however identified a few men that looked like the leaders or managers but they had kept their full suits on even as they climbed into their plain white vans at the end. At least they had about half a dozen license plates. All rentals with bogus names for sure.

The press and Washington were going crazy with their demands for answers and rumors were spreading like wildfire but Carole was doing an outstanding job of keeping them at bay and knocking down any rumor that was too scary to contemplate like one claim from a FOX News analyst that the government was hiding the fact that hundreds had been killed at JFK. They were also reporting claims of a false flag attack that was already gaining traction on the blogs.

Cristal and David both took cat naps in the afternoon because they just couldn't keep awake. The CIA's hastily arranged bunk area was a welcomed relief.

The news from JFK seemed to get worse by the hour. It was confirmed that every terminal had been hit.

It was almost 6 pm on Christmas Eve when Morrison was called out of the room. He was back in seconds.

"This may be a break. That idea of checking with Immigration officers may have paid off. I have an ICE agent on the phone." He clicked on one of the phone lines, "Agent Handyside, I have you on speaker with senior CIA people in the room. Please repeat what you told our investigator."

There was a pause and then the agent spoke, "Well I'm an Immigration and Customs Enforcement agent and I got this Homeland Security Watch and it brought to mind a guy from yesterday afternoon. Just before I signed out at 4 pm this guy came through. Turkish businessman, mid to late thirties, about 6-foot, medium weight, olive skinned, spoke excellent English, almost an

American accent, proper passport and visa, but there was something about him that made me think he had gone to some trouble to disguise his look. For one thing I was pretty sure he was wearing makeup on his lower face. Like someone who had recently shaved off a beard and was covering up lighter skin."

At this everyone in the room straightened as he continued, "You might not have noticed the makeup but our lighting is especially set to pick up little things like that. I hesitated because he looked the full part of a rich business man and not the kind that would often have a full beard, but with the proper paperwork and answering all the questions correctly, there was no reason to question him further.

"Anyways, he said he was in town to see some potential distributors and wanted to catch a couple of Broadway shows. Very pleasant guy too. I know this might be nothing but the watch did ask for any middle-aged Arab businessmen."

The DD spoke first, "Agent Handyside, this is excellent. This might just be our man. It fits the profile. Is there anything else you can remember about him?"

After a pause, "No, sorry, that's it."

"OK. I forgot to ask. Where did all of this happen?"

"Sorry, Terminal 3 International arrivals at JFK. From what I hear I may have the next month or two off."

Half of the room smiled and the other half looked more worried.

The DD finished, "We need you to do one more thing for us."

Before he could finish the ICE agent cut him off, "I know, ID him on the security tape. I'll get right over to Security at JFK and do that."

"Thank you Agent Handyside."

Morrison, head of the New York bureau was the first to say the obvious, "Something does not connect. If he only arrived around 4 pm yesterday and the insect thing started within an hour or two that does not give him much time to orchestrate the whole thing."

Cristal answered, "True but the work all had to be done before he got here anyway. We are working on the theory that he does not actually have to execute the entire attack himself to be able to brag about it or claim a daring role. He just has to be on the scene so he can say he executed it."

Morrison continued, "Still the timing is suspect. Why leave it so close. Why not come in the day before to pump up the troops and make sure everything is ready?"

The DD took over, "It's puzzling but let's leave that for now. You need to go get your people looking not only at the security videos of the fumigation but as soon as we have the pointer to this guy going through immigration we need to track him through the building, get a look at his face and hopefully get a cab number or license plate at arrivals. You need to get all the videos from JFK from 3:30 yesterday. Handyside has already given us the time frame."

"Transfer half of it to Langley as well and get them working on it too if you need to. Phil here can help with that one."

"Also Phil, work with Carole to get me a judge on standby in case we need warrants. It is Christmas Eve and it might be hard to find one."

"One more thing. I know this is Christmas Eve and everyone wants to be home with their families but no one leaves while they are needed and everyone is needed until we catch this guy or verify he has left the country."

Morrison hesitated, "You're talking about New Yorkers many of whom were here on 9/11. You could not force them to go home."

Deputy Director Bill Carter simply blushed and nodded as Morrison rushed off to get his people working on the chase.

They were just regrouping when the DD's phone beeped with a text message, "Call me, Carole."

"Where are you," he said as he stepped out of the room and made the call.

"Back in the office in Langley. Listen I know this is a bit off topic but there have been some significant developments in that other case you had us working on. Just as I got back, I found out that our Jason Fletcher in Nairobi's contact in Frankfurt has been making several calls right after his calls with Jason that according to GPS and time stamps map to a newsstand in a tube station right next to MI6 headquarters. We have access to the surveillance videos of the cameras in the tube station and we have your man.

"We have him clearly on video twice, next to a newsstand triangulated by cells which are very close in the tube stations and talking on a cell phone that is unregistered and encrypted, that according to NSA's data, are at the exact time and duration of the UK calls Kurt Willems made."

"And who is Kurt Willems again?"

"Ex. German Secret Service who tried to hire our Jason Fletcher in Nairobi to kill David and Cristal. We also think it was his guys at the airport and the hotel that tried to kill them.

"Anyway, Jason sent us his call logs and we tracked Willems down and got his call logs through the NSA database of meta data."

Carter was surprised, "We still have NSA meta data out of Germany and the UK? I thought that was abolished back in 2014 when Edward Snowden blew the whistle."

"Yeah, I don't know the detail but whatever they curtailed, it didn't include this metadata that we just needed. So yes, they still have some access to this kind of data. Maybe they have to get it one phone at a time, I don't know but we have him dead to rights on video. And we also have him on the same cell phone with Kurt from his own apartment in one case. Unless there is some miraculous coincidence and he has a reason to be talking to this assassin, then I'm pretty sure we have our man. You may not want to take this up with David right now but we'll need to deal with Sir Richard Brighton on this."

"That high?"

"Yup. And I think you know which one of his directors it is so you know whom we're talking about."

"Wow, that explains a lot. OK, shut that whole thing down if you have confidence we have him and remember 'eyes only'. Make sure this does not leak or we'll lose him. Thanks for the call but I have to get back in the room on this Khalil thing."

"Just before you go, I already had the judge ready on a moment's notice if you need warrants. He knows the background so he'll sign anything we need."

"OK." He hung up and just before re-entering the room thought for a minute. David had kept his side of the bargain saving Cristal and risking his life on several occasions to get this close to Khalil and now he was going to be able to keep his side of the bargain even if they had missed the bomb.

They had been sitting on pins and needles for about two hours when Hank Morrison came back into the room, "Agent Handyside ID'd the guy and we got him and traced him through the security videos out to getting into a car at JFK. As the Agent said, he's dressed as a business man but we didn't get a good look at his face. Looks like he knew how to avoid cameras in the airport.

"The license on the car goes to Hakim something or other and he's on our watch list but not one of the big guys. We have a team on their way over to the address now with some uniforms."

Within minutes they had the bad news. The apartment was empty. Cleaned out.

"Shit!" said the Deputy Director, "I was hoping we had him. Tell them to interview everyone in the building and see if anyone knows where he moved to."

"OK but it's almost 10 pm on Christmas Eve so we're going to have a whole bunch of very unhappy people."

"Can't be helped."

Morrison was back in a couple of minutes, "Carole got us a warrant for Hakim's bank records, credit cards, phone records, you name it. It will take a hour or two to get some of them but we'll start analyzing them as fast as we can."

It was almost 2 am on Christmas morning when Morrison came back, "The only thing odd we've found so far is that he rented that black Lincoln we saw on the security video."

It was a long night waiting for anything to come in. They had an APB out on the Lincoln, watches out at all airports and border crossings for someone who might be Khalil, were tracing any information they had on Hakim and were starting to nod off when the phone in the room went. Hank Morrison looked at his watch, nearly 7 am and put the phone on speaker.

"This is the agent in charge of the Nuclear Incident Response Team at JFK. I was told to call this number and give an initial report."

Bill Carter realized he had asked for this almost twenty-four hours ago but they had all forgotten about the NIRT team's feedback.

"Yes. This is the Deputy Director of the CIA and I have with me a team from New York and Langley. Please proceed."

"Well we've been at it here for almost 24 hours and we don't know a whole lot yet except the attack seems to have been well planned. They used a mixture of magnetized Cobalt-60 and iron filings and something to keep it from coagulating and in suspension, probably a slurry made out of water and corn starch. I've seen the videos and it looks like they were carrying what were probably lead-lined garden sprayers full of this stuff and spraying it everywhere people go and also in some very hard to get to places like the underside of escalators, elevator shafts, and ventilation systems.

"Because it's magnetic it will be a real challenge to clean up. Could take months is a first guess and some metal structures including some supporting beams may have been contaminated themselves and will have to be disposed of and replaced. There are also some planes that are going to need new landing gear at least. They did a hell of a job getting this stuff everywhere. There's a lot of bugs running around too."

He continued, "The rads are not super high because Cobalt-60 isn't the worst stuff in the world and it was diluted with the iron filings so it's not going to kill you real quick but there's enough of it everywhere that your exposure without lead-shielded clothing and a full post-decontamination protocol would have to be under ten minutes to be safe.

Our guys have been very careful not to expose themselves or make this situation any worse by inadvertently spreading the stuff further with our investigation so progress has been slow.

"Essentially doctors will tell you there's no safe level for this stuff and this place is seriously contaminated. So we're not talking about Chernobyl but this airport is off limits for a very long time.

"I'm assuming there is an economical way to clean this up but if too many structural members have been infected and have to be replaced, you just might be looking at bulldozing some of these buildings and maybe the entire complex.

"Even if a building was cleaned up and safe there is a possibility that when you open the doors no one will come once the press gets hold of this. We may effectively be looking at total demolition of the site."

Cristal spoke up, "What about the Cesium?"

"What Cesium?" was the quick answer.

Everyone in the room looked at each other in horror. The Deputy Director took over, "We are pretty certain these guys had a load of Cesium-137. Have you checked for it?"

"Listen, I'm in Terminal 4 so I didn't do all the testing myself. This is a big airport. But these detectors should pick it up if it's here. I've seen none and the other terminals have only reported Cobalt-60. I was not specifically asked to test for Cesium-137 but I'll ask everyone to report back if they find any but my guess on what I've seen and heard so far is that it's not here."

"Thank you very much for your report. Please keep this office updated on any developments, especially if you find Cesium."

The Deputy Director hung up the phone and looked around the room in horror. Where the hell is the Cesium? Are we sure they had some? Maybe they left it at home for a future operation."

Boutet, the Khalil expert spoke, "He didn't leave it at home and yes Pakistan reported they had it for sure. They've been trying to hit the US since 9/11. You don't go to all this trouble and come this far and leave some of your weapons at home. He has broken into the Great Satan and he's going to strike here. And it's going to be today, Christmas Day, not Christmas Eve! JFK was a damned decoy! He is planning something bigger with the Cesium! He is still here. He hasn't left the area because he's not finished!"

Bill Carter exploded, "How could we have missed this. CNN reported hours ago it was Cobalt-60 and none of us thought to ask NIRT about the Cesium. We've wasted hours! Hell we've wasted a whole day!"

Tired as they were having had no sleep for more than a day and Cristal and David having travelled ten thousand miles they were all drained but suddenly wide awake with the adrenalin rush that comes from overpowering fear.

The DD spoke for everyone when he said, "WOW! Bob is right. JFK must have been a decoy. His real target was Christmas Day. He's going to hit us big time today!"

Cristal started, "We can still get him. We now know that he didn't want to kill a lot of people at JFK he just wanted to hurt the economy and scare the hell out of the population. But shutting down one airport is not good enough. He needs something bigger. Something that shuts down more to hurt the economy.

"Again, he's likely not chasing a headcount figure for dead bodies. Like 9/11 the big impact will be the economy. Look at Pittsburgh. Shopping centers all across America would have been emptied if people thought terrorists could drive a propane truck into a shopping mall and kill people. It's the fear factor and the impact on the economy.

"We spent trillions on homeland security and two wars after 9/11. I know we don't like to think of it as a success on their part but when did nineteen men ever do so much economic damage in a war.

"He is after fear and chaos and the economic cost of these attacks. Deaths are a secondary benefit for him and just add credibility to the fear factor. I've had this nagging feeling all day that JFK was too small for Khalil. He wants to beat Osama Bin Laden. He is going to do something that makes 9/11 look puny."

David spoke, "Cristal is right this guy is cunning, arrogant and ambitious. He learned the lessons of 9/11. In some ways he used the perfect tool in JFK. Something that infects metal just enough that a major piece of infrastructure is taken out of service for years.

Not enough to kill very many people but enough to keep them away and scare the hell out of them and force some kind of overreaction.

David continued, "Cristal's right, he wants something much bigger. It has to be something that affects a much larger number of people. Not just people who use the airport or any other single or special purpose target for that matter."

Boutet joined in, "So what is his next target? More infrastructure?"

Phil Harris had been quiet through all of this, "We know Cobalt-60 is or can be magnetic. What do we know about Cesium-137? Is it magnetic too? Do we need to get a chemistry professor in here on Christmas morning?"

Suddenly Phil Harris remembered something from an earlier briefing, "Oh SHIT! It's water-soluble. He's going after the water system."

The panic in the room was palpable. Hank Morrison was the first to speak. "New York gets at least half of its water from the Catskills. It all comes in through a massive pipe about 80 miles long, the Delaware River Basin Aqueduct system. If he drops that stuff at the intake upstate he will contaminate the entire water supply for New York. Once it's mixed in with the other water, it will all be contaminated. We'd have to evacuate the city. Maybe for decades or longer. You're talking trillions of dollars in losses if New York has to be abandoned."

David spoke, "But he can't have dump trucks full of this stuff. It had to fit in whatever was on the bow of that ship and they need to transport it around on land. If he has a limited amount of it, he has to get it into the system where it's a pure stream right into the city. Pull up a map quick of the water system feeding New York."

"What about pumping stations?" Cristal asked.

Hank Morrison responded, "That's the beauty of the system. It's mostly gravity fed and I'm pretty sure water treatment stations are not going to filter out dissolved radioactive material. One treatment center wouldn't do the job. He has to get it into the system upstream somewhere. We're totally screwed if he gets it into the entire system. Even a diluted amount would shut down New York. No-one would want to use any water for decades and all the pipes would be contaminated. The city would be a massive radioactive ghost town."

Within minutes they had the map and their target. The Kensico Reservoir just north of downtown.

It was Hank Morrison again. "I know it. But it's not the reservoir itself, it's the dam. Kensico dam is where they pull the water from. I used to play touch football in the park right in front of the old dam. Its only about fifteen miles north of here just north of White Plains, next to Valhalla."

Boutet added, "Where Norse fighters went when they died in battle."

Collectively they all gave him a dirty look.

Cristal said, "He has spoofed Police cars before, who polices the water system and has access to everything?"

Morrison answered, "The Department of Environmental Protection and they have their own police force, DEP Police ... SHIT ... he's got one of their trucks I'll bet."

Cristal looked at the Deputy Director, "We may be too late. The sun is just coming up and this is when they would plan it. We need something to get us up there NOW!"

The DD had planned for fast action, "I have two specially configured Blackhawk helicopters on standby at Battery Park. We are five minutes away. Three minutes given the streets will be empty for Christmas."

"Hank, tell your people to get DEP on the phone and explain they need to get someone to that reservoir and they may be facing terrorists posing as DEP police."

The DD was right, the streets were empty and they were there in under three minutes sirens blaring. As they got in the choppers, the DD held back, "Sorry folks, no Ops exposure for me. I promised the Director. Hank Morrison here is in charge. Let's hope you read it right and you get there in time."

The three piled into the first chopper. Cristal glanced over at the other chopper that seemed to be filled to capacity with special Ops types in white winter camo which made her smile. New York was having one of its traditional brown Christmases.

She was a little shocked at the combat style take off of the choppers in downtown New York. She instantly realized she had not eaten in a long time and felt immediately nauseous in the chopper.

Hank Morrison spoke into his headset, "Hell, one of my folks just got off the phone with DEP. You'll never guess. That low-level Jihadist Hakim that picked up Khalil at the airport is one of theirs and he's on duty this morning. How the hell did we miss that one?"

A long 5 minutes later Hank spoke again, "I know this area. The main take-up in the reservoir is at the dam straight ahead. The special Ops guys will go in first in case we come under fire. These choppers don't have much in the way of protection."

Just as they approached the dam they saw the chopper in front open fire at something on the ground behind the dam. They had come in at a bad angle from the south-east for the target that was almost directly beneath them near the foot of the dam. As the second chopper came over the dam Cristal was first to see it. A DEP SUV on a dirt road, one guy standing near an open door aiming a weapon at the other chopper and now looking for cover as another jumped out of the back of the truck.

There was what looked like a large cooler sitting on the ground behind the SUV. The cooler appeared to be really heavy as he dragged it towards the water.

By now the attack chopper in the lead had swung around and a hail of bullets chewed up the ground all around the guy with the cooler.

Cristal yelled into her mic, "Don't hit the bomb!"

Whether they could hear her on the radio or not she was not sure but she could see that the gunner was walking his aim towards the guy with the cooler and coming in on the right side away from the cooler. The Jihadi went down quickly in a spray of blood but the cooler started rolling down the hill and on to the reservoir's thin shore ice near the foot of the dam.

The second terrorist jumped in the truck and gunned it. He was only about fifty yards from the road that crossed the dam so the next time they saw him he was turning left on to a highly treed access to the dam.

On the radio, Hank yelled orders. The attack helicopter was to stay with the weapon as they had tools to handle radioactive material while the other chopper would keep the fleeing Jihadi in sight until law-enforcement could catch up with them.

They circled looking for the truck which had ducked into some woods and for the moment seemed to be trying to hide. They could see roads on all sides. He had to come out somewhere.

By now the special Ops guys were on the ground and reported they had the weapon in custody and it had not spilled into the reservoir but that it did get hits for radioactivity when tested up close. They also reported that the terrorist at the scene was a shorter person of less than five foot five.

Cristal spoke into her mike, "Then Khalil is the driver of the truck. Don't lose him."

Through her earpiece Cristal picked up that every law-enforcement officer in the area was closing in on the chase based on information from their pilot. It was only a matter of time before they caught him. Her only fear was that he would try to cause a major accident and take as many infidels with him as possible.

The chopper was almost over head the truck when they spotted it. It suddenly veered dangerously to the right and skidded on the cold pavement causing the chopper to over shoot and pull up in a turn.

David yelled, "Don't lose him. Somebody keep eyes on him."

Cristal tightened her belt as she slid open the door on the chopper and hung out looking below and behind the chopper. The cold wind with a wind chill at this speed of probably ten below caught her breath as she yelled, "I have him. He just took a dirt road. Looks like an access road of some kind."

As the chopper swung around she directed them to the road that was almost invisible from the air. It appeared that the ground was frozen because there wasn't even a dust cloud to help them pick out the fleeing truck.

The tree cover was surprisingly dense given that most of the trees had lost their leaves.

The pilot brought the chopper to a hover about two hundred yards from the dam as shells started penetrating the fuselage particularly in the area of the cockpit. Both the pilot and Hank Morrison screamed that they were hit and the helicopter started to sway back and forth.

Cristal immediately thought of Tiffany. She had lost the only father she knew and she was about to lose her mother and her real father to this damned terrorist.

Smoke was coming from somewhere as the pilot somehow got enough control to pull up and away from the invisible attacker.

"Go right." Hank yelled to the pilot. There are a couple of intersecting roads and a massive park at your two o'clock.

A minute later he found the park and the roads and his experience told him that he had better use the road as it was the first solid and level footing he could see.

With the pilot covered in blood they touched down on the road. David and Cristal checked the two wounded and got them out and far away from the smoking chopper. They had them settled with compression on their wounds that did not appear life-threatening.

Cristal whispered to David, "We're sitting ducks. He could come out of that wooded area right at us and he has an AK-47."

She was the first to react. She unholstered her weapon and sprinted back down the road in the direction of the woods. David was not far behind.

Over the approaching sirens they heard the screeching of tires before they saw him.

The truck came out of the covered part of the road barreling over a small crest. He instantly assessed the situation and floored it aiming directly at Cristal and David. Cristal had no time to fire and simply headed for the frozen ditch. The SUV barely missed her leg as she jumped. David got off two rapid shots at the driver who had slumped down. David followed Cristal into the ditch about ten yards behind her.

Suddenly both felt the heat and light and then the blast and sound of the tremendous explosion as the truck hit the helicopter nearly vaporizing both of them.

Cristal's first thought was of the Cesium. She hoped it had all been in that cooler. Otherwise they were all dead.

She turned in time to see an enormous red and orange fireball ascend into the overcast sky. There was very little of the truck and the helicopter left.

She moved over and sat on the ground with David. Both were a little winded.

She smiled at the thought that they had saved New York. A gargantuan attack had been averted but only by seconds. All of the work. All of the fear of failing at stopping the main attack was now behind them.

Finally her attention turned to the man who had stoned her best friend to death right in front of her. She had no feelings left for the man. Whether it was the fatigue of no sleep for nearly two days or the shock of the last hour, she just felt numb.

Finally this animal had been stopped and would no longer target innocents in his insane hatred for America and the ugly irony was that his last thoughts were probably of his instant transition into heaven. She thought sadly that now they would never know what he looked like. He had gone to his grave with his secret identity.

Three law-enforcement cars and an ambulance were not far behind and over the next five minutes six more arrived including some of Hank Morrison's CIA team from New York. Apparently the fire ball had not been hard to find. Cristal kept them all far back from the fire in case there was Cesium present.

Thankfully, the smoke from the fires was blowing away from them and taking with it hopefully any beta particles from the Cesium.

First aid was being delivered to the two who were injured. Hank's team were gathered around him as his wound was dressed, getting the scoop on what had gone down.

A fire truck showed up and kept its distance but got water from a high-powered hose on to what was left of the smoldering vehicles and small field fire that had been started by the crash.

With the excitement starting to abate and the injured being attended to, Cristal and David got on the headsets in one of the CIA cars and debriefed the DD who was anxiously awaiting their call.

They gave him a blow-by-blow account of the last ten minutes.

The DD took over, "I could not be happier. You two have saved us all.

"The Nuclear Incident Response Team was just choppered into the reservoir and their initial report is that a substantial, maybe large quantity of Cesium is the likely contents of the cooler and none of it was spilled into the reservoir. They are sending some folks your way to check out the remains of the truck.

"Looks like you guys got there just in time to save New York City from near total destruction. We would have had a panic evacuation killing probably hundreds and a likely scenario where no one would ever want to live here again. I know it's not enough but, congratulations and thanks."

Cristal spoke with a smile, "Just as important I think is that we got Khalil. He probably convinced himself in his last seconds that he was a martyr for the cause and I hope he enjoys his seventy-two virgins but he won't be threatening anyone again."

David spoke, "What about Mogadishu?"

The DD smiled at the other end of the call, "We've had armed drones watching Mustafa's every move since the football game. The other chopper informed me they had the weapon so just before your call I ordered a hellfire missile to take him and anyone with him out immediately just in case they heard about New York and went into some kind of a bunker routine. First reports are that we got him and a couple more cleanly. I would say Al Qaeda and the fatwa on you just took a big hit."

David and Cristal smiled at each other.

Cristal said, "So what now?"

"Well David and I have some unfinished business and we need a full debriefing so unfortunately we need you both back here pronto while everything is still fresh. Take one of the CIA cars."

Cristal shrugged, "OK but I'm starving. You are going to have to wait until I get some breakfast."

"I'll be here all day. Take your time. It may not be easy finding anything open. It's Christmas after all. Oh yeah, Merry Christmas."

David and Cristal hung up promising not to be too long. They knew the Deputy Director, Bill Carter was also far from home on Christmas and he surely wanted to get back to Langley.

Cristal's thoughts immediately turned to her beautiful little Tiffany and how she must be spending Christmas morning with Cristal's mom and dad. She couldn't wait to get there and hug her and introduce her to her real dad. David was in for a very special surprise she was sure. But she had to clean up here first.

It was still early so thinking her parents might be sleeping in she made a mental note to call them after breakfast. It had been a long couple of weeks and she wanted to let them know she was fine and the drama was finally finished.

She suspected the DD would spend the rest of the day debriefing the Director, the President and working with the media group to put the best spin on the police actions.

There had been a major interdiction at the Kensico Reservoir in the early morning and there would have to be a decision made on whether to tell the American people about another nuclear attack. Certainly they would want to make the most out of killing Khalil, the most wanted man on the planet.

There would also be progress to report at JFK in the investigation and clean up. He still had to track down and arrest all of the participants in the JFK attack and investigate that ship as well. On second thought, there was no way he was getting back to Langley today.

After seeing that the two injured were receiving good medical help and were being transported they headed towards I-287 in their commandeered CIA black Crown Vic.

As Bill Carter had indicated, there would be nothing open on Christmas morning.

Cristal remembered that the Interstate Service Centers were always open and there were lots of interstates in this area. Their GPS led them across the Tappan Zee Bridge to one just inside New Jersey border on the Garden State Parkway.

Cristal was exhausted to the point of near collapse and starving. MacDonald's was open so she ordered two Egg MacMuffins and David had the Big Breakfast. Neither was impressed with the food but the ketchup helped and the coffee was good. At least it temporarily filled the hole. They both realized it had been a long time since they had had a real meal and this was the closest to American as they had had in almost a month.

The food court was nearly empty with only a few travelers on this Christmas morning. Cristal had just changed the subject to their daughter whom David knew nothing about and she hadn't seen for over a month as a scruffy looking guy with long hair, black leather bomber jacket, chained wallet and shades sat down behind David facing her.

She reasoned some truck drivers still had to work on Christmas Day. She was mid-sentence bragging about how smart little Tiffany was when the guy behind David opened his Egg MacMuffin, removed his shades and proceeded to empty four little sachets of pepper on to his egg. As he looked up and made eye contact there was instantaneous recognition as they both went for their guns.

Cristal's bullet whizzed by David's ear and nearly ripped off the top of Khalil's head as his gun fired into the floor. David was on the floor, weapon drawn and hand to his ear before he realized that Cristal had stopped shooting. Next he realized he was in trouble. He was choking on something he had in his mouth when all hell broke loose.

Cristal was standing over David by now in a broad stance, two hands on her weapon and pointing it at Khalil when she noticed David struggling on the floor. The few people and rest stop staff in the food court were screaming as she crouched down over David and punched him hard on the back dislodging his breakfast.

As his head cleared, David now saw the target. A man missing part of the top of his head and a long-haired wig and a gun lying nearby. Blood was everywhere.

Cristal yelled, "Police officer. Don't panic. Someone call 911."

She looked back at Khalil who was not dead yet but would be soon. She holstered her weapon stepped over David, kicked the other gun away and crouched down beside the dying Jihadist. As she ripped a small wooden cross from her neck, showed it to him and pressed it into his trembling hand, she whispered, "Tiffany would want you to have this.

"And just for the record, this does not qualify as martyrdom you asshole. You're going straight to hell."

Just before he breathed his last gurgling breath, she saw him stare at the little wooden cross in recognition. His gaze returned to Cristal and then those black remorseless eyes closed for the last time.

David was still coughing as he sat up. Between gasps he said, "The bastard wasn't in the truck. He followed us here. How did we not see him from the helicopter?

As he regained his breath and Cristal sat on the floor staring at Khalil he finally smiled, "You saved my life for real this time. I owe you one."

Epilogue

Sir Richard Brighton arrived at the loading dock area of MI6 headquarters with his personal bodyguard. Guards were holding a man at gun point that had been challenged at the door and had a daily password that called for direct contact with the Chief.

"I'll take it from here gentlemen."

"But sir, he has a weapon."

"That's all right, carry on."

As they headed for the elevator he said, "Nice disguise. The leathers, long hair and the sun glasses work."

"I picked up the idea from someone else."

"Well, let me say it's great to have you back. You've had an interesting couple of years from what Bill Carter tells me. I would like to hear all about it someday."

"Interesting is one way to describe it."

"Well let's hope this morning is less eventful. I thought you might want to be in on this given what you have had to put up with."

As they arrived on the sixth floor, heads turned as the Chief of MI6 escorted a man clearly in disguise through the office directly to Jack Hammond's office. Only the Chief and David entered and closed the door while the bodyguard remained outside.

The chief spoke, "Jack, I would like to re-introduce you to the once departed David Crowe. He has quite an amazing story to tell and you're one of the main characters."

The shock on Jack Hammond's face was everything David had hoped for and more. As David removed the wig and the glasses, Hammond reached under his desk. David put a bullet though his forehead before he could pull out the gun.

As the screams from the outer office subsided the chief said, "That wasn't very sporting of him now was it?

"One problem though, now we're not going to find out who the rest of his co-conspirators were."

David looked at him, heart still pounding, "You took a big chance walking in here knowing what you know."

"Why do you think I allowed you to keep the gun. I had a sneaking suspicion that he might have sneaked one in here himself. Anyway, I'll put one of our field guys up against a desk jockey any day of the week."

***

Cristal had rushed home to Cincinnati to see her daughter. She hugged Tiffany hard as the tears flowed. Mom and Dad wanted to know all about it but she could only tell them some of what had happened. Still they got the picture and did not ask embarrassing questions like "Did you ever have to kill anyone?"

Cristal explained she was going to have to disappear for a while with Tiffany's real dad who was an honest to goodness hero and the true love of her life but she promised to call them from time to time. She also promised them she would change her hair back to its natural color.

As she sat in the Cincinnati airport waiting for her flight to Dulles and then London to meet David and introduce him to his daughter she watched the Airport CNN TV network.

Suddenly 'Breaking News' came across the screen. Wolf Blitzer's face appeared. She was amazed at how her old colleague never seemed to age and always seemed to be available when breaking news happened. When she worked for CNN they used to joke that he slept in the studio.

"We have breaking news out of a suburb of Pittsburgh. Authorities apparently intercepted a terrorist attack at the Monroeville Mall. A propane truck was to be used as a bomb. It likely would have penetrated the entrance and when detonated it would have killed hundreds of Boxing Day Shoppers. Authorities are not releasing much information but eye witnesses claim a sniper on top of the Mall took out the driver and completely disabled the truck as it entered the parking lot at high speed."

"This raises many questions that we hope to get answered like why was there a sniper on the rooftop."

"It was just over a month ago, on Black Friday in fact that another large propane truck exploded not far for this very Mall. People are now asking if there's any connection. So far the Justice Department, the Pentagon, the FBI, the CIA and the Pittsburgh Police have refused comment. Stay tuned as we follow this story looking for additional details."

Cristal hugged Tiffany even harder and cried silently into the baby's blanket. "Was it ever going to end," she thought.

***

Before they got on the plane, Cristal dropped a small envelope into the mailbox at the airport. It was addressed to the main holding center at Wichita Police headquarters.

In it was a note to Greg Wiggins that simply read. 'Here, you might need this again', along with her wedding ring.

**

Cristal and David were given an MI6 flat in London for a month while they got their things in order.

There was no talk of marriage but David was immediately smitten by Tiffany, acting like a real daddy and was starting to get the bug of family life. At least for a while.

Sir Richard Brighton had given David a month off to recuperate or rather a delay in reporting back to MI6 after an absence of over four years. He also gave him all of his back pay.

They had only just settled in to the London flat when David announced that he had one more piece of unfinished business that was not particularly dangerous but had to be taken care of and would require him to travel for a couple of days.

**

Sergeant Dick Crawford parked his car in his underground spot and made his way up the elevator to his apartment just outside of Richmond, Virginia. As he opened the door something struck him from behind and everything went black.

When he came to, he was sitting in a kitchen chair, hands and feet bound to the chair and something like a hood or pillow case over his head.

Someone was talking over a very loud radio. Somehow the voice seemed familiar but he couldn't place it.

"So this is your lucky day Dick. I can see by your squirming that you're fully awake now. So we can get started.

"You're going to love this. I know I did at Guantanamo."

Dick Crawford suddenly recognized the voice. It was the Jihadi known as Daniel Boone or Abu Nistal who had mysteriously disappeared about a month ago. His heart rate, already pounding, skyrocketed. He lost control of his bladder.

Suddenly he was tipped backward and the water came pouring onto the towel over his head causing him to gag and gasp. He was pinned to the chair and as hard as he tried, he could not move. The sensation was much worse than he had imagined. All of his primal fears appeared at once. Total helplessness, hopelessness, impending death, and fear beyond anything he had ever known. He knew instantly that he could not take this. He would do or say anything to stop this torture if he lived another second. He knew he was about to die a terrible death.

The torture stopped after what seemed an eternity and he was sat up where he continued to gasp and cough up water. His head, his lungs and his heart were pounding and he had pissed himself again and worse.

Now the loud radio made sense. He couldn't even yell for help if he could even get enough breath to do so.

"Well Dick. That was your first taste of what you put me through and seemed to enjoy so much for a couple of years. I made that one short. Just a sample of what is to come. I find the anticipation adds to the effect.

"Sadly though, you have no way to stop it because you don't have anything I want. I have no questions for you. But luckily for you I'm limited on time. I cannot stay here for two years so we'll just have to make do.

"To add a little excitement I have a special mixture for you coming up. I've added quite a bit of white vinegar and cayenne pepper to the next bucket. I think you'll enjoy it."

"Please, please don't do this. I'll do anything for you. I'll give you anything."

"Oh, don't plead Dick. C'mon you're a tough guy, remember. Listen you've only got ten or twenty more of these to go so let's get started," he said as he tipped him back again.

***

Three days after Cristal left for London Detective Bert Wilson knocked on the Serpe's door. They invited him in.

As he sat down he said, "According to the daycare Tiffany has not been there for a few days. Is she sick or something?"

Frank Serpe had envisaged this and had a story that he now realized didn't hold water so he simply said, "It's over. Our daughter and our granddaughter are safe."

Bert Wilson blushed a little, "Is there anything more you can tell me?"

Frank and Mary looked at each other. Frank continued, "You understand there are things we don't know and there are things we do know but we cannot speak of."

"You were right. Cristal, unbeknown to us was at one time a CIA agent. All I can tell you is that she was kidnapped and there were terrorists involved. That issue has been resolved. And I'll say one more thing. JFK was not the only attack in New York, but it was the only one reported and Cristal was at the center of all of the recent news on that front. It's all clearly classified and we can say no more and you can't quote us on any of this but suffice it to say that we are extremely proud of our daughter and very happy that she and Tiffany are safe."

Bert smiled, said his goodbyes and headed to the car.

Colt Baker was playing with his smart phone as he entered the car, "Well what did they have to say about the kid?"

"As I told you weeks ago, if the kid disappears, all is well. You owe me twenty bucks."

THE END

www.ingramcontent.com/pod-product-compliance
Lightning Source LLC
Chambersburg PA
CBHW071155250626
47159CB00001B/95